Veil of Mists

a novel of the Seven Deadly Veils, Book Two

Diana Marik

Praise for Diana Marik's Veilverse

Veil of Mists

"I am obsessed with this series. Diana Marik has created a high intensity series that grabs you and doesn't let go." – Lisa Reigel Reviews

"Danger and deception know no bounds in this riveting second installment of the *Seven Deadly Veils* series. Complex liaisons deliver the action and suspense paranormal fans crave." –RT Book Reviews

The Blue Veil

"Marik's compelling delivery commands readers' attention; the easy, seamless passion and intensity between characters is a welcome companion to a perfect balance of action and suspense." –RT Book Reviews

"The characters are edgy and intriguing. The plot is suspenseful and sexy. I'm drawn into this series and fascinated by the world that Ms. Marik has created." — Comfy Chair Books

Veil of Shadows

"The suspense is as dramatic and intense as the action, and paired with Marik's steamy sex scenes, will leave readers satisfied on many levels. Off-the-chart chemistry." 4 STARS HOT –RT Book Reviews

"I flipping LOVED this book. I was drawn immediately to the main characters of *Veil of Shadows*. The characters are edgy, sexy, and intriguing. Her writing style drew me in and kept me fascinated; the suspense kept me on the edge waiting to see what would happen next. *Veil of Shadows* is fast paced and action packed. I highly recommend this book to fans of paranormal romance and romantic urban fantasy." –Comfy Chair Books

Dedication

For Heather—may old wounds heal gracefully.

Acknowledgments

I would like to thank all those who have been a constant source of encouragement. When darkness descends, the light that keeps us going is the love our friends freely give to us. Matisse, Lorraine, Jen, Laurie, Theresa, Kathy, Bridget, and Barbara—your affection and support of my work is precious to me. And I would be remiss if I didn't give special thanks to the BOC Book Club, especially to Kim and Janet, whose love of books and passion for the written word keeps me up long nights at the computer when I should be resting in bed or watching episodes of *Game of Thrones*. It is because of your love I strive to write the very best I can. Thank you!

Chapter One

"Make sure you bring up the camera equipment in the green backpack. I want to get some shots before the sun gets too low," Professor Miranda Crescent shouted to her guide, Will Lightfoot, as he made his way down the mountain.

"I won't forget." Will smiled back as he jogged down the narrow trail to the Jeep. Her handsome companion was not only knowledgeable about the glyphs and Native American lore, he was also a PhD candidate in economics. She watched the muscles of his back flex as he made his way down to the Jeep; the fact that he had a body like an ancient warrior had nothing to do with her estimation of him. *R-i-g-h-t!*

Rising from her kneeling position at the base of the rock formation, she deeply inhaled the crisp, invigorating mountain air and smiled. "Magnificent." The majestic vistas in the Carson National Forest in Northeastern New Mexico were spectacular, as were the petroglyphs she'd been examining. As an art authenticator from New York City, Miranda had a deep appreciation for the glyphs.

Two bald eagles gracefully flew against the rock face of a mountain. *There sure were no views like this back home.* Getting away from Manhattan for a few months had been just what she'd needed; evading an involvement with a very powerful and dangerous vampire had been an even wiser decision. When Miranda heard her phone ringing, she checked the number and then chose to ignore it.

"Got it," Will called out as he searched the back of the Jeep. "I'll bring up some bottles of water, as well."

"Good call!" After her relationship with Gabriel had gone bust last spring, Miranda had jumped at the opportunity to take a seminar in ancient Indian art. *Indian*—not Native American, as Will's grandfather, Chief Angel Fire had informed her. Near Taos, the chief had shown her his assortment of silver and turquoise jewelry he had designed, and Miranda had bought several pieces for her best friend, Lizandra, the Were Queen of New York.

"Make sure you stay hydrated." After handing her a bottle of water, Will laid her equipment by her feet. "You nearly got yourself dehydrated yesterday when we were exploring the lake region."

"I'm fine. I think it was the altitude that got to me more than the lack of fluids. Remember, I live at sea level." She grinned. "Stupid altitude sickness."

Miranda watched the muscles in Will's throat as he swallowed his water. After tying his hair back, he sat beside her on the rocks as they looked out over the forest. He playfully tugged at the tips of her hair. "What, they don't have mountains in New York?"

Elbowing him, Miranda smirked, then became serious. "You know my grant expires at the end of the week."

Scanning his attractive face, Miranda realized she'd never met anyone with two different eye colors—one eye was brown and the other green. She'd loved hearing him tell her legends of his people when the ancient tribes had mated with different animals. His ancestral tribe had been eagle worshippers, and Will had a tattoo of an eagle with a full wing span across his upper back. Miranda had studied the colors and, at times...it appeared as if the eagle were trying to break free. The eagle's head was tilted so the eyes looked straight at her, but what was most intriguing—the eagle also had one green and one brown eye.

"Yeah, I know," he said quietly. "But you're still staying for my grandfather's birthday, aren't you? He's going to be seventy-seven."

"Of course I'm staying. I wouldn't miss it." Miranda had enjoyed her friendship with Will, but they had lives to get back to. Soon, he would start work on his PhD, and she would be returning to New York.

When her phone rang, yet again, she silenced it. Exhaling, Miranda picked up the camera equipment and started setting up the last of her shots.

Later that night, with only a blanket covering their bare bodies, Miranda and Will stared up at the starry sky. Their fire kept them warm against the night's cool breezes. "I still can't get over how bright the stars are." Miranda closed one eye and raised her hand to the sky. "You can almost touch them."

"Almost magical." Will smiled as he bent to kiss her, then heard a buzzing noise. "Your phone's ringing. Again." Laying back down, he flexed his fingers behind his head.

"I know." Grimacing, she checked the number and then shut the phone off. As far as she was concerned, she was on vacation. She exhaled. Whatever concerns New York had could wait until she returned. Even if the concerns were that of the vampire high lord himself—Valadon.

"He sure is persistent." Will ran his thumb down the side of her cheek. "You know, in the firelight, it looks like your eyes glimmer red."

Miranda played with the beads in his thin braid. "He's stubborn and not used to anyone saying no to him." Knowing his spicy taste, she pulled Will down for a kiss. Will was a patient lover who liked exploring her body by slowly smoothing his hands over every inch of her skin. After being with a vampire for nearly six months, she appreciated the darker skin tones of Will's warm body and slid her hands over his taut muscles as their bodies melded together. It felt as if magic floated on the air; the earth's vibration seemed to be humming.

***

High Lord Valadon, the ruling vampire of New York City, paced the floor of his penthouse office suite and then paused to look out at the darkening sky. A storm was coming in over the water, creating a veil of mist over his city. After he defeated the sinister ancient, Mulciber, Valadon's status had been elevated to high lord, and his powers had grown exponentially, but there were still some things he could not see. Even the moon appeared to be hiding from him—not unlike a certain woman.

After Miranda's relationship with his progeny, Gabriel, had ended, Valadon had secretly rejoiced. Remare, his second in command and oldest friend, had been right when he'd said the relationship wouldn't last. Valadon was growing frustrated at her lack of response.

He had been certain she would have returned to him by now; he was perturbed she had not. When Miranda had chosen to leave New York, rather than join him by his side, his temper had spiked. He needed her here with him— especially after the last message he'd received from his agents in the Vampire High Court in Europe.

He tried calling her again and nearly crushed his phone with his bare hand when he was directed to voicemail.

Remare appeared in his doorway. "Is the art professor still refusing your calls?" Having shared blood with the leader of his Torian guard, Valadon knew Remare sensed his frustration. "With the disturbing reports coming from Europe about those conspiring against you, I would have thought you had enough to be concerned about."

Valadon continued scanning the lights in the other office buildings of the Financial District, then glanced back at him. "She should have contacted me by now."

Remare leaned against the doorframe. "Miranda never struck me as quite one to follow anyone's orders or do what's expected of her." He stroked his bare chin with his thumb. "She's a woman of strong beliefs, her *own* beliefs."

"Stubborn." Valadon faced Remare. "Has there been any more news from Europe?"

"Since the last transmission of the High Court's desire for '*an arrangement*'? No." Remare strode to Valadon's side as he viewed the neighboring buildings. "Even though you answered the VHC's ambassador's questions, apparently, there are still those in the High Court who are not completely satisfied."

"I will deal with them when the time comes. For now, I want Miranda here. With me."

"What could she do here?"

"I'm not sure." Valadon straightened his spine. "But I want her here. Now." Valadon bent his head back and closed his eyes. Not many vampires could enter the mind of a human at so far a distance, but not many vampires were high lords. Valadon was over a thousand years old, and in his veins flowed the power of the Bluebloods—purebred vampires. He concentrated on the image of Miranda and let his power travel distances over cities, highways, mountains and valleys until he found her.

***

"*Miranda?*"

Miranda thought Will was whispering to her as he thrust inside her. As she clutched the muscles of his back, the passion flowed freely between them. The energy swirled around them as their hearts beat in unison. Something about being in the old, primal forest at night played with her

Elemental senses, heightened them, and she felt herself absorbing his heat and the magic they were creating. She couldn't remember a time when her senses felt so finely well-tuned.

"Miranda."

Bloody hell! That was *not* Will's voice in her ear, but Valadon's. She silently shrieked at him, *"Get out!"*

"We need to talk."

"Not now!" Her climax building, Miranda had to fight not to scream her thoughts aloud.

"Now! You've refused my calls."

"Not now! Damn you!" Miranda opened her eyes to see the passion gathering in Will's eyes; their combined scents of arousal permeated the air around them, adding to the magic. Sweat glistened on their bodies as he continued his thrusting, and she could feel her body tightening as it neared ecstasy.

"MIRANDA!"

"DAMN YOU!" Miranda let down her shields and let the High Lord of New York see exactly what she was doing and who she was doing it with. It would serve him right. She arched her back and screamed out Will's name.

***

Valadon bellowed a howl of frustration so loudly Remare thought the windows would shatter. He backed away to give Valadon the space he needed and watched as the high lord stormed over to the bar and poured himself a glass of blood wine. He wasn't sure what had transpired between Valadon and Miranda, but he could guess. Remare silently stepped down to the sunken conference area and, slowly exhaling, relaxed on one of the couches.

He should feel sympathy for his friend; each of them knew well the anguish females caused. But, instead, Remare found himself inwardly smiling. He was pleased

Miranda was safely out of New York and away from the machinations of the vampire courts. Her involvement with Valadon had nearly cost Miranda her life and that was something he did not want to see repeated. He had thought often of her since she'd left Valadon House—usually late at night when he was alone in his cold, empty bed.

Remare had one regret. He had erased one memory of hers, one that could be potentially dangerous, one that had been precious to them both.

***

The party was in full swing for Will's grandfather in the elder's backyard. Chief Angel Fire, who had his long white hair tied back, kissed Miranda's cheek. "I'm glad you were able to make it tonight," he said in his deep voice. "This night is special to us all."

"I wouldn't have missed it." Miranda liked the elder chief—the old man simply radiated warmth. When she looked at Will, he grinned back at her. Will wore a light blue denim shirt with indigo jeans; his brown boots completed the outfit, and with his hair tied back, he could have been an actor in Hollywood with his high cheekbones and handsome face. Surrounded by his family, he glowed with vitality. She sensed his natural rhythm was stronger, more intense.

After Miranda feasted on food and drink, the birthday cake was served. Everyone sat around listening to the elders tell stories. Miranda was fascinated by them. When Chief Angel Fire told his tale, her eyes began closing and she felt the edges of sleep pulling at her. In a half dream-state, she heard the chief recounting a time when the clan had turned into eagles and soared high above the mountains. He spoke of chants and shamans who believed, when the planets were lined up in a confluence of power, the magic of their tribe became elevated and they had the power to spell-cast others.

Miranda imagined the gift of flying, of soaring free as the clan chanted in their native language. She peered at Will, who smiled at her through a veil of mist that engulfed the revelers. She blinked once and saw him wearing a coat of feathers, then blinked again to see others wearing headdresses of eagle feathers and dancing naked by the fire as the chanting grew louder.

She gazed upward at the full moon and belatedly realized it was nearing the midnight hour. Miranda watched in amazement as each member of the clan began morphing into their eagle forms. Suddenly, they were half-human/half-eagle, and she was mesmerized by the sight. Her last coherent thought was that maybe her drink had been spiked.

Miranda sensed strong arms lifting her and saw Will smiling down at her. She watched as he undressed her. He was covered in black and red feathers and pressed a shiny, dark totem onto her forehead as he chanted words she didn't understand.

Images of darkness and light filled her mind as colors exploded and contracted as she was raised high into the night sky. A feeling of disassociation enveloped her as she flew over the tops of trees on the mountain in awe of the sights. A black eagle was flying by her side. Beads were woven into the feathers, the same beads Will wore. She turned her head to see the other eagles flying higher and could hear their distant cry over the mountains.

Miranda knew she was dreaming—had to be—even though she could taste the cool, clear air in her throat. She should have felt cold as the night breezes caressed her naked skin but, instead, felt only warmth. She looked at her arm, and it was covered in feathers the chestnut color of her hair. Miranda should have been terrified, but flying made her giddy with laughter, and she simply savored the sensations of being airborne. When she tried to speak, the cries of an eagle emitted from her throat.

The eagle beside her kept pace with her, cawing his own sounds of joy, his wingspan strong and powerful as he wove his way on the air currents. When Miranda felt herself growing slower, she followed behind him, flying on his wake. Will flew with the easygoing manner he did everything else—his power a living, breathing thing.

The mist had finally cleared the moon, and the brightness lit up the forest. Miranda could see far better than she ever had, noticing the movements of the animals in the forest—a deer treading slowly through the trees, a rabbit hopping over a fallen branch and a rattler slithering across a road.

Drunk on the sensations her new body was experiencing, she felt the rush and excitement of flying, the sense of clan unity as they flew in formation and then in solitary splendor. Nothing could ever compare with the freedom of flight. Sensations were too complex for meaning. Time didn't seem to exist.

The last thing she remembered were the cries of the other eagles far off in the distance.

***

The next morning, in her hotel room, Miranda woke with the mother of all hangovers. She threw the covers off and crept into the shower to clear her head and get the awful stiffness out of her shoulders. *Must have slept funny.* She rubbed her arms and neck, letting the warm water wash away the night's revelries. Quickly rinsing off, she towel-dried her body. It was only when she was standing sideways in front of the mirror that she noticed the tattoo of a soaring eagle on her left shoulder blade. *What the hell?*

Miranda had no memory of getting a tattoo.

On the taxi drive to the airport, she tried Will's phone three times, but there was no answer. At the airport, she called the university and was told politely by the department's secretary they had no knowledge of a Will Lightfoot and no grad or undergrad students were registered under that name.

Miranda was stunned silent. She Googled his name, and nothing came up. Her heart raced, and she checked her purse; her credit cards, cash. Everything was there. At the bottom of her purse, she found a dream catcher. The feathers were black and red—Will's colors.

Miranda peered around the airport and sighted the tourist sign: *Welcome to the State of New Mexico: The Land of Enchantment.*

I'll say! She had left New York to get away from the vampires and the werewolves, wanting something more normal.

Was normal even something that existed? She looked down at the tips of her fingers and saw that her nails were sharpened to points. Like talons.

Normal?

Apparently not.

Chapter Two

Miranda smiled as the cab drove over the Brooklyn Bridge. Even in the late afternoon, Manhattan's skyline was spectacular. Nothing beat the view of downtown New York. Some of the oldest and most architecturally inspiring buildings were located here. The city may not have the majestic vistas of the Sangre de Christo Mountain Range in New Mexico, but the breathtaking view of the skyscrapers meant only one thing—home.

She opened the window to breathe in the myriad of fragrances that made up New York—the brine of the East River, the various scents of the diversified ethnic restaurants, and of course, the exhaust of all the cars and tourist boats near the piers.

To Miranda, it smelled like heaven.

After paying the cab driver, she turned around to make sure she was really home. Having been gone for two months, it felt strange being back, almost unreal. After unlocking the door and resetting the alarm, she went to see if there was anything edible in the fridge. Thank God, there was some fresh orange juice, which she quickly drank.

She was glad the stack of mail on the kitchen table had been sorted by Orion, her trusted musician roommate and best guy pal. Speaking of which—

Miranda peered up at her ceiling; with the rhythmic sounds coming from above, he was busy entertaining his girlfriend. *No wonder he couldn't pick me up at the airport!* Orion was drop-dead gorgeous with his black hair, blue eyes, and killer smile. Whenever he played the clubs, they sold out quickly with a predominance of female fans.

Miranda liked his girlfriend, Max—short for Maxine. Both were Weres in her best friend's clan.

Another loud groan reverberated throughout the house; the banging of a headboard signaled to Miranda it was time to toss in a load of laundry in the basement. She paused when she heard the female's moans. *Uh-oh!* Miranda was pretty sure those sounds weren't Max's.

After making her way back upstairs, she heard the combined howls of two spent werewolves. Then, Orion finally made an appearance, wearing only a pair of black jeans that hugged his toned body and screamed, *"Do me."*

And, apparently, someone just had.

"Hey, beautiful." Even after a quick shower, Orion still smelled gloriously of sex. Grinning, he gave her one of his famous bear hugs that threatened to cut off her air supply, then kissed her on the mouth. "When'd you get in? I thought you weren't supposed to be back until tonight." He grabbed the carton of orange juice and took a few swallows while she gave him the evil eye.

Orion's mouth curled. "Yeah, yeah, I know, no drinking from the carton, but I'm running late." He gave her one last hug and, this time, kissed her cheek. "Welcome home, Mira. I missed you. There's food in the freezer. Chicken kebobs with rice and veggies from Amna's." He wagged his eyebrows. "There's even baklava—with pistachios—no walnuts."

Her mouth watered at the thought of a delicious meal from her favorite Mediterranean restaurant.

Miranda adored her roommate, and if she could ever wish for a brother, Orion would be it. "Well, I'm glad to see the house is still in good shape." Miranda glimpsed the ceiling. "Anything I need to know before you rush off?"

Orion ran both hands through his damp hair, giving her a good view of his six pack. Like all Weres, he liked to flirt, even though their relationship had always been platonic. Weres had different notions about sex; they simply didn't have the hang-ups humans had about nudity. The first few months after he had moved in, she had to constantly remind him not to walk naked around the house.

"I left your messages by your bed. Mail's sorted out." Glancing at the ceiling, he seemed to hesitate. "Lizandra said she wanted you to call her as soon as you got in." He pulled his T-shirt over his head and tucked it into his jeans. Then, he pulled his baseball cap down low. "We'll talk later, okay?"

Miranda shrugged. "Okay." She sensed something was wrong.

When Orion reached the door, he stopped and turned back toward her. "Valadon stopped by. He asked a lot of questions about when you were returning." Orion grabbed his keys and sunglasses from the bowl on the table near the door.

Miranda leaned against the archway with her arms casually folded against her chest. "What did you tell him?"

Orion lifted a shoulder. "What you told me to tell him. Nothing else."

"Good." Miranda knew how persistent Valadon was and wasn't surprised by his stopping by. Her privacy didn't seem to be on his list of priorities.

Orion was halfway out the door when he remembered something else. "Oh yeah, the other vampire stopped by, too."

A shiver went up her spine. "Who?" Fragments of an erotic memory surfaced.

"Remare." Orion put on his sunglasses. "He asked about you, too. Said he just wanted to check the alarm system."

Miranda's body stiffened at the mention of Remare's name. Months ago, they had gotten close—*too close*—and he had been one of the reasons she'd taken the assignment in New Mexico, even if they had reached a mutual understanding. It wasn't until she'd been away from New York that broken pieces of a dream had begun haunting her, and she suspected he might have erased a memory.

"Did you ask him to change the password?" Jerk had programmed a ridiculous password for the alarm she had yet to figure out how to reset.

Orion gritted his teeth like he just remembered. "Sorry. I forgot."

"Go." She joined him by the door. "I'll check my calls."

"Miranda." He hesitated, again. "I'm really glad you're back."

"Me, too."

"I kinda broke up with Max." He winced as if ready for an argument.

Miranda glanced upstairs. "Really?"

"Yeah. Don't be mad, okay?"

"It's your life, not mine." With the way her love life had turned out, Miranda was the last one to criticize anyone. "So, who's the new hottie?"

"I think I'll let her tell you." He quickly glanced at the stairs. "I gotta run. See you later tonight, okay?"

"Sure."

Orion kissed the top of her head and was gone before she could ask him any more questions.

Well, that was strange. Miranda closed the door and wondered who the new girl was but decided the mail and phone messages needed her attention more. Returning the orange juice to the fridge, she detected a familiar scent entering the kitchen—a scent she knew almost as well as her own.

"Welcome back, girlfriend. We were going to have a welcome home party for you...but decided to celebrate a little early."

Miranda grinned. She'd recognize the throaty purr if she were deaf. She turned to see her best friend. At nearly six-feet tall, even without the three-inch stiletto boots, and dressed in a sleeveless bronze jumpsuit that showed off every curve and well-toned muscle, Lizandra stood against the archway and raised an eyebrow. "Welcome home, Mira."

Miranda hugged her as thoroughly as Orion had embraced her. Pack mentality was, if you were pack, you were family, and pack members embraced their own. And as *Friend to the Clan*, she felt cherished. "It's good to see you." She inhaled Liz's scent and then let her go. "I've missed you." She looked back at the archway. "Seriously? Orion? What the hell happened with Gavin?"

Slowly, Lizandra circled the kitchen table, taking her time to respond. "Oh, pretty much the same as you and Gabriel. Just not as extreme."

"Not as extreme, huh?" Miranda nodded above. "You had my ceiling vibrating."

"Hey, I'm Were Queen." Liz thrust her long black braids behind her back. Her café mocha skin glistening, she placed her manicured fingernails on the table and smiled deviously. "I can have whoever I want."

"And did!" Miranda sat as Liz joined her. "I didn't know Orion was one of your favorites."

"He wasn't. But, I wanted something different." Relaxing, Liz crossed one leg over the other. "So. Tell me about New Mexico." She raised one eyebrow. "I hear you did *something* different, too."

Miranda rolled her eyes and then told her about Will and her dream. "But the deal is..." Miranda shook her head. "It felt *real*. Like I was actually flying."

Liz watched her with her arms crossed over her chest. "I should think you'd be more careful with your drinks. You, of all people, should know better. Someone must have slipped you a powerful hallucinogen."

Remnants of nightmares long buried echoed in her mind, and Miranda quickly slammed the door on them. "So, there's no way it was real?" Miranda met her friend's eyes. "But I felt it—I felt the wind on my face and saw the tops of the mountains. I looked down on them!"

Liz leaned forward and took both of Miranda's hands. "Listen to me. There is no way they turned you into an eagle. Weres are only born this way. It's not something that can be transmitted from one person to another or the whole damned world would be populated with Weres."

Miranda's shoulders relaxed. "You must think I'm the biggest idiot on the planet."

"Hardly." Liz rose and walked around the kitchen. "This place is too small. Come to Werehaven, and we'll talk more."

"I can't. I've got laundry to do and mail to sort through."

Liz raised her eyebrows and gave her a look.

"Okay." Miranda relented. "But it will have to be later."

"That's fine. Just make sure you get your well-used ass there tonight."

Miranda smirked. "*My* well-used ass? I think your ass got used more than mine from all the moaning I heard."

"Orion is very...tasty." Liz decadently smiled as she played with one of her braids. "You would know that if you nibbled more."

"I don't nibble on roommates." Miranda wagged her finger. "You lose them that way."

"Speaking of nibbles, your former employer has deigned to enter my stronghold. He's been trying to get ahold of you."

"Yes. I know." Miranda didn't bother to tell Liz about Valadon's mental link and what he had interrupted. "I'll call him." When Lizandra glared at her, she said, "I promise."

"See that you do." Liz hooked her bag over her shoulder and opened the front door, then said in her exaggerated Caribbean accent, "Da man get very peckish...when he don't get his way."

"Peckish, my ass," Miranda grumbled as she eyed the phone. Perhaps, this was one conversation she needed to have in person. It had been months since she'd seen the vampire high lord. He had haunted her mind with whispers for months after she left ValCorp. Maybe he was over her by now. She sighed. From the enraged voice she'd heard thundering in her mind when she let him glimpse her with Will, she didn't think so. It was probably not the smartest idea to let him see her in the throes of passion with another man.

She was entitled to her privacy. Wasn't she?

***

In the penthouse suite of ValCorp, Remare relaxed on the sofa and read his text message. "It seems Professor Crescent has arrived safe and sound from her trip."

"About time," Valadon murmured.

"And you still think it wise to involve her in our business abroad?" Remare casually uncrossed one leg from the other, not certain at all about involving a human in vampire affairs, even if that human was an *Elemental* who had extraordinary talents. And Miranda's gifts were exceptional. Remare fondly remembered the time she had thrown a fireball at him and felt himself growing hard.

"Who else can I send?" Valadon bellowed as he gestured with his open hands. "Vivienna knows all of our people, our most trusted people. She seduced the last two I sent, and we wound up with nothing. I want someone we can trust impeccably. Someone Vivienna has no power over, someone she can't seduce." Valadon turned to face his second. "I would send you," he smirked, "but the two of you would wind up killing each other."

Remare smiled at the thought. Valadon was half-right. He would succeed in killing Vivienna, though she would have no chance at ending his life. He valued his existence too dearly to let the scheming vixen end it. Unfortunately, Vivienna was the adopted niece of Caltrone, a high-ranking member of the Vampire High Council—the council that ruled all vampires, for which Vivienna worked. If he did kill Vivienna, they would lose valuable allies in the High Court they couldn't afford to relinquish.

He read another text message. "Miranda's now at Werehaven. Shall I fetch her for you?" The more Remare thought about it, the more intrigued he became. He would see to it Miranda was protected, of course. But if she could pull this off... Ah, the possibilities.

Valadon stared down at the city below him. "I've spent centuries building up ValCorp, and now, the High Council has become interested in *my* corporation—as if they could take it from me. I'll never let that happen." He turned to face Remare. "Bring her to me."

"With pleasure," Remare said as he rose to leave.

Chapter Three

"Really, Caltrone, with all the finer places in Paris, I would think you could have found some place better to meet than these damned Catacombs." Vivienna, Madame Lord of Paris, bristled at her sometime lover and companion as she followed the stairs leading far below the darkened caverns.

"Yes, of course." Caltrone ran his eyes over her chic dark suit and killer heels. He'd advised her to dress accordingly, but as head of one of the top fashion houses in Paris, Vivienna always dressed elegantly with fine attention given to every detail of her appearance. Even with the high heels, she could walk silently on the stone floor, a skillset she shared only with other Blueblood vampires. He admired her aristocratic beauty as well as her cunning and had seen to it she was made madame lord nearly a century ago. Even though she was one of the most powerful vampires in the city, he was Council—older and far more powerful.

Caltrone used his electronic keycard to open the heavy metal door and waited until Vivienna entered and then locked the door behind him. "But here," he gestured around the vast subterranean room with a long conference table in its center, "there is no chance of being monitored. The Elders had reasons for using the Catacombs, however dismal." He eyed all of the vampires present. "The chamber is secure, and what we are about to discuss will *not* leave this room."

"We're all here for the same reason." Tobias finished pouring himself a glass of blood wine and then resumed his seat at the long table. He was a businessman whose accumulation of wealth knew no bounds, but it was the vampire sitting next to him who posed the greater threat.

"I agree the setting leaves much to be desired, but will suffice, for now." Merlinder nodded in agreement. As calculating as he was intelligent, he reserved his opinions until those around him had made their intentions known first. Caltrone was wary of him; if there was anyone who could challenge him and had the slightest chance of winning, it was Merlinder. Therefore, he was carefully watched.

Caltrone escorted Vivienna to her seat at one end of the table, then took his seat at the head of the table. "Yes. It seems Valadon has already intercepted one of our transmissions." He gazed in the direction of one of his strongest allies, Lysette. She was as beautiful as she was deadly with her fall of blond hair and pale complexion. Although Lysette was petite, no one present at the table was fool enough to doubt her powers or that she enjoyed using her gifts in the most ingenious ways. He smirked. "I believe Lysette has handled that bit of inconvenience."

Lysette nodded with a hint of cruelty in the twist of her lips. "There will be no other communiques from my end. Or they will wind up as Emil did." She clicked the remote, and a video appeared on the large screen. They watched silently as Emil was staked to the ground. One of his executioners took a long blade and removed his heart and entrails as Emil's horrified screams echoed throughout the cavernous room. As his body thrashed about, liquid silver was poured into his empty cavity. After Emil's bloodcurdling shrieks had died, the heart and the rest of the body were torched. Satisfied, Lysette clicked the video off.

There was no sympathy for the traitor from anyone present at the table.

Vivienna glanced across the table at Lysette. "Had you control of your courtiers, this meeting would not be necessary."

Lysette hissed, "And you think *all* your people are loyal, Vivienna? Valadon's arm is long and strong. His wealth buys many tongues."

"And has Valadon bought yours, Lysette?" Vivienna smirked as her lavender eyes glowed. "I seem to remember you having a fondness for our former Minister of Finance."

Lysette rose in indignation. "I am loyal to the High Court, as I've always been. No one here *dares* question my allegiance."

Caltrone watched the interplay between the two powerful female vampires and knew the situation could easily escalate. "No one here questions your loyalty, Lysette." He watched the ice forming in Vivienna's eyes, turning them a darker shade of purple. With her mane of raven hair and fair complexion, she was truly one of the world's most beautiful women. He knew when Vivienna gave the illusion of being serene, she was at her most calculating. Her lack of sentimentality had helped forge their alliance long ago. "But with our failing economy and the value of the euro dropping, it is prudent we take steps now to avoid any further financial calamity."

"My wineries continue to produce a substantial profit, and my donations to the High Court and our ruling council remain steadfast." Lysette glared at Vivienna as she resumed sitting. "Can everyone here make the same claim?"

Caltrone understood the bitterness between the two women; jealousy was a powerful emotion, better to remain detached from such pettiness.

However, he wasn't so sure Vivienna would allow such a slight to go unanswered.

"Paris has always been the world's leader in fashion and continues to be so. As with any business," Vivienna bit into a peach she had taken from the assortment of fruit laid out on the table, her fangs fully elongated, "some years are more...fruitful than others."

"The fashion and wine industries continue to be profitable, but some of us have not had the good fortune you have enjoyed." Calisar, the oldest, but not the most powerful of the vampires seated at the table, turned to Caltrone. "We now look to the High Council for guidance."

"And that is precisely why we are here." Caltrone leaned back and observed those present. Syrio would soon be stepping down as chancellor of their council, and Caltrone planned on being his successor. But, for that, he needed the support of all the vampires present. And that took not only political influence, but a great deal of money. "Syrio has had no answers. We've poured money into the failing economies of our southern regions without significant improvement." His eyes focused on Vivienna. "We need Valadon back."

"He will never willingly come back to Europe," Merlinder huffed. "His empire in America is strong, and he no longer has the loyalty he once did to our High Court."

"It is true we cannot force him to return." Caltrone looked approvingly at Vivienna. "But I've always found persuasion a more viable choice."

Vivienna smiled devilishly as her well-manicured fingers stroked her arm leaving tiny rivulets of blood that instantly vanished. "Valadon has had few weaknesses over the long years he's been away. I suggest we dig deeper into his personal life...and find one."

Caltrone listened silently to the thoughts of those around him. Soon, it would be time to set his plans in motion. Mulciber had been a powerful ally—the ancient's death was unfortunate, but his mole at ValCorp was still loyal to the Council and, as a senior member of the Council, to Caltrone. No one at the table knew about the mole, not even Vivienna.

Merlinder asked, "How do you plan to lure Valadon to our shores? He's not deigned to visit us in nearly a century. Why would he come now?"

Vivienna cocked an eyebrow. "Everyone has at least one weakness, Merlinder."

"In that regard, I may be of some assistance," Isabelle, the youngest member of their group offered. "My brother, Bastien, has informed my parents he will soon be coming for a visit. If anyone knows of a weakness of Valadon, surely one of his elite Torians will be aware of it."

Smiling, Caltrone leaned back in his chair and tapped the tips of his fingers together. "Well done, Isabelle, well done."

The Madame Lord of Paris turned toward Isabelle. "Do tell."

Vivienna was like a lion—a predator patient enough to learn her prey's vulnerability and shrewd enough to wait until she uncovered what she needed to wage her attack. And she would attack; there was too much at risk not to. He knew this because he'd been the one to train her. As an agent of the VHC, she had been one of his best operatives.

Only one other had been superior to her.

But Vivienna also had a vulnerability, and he knew exactly what that was if she should ever set her sights too high.

Chapter Four

Not far from the Museum of Natural History, burrowed deep below Central Park, Werehaven was Black Star Clan's dance club and sanctuary. For Miranda, it was her home away from home. Or at least it had been. She sighed. Arranging her messenger bag high on her shoulder, she quickly exhaled and carefully took the spiral steps leading down to Lizandra's private playground. Striding past the long, curved bar, she made her way to the VIP lounge.

After the tragic death of one of their own, she'd been hesitant about visiting. Even though Lizandra emphatically denied any Weres in her clan held Miranda responsible for Dane's death, she knew the truth. Dane would never have been murdered if she hadn't asked him to research Valadon's enemies. The fact that several members of the HOL also lost their lives did little to assuage her feelings of guilt. The nightmares still haunted.

At the bar, most of the Weres nodded or tipped their drinks in her direction. When she climbed the few steps to the lounge, she saw Brent, Black Star's chief accountant and his lover, Quint, the clan's top legal counselor, relaxing on the couch as they spoke with the Were Queen. Miranda closed the door behind her. "I see the glass partition works fine."

Liz rose from her leather recliner. "Yes, since we seem to hold more of our meetings here rather than in my rooms, it was best to have it soundproofed." She hugged Miranda. "Come sit."

A waitress entered and took her drink order. "Cranberry juice, please."

Miranda knew Lizandra still watched how much she drank. Last winter, she may have drunk a bit too much when her nightmares were at their worst, but she had dealt with her issues. Mostly.

"You know you can only stay until ten, right?" Liz asked.

"Ah, it's still the full moon." Placing her messenger bag down, Miranda sat on the couch facing Brent and Quint. At midnight, all the Weres would change into their wolf forms and traverse the park in their Lunar Run. It was no time for humans to be anywhere in the vicinity.

"Haven't seen you around for a while." Brent leaned over and kissed Miranda's cheek. "Welcome back. We missed you."

Quint nudged her boot with the toe of his shoe and smiled. "Yeah! It's about time you showed your face. We were afraid some sexy beast out west captured your heart and you decided to relocate."

"Never happen." Miranda shook her head. "New York's home and always will be."

"Chic boots you're wearing." Liz eyed her sleek black suede boots.

Ever since she'd been burned on her lower legs by an evil vampire, Miranda had worn leather boots almost constantly in the cooler months. With the tight black jeans and the black leather-look top revealing her tanned and toned arms, she looked like a warrior. "Like them? I thought they were kind of kickass myself." Miranda reached inside her bag and handed out gifts.

Liz unwrapped a pair of coral and silver earrings. "Oooh! These will go great with the new outfit I got. Thank you."

Brent said, "Look, I got a brown leather bound book with my name engraved on the cover."

Miranda smiled at the dark-haired Were. "Something to go with all your electronic toys."

Quint held his gift up. "Sweet! It's an engraved money clip. I could use this for all my papers."

"Half the fun of going on trips is shopping for you guys. I brought a few other things for Gavin, Max and Tia." Miranda took out a few similarly wrapped gifts and laid them out on the coffee table.

When Liz widened her eyes to Brent and Quint, they got the message it was time to leave. Quint playfully nipped Miranda's ear. "Don't stay away so long next time."

The waitress arrived with Miranda's drink and then left with the men.

Liz watched as Miranda sipped her drink. "Did you call Valadon?"

Miranda rose and went to the huge tinted window to observe the crowd dancing. "I'm going to ValCorp after I leave here." She crossed both arms over her chest. "I'll see what he wants."

"Good." Liz stood beside her. Mirroring Miranda's pose, she asked, "Have the nightmares stopped?"

"Not completely." She glanced at Liz. "But they have lessened considerably." She used to think the horrid images of how Dane was tortured before he died were the worst. But she'd been wrong. It was the dreams where he was still alive and she was having a casual conversation with him, seeing him smiling, which haunted her the most. When the harsh light of reality hit her like an anvil that he was truly dead, she experienced the same sense of loss, yet again.

Like a mama bear watching over her cubs, Liz eyed her people dancing. "How not completely?"

"Out west, I only had a couple. I think getting away was good for me." Miranda faced her friend. "So, you don't have to worry every time I take a drink. Liquor was never my choice of poison, anyway."

"Never?" Liz raised one eyebrow.

Miranda returned her look. "I'm not a kid anymore, and childish lunacies have long since lost their appeal."

"Good to hear. Then, maybe you'll start to hang out with your friends who love you."

"How could they love me?" Miranda's voice sounded gravelly, even to her.

"I have told you, *repeatedly*, it wasn't your fault."

Miranda's lids closed as she exhaled.

"Do you know how much effort the clan put into your welcome home party?"

Frowning, Miranda looked around the club. No evidence of any planning was in sight.

"Not here, you idiot." Liz threw her hands in the air. "We figured you would need time to rest. It's still too close to the full moon. We planned it for next weekend, so don't make any plans."

Miranda was touched by the gesture. "You're giving me a party?"

"Yes, it was Max's idea, actually, but everyone agreed that a party was in order, so see that your white round ass shows up next weekend."

"I will." When the silence stretched on, Miranda sensed something else was troubling her friend. More enforcers than usual were scattered throughout the club. "Now, you mind telling me what's with all the extra security?"

"We've had a few altercations with Red Claw."

Red Claw was a rival clan that claimed Riverside Park as their territory. Their pack master, Edgar Renworth, sought to infringe on Lizandra's territory. "You told me you won the case against Red Claw."

"We did." Lizandra slowly exhaled. "But that hasn't stopped the more hostile members from trespassing. Some of the incidents have turned bloody."

Christ! No wonder Lizandra looked so grim. "How bloody?"

"We've suffered a few injuries." Liz continued watching her people. "But so has Red Claw."

"You expect more retaliation, don't you?"

"I expect things will get far worse before they get better." Liz glanced at Miranda and gestured to the bar area. "See that blond waitress. She's new and, I suspect, a plant from Red Claw."

"Is she now? And what are you doing about it?"

"For now...nothing. She's not privy to my conversations, and I only let her hear what I want her to hear. Can you read her? With that gift you have?"

As an *Elemental*, Miranda had some empath skills. "I'll have to get closer. Touching her would be best, but remember, I only read emotions, not thoughts."

"Right now, that's enough. Why don't you go mingle in the bar area? We'll talk again soon. There are things I need to discuss with David and Sam."

Lizandra's brothers entered the lounge. Like Liz, both had mocha-colored skin and green eyes, but David—the older of the two—had long dreadlocks that went halfway down his back. He was muscularly built with biceps and triceps accentuated by his black muscle shirt, and he made the best BBQ this side of the Mississippi River. At six foot-six, David was an imposing figure, until he smiled and then became one of the most amicable people she'd ever met.

Sam was a lieutenant in the NYPD and kept his hair regulation short. Not as friendly as David, he kept to himself and didn't hang out at Werehaven as much as David did.

Lizandra confided in Miranda concerning many aspects of Were culture, but there were meetings she had never been invited to and never would be. Liz had simply stated, *Were business,* and that was the only explanation Miranda ever needed. She kissed Liz's cheek and whispered, "I'll be in touch."

Miranda made her way to the bar area and spotted one of her favorite Weres at one of the high round tables by the balcony. "Hey there, Max."

Max's entire face lit up. "Mira, you're back!" Her hair was black with silver stripes; her nails were painted the same colors. Barely twenty-one, Max still had her youthful enthusiasm and the face of a pixie. She lunged out of her chair to give Miranda a tight hug.

Miranda laughed. "Hey, I'm glad to see you, too!"

"When'd you get back?"

"Just today." She was careful not to mention Orion's aerobic workout session with Lizandra. "I've missed you. How've you been?"

"I'm getting by." She looked downcast. "I suppose you heard."

"Yeah, I'm so sorry, Max." Breakups were tough, even when the parties involved considered it mutual. But Max was young. Miranda was sure, in time, she would find someone else. "Is there anything I can do to help?"

"Not really. But tell me about New Mexico." Max's exuberance had her bouncing in her chair. "You made it sound so wonderful in your texts."

"It was. It really was...enchanting." Miranda was *not* going to bring up her flying adventure. "I brought you back something, but I left it on the coffee table in Liz's lounge."

Max made a face a child would make if Brussels sprouts were being served for dinner. Miranda tried not to laugh, but failed. "Ah, Max, she is the queen."

"Grumble, grumble," was all Max said. "I know she is, and I love her, too, but—"

Miranda didn't know what else to say so she let the silence stretch out.

"I thought I had it bad," Max munched on a pretzel, "but have you seen Gavin since you got back? He was really upset with Lizandra. He got real quiet and wouldn't talk to *anyone*."

Miranda sighed. These were her friends, and they were suffering, yet she had neglected them. That was about to change. "Max. Just how much trouble has Red Claw been giving Lizandra?"

The Brussels sprout look was back. "I'm not supposed to talk about it. Were business."

"Max, I'm her friend. I know I've been away for a while, but you're all the family I have. Tell me what I need to know."

Max gradually let go of her veggie look. "There've been a few skirmishes." She started playing with her hair, again. "Lawe got cut bad across his side, but Liz stitched him up. Mostly, they've been testing us. Liz says they're studying the way we fight."

Just then, a familiar scent hovered in the air. Gavin, aka the red wolf—Lizandra's ex. "How are two of my favorite females doing tonight?"

Affectionately, he ran his hand across Max's back and kissed her temple. When he turned to Miranda, he held her eyes for a moment and then hugged her tightly. He kissed her, as well, but on the lips as a *fuck you* to Lizandra, apparently not caring if she saw or not.

Miranda bet he did care. "Gavin, it's good to see you, too."

"Miranda just got back from out west."

"I heard you went away for a while." He cocked his head. "How was your trip?"

Before Miranda could answer, Sasha appeared and stood beside Max. The former Red Claw had been horribly mistreated in her own clan until Lizandra had adopted her.

Miranda smiled. "Hi, Sasha, you look great."

Dressed in a black miniskirt and blue blouse, she looked radiant.

"Welcome home, Miranda."

"We gotta get ready for later tonight." Max said as she gathered up her purse and downed her drink. "Come around more often, okay?"

"Sure." Miranda hugged her goodbye and waved to Sasha, who was still the only Were who didn't touch as freely as the others.

Alone with Gavin, Miranda found it hard to believe Liz had walked away from him. He was gorgeous with his mane of reddish-brown hair, bourbon-colored eyes and constant tan. Of all the Weres, his muscular build was one of the strongest. She considered him a good friend and thought he and Lizandra had made a great couple.

"I'm glad you finally deigned to honor us with your presence." He smiled as he tipped his beer bottle in her direction.

"Okay, okay. Everyone's gotten on my case about it." She finished her drink. "If I promise to show up more often, will you drop it?"

"Of course. I'm just glad to see you or did the kiss not register?"

"Oh, it registered." She patted the seat vacated by Max. "Sit; maybe you could tell me what's been going on around here since I've been gone."

Gavin gazed up at the lounge. "I'm sure Liz has already informed you."

Miranda leaned back in her chair. "To a degree."

"That's Liz for you. She keeps her cards to herself." He drank another gulp of his beer. "With good reason."

When the silence dragged on, Miranda figured that was all she was going to get.

"Red Claw's been testing the boundaries." Gavin sat back. "They want to see where our strengths and weaknesses are."

She grew pensive. "That doesn't sound good."

He paused in scanning the crowd and just looked at her. "It's not."

Miranda turned to see where Gavin had been looking. "What do you think of the new waitress?"

"I'm not sure." He swallowed his beer. "Some people are harder to get a bead on than others." After another lengthy silence, Gavin asked, "How was your trip?"

"Fascinating." She gave a brief account of her studies. "So, if there are Were eagles and Were wolves, what else is there?

He laughed. "With all that you've seen in the last few years, you still have to ask that question?"

She didn't see the humor in the question. "Fine, don't answer."

Gavin grinned. "Miranda, there are *many* wondrous beings that walk this world." He tilted his beer until she looked around the club and spotted an elegantly dressed vampire making his way to them. "One just walked in."

Miranda caught a whiff of a woodland scent and swore her enhanced sense of smell came from hanging out with the Weres. Despite her attempt to restrain her reaction, her body instantly quivered.

Only one vampire smelled like the forest.

Chapter Five

Through the haze of flashing lights and pounding music, the vampire strode gracefully toward them. She almost didn't recognize him without his goatee. With or without the slight beard, Remare was one of the handsomest vampires to walk the planet. And, damn him to hell, an intelligent conversationalist, one with a wicked sense of humor. She'd even had a few erotic dreams about him. Her body tightened in arousal as the butterflies danced in her lower belly. Remare was the only vampire who affected her this way. Miranda knew it was totally illogical; he was Valadon's second and loyal to no one else, a deadly assassin.

When the blond waitress slithered up to him, a low growl emitted from Miranda's throat. She tried to suppress her response, but not before Gavin saw it.

After acknowledging the Were Queen in her lounge with a bow of his head, Remare moved toward Miranda. He was dressed in a designer black suit. Even with the warm weather, he still wore his black leather gloves. Miranda had seen him fence before and thought he had the grace of a dancer or a leopard. All svelte muscle moving in sync with his natural rhythm—a predator who knew no fear.

"Mir-randa. How nice to see you, again."

Miranda nodded. She adored the way he pronounced her name with the rolling *r*'s. It never failed to send shivers up her spine. "Hello, Remare." She met his dark brown eyes—eyes that held a hint of cruelty tinged with amusement. But, tonight, they were more inquisitive than lethal. "I didn't think vampires frequented Were establishments."

"Gavin." Removing his gloves, Remare tilted his head to the Were. "I never thanked you for assisting Valadon when there was need. You fought bravely."

"Vampires from House Valadon are always welcome at Werehaven." Gavin shook Remare's hand. "They're our allies, Miranda."

She was afraid Gavin had seen the eye sex between her and Remare, when he rose to leave. Quietly, she exhaled.

"I see you two have business to discuss, so I'll leave you to it." Gavin bent to kiss Miranda's forehead. "Don't be a stranger now that you're back."

"I won't."

Gavin wove his way through the crowd and disappeared into the shadows. Miranda faced Remare as the blond server—*Dori*, according to her name tag—waited to take their drink orders. Miranda furtively brushed her hand against the Were's back and didn't like the vibe she got. Something was off. The Were's pitch was faster than most of the Weres she had read, but there were too many conflicting emotions to get an accurate reading. In truth, Miranda wasn't sure if her negativity was because Liz didn't trust Dori or the way she was smiling at Remare.

Miranda turned her focus to Remare and noticed his hair was cut shorter than the last time she'd seen him. She couldn't tell if she liked him better with the goatee or not; either way, he was sexy as hell. Was it any wonder he was always surrounded by beautiful women?

"Cabernet," Remare ordered as he sinuously slid into the seat vacated by Gavin.

"I'll have the same, but ask the bartender to make it half cranberry juice."

At his raised eyebrow, she added, "Lizandra's monitoring me."

Remare narrowed his eyes. "Why would she need to do that?"

"You need to ask that after what happened with Mulciber?" She shot back, and then softened her voice. "People I cared about were killed, the break up with Gabriel," she waved her hand in the air, "and other...stuff," she murmured the last to herself. "Is it any wonder you paranorms give me nightmares?"

Remare frowned.

"Forget it. I had a few nightmares and drank maybe more than I should have. It was really no big deal." Miranda shrugged. "Lizandra worries too much." She met his eyes. "So, why are you here?"

"You need to ask that, Mir-randa?" He cocked his head, then leaned forward, laying one arm on the small table. "Really, I should have thought you would have guessed by now." His seductive grin never failed to arouse something primal in her.

Miranda sat straight back in her chair. "Valadon."

"Correct."

Dori came back and placed their drinks on the table. Miranda swore Dori's skirt was shorter and her neckline lower than before. Remare left a hefty tip that had the waitress smiling and winking at him as she left. "I was going to go to ValCorp in a little while. I take it he sent you to facilitate my progress."

"I volunteered." He smirked as he sipped his drink never taking his eyes off of her. "Your trip out west obviously agreed with you. You look healthy." He gestured toward her arm. "You have a tan, and your arms are toned."

Of all the people Miranda had met in her life, Remare was the one she could never quite get a complete sense for and that infuriated her. As an empath, she could *read* people's emotions, but this vampire hid his emotions behind titanium shields. Iceman, she thought. At times, he was like a block of ice, impenetrable, other times... Yeah, well, she was *so* not going there.

Seeing Lizanda behind the lounge's tinted window—her stance a clear warning that it was time to vacate the premises—Miranda finished her drink. "The moon is still close to full; maybe we should get going?"

"After you." Remare rose and handed Miranda her bag. He looked up at the lounge and saluted the Were Queen.

While they waited to cross Central Park West, the breezes were ruffling the trees. Even though late summer was usually warm in New York, there was a chill in the air, hinting at an early autumn. Ever vigilant, Remare scanned the area around them. Even in the dark, she knew his eyes didn't miss anything.

When the light changed, they swiftly crossed the street to where Remare had parked his car. Miranda had ridden in his black Mercedes SUV before and liked the luxurious feel to it. His dashboard was complete with all the latest e-toys, resembling the cockpit of a jet. He started the ignition and adjusted the radio. Miranda nearly laughed, certain that a vampire as old as Remare would choose a classical station. When Led Zep's "The Immigrant Song" came on, she did her best not to snicker.

"Too much?" Remare questioned when he saw her face.

"Just a bit." She chuckled as he adjusted the music and decided on a classic rock song by Depeche Mode. She liked Martin Gore's voice and considered her tastes in music eclectic. She liked everything from Justin Timberlake to Josh Groban. But the rock classics were her favorites— especially alternative rock.

Miranda wondered if he had discovered that when he'd investigated her.

Remare pulled into traffic and made his way to the West Side Highway which would take them down to the Financial Center and to ValCorp. In such close proximity, his seductive scent of woodlands was getting to her, so she lowered the window to breathe in the fresh air rolling in from the Hudson River. Riverside Park was an endearing sight with all the trees and bike trails. Miranda liked this part of the drive; she could see across the river to New Jersey.

She smiled as a mist was clearing the moon. Even if it had only been a dream, she had been up close to that moon and knew what it felt like to fly.

After the silence stretched on for a while, Remare asked, "Why haven't you contacted Valadon before this?"

Miranda exhaled. If there was one question to ruin her tranquil mood—that was it. "Because...I didn't want to."

When Remare continued staring at her, she merely grinned, daring him to question her.

"You're being impertinent." Remare drove with one hand on the wheel and the other stroking his bare chin as if he missed his goatee.

"Really? I'm not the one who interrupted...a private moment." Miranda wasn't comfortable discussing what happened in New Mexico when she'd been with Will. Another fragment of being in Remare's arms barely surfaced and then was suddenly gone. She wanted to ask him if he'd taken a memory, but feared he would only erase it more thoroughly this time. When she had time, she'd ask Blu if he could restore a memory.

"If you are referring to the time he intruded on you and your lover in New Mexico, I already know."

She narrowed her eyes. "How do you know about that?"

Remare exhaled evenly, and Miranda barely detected his low growl. "I was in the room when Valadon tried contacting you." He turned to look at her. "If you had bothered to return his phone calls, he might not have...interrupted you."

"It wasn't the first time," Miranda murmured. "Your boss doesn't like it much when someone says no to him." She turned away from him, preferring the view of the trees and the river. The moon cast silver crests to the swells on the Hudson River Miranda found relaxing.

"Valadon has been lord for centuries—nearly a millennium—and now that he is high lord, he is used to his authority and having his commands obeyed."

Miranda mumbled, "He can command this," and slapped her hip.

Remare fought a smirk as he watched the highway. "Nick's been asking about you. He's quite smitten with you, you know."

Nick was Valadon's college-age nephew, who also happened to be her student at NYU. Of all the vampires at ValCorp, she missed Nick the most and hoped he registered for one of her classes in the fall. She lamented that they never completed the catalog Valadon had hired her to finish. "I miss him," she whispered.

"He misses you, too. So does Valadon."

She thought she heard him say, *"And me,"* but the way her mind had been working lately, she figured she imagined it.

As they neared the Financial District, he pointed to the pier where boats were moored. "I need to stop there for a moment."

Miranda had always admired the boats and the people lucky enough to be able to enjoy the water any time they wanted to. When Remare parked the car, she accompanied him to his boat. She was tempted to make a comment about vampires not being able to travel over water unless it was the slack of the tide, but decided to keep quiet. Vampires had such little regard for Stoker.

As if hearing her thoughts, Remare smirked. "What? No comments about vampires and the slack of the tide, Miranda?"

"I didn't say it." She tried not to chuckle. "I didn't say a word."

Remare held her hand as she descended the few steps into his boat then went below deck to search for what he needed.

Miranda immediately liked the forty-footer and wandered around the galley and the living room. She noticed the painting of a villa in Tuscany above the electric fireplace and approved of the glass enclosure. She'd done authentications for some people who had expensive yachts, but didn't realize how the salt air could ruin a painting and often left them unprotected. When Miranda moved closer, she studied the artist's name, but didn't know who Asanti was. She remembered Valadon had several paintings by the same artist in his archives.

Remare walked toward her. "I see you've found *The Requiem*. It's one of my favorite paintings."

"It's exquisite, but I don't recognize the artist."

"You wouldn't." He came beside her. "Asanti is a vampire artist. He only sold his paintings to other vampires or gave them away as gifts. He lives here in New York. On the Upper West Side. Actually, not too far from Werehaven."

"He's brilliant with his brush strokes. Look how he uses light and shadows to augment the villa in the painting." Pleasantly surprised, she felt Remare stroking the ends of her hair and then eyed the old bottle Remare had tucked under one arm. "I see you found what you were looking for. Are you celebrating something?"

"It's not for me, but for a friend." Remare led her into the galley. Behind the breakfast nook, he reached beneath for another bottle. "Would you care for a drink? We still have a few minutes."

"Got any Pepsi?" Miranda tilted her head, feeling more comfortable with him than she thought possible. She slid onto the stool on her side of the counter space.

Remare examined the contents of his mini-fridge and held up a small bottle. "Is ginger ale all right with you?"

"It's fine."

He poured her drink and handed her the glass. "The last time I was on this boat I had to bury a friend."

Miranda blinked and quickly looked around her, realizing too late they were completely alone. The butterflies started dancing again.

Shaking his head, Remare laughed at her nervousness. "Mir-randa, do you really think I still harbor any thoughts of harming you?"

"Not at all." Slowing her breaths, she took another sip of her soda. "Who did you have to bury?"

"You met him once." He watched her eyebrows gather in thought. "His name was Kristoph."

Miranda remembered the flirtatious vampire with the androgynous looks. Kristoph had been polite to her, but underneath his playful, seductive aura, she had sensed a pervasive loneliness as if he had suffered a despairing loss and had never completely recovered. "What happened to him?"

Remare's eyes darkened. "He was murdered. From the descriptions he gave me before he died, I believed it was Scherer."

Miranda recalled the malicious bodyguard of the HOL, the hate group who had plotted against Valadon. Scherer had once pursued her down Fifth Avenue with death in his eyes. Later, he had tortured Remare, and Miranda had killed him for it. "Kristoph was your friend."

"Yes, but as he had no standing in Valadon House, his burial was quiet at sea. Vampires prefer burials at sea; the place where we *all* originally came from."

Miranda wasn't sure if Remare was talking about vampires or all people. She supposed he was referring to all beings as she recollected vampires believed they evolved as humans did, just that their evolvement had occurred underground. "Did you bury Cyra, as well?" Cyra had been her vampire friend who had hung out with her and Lizandra.

"Cyra was popular at Valadon House and at ValCorp. We used a far larger boat for her funeral. Our sage, Victor, presided over the ceremony." Remare took a sip of his drink. "Morel is still overcome with grief. Even now, he prefers solitude. It will be quite some time before he fully recovers, if at all."

"I would have liked to have attended her funeral. She was a good friend."

Remare bowed his head and appeared reflective. "You were in a coma at the time."

Miranda lamented she never had the chance to say goodbye to her friend who always had a quick and endearing smile. "Could you take me to the place where you buried her sometime? I would like to place some flowers on the water."

"If you like." He nodded in her direction. "But come now, Valadon awaits."

When they were both on deck, Miranda took one last look at the waves on the water. From their vantage point, they could see the Statue of Liberty brightly illuminated in the distance. "Look." She gestured. "Lady Liberty is all lit up." Feeling a strange sense of contentment, Miranda met his eyes as a cool breeze stole over them. "Thank you. For bringing me here. I think I needed this moment." Somehow, being with Remare gave her the strength she needed to face Valadon.

Odd, now that she thought about it, she often felt stronger when she was with Remare.

"You're welcome." Remare breathed in a whiff of her hair. Miranda smelled like orange blossoms. Closing his eyes, he inhaled her scent deeply into his lungs. Lifting a hand to rest gently on the small of her back, he allowed himself to enjoy one moment of peace as they watched the waves and the distant statue.

He, too, needed this moment. But for different reasons.

Remare brushed a strand of hair away from Miranda's face. He hoped Valadon knew what he was doing. Miranda was dear to Remare, and he didn't want to see her harmed. She had suffered enough at the hands of vampires. Remare remembered the damage done to Miranda's body in the wake of Mulciber's violence. She'd been bleeding from all the orifices in her face, and he had feared she wouldn't survive. He had shared some of his blood with her to ensure her survival.

As she calmly gazed over the river, he had to force himself to keep from kissing her. He could easily understand why Valadon and Gabriel had been attracted to her. The look of grace on her face was mesmerizing. No other woman he knew—and he had known many in his long years—could match the serenity Miranda possessed. He wondered if she was aware of what her face looked like at times like these. When he had first entered the state room, he'd enjoyed seeing how rapt Miranda was in his painting.

The professor was alive and well tonight, but he wondered more about the woman—a woman he found impossible to forget.

Chapter Six

Walking hesitantly down the hall to Valadon's penthouse office, Miranda remembered the last time she'd been here. She'd almost betrayed Gabriel, if common sense hadn't penetrated the hazy, sensual rapture the high lord had cloaked her in.

Disillusioned with his cunning, she realized too late Valadon had never stopped trying to win her favor. However, when she'd been in New Mexico, his interest in her seemed to lessen. At least that's what she'd thought—until he had tried to contact her at the worst possible moment.

Entering his office suite, she paused when she saw him staring out the window. The moon's glow made his face appear paler than she knew it to be. How any human could mistake the vampire for a human was beyond her. Slowly, she covered her heart with her hand and bowed her head, needing a moment to collect herself. That otherworldly essence that proclaimed him *other* always hit her hardest when she was alone with him. Even with her eyes closed, she could feel his magnetism and the unrelenting desire to know the unknowable.

At nearly six foot-three inches with an athletic build, the High Lord of New York was an imposing figure. And that was before anyone saw his mesmerizing emerald eyes—eyes that turned a turbulent sea green when he was angered. The intensity in those eyes defined the vampire. He ran his empire, ValCorp, here, high in the sky, but deep below the surface in Valadon House, he ruled over the vampires.

In those subterranean levels, Miranda had seen the depth of his power when he had faced off against the maleficent ancient, Mulciber. She'd been told no vampire lord had ever defeated an ancient until Valadon had. His display of supremacy was something Miranda would never forget. Of course, she had loaned him what *Elemental* energy she could. And she'd had one helluva power source. She fingered her blood amber necklace.

"There's a mist over the moon. I believe that means we're in for a night of terrible weather," Miranda ventured cautiously, not knowing how Valadon would react to seeing her.

"Is that something you learned from your Native American friends?" The high lord kept his eyes locked on the window and his arms folded over his chest.

Miranda steeled herself against the deep, melodious tones of Valadon's voice. "Actually, it's something I heard on the weather channel earlier tonight." She grinned as the vampire turned toward her. With his dark brown hair and sculpted cheekbones, he could put any Hollywood heartthrob to shame. His sensual lips cried out for every woman's kiss, but it was his indefinable aura of power that held Miranda in awe. And that had frightened her. Just one of the reasons she had chosen to be with Gabriel.

Something Valadon had yet to forgive her for.

He scrutinized her from head to toe. "You look well."

"As do you." Miranda stood beside him and gazed out the window. Mirroring his pose, she folded her arms over her chest. "How have you been?"

"Patient. Waiting for *someone* I hold dear to make her presence known to me."

She smiled as she met his eyes. He wasn't trying to manipulate or overwhelm her. He was obviously displeased she'd ignored his messages, but underneath it all, she sensed he was happy to see her...and something else.

"*Someone* had the right to make her own decisions." Miranda admired the lights in the buildings across the street that made up New York's majestic skyline.

Something resembling a growl broke from his throat as he studied the lingering mist for a moment longer. "I would like to talk to you about what's been happening here." He turned toward the door.

Miranda wasn't sure it was a good idea, but if all he wanted was to talk, then she would listen. "I'm here now."

"Not here. Let's go below," his eyes narrowed, "or are you still frightened of the lower levels?"

She remembered the scar Mulciber had given her across her face and inwardly cringed at the memory of being imprisoned in one of the underground cells. But she knew she was safe with Valadon. "I hear you're a high lord now."

"Yes." He went to take her elbow, but she carefully maneuvered away from him.

"If I appear distant, I have my reasons." She met his eyes. "Do you understand?"

Valadon seemed to study her, then nodded. "We can go to one of the conference rooms here if you prefer."

"No." She shook it off. "It's all right."

She accompanied him to his private elevator that would take them far beneath ValCorp's façade. Down below, not unlike Werehaven, a whole world existed where the vampires congregated to enjoy each other's company. It was where the magnificent archives housed Valadon's vast collection of art and rare books.

She had fallen in love with the archives the moment she'd seen it. Unfortunately, it had also been where Mulciber had slashed her.

"So, tell me what it feels like to be high lord. I hear it's quite an honor." When the elevator doors closed, she felt Valadon's energy brushing up against hers.

"Come into my parlor, and I will tell you secrets beyond your imagination." He smiled as he keyed in his code to the elevator that would take them down to Valadon House.

Miranda smirked at the sense of humor Valadon so rarely displayed. "Secrets, huh?" She inhaled his masculine scent. Something about his scent always reminded her of the ocean at night—something dark and deceptively dangerous.

"Some secrets you have to work to uncover."

Miranda didn't bother asking which secrets those were.

The elevator doors opened, and Valadon led her to his luxurious living room with the plush couches, elegant chandelier and white brick fireplace. Here, the vampires of Valadon House had been very attentive to her. Cyra, Morel and the others had made sure she felt welcomed in their home.

When they were comfortably seated and Escher, Valadon's butler, had served them Turkish tea—one of her favorites—Valadon finally spoke. "There's a painting that's become available, and I wanted you to examine it before I purchased it."

Miranda was confused as she sipped her tea, delighting in its aroma. *This is what he's been trying to get ahold of me for?* For months, she had believed he wanted far more from her. "A painting?"

"Yes, it is an exquisite work, and I want you to authenticate it before I acquire it."

She carefully studied his eyes and face. Clearly, there was more going on than she was privy to. "What's the catch?"

Valadon smiled. "So suspicious of me, Miranda?" The high lord sat back as he drank his tea, never taking his verdant eyes off her.

Miranda watched as the king of vampires reclined comfortably. And knew, without a doubt...she was being played. Every gut instinct she had was going off inside her head that there was far more going on than Valadon was saying.

She wasn't going to give him her speech on trust or how some people violated that trust and lost it. But she was thinking it. Real hard.

"There has to be more to it." *Gotta be.* "What's the painting, and who's the owner?"

"It's a beautiful Degas, and the owner has recently passed away; that is why it is up for sale, now. The estate of the deceased has been settled, and it has now become available." He looked directly at her, the red rims around his irises glowing. "It's something I've wanted for a long time."

Eyes narrowing, she considered all the things he *wasn't* saying. Trying to get a read on him with her empath talents—especially now that he was a high lord—was nearly impossible. "Where's the painting, now?"

Valadon met her suspicious look. "In Paris."

"Paris?" she asked, bewildered. "Did you say Paris? I can't go to Paris." She put down her tea. "The museum would never let me leave. I just got back from a two-month leave. They're never going to let me go, now." Completely astonished, she rose and started pacing.

"Yes, they will. I'm on the board, Miranda, and I've already talked to Jordan Knox. You can leave at the end of the week and even take a day or two to get some sightseeing in. Paris is a wonderful city. As I'm sure you know."

Miranda wondered if he was aware Paris was where she'd completed her Master's degree at the American University. *Of course, he does.* "I suppose you would be coming with me?"

"Unfortunately, no. Paris is the territory of a powerful vampire, one connected to our ruling council." He leaned forward. "And as High Lord of New York City, I cannot enter her domain without permission. The same goes for any other vampire lords who wish to visit my city."

Miranda tilted her head. "Would permission be so very hard to obtain?"

She knew Valadon sensed her suspicions by the way he smiled. "In this case, yes."

Vampire politics. Miranda shook her head as she considered the possibilities. Her desk was probably stacked high with work. Jordan would *not* be okay with her leaving, again, even if Valadon had persuaded him to release her for the few days she'd need to validate the Degas. She made up her mind. She couldn't do it. "Valadon, you know there are many authenticators all over Europe; you could easily hire one of them for the validation papers."

"I could. True." He sipped his tea, then put the cup down. "But I won't. I trust you, and it's you I want to validate my painting. I don't appreciate others knowing what I'm interested in, and I prefer them not knowing what it is I accumulate."

And what High Lord Valadon wants, he gets. She continued strolling around his living room then turned in his direction. "Can I have a day or two to think about it?"

"Of course. But please make your decision soon." He sat back and crossed one leg over his knee. "I don't want to lose this opportunity."

"Jordan is not going to be thrilled with this." Miranda tapped her fingers on her hips.

"The museum will be generously compensated for your time away and acquire the loan of one of my paintings." Valadon's voice radiated dulcet tones. "They will be quite happy, I assure you."

Miranda stopped pacing. Something was off here, she could feel it, but couldn't comprehend what. Valadon seemed rather pleased with himself. Too pleased. "I'll give you a call tomorrow?"

He nodded as his phone went off. She wandered toward the kitchen area to give him privacy.

"Miranda, I have to check something in my rooms. I'll be back in a few minutes."

"Sure," she murmured as she walked around. When she found herself at the end of a long corridor, staring at two carved oak doors, she wondered if her old key card still worked. *Let's find out.* When the mechanism clicked, she walked in, flicked on the lights, and smiled.

Valadon's archives were a sight to behold. A world of beauty and enchantment. His vast collection of books belonged in a museum, and his art collection was one of the finest in the world. It was a shame the masses would never enjoy his works. But collectors valued their privacy as much as they valued their possessions.

And they valued their possessions immensely.

By the intricately designed balustrade, she glanced at the two levels below. The oldest and most valuable of Valadon's possessions were on the lowest level. Peering down, she saw a figure moving in the shadows. From this angle, she couldn't make out who it was, but when he looked up at her and held her gaze, Miranda gasped sharply as a feeling of unease gathered deep within her.

***

Valadon finished his call and leaned back in his chair. Exhaling, his thoughts turned to Miranda. With her chestnut fall of wavy hair and her whiskey-colored eyes, which held more knowledge than any mortal should have, she was as beautiful as he remembered. He had been attracted to her from the moment he first saw her. The fact she was human had been the only reason that had kept him from approaching her sooner. But her courage and compassion had inflamed his desire for her.

There were few in his house who would dare address him the way she did and even fewer he would tolerate it from. He smirked. But he was content to have her by his side, once again.

Valadon didn't appreciate her cool detachment, but he did understand. He'd seen what Mulciber had done to her and how far she'd gone with her own power to defend herself.

He never wanted to see her battered and bloodied again.

But Valadon was a high lord, now. And it was not only his status that had been elevated. His power had surged dramatically when he'd killed Mulciber, as if he had absorbed some of the ancient's strength before he died. He looked down at his clenched fist and felt the vibrancy he'd been able to wield, then slowly flexed his fingers. He'd become very powerful, much more than most vampires could guess. Therefore, he should be able to protect Miranda from any of his enemies.

Even though he was the one planning on opening the lion's cage.

Chapter Seven

The moon's glow was bright in the midnight sky over Central Park; the earlier mists having vaporized into the crisp New York air. Standing naked and proud, Queen Lizandra of Black Star Clan relished the mild wind blowing against her heated skin. Weres were warmer than humans, but during the full moon, her blood boiled hotter than usual. The Lunar Run would help her work off the intense heat they were all feeling.

Tonight, the chase would be especially exhilarating.

High on the rock precipice, Lizandra looked out over Central Park and peered down at her clan, a clan that had a Wells as a leader for as long as she could remember. Before she was clan leader, her father, Charles, and before him, her grandmother, Victoria, who had first dreamed of the sanctuary that was now Werehaven. Liz would do her ancestors proud with leading the clan in their run.

She surveyed the Weres slowly morphing into their wolf forms. With the true essence of a huntress, a thick black pelt emerged from her arms; her nails, already lethally long, turned into viciously sharp claws. Her snout protruded as her sharp canines elongated. When her body had completed its transformation, she arched her back and bayed gloriously at the moon. Hearing her howl, the wolves in the pack echoed her melodic tones, creating music in the night.

The run began, and Lizandra proved why she was queen. She sent her two lieutenants, Brent and Quint, ahead as scouts. They didn't have the bulk most of the Weres had, and because they were lighter, they moved very swiftly. Her own speed was unmatched by anyone in the clan—except for one. She smiled. But, tonight, Gavin's job was to watch the flanks of the pack.

The Were Queen led the wolves gracefully down the trails leading south along the lake. The fastest were in front, sprinting, howling, showing off their strength and agility. Their cadence in harmony as they passed Belvedere Castle, then they hit their stride near Strawberry Fields. Their pace, already strenuous, quickened when they passed Sheep Meadow, and finally, they gathered at the carousel to regroup. Max and Sasha were the last to join them. None were ever left far behind.

Liz was pleased her wolves were howling their song of joy—their cry an avowal of pack. Her snout pointed at the moon as her howl pierced the cool, dark night. The blood pulsing through her veins was an affirmation of what it felt like to be truly alive.

Humans would be terrified if they ever witnessed the Weres in their full glory and heard the majesty of their voices singing to the moon. Lizandra snorted. These were her people. Strong, proud and protective of each other.

Not wanting to rest long, she led them on, sensing Gavin had enough of guard duty—Lawe usually was assigned that duty. Gavin might not be Were King, but he'd been her consort for a reason. He was the fastest and strongest of the pack, but the way he was nearing Orion caused her concern.

As they rounded Wollman Rink near the zoo, Liz heard the excited shrieks of the caged animals. Gavin sprinted ahead in a burst of speed unrivaled by any of the others. When he pulled alongside Orion, he bit down on his flank—not enough to cause a severe injury, but enough to show the younger Were exactly what he thought of him.

Lizandra snorted as he ran past The Boathouse. In her wolf form, she could hear every bird cry, smell every scent of the pine trees and see all the wonders Central Park offered. When she reached Bethesda Fountain—her favorite place in the park—panting from her exertions, she stared above at the statue of the angel. She then looked over the lake as it mirrored the moon's glow and stood in awe of its radiant beauty.

By now, the other Weres were hunting prey on their trek through the tree-lined paths, devouring squirrels and other wildlife. She could hear the mating cries of the more festive members of the clan and one plaintive howl of frustration echoing loudly through the trees. She knew taking another lover had made Gavin's blood boil. He'd been anguished over his demotion, but she hadn't expected such riveting sounds of torment.

She led the pack to the monument known as Cleopatra's Needle, near the Metropolitan Museum, for their cooldown. Here the more ambitious members of the clan would journey north around the reservoir and then return to Werehaven.

Declining that part of the run, she decided she would save herself for another type of workout—one equally vigorous.

Later that night at Werehaven, Lizandra sat naked in her human form in front of her vanity, examining her face. A shower had cooled her body, but her face was still flushed. The Lunar Run always energized her, and as taxing as the demanding run was, she still felt her power throbbing in her veins. Smiling, she applied her favorite rose-fragrant moisturizer and sensed someone entering her private chambers.

Glancing in her mirror, she saw Gavin breathing her musky perfume deep into his lungs. His reddish-brown hair was still damp from his shower. In his current state, their combined scents did sensuous things to his naked body.

He pulled a chair near her and sat. "You missed a place on your left shoulder." His voice sounded husky. "Do you want me to rub it in?"

Lizandra was glad Gavin had come. If he had not shown, she would have gone to him. "You broke ranks tonight." She handed him the bottle of lotion and let him massage her tired shoulders. She had stretched her muscles to their maximum tonight; there was no pain, but rather a tender ache that signaled she'd had a great workout. Her eyes slowly closed at the sensations he aroused with merely the touch of his hands on her shoulders.

"Yes, I did. But you were expecting that."

This close, she inhaled Gavin's spicy scent and took it deep into her very being. He had been her lover for years, so he knew every caress, every touch that drove her to wildness. She knew Gavin could tell by her arousal how his touch was affecting her.

"Do you want me to do your calves?"

Lizandra slowly lifted one foot to Gavin's chest; she could feel his heart thundering against the sole of her foot. His muscles rippled as he worked her calf. Gavin looked at her with heated eyes. When he first had walked into her room naked, his presence didn't register as something sexual. But the look in his bourbon-colored eyes said his thoughts were highly sensual.

As a chiropractor, Gavin gave exemplary massages. Every touch, every caress was designed for one purpose— stimulation. And she was as hungry for him as he was for her. When he finished with her calves, he moved his hands up her thighs. "Put your foot on my shoulder."

Liz slowly moved her foot high enough to brace on his shoulder; she knew by doing this, she was exposing her most intimate flesh. Having been denied for weeks, Gavin stared, eyes burning with desire. She liked Orion—they had made beautiful music together—but he wasn't Gavin, whose only flaw was that he'd made her feel vulnerable.

Gavin used the tips of his fingers to massage her inner thighs. His eyes boring into hers, he moved his thumbs to massage the heated flesh between her thighs. He was purposely not rubbing the one place she wanted him to touch most. He rubbed, caressed and touched her everywhere but her clit. When she emitted low warning growls, he snickered. "Denial is one of the worst sins a person can inflict on another."

"Only if the reason is lame. I had my reasons, Gavin." She pulled him close, running her nails up his pecs and kissed him passionately.

By tomorrow, they would both be sore and achy from their lovemaking. There was a time to be tender and loving; tonight wasn't it. The moon's magic was too strong, the forces controlling their animal natures too intense.

Tonight would be mercilessly rough.

In a burst of speed, Gavin whipped her body up and fisted her long braids as he pulled her head down and kissed her with the passion borne of a starved man. Rough kisses weren't his usual, but tonight, he was obviously in a demanding mood.

Liz knew this side of Gavin, flirted with it, even encouraged it. Tonight, they would unleash their appetites, drive each other insane with their animalistic instincts.

But Lizandra was pack leader, a queen, and she liked to dominate. It was her right, her preference, and she would fight Gavin for dominance. She caressed his male flesh, her nails digging in a fraction too deep.

Gavin reluctantly lessened his hold on her hair. Then found himself flung against the wall of her bedroom. Rising to her full height, Lizandra smiled at her prey. Gavin had never been threatened by her statuesque physique. She wanted him to enjoy his view of her body flushed with arousal. If her scent didn't drive him insane enough, she knew how to stroke him to have him nearly begging.

Looking at him with hooded eyes, she decided she would test that fine line between pain and pleasure. She caressed her sides to entice and then ran her hands up to her breasts and stroked her own nipples. When her moans turned euphoric, Gavin charged her.

She would be bruised come morning.

But so would he.

Chapter Eight

"Miranda, it's great to see you," Morel said as he embraced her.

Miranda hugged him tightly. "I've missed you." At six foot-five inches, he was the tallest of Valadon's Torians. With his long blond hair and golden-green eyes, he was a strikingly handsome vampire. Miranda remembered after his wife's death, he'd preferred his solitude and refused her and Gabriel's calls. Perhaps, now, the numbing frost of death would start melting.

Morel led her to the sofa in the sitting area of the archives. "I heard you were traveling out west. How was your trip?"

Aside from a bout of lunacy? "Interesting, to say the least. I learned a great deal about petroglyphs and New Mexico's terrain." Sitting next to him on the sofa, she tugged one leg under her body. "But it feels good to be back in New York."

Miranda studied his face with the discernment that made her a good authenticator. It saddened her to see that the usual glow in his eyes had greatly diminished. She tugged on a strand of his hair. "I see you let it grow long."

"Laziness on my part." He offered her a crooked smile. "Eventually, I'll get it cut." Turning towards her, he relaxed into the sofa. "So, what brings you here? Not that I'm not glad to see you, but it's been months."

Miranda exhaled, then rose and walked to the fireplace, the heat from the flames soothing her. "Your boss wants me to fly to Paris to authenticate a painting for him." She peered sideways at him. "I told Valadon I would give him an answer by tomorrow." She gestured to the staircase. "I just left him in the living area. He's taking an important call."

"He's missed you, Miranda. We all have." Morel watched her as she paced in front of the fire. "Why did you stay away for so long?"

Closing her eyes, she bent her head back. "Things got...a little complicated." When she opened her eyes and saw him waiting, she thought he deserved a better explanation. "I was with Gabriel for nearly six months. He wanted to cut his ties with Valadon—start a new life—sort of flex his wings a bit." She shrugged. "I thought it was for the best."

Morel crossed one leg over the other. "Nick's missed you a lot. After you left, he talked a great deal about you."

Miranda felt the guilt kicking in. The vampires had been generous with her, and she had turned her back on them. "I missed him, too." She grinned at Morel. "Nick holds a special place in my heart."

"Would you like to see him?" He smiled as he nodded toward the stairs. "He's upstairs in the training room with Bastien. They're practicing their martial arts. C'mon." Morel slipped his hand in hers and led her up the stairs to the second level. "I'll let Valadon know where you are."

"Okay." Sighing, Miranda looked around the magnificent library. Just being in the archives brought back good memories of working with Nick.

Morel opened the door that led to the training area. Halfway down the hall, she could hear grunting as a body hit the mat and someone panting from exertion.

Entering the room, she saw Bastien bending down to give Nick a hand up. Both were covered in perspiration.

"Again. This time, Nick, watch his shoulders. See which arm he leads with," the leader of the Torians instructed.

Miranda's eyes immediately flew to Remare, who was wearing a black sleeveless gi with three red Asian characters embroidered across the back. Wondering what they meant, she watched as each fighter moved into position.

"I'll go find Valadon. Watch Remare; he's one of the best instructors in the world. He keeps us all in impeccable shape," Morel whispered. "He once trained in Asia when he was a member of Qui Ti Huay's court. No one can match him for speed...or skill."

Barely aware of Morel's departure, Miranda exhaled softly. "I'll bet." She'd once seen Remare fight nearly a dozen Rogues. It took only minutes for him to behead a few as the others had run off. Of course, she'd gotten an unwanted haircut in the process. She smirked as she remembered the throwing star. Maybe she should have waited in the car as he had requested, but that just wasn't her style.

Nick hit the mat, again, groaning as his shoulders went slack.

"Once more," Remare ordered as he helped Nick up.

Concentration blazing in his eyes, Nick watched every movement of Bastien's fighting style.

Miranda tried to focus on the sparring match, but her eyes kept drifting to Remare, who was as tough an instructor as Lizandra. She enjoyed observing him as he scrutinized every movement Nick made. Like the Were Queen, Remare apparently liked his people to be in optimum condition. Sympathizing with Nick, Miranda could still feel the aches and pains from Liz's workouts.

In a move almost too quick for her to follow, Nick was able to get the jump on Bastien and had him pinned on the mat. Miranda let out a whoop of approval and clapped her hands. Suddenly, aware all eyes were on her, she slowly stopped clapping. *Right!* What not to do when watching a sparring match.

"Miranda!" Elated, Nick shouted with joy and moved in her direction as Remare snaked out a hand to stop him.

"And the last thing you do is become distracted when a beautiful woman enters the room. Now, explain to me where you were screwing up," Remare ordered Nick.

Beautiful? Remare thought she was beautiful? Miranda was stunned. With the women he hung out with, that was high praise. A smile tugged at the corners of her mouth.

"Now, observe what you should be doing." Remare took Nick's place on the mat. "Bastien, repeat Nick's last few steps."

Bastien complied, bowing to the grand master and immediately taking his position.

After Morel returned, he said, "Remare's been instructing us for centuries. He knows all our moves. Bastien is one of the best hand-to-hand fighters in the Torian guard. Next to Remare, he has the ability and speed to rival the best martial arts fighters in the world."

Remare and Bastien went through their moves with precision so that Nick could see where he needed to be quicker with his kicks and punches.

Miranda admired the natural grace of the two combatants. Remare moved with the fluidity of a cobra, and she wondered if that's what the lettering on his gi meant. Bastien was fluid, as well, but he didn't have the quickness Remare possessed. In a blaze of razor sharp twists and turns, Remare had Bastien on his back in seconds. When they finished their exercise, Remare spoke a few words to Nick, then bowed and went to the door at the end of the room. Before leaving, he met her eyes, briefly nodded, and then disappeared.

"Miranda! It's good to see you." Nick grabbed Miranda in a tight hug and whirled her around. "I'm glad you're here."

Dear God, Nick had filled out a lot since she had seen him last and had put on at least ten pounds of muscle. Miranda imagined the full-grown male he would become one day. She returned his enthusiasm and nearly laughed. "I'm glad to see you, as well. You have one helluva tough instructor there." She nodded in the direction Remare had just gone as Nick lowered her to the ground.

"Remare never settles for second best. He'll bring out the best in you—even though you're cursing him under your breath."

Yeah, that pretty much summed it up.

Smiling, Bastien handed Nick a water bottle and used a small towel to wipe his face. "Good to see you again, Miranda."

"I signed up for your Nineteenth Century Art History course," Nick guzzled some water, "and so did some of the other students in our last class." A trickle of water ran down his chin and neck. He grinned at her mockingly. "I thought with the title, *Friend of the Court*, you would have stopped by sooner."

"I'm here, now."

Morel's ringtone sounded, and he read his text message. "I have to let Remare know to check his messages."

"I'll tell him," Miranda volunteered as the others looked exhausted from sparring. She walked to the door Remare had used as she heard the men commenting and laughing about the sparring match.

***

Closing his eyes, Remare dropped his head back, letting the cool water of his shower run over his too-heated flesh. He had his own luxurious bathroom in his apartment, but the shower in the training area was closer. The workout had felt good, but more importantly, it had relieved some of the stress that had been bothering him. At the sound of a door opening, he turned his head and saw Irina striding toward him. With her long white-blond hair and blue eyes, she was as beautiful as she was deadly. And one of his best assassins.

"I've spoken with our contacts." Irina leaned against the frame of his shower door. "There have been no sightings of Brandon."

"I did not think there would be." Remare sighed, aware Irina was watching the water sluice off his naked body—a body she'd been intimate with for decades, even though it had been a long while since he had chosen to share his bed with her. "Brandon is far too clever to make it easy for me." He turned the faucet off and used a towel to dry off. Irina's look of hunger did not escape him, though his body remained unresponsive.

If he was still hard at all, it was because of the rush of the sparring. Miranda's presence had absolutely nothing to do with it. At least, that was what he told himself.

Noting his partial erection, Irina didn't wait for an invitation. She opened the short door to his stall and went down on her knees before him.

Remare saw the longing in her eyes and felt...if not pity for the woman who had been his sometime lover, a certain remorse—regret that he could not be what she most desired. The others thought her an ice queen, but he had seen her vulnerable when he had helped free her from a cruel lord in Russia. When she tried to take him into her mouth, he stopped her with a hand on her shoulder. "No. Not now." *Not ever again.* Hurt and confusion marred her eyes when he heard the door opening, again.

"Sorry to disturb you, Remare," Miranda called out, "but Morel asked me to tell you that your phone is off and to check your messages."

Remare glimpsed the surprise on Miranda's face as
Irina rose from behind the shower door. He watched as one
eyebrow slowly lifted and didn't have to read her mind to
know what she was thinking. *Only one reason a woman
would be on her knees. Ri-ight!* Miranda gracefully tried to
cover her disappointment, but he'd seen it. Before the
silence dragged on too long, he said, "Thank you, Mir-
randa."

"Okay, then." She turned and left.

Irina eyed his face and then watched as Miranda closed
the door behind her. Unfortunately, when she gazed down,
he was fully erect. "You get hard for the human woman?"

Remare heard the accusation in Irina's voice and
resented it. "Don't be ridiculous." He narrowed his eyes as
he chastised her and hardened his tone. "She's a human.
And Valadon's human." Not liking the look of scrutiny in
Irina's eyes, he quickly tied the towel around his hips.

***

"I see you've found Nick," Valadon said to Miranda as
he joined the group and nodded to Morel and Bastien. He
spoke silently in her mind. *"Thank you for getting Morel to
join us."*

Miranda understood his preference for the silent
communication and allowed the non-verbal intimacy. "Yes,
we were just getting reacquainted." She stood beside him.
"You should have seen the way Nick put Bastien on his
back."

"Yeah, it only took him three tries." Bastien snorted.

Escher came quietly to them. "My lords, I've prepared a
midnight meal if you are hungry—sliced marinated steak
with grilled vegetables and garlic roasted potatoes."

Bastien sighed with near-orgasmic pleasure. "The
marinade with the merlot and Montreal spices? God, that's
my favorite."

"Mine, too!" Nick looked at Miranda. "Escher's the best. You've got to sample his cooking."

Miranda's stomach picked that moment to emit a soft grumble. She prayed the others didn't hear, but when Valadon grinned, she knew that they had.

He winked at her. "Would you care to join us?"

When the others encouraged her to stay, Miranda decided she could do with some food. Valadon guided her to the dining room that could easily seat twenty people.

Valadon sat at the head of the table, and Miranda would have joined him, but she wanted to see where everyone else sat first. Morel stood to the left of Valadon, and Remare then entered and took the right. Of course, Remare was his second and would be seated on his right, but only now did she realize Morel was his third.

Morel motioned for her to sit in his seat, then took the one next to it.

When the other Torians entered, Escher removed the lid to the meal, and Miranda nearly drooled at the aroma of deliciously cooked meat. He served the steak the way she liked it, the outside darkly crisp and the inside a juicy pink. The others chatted and recounted highlights from the sparring match—her heart warmed at their sense of camaraderie; it was admirable—except for Irina, who ate silently as the others talked and kidded each other.

"Miranda," Valadon whispered in her head, *"how come you don't look at Remare? Has he said or done anything objectionable?"*

Miranda looked up at Remare, not knowing how to answer Valadon. She went with the truth. *"I kinda walked in on him and Irina...when she was giving him...a moment."*

One corner of Valadon's mouth rose. *"I see his silence is for your benefit, then. Thank you for joining us tonight. It means a lot to Nick and..."* he nodded at Morel, *"everyone else."* He then turned to Remare. "You don't speak to our guest?"

Remare seemed surprised by Valadon's question, but answered, "I spoke to Miranda plenty when I brought her here earlier tonight as I'm sure she could attest to." He lifted his glass of Cabernet in her direction. "Her trip was very enlightening, and she is happy to be back."

Miranda nodded to Remare. She wasn't about to admonish Valadon for entering her mind. This time, he spoke politely and not in his usual demanding voice, so she didn't feel susceptible to his power. As she watched his eye contact with Remare, she knew they were also conversing silently and wondered what they were talking about.

Nick said, "Miranda, tell us about your trip."

"Do you really want to hear about ancient Native American petroglyphs? I think everyone at this table would be bored."

"Tell us," several voices echoed.

Miranda gave them the short version of her trip, leaving out any mention of visions of flying. When she was done answering their questions, she sat back and observed the dynamics of the group. She realized, not for the first time, how lucky Valadon was to have such loyal men and women in his house and how paternal Valadon was with them. She found it an attractive quality.

"Miranda, you look tired." Valadon asked, "Would you like someone to drive you home?"

She was grateful for the affability of the vampires around her, but exhaustion was beginning to set in, and she just wanted to crawl into her own bed. "Thanks." She nodded. "That would be great."

Valadon accompanied her to the elevator. "Thank you for coming. It was a pleasure to see you again after such a lengthy absence." He bent to kiss her temple.

"It was good to see everyone tonight." Hesitating for just a moment, she met his eyes. "Including you. I'll give your request serious thought and call you tomorrow."

Valadon bowed and then turned to walk down the hall. Clever vampire. He knew she resented his authoritative posture with her so he had acted humbly and informally with her. Hard trick, she thought, for a vampire high lord, and smiled.

When the elevator doors opened, Katya, Valadon's other elite female Torian, stepped out and greeted her. "Hello, Miranda. I hear you might be going to Paris?"

"Hi, Katya. That hasn't been settled, yet. I'm still thinking about it."

"Well, if you do decide to go, I was wondering if you could do me a favor."

Miranda raised an eyebrow. "Such as?"

Katya laughed. "Come to my room. It will only take a minute." Miranda followed her down the corridor. When Katya opened her door, she pointed to a wall covered with shelves of miniature glass bottles of various sizes and shapes. "I've been collecting them for decades."

Miranda was in awe of all the sparkling colorful pieces of glass. She had a friend at work who collected Murano glass, but didn't know anyone who collected tiny bottles resembling antique perfume bottles. "Impressive."

"I was going to ask you, if you went to Paris, to visit a shop." Katya reached in her desk drawer for a card and handed it to Miranda. "The proprietor is a master craftsman. I sometimes order online, but would appreciate it if you could pick up a piece for me. That is, if you do decide to go. Just tell the owner it's for me. He knows the ones I like."

Miranda put the card in her bag. "Okay. If I do go, I'll get this for you."

Katya smiled warmly. "Thanks."

Well, that was strange, Miranda thought, exiting the elevator. However, her face heated and she nearly gasped when she discovered who was waiting to drive her home.

Chapter Nine

The dark, lonely streets off Sixth Avenue passed by as Remare drove her home. Miranda cracked the window open because his masculine scent was playing havoc with her hormones, and her body felt increasingly warm. A light breeze made the trees rustle as the falling leaves danced in circles on the curb. After the silence stretched on a little too long, she turned to him. "Was it bad news?"

When Remare remained silent, his eyes on the road, she added, "The phone messages?"

His eyes, darker than usual, glanced at her. "Not particularly."

Okay, not in the mood for conversation—Iceman. The tension in his body, present ever since he got behind the steering wheel, hadn't lessened.

Hesitating for a moment, he cleared his throat and then, in an even voice, said, "Valadon was glad you came tonight."

"Yes, he was," Miranda agreed. Either the vampire lord had mellowed or he was on his best behavior. *He's up to something!*

"You shouldn't lead him on like that." Remare slanted her a look. "The way you did at dinner."

Shaking her head, Miranda narrowed her eyes in affronted confusion. "What the hell are you talking about?! I didn't lead anyone on tonight."

Remare glanced at her and then back at the road. "Yes, you did. You might not realize it, but you did. Valadon is very *sensitive* where you're concerned. You shouldn't play on his emotions."

Play? Play!? Miranda wasn't sure she was hearing him right. "*Exactly* when did I play on his emotions?" She heard the heat rising in her voice.

Nearing NYU, Remare exhaled deeply as he turned down Miranda's block. "At the dinner table, when you put your hand on his."

Miranda remembered barely brushing Valadon's wrist. "I didn't put my hand on his."

"Yes, you did." Remare's breaths increased as he parked the car. "And then, you started flirting with him."

Outraged, Miranda shrieked, "I *certainly* did not. I was being social. You were the one who was so silent."

His dark brown eyes bore into hers. "I *wasn't* silent."

"Yes, you were." Tilting her head, Miranda leaned closer to him and tried not to inhale his intoxicating, woodsy scent. "You barely glanced at me."

Remare's voice grew loud. "You were sitting right in front of me. *Obviously,* I saw you."

"Saw me, maybe. But you didn't say a word."

"Of course, I did."

Miranda muttered, "Did not."

"I..." Remare seemed to be grinding his molars as he stared at her with heightened awareness. But, instead of coming up with a pithy remark that would sting, his lips suddenly crushed hers, and he pulled her tightly into his embrace. His lips were like rose petals, soft and firm. Not wanting the kiss to end, Miranda dug her fingers into his back. Her world turned on its axis, and she wondered if they somehow hit the switch on the heating unit because the car suddenly felt like an inferno. She tasted wine on his lips and felt the butterflies in her belly dancing all the way to her toes.

Miranda didn't know exactly what had just transpired between them. One moment, Remare and she were fighting.

What the hell had they been fighting about? She couldn't remember and decided she didn't care. Remare was kissing her. Remare. Was. Kissing. Her! *My God, the vampire could kiss!* She ran her fingers through Remare's hair, loving the way his thick waves felt as she massaged his nape.

Breathing heavily, they silently moved away from each other, each stunned by what had just happened. Miranda was reluctant to drop her hand that was still woven around his neck. She could taste him on her lips and felt her heart pounding as she looked up at him. From the stricken expression on Remare's face, he too had been overwhelmed by the intensity of their kiss.

"What just happened?" she asked in a voice that was sultrier than she'd intended.

"I don't know," Remare whispered softly, "but I think you should go inside."

Still panting, Miranda shook her head, hoping the cobwebs would clear. Remare sat back in his seat and focused on the road—his eyes cold as the night. Reality—the mother of all bitches! She sighed. Remare's loyalty was to one person only, Valadon. Always was and always would be. Resigned, she shook her head at the futility. Remare was right; it was time she went inside. Exhaling, she said, "Okay," then opened the door and slowly closed it behind her.

Her mind still fogged with crazed lust, she slowly climbed the few steps to her home.

Remare watched as Miranda closed the door behind her. His hand tightened on the steering wheel as reason crept through the mind-numbing mist clouding his brain. *Damn it!* What the *hell* had he been thinking, kissing Miranda?

He hadn't meant to, had he? He'd simply turned to admonish her, and her lips had been right there, parted in sensual invitation. He really should have ended the kiss sooner and not allowed himself to get caught up in the way she felt—so warm and responsive in his arms. Her gentle sucking on his tongue had aroused him, again.

He had vowed never to let his desires interfere in his duty to Valadon; he knew the high lord loved her and she was *not* to be touched by any other. He knew this, and yet...

Frustrated, Remare banged his fist against the steering wheel. Breaths harsh, he checked his mirrors and pulled out into the street. At the traffic light, he couldn't remember where he was going. That was the depth of the effect the woman had on him. *Smart, Remare, real smart!* He shook his head at his idiocy; he never should have kissed her. He was a vampire who did not give in to his base emotions lightly; he had learned centuries ago to keep himself distant, detached, and vigilant.

But the sensations Miranda elicited in him made his body feel riveted, alive. He had not felt such passion in some time. And something dark inside him, long dormant, had finally awoken.

Miranda was a passionate woman; he had often thought so. Even though she hid it behind a cool, detached exterior, he had always known a fire burned within her. Remare had once before experienced the depth of her desire. Sensual images of them on a cave floor flooded his mind, and he quickly locked them away. Her female scent then had haunted him, and continued to do so.

Breathing deeply, Remare tapped his fingers on the steering wheel as he pondered his next move. Now, the question was: What the hell did he do about his awakened desires? Did he pursue an avenue that would only lead to certain destruction or did he remain loyal to his liege? He had sworn a blood oath to Valadon never to betray him.

It chafed to realize he was considering doing just that.

Locking her door, Miranda rested her forehead on it, still stunned from kissing Remare. She wondered if he was as perplexed as she was by the ardor that had stirred between them. Fragments of erotic dreams flashed through her mind. She quickly shook herself free of them.

Miranda tried to get a hold of reality and heard someone playing Josh Groban in her house. No one should be home. Orion would still be at Werehaven this close to the full moon. Cautiously, she moved down the hallway and noticed a light on in her bathroom.

Moving the door open a few inches, she spotted a freshly-showered and naked Orion trying to put a bandage on the back of his upper thigh. From the bruising on his leg, the puncture wounds had to be deep. "What the hell happened to you?"

"Oh, hey, Miranda. Yeah, I know I'm not supposed to use your bathroom." He lowered the music. "But I didn't have any bandages."

"You're *supposed* to wear clothes, too!" Miranda chided.

"Right." Orion took a washcloth from the shelf and tried to cover himself. Tried and failed as Weres were typically larger than the average human male. "Listen, can you give me a hand here? The tape won't stick."

Miranda admired Orion's form. He truly was a handsome male with his broad chest and slim waist, but he was her friend and her roommate so the *No Touch Rule* was still in effect. "Give me the gauze."

She bent down to examine the wound and was eye level with one of the most perfect asses God ever gave to man. *NTR, NTR,* she kept repeating to herself, and really, it was

Orion—he was like a brother to her. "No wonder you can't get the tape to stick, you used too much ointment." She grabbed a tissue and wiped away the excess.

"Yeah, I know. It was kinda hard trying to figure out how much to put on from this angle."

"You going to tell me what happened?" Miranda reset the gauze over the wound and cut new strips of tape to keep it in place.

"Gavin bit me—hard! When we were running with the moon, he grabbed my flank."

Miranda didn't need to ask why. "Serves you right," she mumbled.

Orion seemed surprised and hurt by her response. "Miranda, you don't get it. Lizandra is your friend; mine, too." He shut off the music. "But she's also my queen."

"Save it. I've already heard this argument."

Miranda went into her bedroom and began to undress until she was as naked as Orion and then slipped on her favorite sleeveless T-shirt and a pair of old shorts. All she wanted to do was get some sleep when she noticed Orion standing in the doorway.

"Can I come in for a few minutes?"

Miranda glanced at his nude form as she slid between the sheets. "Not if you don't put some boxers on."

Orion looked around the room and spotted the laundry basket and found a pair of clean underwear. Slipping them on, he asked, "Decent enough?"

"Sure." She rolled on her side in his direction. "What's going on?"

Striding to the bed, Orion made puppy noises—his way of asking permission to join her.

The thing about Weres, Miranda reminded herself, was that nudity and sleeping, actually sleeping, with friends was no big deal. To them, it was natural and not especially sensual. When she looked up at Orion, she could tell something was troubling him—had been for some time. She pulled the blankets back as Orion moved in beside her.

"Thanks."

"Tell me," she said, remembering the phrase Remare had often said to her.

"I will. But could you just hold me for a little while?"

Any other guy and Miranda would have raised an eyebrow, but Orion was different. Sure, he could be playful, but they had an understanding, a line neither one of them crossed. She lifted an arm, and like a wounded animal, he burrowed into her embrace. Miranda stroked his hair and then rubbed his back.

"That feels good. Don't stop," he mumbled to her chest.

Miranda could feel the tension easing from his body as he snuggled closer to her. "You don't have to talk, Orion." She yawned. "It can wait until tomorrow."

Orion's body shuddered. "I'm afraid."

Sensing his fear, she stroked his arm. "Of what?"

"That I'll be homeless, again. Not here, but with the clan. I think I screwed up. Big time. And not just with Lizandra."

Miranda turned to face him. "What do you mean?"

"Remember when I was a lone wolf?" He exhaled deeply. "I was so damned cocky, as many young wolves are. I thought I didn't need a clan, that I was independent. How wrong I was." His voice seemed to trail off then got strong again. "Lone wolves don't last long in the wild. It's doubly true of the city. If you hadn't found me when you did...I very well could have died."

Miranda remembered that particular nightmare very well. "That's long over with. You're with Black Star, now."

Orion turned to face her. "I'm afraid Lizandra is going to kick me out of the pack."

Miranda snorted. "No, she won't, Orion." Lizandra was selective about who she chose to lay with from her clan. "You're one of her favorites or can't you tell?"

"She doesn't want me, anymore. I think she's back with Gavin."

Miranda wasn't surprised. Gavin and Lizandra made a good couple. They seemed stronger together. "Just because she's with Gavin doesn't mean she's going to kick you out. You would have had to do something intolerable, like break one of the clan's rules to get kicked out." Miranda looked at him. "Did you?"

He shook his head. "No, of course not."

Miranda exhaled quietly. "Then, what's got you so upset?"

"The clan wants me out because I was with Lizandra. They saw when Gavin bit me, and no one helped. They just howled their laughter. They let me limp all the way back to Werehaven." He looked up at Miranda. "They knew I was in pain, and they left me behind."

Clan rules, Miranda thought. Gavin was a definite favorite, and as Beta, he had the loyalty of the Weres. Could they be jealous of Orion's burgeoning success as a musician? Maybe, but she would hardly call it a shunning. "If they wanted you out, they would have locked the doors and barred your entrance. Did that happen?"

"No." Orion trembled then pulled the blankets around him closer as if cold.

"It's just the full moon, or almost full moon," Miranda whispered as she continued stroking his arm. "It makes us all a little crazy." No wonder she had kissed Remare the way she did. Apparently, it had affected Remare the same way. A wave of heat warmed her.

"It's not just that. Lizandra's been hinting at it, for some time. Some in the pack have grown, I don't know, jealous maybe, of my singing career. They've let me know in very subtle ways." He was silent for awhile, then looked at her. "But I have something else to tell you, and I don't think you're going to like it very much."

Surprised, Miranda looked at him. "After what we've been through, you can say that?"

Orion sat up. "I love you, Miranda." He shrugged. "Maybe not the way most males love females, but I love you like a friend, maybe more."

"Say it," Miranda cajoled. "I promise I won't hate you."

Orion raised his eyebrows. "Promise?"

Miranda saw how upset he was when the light from outside illuminated his downcast face. He truly was miserable. This was more serious than she suspected. "Orion, just tell me."

Orion studied her for a moment and then shook his head. "Dane and I were pretty close—maybe a little closer than you might think."

Miranda's jaw opened, and nothing came out. She couldn't *possibly* have heard him right. Orion loved women. When he sang, it was as if he were singing to every woman in the club. And Dane—he'd been her friend *and* lover. "I think you need to explain that." His face held guilt and something else. Remorse, maybe.

Orion shook his head. "You heard me right." He laid his head on his pillow and put the back of his hand over his eyes. "It was a long time ago. Before you got involved with him." He exhaled. "It was just one night."

Miranda thought it was certainly a night for surprises. "Orion, are you gay?"

"No. It wasn't like that. Sort of. But I gotta tell you. It was my idea."

Miranda sat up. "I'm listening." She removed his hand from his beautiful face.

"It was after one of my shows, close to the full moon, and Dane and I were drinking. Heavy. I wanted to celebrate, and he was with me. We started talking about what-ifs, things we wanted to try but never did, shit like that. I don't remember who said what after that. We were both pretty drunk."

Miranda narrowed her eyes. "Just how drunk were you?"

He lowered his head. "I cared a great deal about Dane, considered him one of my closest friends." Orion seemed to be remembering things he wasn't ready to share. "The strange part of it all, when I asked Dane if he wanted to, he didn't hesitate."

"You're one of the handsomest men I know, Orion. Who wouldn't want to have sex with you?" Miranda now had images in her mind of the two of them together and probably would for some time. "Anyone else?"

"Huh?"

"Was there anyone else you decided to *experiment* with?"

"No, only Dane."

"You're sure? And you never felt the need to repeat the experience?"

"No. Believe me, if I was gay, I would know. Dane wasn't gay either. We were just curious." He shrugged. "Curious fools, I guess." He examined Miranda's face as if looking for any sign of disgust or reprimand.

Miranda wondered how he would react if he knew about her more reckless nights when she'd been younger. Some secrets deserved to be buried in the past where they belonged. She contemplated all the things Orion wasn't telling her and smiled. "You do know I would still love you if you were gay, bi, or even...part vampire."

He looked up at her in disbelief, shook his head and then sniffed her arm. "Speaking of vampires—"

Miranda waved her index finger and shook her head. "Don't go there."

"Okay." He hugged her closer, anyway. "I wanted to tell you about Dane so maybe you wouldn't drink as much."

Miranda sighed. "I'm not an alcoholic, Orion. I hardly drank at all when I was out west. And I don't miss it."

Orion scratched his head. "What about the bottle of vodka I found in the back of the freezer. You never used to hide the liquor."

Miranda rolled her eyes. "It was summer. Lots of people freeze vodka." She exhaled. "I know I drank a lot after what happened last winter with the vampires. I'm over it."

"You're sure?"

"Yeah. The nightmares have lessened, too. They're not completely gone, but I don't have them as frequently. You don't have to worry, and you can tell Lizandra she doesn't have to keep sniffing my breath."

"You would tell me if you were having problems, wouldn't you, Miranda?"

Miranda smirked. "I let you sleep in my bed, don't I? Stop worrying." She exhaled as she gently patted his arm for reassurance. "I don't live in that time zone, anymore."

Orion's gaze didn't move. "All right, then. There's one more thing. I don't think I'm going to travel as much, anymore."

"Why? You've always loved going on tour."

Orion rubbed his brow. "In the beginning, it was a lot of fun. All the different cities, the crowds, the applause." He ran a hand through his hair. "It's not so much fun, anymore. The last show—there was an incident." Orion looked at her. "The band picks out certain people from the audience to visit with us backstage. Some of them know members of the crew and get sneaked in. We have a few drinks and relax."

"Relax?" Miranda raised an eyebrow.

"Okay, sometimes, we have sex, but not like other bands." He exhaled. "It's not as exciting as it used to be. Anyway, after the last show, when I was relaxing in my room and there were a couple of college-age fans there, I thought my beer tasted funny and then I started getting a killer of a headache."

"They spiked your drink?" Miranda sat up quickly. She'd heard all kinds of stories about women given ropheonol and other drugs, but never imagined it would be done to a guy.

"Yeah. What's worse, they tried to take pictures of me half-dressed with one of the girls. I had to wrestle the camera away from them. I think they were on something, too, because they were stronger than they should have been. They wanted to have sex with me, and when I told them I wasn't interested, they started yelling obscenities."

"What did you do?"

"My road manager heard the noise and came running in and got them out. I was so angry I crushed their camera phones. I was violently sick afterward. Thank God I'm a werewolf and was able to sweat out the drug before it took hold of me.

"Orion, I'm so sorry." Miranda was horrified at what could have happened. "But you can't let one incident prevent you from doing what you most enjoy."

"I'm not. I just want to stay closer to home is all. There are lots of clubs in the New York area. I told my manager no more clubs outside the tri-state area." His voice sounded sleepy as he yawned. "If I get bored, I'll take more bookings."

Miranda thought there was more to the story, but for now, she'd let it rest. It was late, and they were both exhausted. She snuggled closer to Orion, who seemed spent. His body was relaxed, now, and she was glad. People didn't need sex to have intimacy. They just needed to share their most intimate thoughts with someone they trusted.

She looked down at Orion and could tell from his breathing he'd fallen asleep. Sometimes, when the night grew too dark and the nightmares came, she had climbed into bed with him. He had never asked why, never asked her about the dreams or why she woke up screaming. He merely held her in his arms, giving her the strength and warmth she needed. That's what friends did. They loaned you strength when your own wasn't strong enough.

Fear was an old friend of hers she had known all too well. Sometimes, he came in the night; other instances he came when she was awake. But thank God she had someone who sent him back to the hell he belonged in.

Tonight, she would sleep without any dark visitors, as Orion would.

But, in time, she knew the demons would return.

Chapter Ten

"Jordan, are you sure this isn't going to cause a major inconvenience?" Sitting in the museum's cafeteria, Miranda pushed away her finished lunch plate. Somehow, she didn't think her boss would be willing to see her go on another trip after she'd been away for two months.

He waved his hand in the air. "No, this summer has been particularly quiet, and as I've already told you, the museum knows summers are when most of our people take vacations so we planned accordingly." He smiled beneficently at her. "Besides, Lord Valadon has been *very* accommodating with us. He's even loaned us his Seurat, which no one has seen in...ever."

"Yes, I know." Miranda exhaled. "Valadon can be quite persuasive when he wants something."

Jordan peered at her over his dark-rimmed glasses as he cleared his throat. "Valadon didn't happen to mention the availability of any other paintings, did he?"

"No. I'm only going to validate the Degas. If there are any other paintings available, I know nothing about them." She raised a hand before he could interrupt. "And, before you ask, yes, I'll inquire if the estate has any other works they want to negotiate."

"Good girl." He nodded. "I knew there was a reason I hired you. I just wish we knew the name of the estate. We could research the family and speculate what other works may go on the market."

Miranda knew the name of the family she was going to see in Paris, but if she ever divulged that information, Valadon would have her head. "You know collectors are a funny lot when it comes to secrecy. They don't like advertising when they have to sell off their art to pay for otherwise risky business pursuits that didn't pay out as expected."

"Just keep your ears open when you're over there and don't be afraid to ask questions... discreetly." Jordan handed her a few of his business cards. "Just in case a family member might want to sell something the museum may want to procure. Let the lawyers know you would be interested if any other works should become available."

"Of course." If she hadn't respected and genuinely liked Jordan, the guilt at leaving so soon after she just returned wouldn't tug at her as much. "I'm going to go over the files on my desk and clear up as much as I can before I leave. And I promise I'll put in extra time when I get back."

He waved his hand in the air again as if it was inconsequential. "If you can get Valadon to loan us more of his paintings, that won't be an issue. I've heard his collection is extraordinary."

Miranda knew a fishing expedition when she heard one. Usually, Jordan was more subtle than this. "Yes, that's what I've heard, too."

He exhaled in defeat. "And you're sure he's providing security for the transfer of ownership. If not, I could—"

"Everything's already been arranged. I'm going to meet his security people on his private jet, so that's not an issue."

Jordan smiled appreciatively. "I'm glad you're back, Miranda. I've missed you. We'll have to have dinner when you get back from Paris so that you can tell me all about your trip."

Her phone buzzed. "We will."

"You know," he hesitated, "there was talk about you, months ago, that you might be romantically involved with Valadon."

"I was dating a doctor." Miranda sipped her water. "Really, Jordan, you can't believe everything you read in the papers." She checked the caller ID. "I'm happily single now and plan to stay that way."

"Whatever became of Jason Morgan? Weren't you two involved at one time or another?"

"Jason is the biggest playboy on the East Coast." *Or used to be.* Miranda smiled at the mention of Wilson Morgan's notorious son who seemed to love the spotlight. "And, no, we were never dating. Just friends." She read her text.

Jordan exhaled. "Pity, he would have been a good match for you."

Miranda didn't think so. Jason hadn't been known for his fidelity. Yet, his relationship with Rosalyn, the proprietor of Nightshade, seemed monogamous. Because of business concerns, neither one of them wanted their relationship to go public.

Months ago, she had promised Rosalyn never to mention it after the vampire had driven her home from Nightshade. She had sensed a good vibe from the affable Rosalyn and decided to make it a point to visit her before she left on her trip.

"It's Valadon." Miranda put down her phone. "I'm going to stop at ValCorp after work to talk to him one last time before I fly out this weekend." If she'd had any second thoughts about going, they evaporated when Valadon told her how much he would compensate her for the validation. As always, he'd been exceedingly generous. That's how she *knew* there was more going on than what he'd previously told her. That and the look in his eye when he discussed Paris with her. Something was up. Valadon wanted her in Paris for another reason. *But what?*

Miranda knew only one other person who might know what that reason could be.

***

During the elevator ride down to the sub-basement of the New York Public Library, Miranda still experienced feelings of excitement and awe ever since Felicity had introduced her to a world she'd never imagined. An ancient vampire made his home there, and Miranda called him friend. She had known many exemplary scholars; however, none came close to the erudite Blu. But then again, none had lived for thousands of years. With his golden hair and hazel eyes, Blu resembled a grad student more than the primordial vampire he was; his penchant for wearing blue jeans and T-shirts didn't help.

"Miranda, how nice to see you again." Guy de Montglat, aka Blu, embraced her as he welcomed her into his opulent living room where the pale blue walls showcased several works of art and his bookcases were filled with many leatherbound books. "I'm afraid Felicity's not here at the moment."

"That's okay. It's you I was hoping to see. I wanted to ask you a few questions about the vampire courts in Europe—one, in particular." She snuggled into one of his plush couches. "I'm leaving later in the week to go to Paris, presumably, to validate and procure a painting for Valadon."

"Paris?" Montglat's expression was that of confusion. "He's sending you all the way there to do a validation?"

Blu handed Miranda a glass of wine as he joined her on the couch. "Why doesn't he have a scholar there authenticate it instead of sending you across an ocean?"

"My thoughts exactly." She sipped her wine. "Valadon likes his privacy." She nodded at Blu, who she knew also valued his solitude. "But he hasn't always been completely honest with me." Miranda's eyes narrowed. "He's holding out on me. I can *feel* it. I just don't know what it is."

Blu smiled. "Then, why go? If you don't trust him?"

"It's just for a few days, and Valadon was *very* generous with reimbursement." She relaxed back into the cushions and blew out a breath. "I haven't been to Paris in a few years. I did my graduate work there."

"Yes, Felicity told me." Blu studied her for a moment. "You know, Miranda, with the current turmoil in Europe, Paris can be a dangerous city." He set his glass down and faced her. "I'm not entirely certain I like the idea of you going there alone. Some of the world's oldest and most powerful vampires call Paris home."

"Oh, I won't be going alone. Valadon told me he's giving me one of his elite Torians to safeguard the painting."

"Do you know which Torian?

Miranda wasn't sure if she was breaking any confidences, but Blu had once saved her life. "Bastien."

"Ah, Sebastien de Rosemont. His family is one of the oldest. Very well-respected. Where is the transaction to take place?"

"I'm meeting with Valadon later tonight. He said he'd fill in all the details then."

"But you don't trust him?"

Miranda leaned forward and tapped the tips of her fingers together. "Not completely. It's just a feeling I get in the way he smiles." She arched a brow. "Like he knows something I don't."

Montglat appeared contemplative. "I haven't been to Paris in years, as well. That's Vivienna's territory. She and Valadon were once involved centuries ago."

Her curiosity peaked. "Who's Vivienna?"

"A very powerful vampire who presently holds the title of Madame Lord of Paris. Through the centuries, she carefully made her way up the ranks, choosing her allies with coldhearted calculation."

Miranda wanted to learn more about her. "How'd she become involved with Valadon?"

Blu grinned. "Miranda, are you jealous?"

She rolled her eyes. "Curious. No one's ever told me any back history about him. Just the economic, political stuff."

"The story is quite sordid. I'm not entirely sure of all the facts. I've only ever heard rumors and speculation from those in the courts."

"That's more than what I know." Miranda shrugged.

"Very well. Vivienna is the type of woman who would never be content long with her position. She always had her eye on advancement. Those of us who knew her weren't surprised when Caltrone, one of the elders in the Vampire High Court, made her the ruling vampire of Paris." Blu had a faraway look in his eyes. "She was quite adept at becoming familiar with those who could help in her advancement."

"Sounds like a social climber."

Montglat scoffed. "Don't let her hear you say that." He sipped his wine. "She was far more cunning than most gave her credit for."

"How'd she meet Valadon?"

Montglat closed his eyes in memory. "Centuries ago, she was involved with a general in one of our many wars. The courtiers were notorious for their grand way of living. At the time, we were still in the closet, so to speak, but Vivienna liked parties and insinuating herself in the most prestigious courts—vampire and human. She liked seducing and manipulating high-ranking people who could be of use to the VHC as well as herself. When her general, who was later promoted to Minister of Defense, was away fighting, she met and seduced Valadon, who was our Minister of Finance."

"Sounds like Vivienna wasn't much on fidelity."

Montglat laughed. "You have to remember, Miranda, those of us who lived through different time periods associated with humans at the highest echelons—it was necessary for our survival. Vivienna considered the courts her private playground. Fidelity was not a concern. She was, however, a most extraordinary spy."

Miranda didn't doubt it. "What happened between her and Valadon?"

Blu crossed one ankle over his knee and seemed transported to another time and place. "The question you should be asking is what happened to Valadon before he met Vivienna. Now that is far more interesting."

Miranda smirked. "Ask the right questions, get the right answers?"

Blu grinned. "Something like that."

"Okay, I'll bite." Knowing how cryptic vampire were, she asked, "What happened?"

"Valadon had taken a leave from court politics and the ministry. He told the elders he needed time to himself. There was talk he had fallen in love with a human woman who had recently passed away and he needed time to grieve. He took, however, more time than any of us would have expected. Anyway, Vivienna was either ordered by the VHC to break him of his malaise or she took it upon herself to become his lover. One thing was certain, the court wanted him back. Economics, especially when there was a war going on, made the financial empires volatile, and the elders grew impatient with Valadon's absence. Either way, she became involved with him."

Miranda thought Vivienna calculating, indeed, if she set her eyes on Valadon when he was most vulnerable. "What happened to the war general?"

"Ah, he, too, was a court favorite, winning victory after victory in the many battles we financed. Some wars were human, some were vampire, but our wars have always intermingled, and our futures depended on the outcomes of those battles. It was rumored the general had the misfortune of falling in love with the beautiful temptress and intended to marry her—rare in our world. When her seduction of Valadon became common knowledge, he ended all involvement with her. Some expected a duel to result, but the two were close friends and even rumored to be lovers themselves."

Miranda's stomach began to ache. She'd heard similar rumors in Valadon House. "Who was the war general?"

"A vampire still in Valadon's employ." Blu looked directly at her, and she could see the golds and amber striations in his eyes. "I believe you've already met him. Valadon's second, Remare."

Miranda nodded. She knew there had to be more to the story, but she wasn't sure she wanted to know. "I have no plans to meet with this woman in Paris. I'm just going there to procure a painting for Valadon."

"I hope you don't meet her, Miranda. But, if she wants to meet you, she will find a way."

"How do you know so much about her?"

"If you're asking if I ever became her lover, the answer is no. Women who resemble vipers have never held much interest for me." He smirked. "But, I intercepted some of her letters to Caltrone and found a journal of hers she inadvertently left behind in the home of a friend." Montglat met her eyes. "Would you like to read them?"

One corner of Miranda's lips curved as if they had reached a silent accord. "Yes, I would. But, before that, I wanted to ask you something."

"Go ahead."

"If a vampire erased a human's memory, could you restore it?"

Montglat narrowed his eyes. "First of all, we don't erase memories. The memories are still there; they are just covered with a veiled layer. Most vampires don't touch a human's memories without having a good reason."

"Could you lift the veil?"

"Yes. Why do you ask?"

"Because I suspect someone stole a memory, and I want it back."

"Someone associated with House Valadon?"

"Yes."

"I see." Montglat rubbed his chin. "How long ago do you think this occurred?"

"A few months ago."

"Ah, rather recent, then. I was afraid you were going to ask about something longer ago." He joined her on the couch and met her eyes. "What will I be looking for?"

"I get these fragments, mostly in dreams, but I remember being in a cave with Remare."

"And you think he covered a memory? Interesting."

"Yeah, I do."

"All right then. I need you to concentrate on my eyes. This won't hurt. It's only been a couple of months, so if there is a veil on your memories, it should be rather easy to find."

"Okay." Miranda hesitated, but was determined to find out if her dreams were real. She felt a whisper in her head, as if a cool breeze had entered and was wafting through her mind.

"Can you tell me— Holy hell! Miranda!" Panting, Blu rose and took several steps back. "Why didn't you warn me!?"

Miranda's breaths became labored as graphic images of Remare and her rolling around nearly naked on the cave floor surfaced. *Son of a bitch!* He *had* tampered with her memory! The fragments that had haunted her were real.

"I think I'm scarred for life. When the hell did you become involved with Remare? I thought it was Valadon who was interested in you."

"Take a breath, Blu. It was only one time, and I'm sure you've seen others in the throes of...whatever." Miranda was fanning herself. "It *was* just one time?"

"If you're asking if any other memories were tampered with, I can tell you I didn't see any other veils, and I would have noticed, I assure you, if there had been."

"Good to know." Miranda rubbed her head as she gazed downward. "That SOB; I knew it. I could sense something was missing when I saw him."

Blu seemed to collect himself. "If he covered the memory, he must have had a good reason. I take it Valadon is unaware of the situation?"

"There is no situation. Remare and I agreed it would never happen again. We're just friends." She sighed. "Anything else would divide House Valadon, and I'm not going to let that happen."

"That's probably a wise decision."

"Listen, Blu, I gotta go."

"Wait, I'll get you the letters and journal." He disappeared into his other room and then reappeared with the articles. "Take whatever time you need to read them, but promise me you'll return them when you're done."

"I will. Blu, I need to know this. Is there a way a human could block a vampire from entering her mind?"

"Yes, there's a way you can prevent this from happening, again. Gaze at my eyes, Miranda. If you ever suspect a vampire is invading your mind, fortify your defenses."

"How do I do that?"

"Imagine a wall in your mind built of the densest metal. Impenetrable. Throw all your energy there. With your abilities, I should think you'd be able to sense when a vampire is trespassing."

"How come I didn't feel it with Remare?"

Blu sighed. "I suspect you were too busy at the time to notice."

Miranda's brow arched. *"That won't be happening, again."*

"I hope not."

"Miranda! How wonderful to see you."

"Hi, Felicity. I'm sorry, I gotta run. We'll talk soon, okay?" Miranda hugged her friend and then beat feet to the door.

"Did you know Miranda had become romantically involved with Valadon's second, Remare?"

"No, the last I knew she'd been seeing Dr. Gabriel." Felicity put her parcels down. "But that ended months ago. What's this all about?"

"Miranda asked me to restore a memory Remare had covered, but she didn't tell me it was of her and him—" Blu took a gulp of his drink. "I don't think I'm quite comfortable with the idea of her with him. He has a reputation, you know."

Felicity huffed. "Miranda is old enough to make her own decisions. No reason to get disturbed by it."

"Easy for you to say. She's not your granddaughter." Blu shuddered at the memory. "How would you feel if you walked in on Miranda while she was having sex?! It was most disconcerting."

Felicity rolled her eyes. "Let it go, Guy. I rather like Remare."

He sighed, deeply. "You would!"

Chapter Eleven

The next few days went by quickly as Miranda tried to clear up the work on her desk. If she made decent headway, there would be less to come back to. Valadon had called twice, trying to set up a meeting, and Lizandra also wanted to get together. But Miranda needed to unwind and wanted some alone time. She'd been staying late every night at work, but tonight, she went for a long bike ride along the boardwalk near the Hudson River Park.

Miranda found the fresh air and the scent of the brine from the river soothing. Stopping at Teardrop Park to admire the view of the river, she looked back at the Financial District and wondered why, whenever she wanted to be alone, she found herself in the vicinity of ValCorp. *I just can't get away from you, can I?* Swallowing a few gulps from her water bottle, Miranda wondered how the vampires of Valadon House were doing. In particular, Remare.

Sighing, she thought she would have heard from him by now, but true to his word, he wouldn't do anything disloyal to Valadon.

Continuing south, Miranda neared the docks where Remare kept his boat. The night they'd stopped there and admired the Statue of Liberty, she had thoroughly enjoyed his company. She was tempted to look in his boat to see if he was there, but that would be inviting trouble she didn't need. As much as she wanted to hate him for veiling her memory, she understood why he had done it. She would not cause a divide in Valadon House.

Turning her bike around, she headed home.

After a very long, cold shower she decided to go visit Rosalyn—a vampire she had instantly liked. And, more importantly, trusted. After all, the manager of Nightshade told her she was welcome any time in her club.

With or without her cantankerous companion.

***

Unlike Werehaven, which had a more earthy and relaxed ambience, Nightshade was sophisticated and chic with its smoked mirrors and crystal designs. Here, the cool detachment of the elegantly dressed vampires reigned supreme, along with the willing adoration of the humans who wanted to be seduced. Miranda had no desire to be seduced by anyone. She was in no mood to be someone's chew toy and had never liked the idea of being fed on.

Until a certain vampire had introduced her to the pleasures of a vampire's bite.

She spotted Rosalyn's luxurious mane of red hair at the top of the stairs.

"Miranda! Good to see you." Rosalyn returned her smile as she took her hand and led her to her office. "It's been months. Why on earth did you wait so long to call?"

Miranda tried to place the vampire's accent and failed. The stunning vampire had a welcoming smile and a genuine quality to her Miranda rarely sensed in other vampires. After closing the door to Rosalyn's office, Miranda said, "I've been out west studying Native American Art. Listen, can I get a drink?"

"Of course. Fiona will get you whatever you want."

A moment later, a waitress with short dark hair appeared and took their drink orders.

Apparently, Rosalyn had already mentally contacted her waitress. "Cranberry juice and vodka."

"Bring the bottle and also some vermouth." After Fiona left, Rosalyn joined Miranda on the couch. "How's my favorite benefactor doing?"

"If you're talking about Remare, I'm not sure. He's been distant since I've come back." Miranda shrugged and exhaled. "I suppose it's his way."

Rosalyn played with a long curl of her hair. "And you were hoping absence would make his heart grow fonder?"

Surprised, Miranda gazed at Rosalyn's golden brown eyes. "No, of course not. We were friends. That's all. I helped him locate a painting. We were never involved."

Rosalyn's grin reached her eyes. *"Um-hmm!"*

Miranda glared at the smiling vampire. The woman was good at staring her down, but she had nothing on Lizandra, who had a surgeon's precision at getting to the heart of the matter. Miranda changed the topic. "How's Jason?"

"Delicious, as always." Rosalyn laughed when she saw Miranda's eyebrows rise.

She knew Rosalyn was just being playful. "You don't mind keeping your relationship secret?"

"Why should I mind? We see each other when we can. I love him, and he loves me. We're happy. It is best for both of us this way." Rosalyn flipped her hand nonchalantly in the air. "Vampires who would take exception to me seeing him, and would take their business elsewhere, don't have to know. And his kind, those who would frown upon our relationship, who cares what they think?"

There was a quick knock on the door, and then Fiona entered. After setting their drinks on the coffee table, she asked, "Is there anything else I can bring you?"

Rosalyn looked at Miranda in expectation. "Perhaps something to eat?"

"No, I'm fine. Thanks."

"That will be all, Fiona." After the door closed, Rosalyn turned her attention to Miranda. "Somehow, I don't think you came here tonight to ask me about my relationship with Jason."

Miranda sipped her drink. "No. I'm leaving for Paris on business this weekend, and I wanted to ask you about the Parisian court."

Peering above her glass, Rosalyn made a face that amused Miranda. "Vivienna's territory. If you can, avoid her as much as possible."

"Why?"

"How much has Valadon told you about her?"

Miranda didn't like lying and tried to stay close to the truth. "Not much, but from what I gathered, she's kind of venomous."

"A viper, for sure." Glass in hand, Rosalyn gracefully rose and gazed sullenly out her window down on her patrons. "She has no heart."

"You knew her." Miranda said it more as a fact than a question.

"Yes. Unfortunately, I did." Rosalyn turned to Miranda and then at the dancers below.

Miranda didn't think the redheaded beauty was watching her people; from her solemn expression, she believed Rosalyn was reliving a particularly poignant memory.

"It was centuries ago. I had fallen in love with a young soldier in Paris. He was incredibly handsome and enjoyed the opera as much as I did. We were happy, for a time. News must have reached Vivienna, evidently. She was already involved with a high-ranking member of the court, but she was never one to let a challenge go unanswered." She downed her drink. "And anyone who was happy was a challenge to her."

Miranda wasn't sure she should ask any more questions. Somehow, she didn't think this story was going to end pretty. "What happened?"

"She seduced him, as was her way. She believes everyone is hers to toy with as she sees fit. Not long after, I returned to Finland."

Miranda joined her by the window. "Did he ever try to find you?"

"You don't understand." Rosalyn turned toward her. "You've never met Vivienna. Of our kind, she is one of the most beautiful and dangerous. I'm sure he had no memory of me when she was done with him." She sighed. "Why is it you're going to Paris?

Miranda wasn't sure how much Valadon wanted her to share with others, but she liked Rosalyn, and if Remare trusted her, so would she. "Valadon wants me to authenticate a painting he wishes to purchase. I'm going there to procure it for him."

"I see."

Miranda didn't want to bring up any more painful memories for Rosalyn so she changed subjects. "What can you tell me about Irina?"

"The Ice-Queen? I know a little."

Miranda saw the same look Lizandra used, as if she were asking, *"Seriously?"*

"I'm curious, that's all."

"Um-hmm." Rosalyn chuckled. "I'll bet."

After Rosalyn stopped laughing, Miranda gave Rosalyn her Grinch smile.

"I'll say this for our mutual friend, he does pick the most dangerous women to become entangled with."

Miranda motioned with her drink. "Go on."

"Irina was originally from Russia. I hear she is one of Remare's best assassins. Not as bad as Vivienna, though in some ways, deadlier. I'd watch my back around that one."

"No need to." Miranda smirked. "I'm not involved. Remember?"

"If you insist." Rosalyn smiled slyly. "She's one of the deadliest Torians—a master in the arts of killing. When they come in here, she never strays far from him. She is very observant. I don't remember her being involved with anyone else but Remare. Even though there is one who watches her from a distance."

Slowly, Miranda shook her head. Rosalyn was right about Remare hanging out with dangerous women. "Didn't he ever date anyone less lethal?"

"Perhaps." Rosalyn gracefully walked to her desk and sat. "He's been with you."

Miranda didn't know how much Remare might have told her. Her face flushed at the memory of what they had done and tried to avert her eyes. But too late, Rosalyn had seen her blush. "Nothing really happened between us. Never will. He told me his loyalty is with Valadon. Not me." Miranda finished her drink. "Gotta respect a guy for knowing his priorities."

"But he wanted to be with you, did he not?"

Damned vampire instincts. "It doesn't matter. He's Valadon's main man, not mine."

Rosalyn narrowed her eyes. "The night he brought you here to my office, he was very specific that everything was to be perfect—from the flowers to the meal he had catered. He never made those arrangements for Irina or any others. I know Remare. I watched him when he embraced you out by the railing. He was happy. It was good to see him that way."

Miranda thought so, too. "It matters not. He told me there's no way." She shrugged. "I'm respecting his wishes." It was one of the reasons she had taken the job out west for the summer.

Rosalyn smiled. "I have faith in Remare. I've never known him to give up so easily when he has wanted something. If he truly wants to be with you, and I believe he does, he will find a way."

Miranda grimaced. "You haven't seen the way Valadon looks at me. He's very proprietary as if he branded me *his*."

"So, both of them desire you." She laughed heartily. "Not the worst possible circumstances I can imagine."

Now, it was Miranda's turn to give the *"seriously"* look.

"It would not be the first time they shared a woman."

Miranda shook her head. "No, thanks, that's not my speed."

"They shared Vivienna for a while. Until she betrayed them both."

Miranda visualized all that Rosalyn wasn't saying. "Remare loved her, didn't he?"

"Yes, and she betrayed his trust and loyalty. As she did with Valadon. Vivienna doesn't love. She manipulates people for her own ends. Caltrone, a high-ranking member of our council, had ordered her to seduce Valadon to bring him back into the fold. She only pursued Remare to get close to Valadon. As soon as Remare went away to war, she moved on to Valadon—her true mark." Rosalyn seemed reflective. "I don't think Remare ever let himself become close with another woman after her. That's why his relationship with Irina lasted so long."

It made sense to Miranda, why, at times, Remare seemed so cold, so distant. "Thanks for the info." Miranda put her empty glass down on her desk. "But I probably won't be meeting Vivienna. I'm going to be wrapped up in my work. I'm not going there to socialize."

"I hope you don't meet her." Rosalyn accompanied her to the door. "But, if you do, be on your guard. Remember what I said about my lover losing his memories. All vampires have different talents. Vivienna's is getting inside your head. She's sleek as a snake. She can get inside your head without you even knowing she's there. Be careful, Miranda."

Miranda shivered. The last thing she needed was for a vampire to screw around with her head. Mulciber and Brandon had played with her while she'd been their captive.

Fighting off one vampire had been tough enough—two had been impossible.

Chapter Twelve

Gazing out the tinted window of Valadon's limo, Miranda watched the buildings pass by. The high lord had insisted on having dinner at Le Cirque her last night in New York. Although dinner had been spectacular, the horde of paparazzi waiting for them as they emerged from the restaurant had been terrifying. She knew, within moments, images of them together would be all over social media. Again.

"This is the contact you will be meeting." Valadon removed a case from a hidden panel in the limo and handed her a black leather binder with ValCorp's gold insignia of a flame-tipped staff. "Henri Duchamp, my solicitor in Paris, will meet you at the airport and see you to the hotel. Once you're settled in, he will make arrangements to introduce you to Andre Brevet, who is handling the estate of Marta Venier." His emerald eyes shone with male smugness. "I trust the accommodations at Le Grand Hotel will be suitable, though you will probably be spending most of your time at Château Venier."

Miranda remembered Valadon telling her in the archives his first investments had been in real estate. "You own Le Grand, don't you?"

"Of course, I do. I would not send you to a hotel I *didn't* own."

"This is a business trip." She smiled. "I'm only going to be there a few days, and if you picked the accommodations, I'm sure they will be more than adequate." Valadon had exquisite taste in everything from the luxurious interior of the limo to the elegant clothes he wore. Even his cologne implied wealth and sophistication.

Miranda glanced down at the black dress Cesare, ValCorp's head designer, had made for her and felt chic. After spending the last few months studying petroglyphs in New Mexico's wild, it felt good to be wearing designer threads. She'd enjoyed their dinner, especially since Valadon hadn't been overbearing. She liked this more subdued version of him, even though a niggling voice in the back of her mind kept asking, *what is he not telling me?*

After checking his messages, Valadon said, "I've already informed Bastien he is to be with you at all times when you are authenticating the painting. And Remare has made arrangements with our people there to insure your safety as well as the Degas."

Miranda was disappointed Remare hadn't come by to say goodbye, but reluctantly, she understood his reticence. She glanced at Valadon and whimsically wondered which was more important to him, her or the painting. "Do you really think I need a bodyguard?"

"Yes. I would not take the risk," he said in his melodic, deep voice as he gently squeezed her hand. "These are troubling times, Miranda."

She pondered what Valadon was thinking as he stared out the windows. He seemed more preoccupied than usual, but she couldn't get a read on him. Covert bastard was good at shielding his emotions. "How does Bastien feel about going to Paris?"

"He's looking forward to it. His parents still live there. If you're lucky, you might actually get to meet Auguste and Giselle de Rosemont while you are there. They are good people and friends of mine."

The limo driver pulled up to her brownstone.

"Everything you need is in the folder. Bastien has his copy. Your itinerary and my credit card is enclosed for your expenses. Try not to cause me too much damage." Valadon winked and then pulled her into his embrace and kissed her forehead. "Have a good trip and remember—Bastien stays with you at all times."

As the limo driver opened her door, she nodded. "Thank you. I'll make sure your painting is well taken care of. See you in a few days, Valadon."

His verdant eyes seemed to be glowing. "Miranda."

She watched as the limo drove away. The license plate, ValCorp 1, caught her attention. No wonder the paparazzi knew they were at the restaurant. After she entered her home and kicked off her shoes, she went to the fridge to get a cold bottle of water and then relaxed on her sofa. Perusing the binder, she found Valadon's card—it was the Black and Gold one—*Unlimited*. A low whistle emitted from her lips. The last time Miranda had been in Paris, she'd been a student on a budget. But, now—*thank you, Valadon.* Damage, indeed; she laughed. She was definitely bringing home goodies for Lizandra and the rest of her friends.

Speaking of the Were Queen, she checked her messages.

Have a good trip, Mir, and if you have time, bring me back something shiny. By the way, you can thank me for your surprise the next time you see me. It's already waiting for you on Valadon's jet. Au revoir—Liz.

Surprise? What surprise? Miranda shrugged, thinking she'd find out soon enough. *Shiny, huh? Oh, I think I can manage that.* She was disappointed Orion didn't leave any well-wishes, nor did anyone else. Shaking off the glum feelings, she changed into comfortable travel clothes then checked, one last time, that everything was secure. No dishes in the sink, all windows locked, plants in her rooftop garden watered.

When the car pulled up to take her to the airport, her luggage was already waiting by the door. What she wasn't ready for was the driver.

"Valadon said you were all set to go to the airport. Are these the only bags you're taking, Mir-randa?" Remare scrutinized her outfit—clothes he personally had Cesare create for her.

Miranda stifled a grin as a thrill shot through her. "Yes, I always travel light. I'm only going to be gone a few days. Lizandra said the same thing. I just don't pack much." She was glad Remare was taking her to the airport; his presence alone had a soothing effect. Sighing, she wished he was the one accompanying her to Paris instead of Bastien.

She sensed Remare thought the same thing. "Are you ready?"

Miranda looked one last time around her living room and then at Remare. "Yes, I think I've got everything."

He opened her door to his Mercedes SUV, then secured her luggage in the rear compartment. Breathing Remare's scent deeply into her lungs made her feel more alive— stronger. Goosebumps tingled her skin. Soon, they were on the highway to the terminal where Valadon kept his private jet.

After driving in companionable silence, Remare said, "When you get to Paris, I have an associate I want you to contact." He reached inside his jacket pocket and handed her a card. "Francois Pascal is an old friend of mine. We go back centuries, and he will look after you. More than likely, Bastien will not always be able to accompany you, so I've asked Pascal to keep an eye on you, as well."

"All this for just one Degas painting?" Miranda believed in security, but she was convinced there was a lot more going on Valadon had neglected to tell her.

"Paris is one of our oldest cities, Mir-randa. There are some very old vampires still living there. Be aware that not all of them follow the rules Valadon has set forth concerning humans." Glancing in her direction, Remare lifted his hand to briefly cup her cheek where a malevolent ancient had once slashed her. A wound Remare had healed. "But I'm sure you already knew that."

Miranda was elated he still rolled the *r*'s whenever he said her name and wondered if he'd been in contact with Rosalyn. "Anyone, in particular, I should watch out for?"

"Just remember to call Pascal if you should run into any unpredicted situations."

"Okay." Feeling content, she put the card in her handbag and watched Remare drive. "I didn't know you'd be the one driving me. Thank you."

"I wanted...I wanted to make sure you arrived safely. And to warn you—"

She watched his lips thin. "Warn me about what?"

"Don't stray too far from the hotel. I know you will be working the majority of the time. But try to stay in public places and avoid—"

"How come you're not coming with me?" Miranda interjected, surprised as he was at her spontaneous question.

Remare looked at her with longing in his eyes. "I wish that I could, but as Valadon's second, I would require permission from the reigning vampire in Paris. And that's not something forthcoming. Do you still have the phone Valadon gave you?"

Miranda fished for it in her purse and then waved it. "Yes, right here."

"Good. Keep it with you at all times."

She saw the exit sign for the airport and regretted they didn't have more time to talk. "Remare...I wish you were coming with me."

He slowly exhaled, then looked at her as he turned into the terminal. "That is not possible. Valadon needs me here."

He had reminded her again of his loyalty to Valadon. There was much she wanted to tell him, but as they approached the inspection station, that possibility was now gone.

After Remare showed his ID to the security personnel and they were waved through, Miranda gawked at Valadon's plane. Never did she imagine she'd be flying on someone's personal jet. "Impressive."

"Lizandra called Valadon earlier insisting certain protective measures be implemented where you were concerned." Smirking, Remare opened his door. "She didn't think Valadon had done a proper job of it the last time you worked for him."

"She did, huh?" Miranda closed her door and smiled at her friend's protective streak.

"Yes, she insisted one of her people accompany you on your trip." Handing Miranda's luggage to one of the attendants, Remare nodded to the jet waiting on the tarmac. "He's waiting on the plane."

When they walked together to the plane, Miranda hesitated to look at him, but then, Remare leaned in to embrace her. She closed her eyes as she breathed in his masculine scent. Hoping he would kiss her, she was disappointed he did not. Until she felt the tip of his tongue lick against her jugular. Her body shivered at the sensual touch. To a vampire, it was the most intimate of kisses. Staring into his chocolate brown eyes, she saw his red rims glowing.

"Be safe, Mir-randa." He nodded to her. "I'll see you when you get back."

When he turned to leave, she immediately felt an emptiness—as if a piece of her had slowly drifted away. It stung more than she thought it would. Shaking off the bitter sensation, she murmured, "*In a few days.*" Then, she turned and climbed the stairs to the jet.

Once inside the fuselage, she grinned when she saw her traveling companion.

Wearing his NY baseball cap, an exuberant Orion raised his glass to her. "Lizandra said I should see Paris while I'm still young."

"Hello, Miranda." Sitting across the aisle was Bastien.

Miranda rolled her eyes when she heard them arguing over who the better hockey player was on the Rangers. She thought Nash, but wasn't going to interrupt them. Were and vampire were similarly dressed in button-down shirts and dark slacks, except Orion's boots were black and Bastien's were brown. Both men were exceedingly handsome, and Miranda's sense of pitch went haywire with the two so close together.

Miranda grinned at Orion. "I am so glad to see you. Why on earth didn't you tell me you were coming with me?"

"Lizandra said not to." Orion shrugged. "She wanted you to be surprised."

Miranda sat next to him and hugged him tightly. "You're going to love Paris. I'll show you the Eiffel Tower and take you on a boat ride on the Seine."

"Nice to see you, again, Miranda. But don't make too many plans." Bastien checked his phone. "He's on guard duty, as well. We're supposed to be taking turns watching you."

"I think Valadon worries too much. I went to grad school in Paris, Bastien, and lived there for almost three years. I *know* the city."

"But does Paris know you?" Bastien reclined in his seat and closed his eyes. "You two should get some sleep. It's a long flight, and we're going to be busy as soon as we get there."

Miranda wondered at Bastien's remark and then shrugged it off. Vampires could be so cryptic. Of course the city knew her. She'd studied at the museums, hung out at the cafes, and visited all the touristy locales like all the other grad students. She'd even done some modeling for an old local artist who'd been her mentor and friend, Monsieur Dourdain. She'd visit him as soon as she could, she decided, as a cold shiver ran through her. It had been some time since they'd been in touch.

***

After watching Miranda's jet take off, Remare called Valadon from his car. He did not like the game the high lord was playing, but resigned himself to the necessity. "Miranda is now on her way to Paris, as are Bastien and Orion."

"Good. We'll soon learn quickly enough what our European cousins are up to."

"Your photograph with Miranda is now all over the social media sites, as you requested. The Council members have surely seen it by now."

"As planned."

"You still don't believe we should have warned Miranda what she might be up against?"

"No. It's better she doesn't know. She'll be safer that way."

After he ended his call, Remare wondered at Valadon's wisdom and began favoring his sapphire ring he wore on his left hand. Miranda had many good qualities, but she had yet to master the art of deception—her emotions were always written on her face. He grimaced. Unlike the Madame Lord of Paris who was a master at disguising her motivations, spinning one web over another to lure in her prey.

And, now, Remare was sending Miranda straight into the webmistress's snare of deceit. He hoped to hell Valadon was right, because Remare was seriously contemplating catching the next flight out to Paris. "Be safe, Miranda," he whispered to the moist night air. "I would be with you if I could."

At the sound of another plane's engine preparing for take-off, he thought he heard the shrill laughter of the bitch queen of Paris, Vivienna.

The nightmare had just begun for Miranda. But for him, it had been a haunting experience. Alone in his car, Remare leaned his head back and closed his eyes as a bitter memory surfaced.

Paris, 1640

France had just lost a major skirmish to the Spaniards in the Battle of Arras, and Remare was reporting their loss to the Vampire High Court. As he walked the majestic halls of their gilded palace, he could hear the snickering of the guards. When he passed the courtiers, courtesans and other visitors to the court, he could detect more whispering. He scoffed. Surely, one defeat in battle wasn't something that would have them gossiping.

Remare looked around the court at all of vampire aristocracy and could not discern why his presence was eliciting such attention. It was no matter to him; as soon as he delivered his report, he would see his beloved, Vivienna, once again before joining his fellow soldiers in the field.

One of the leaders of the Council of Elders, Magritte was holding court. Seated high on her dais, she was as beautiful as she was deadly. The power of the two-thousand-year-old vampire could be felt throughout the room. It had been her acumen in vampire/human détente that had netted them prime hunting grounds and beneficial business associations. When she motioned for him to come forward, he bowed and went obediently.

"Madame, the loss at Arras is a minor setback. We were winning the battle until the enemy was aided by unforeseen circumstances."

"Do not apologize, Remare; word of the duplicity of our enemies has already reached this court. I am sure you did everything you could under the circumstances. You are hereby granted leave to return to your duties."

Bowing again, Remare turned to leave when a side door opened and Vivienna stepped out in a stunning dress made of pearls and silk. Her raven hair was fashioned high in curls with long ringlets down her back. His heart raced, and his face broke out in a wide grin. He moved to join her when Caltrone appeared from behind. It was obvious they had been sharing blood...and from their combined scents, he could tell they had shared their bodies, as well.

Remare went to dislodge his sword when he heard Magritte's voice in his head. "Do not! Caltrone has ascended to the Council of Elders. He is to be accorded every respect."

Seething, Remare watched as Caltrone climbed the stairs to take his place at Magritte's side. "I see your machinations have garnered favor with our High Court, Caltrone. You are to be congratulated."

"Thank you, General. Too bad I can't say the same for your maneuverings on the battlefield." Caltrone glanced at Vivienna. "Or in the bedroom. In either case, you've come up lacking."

The whole court burst out in derided laughter, and Remare's blood began to curdle as he looked at Vivienna's mocking smile. He wanted to strangle her with his bare hands until he felt the freezing cold of Magritte's touch as her power stopped his hand. When he saw Caltrone's mocking grin, Remare swore he would kill Caltrone at the first opportunity.

When Magritte raised her hand for silence, the court became quiet. "In your absence, Caltrone has adopted Vivienna as his ward. She is now a full member of this court and a member of my entourage. We thank you for your service to the court."

Remare bowed to Magritte and stared with hot eyes at Caltrone. With one last scathing look at Vivienna, he turned and marched from the room amid jeers and snickering. She had used him to gain access to others in the court. And he had been too blind to see it. A friend had warned him about Vivienna, about her duplicitous nature, but he had brushed off his comments, dismissing them as jealousy. Vivienna had always been ambitious, but he had never dreamed she would sell herself to the highest bidder.

And, now, the whole court knew of his humiliation.

Chapter Thirteen

Valadon rode his private elevator down to the lowest level of Valadon House his Torians nicknamed Caina. He thought it a fitting name as he walked past relics of bygone eras—testaments to the epochs they had fought through and survived. When he reached the last chamber of the vast cave, he glanced once around to make sure he was truly alone, then he pressed a stone, opening the entrance to the Hall of Memories.

Using a torch to light his way, he walked to where his mother's tomb was located and ran his fingers tenderly over her plaque. Vampires preferred funeral pyres, usually at sea, but kept mementos of the dead to honor their memory. Opening the vault, he retrieved a box containing jewelry and other items dear to him. He searched the box until he found the piece of canvas with the likeness of his beloved Lena. The beauty and feistiness of Marlena de Avignon had captured his heart centuries ago.

Valadon sat on the stone bench facing the vaults. Regret burned in his soul that he was never able to grant her the one wish she had asked of him.

Marseille, 1630

Valadon stood on a bluff, watching the ships pulling into the harbor. As Minister of Finance, he often came to Marseille to conduct business with the merchants—vampire and human—who contributed heavily to the Parisian courts.

"If I could wish for one thing, it would be to accompany you on one of your voyages."

Valadon smiled. He was heartened that his love had chosen to see him off. Lena loved hearing of his tales of distant lands, and knowing her love of literature, he often brought her back books from the countries he visited. "I was not sure you would come, Lena." He turned to see her golden locks blowing in the wind and her whimsical smile that had first caught his attention. "Are you still angry with me?"

Sadness, but also a stubborn resolve, etched her face as she pulled her shawl tightly around her. "No. I suppose I will always be disappointed, but I know you did what you could."

"Lena, I tried—very resolutely." Valadon reached for her, but she pulled away. "I asked our ruling council for permission to make you my bride and to turn you. They refused to grant my wish. Unequivocally." His heart ached that those in the court would not grant his request. "Please believe me, no one is more remorseful than I."

"I know. You've already told me." She sighed. "I'm to marry Monsieur Rocheforte. My father insists on it. He's warned me for years of the arranged marriage." Lena looked at him with tearful longing in her eyes. "I had hoped, prayed to God, you would find a way."

Valadon's heart was breaking. Only human aristocrats of the highest echelon knew of the vampires, and the treaties they had with them were finite. The Vampire Council members had insisted on the marriage of Lord Avignon's youngest daughter to Rocheforte, citing how the marriage would cement the continued trade and profits that poured into Paris. Their greed had known no bounds.

Valadon exhaled. He'd even gone to Magritte, one of leaders of the Vampire Council, but she too had turned down his request. No one in the vampire hierarchy wanted their Minister of Finance wedding a human. "Look to your own kind," Magritte had urged. "If you must marry, there are many in our court who would make a suitable partner for you. Why not one of them?"

He had responded, "I do not love any of them."

Magritte had scoffed at his admission of love and told him marriage was a contract, a business transaction, and that, of all the members of her house, he should know that. "If it is love you want so very badly, take her as your mistress."

Valadon knew it was impossible for Lena to become his mistress. If her husband were to find out she'd taken a lover, he would do unspeakable harm to her.

"There is no way. I am sorry, Lena. But I am not sorry for having met you and for loving you. I take you with me in my heart."

"I wish to give you a gift before you leave." Lena reached into her purse and drew out a piece of canvas containing her likeness. "There was no time to have a proper portrait done, so I had one of the villagers draw this. Keep it, and from time to time, think of me."

Valadon pressed the canvas to his heart. "Know that I will." He kissed her gently and tasted the tears that fell from her eyes.

Valadon closed his eyes in bitter memory. He folded the canvas and returned it to the box. "I still think of you." He prayed to the stars above that the dead found peace— something he could not.

Remare watched as his friend suffered in quiet dignity. "You still come down here, even after all these long years?"

"On occasion." Valadon looked up at Remare. "Tonight seemed most worthy."

"You're nostalgic because Miranda is now on her way to Paris."

Valadon's voice was coated in quiet fury. "I don't think I've ever fully forgiven those in the court who refused my petition to turn Lena. I'd almost forgotten how childish their petty concerns were." His voice softened. "Did I ever tell you I went back to Marseille after I'd received word Lena was dying?"

"No. I don't believe you ever did."

"It was winter, and she had been taken ill. I held her in my arms. She was only thirty-seven years old." Valadon seemed lost in his reveries, and not wanting to disturb him, Remare waited for him to continue. "She told me she never really forgave me for not taking her with me on my voyage and that she had kept a secret for nearly twenty years."

"What was the secret?"

Valadon exhaled. "When I told her I could not marry her, she was already pregnant with my child. Not long after I sailed from Marseille, she gave birth to a boy. With her father and fiancé long at sea, she was able to hide her pregnancy from them. A midwife she had confided in told her she knew of a noblewoman who desperately wanted a child. Lena knew there was no way to keep the baby. Her father and fiancé would have shunned her or worse; therefore, she gave away our child." Valadon hung his head in despair. "The midwife told her the baby died soon thereafter."

Remare remembered, centuries ago, many human and vampire children died in infancy. He felt sympathy for his friend and his grief at suffering such a loss. "You told me Lena had three other sons with her husband."

"Yes, I made sure they were all well provided for, as I did her grandchildren and all the children who followed until—" He shrugged. "But there was one I never lost track of."

"Who?"

Smiling, Valadon only said, "One I have great affection for."

Exhaling, Remare put his hand on Valadon's shoulder. "You did what you could. Back then, we could not defy the court or our ruling council. Magritte once loved you. This was her way of getting revenge on you for not returning her affection."

Valadon nodded. "As if she hadn't already gotten her pound of flesh. You know of what I speak."

He did. Centuries before, Magritte had become spiteful after Valadon's rejection and had them both punished in front of the court. Vampire memory could be long and brutal.

Remare had been humiliated in the court by Vivienna, but Valadon had suffered far worse with the loss of his love. Remare closed his eyes. His heart felt like it was being squeezed in a vise. He knew Valadon had found a new chance for love with Miranda. How could he possibly take that away from him?

Valadon's eyes turned to ice as he looked up at him. "But we did defy them, didn't we?" He rose and placed the box back in the vault. "For all their manipulations and their cunning, we were able to outwit them." His voice turned to granite. "And we will, again."

***

"There may be a problem with our plans, after all, my darling." Caltrone looked up from the latest set of photos one of his assistants laid out on his desk. "It appears Valadon has taken up with the young art historian he was involved with last year."

Brushing her mane of raven hair, Vivienna slid behind Caltrone and ran her red-tipped fingernails along his chest as she glimpsed the pictures. "Problem? I see no problem."

Vivi waved her brush in the air. "She's a minor irritation—easily dealt with, easily disposed of, like so many others."

Caltrone felt the bite of Vivienna's nails on his shoulder. He enjoyed watching her walk naked around his bedroom with his scent still clinging to her skin. "Our spies informed me Mulciber thought the same. Where is he now?"

"Mulciber was a blood addict and a fool." Vivienna continued brushing her long wavy locks. "At least he was smart enough to have his mole report to us. If this human woman was a threat to our plans, we would have heard more about her by now."

"Valadon is not to be underestimated." Caltrone leaned back in his chair and rubbed his chin. "He's a shrewd businessman. He didn't get to where he is today by being predictable."

"And I didn't become Madame Lord of Paris by being obvious. I'll have this woman looked into. She's human, and humans have weaknesses." Vivienna put down the brush and waved her hand in abject dismissal. "Valadon is far more interesting prey." She smiled wickedly at Caltrone. "I've played with him before. I know him and his second. I'm looking forward to playing, again."

"As we all are." Caltrone snaked his hand around Vivienna's waist and pulled her to him. "Our plans are secure, but for now, let's enjoy the night." He kissed her passionately as her nails dug trenches in his back. One of the oldest living vampires, he healed almost immediately, and instead of feeling pain, his arousal surged at the thought of having her, again. When he felt her cupping him, using her nails to torture him, he picked her up and tossed her on his bed.

Vivienna laughed. "Should we celebrate, yet again, *mon coeur*?"

Caltrone's fangs lengthened, and his eyes glowed as his red rims pulsed in anticipation. She called him her heart, but he knew Vivienna had no heart. Those who held power could not afford that particular luxury. He would have thought that was something Valadon would have learned by now. He stared down at Vivienna as she plucked her nipples in open invitation. Her appetite for sex was as lustful as his own. Of all his associates, he enjoyed Vivienna the most; she had never failed him in all of their clandestine operations.

He knew she would not fail him now.

***

"Whoa! Never been in a room like this before." Orion laughed as he opened the double doors to their magnificent suite, which looked more like a wing in the palace at Versailles.

"I have," Bastien murmured as he tipped the bellhop and locked the door after him. He checked out their rooms. The living space was decorated in true Sun King fashion with Louis the fourteenth furniture; the walls were a pale blue and held reproductions of the Impressionist paintings Paris was so famous for. His parents owned many of the originals.

Even if he hadn't been one of Valadon's elite guards and enjoyed an industrious lifestyle, he still had an appreciation for the finer things in life. He'd grown up with wealth and privilege as most Blueblood vampires did. But, unlike the others, he had walked away from his position to become one of Valadon's Torians—a decision his family never quite accepted or had completely forgiven him for. Especially Isabelle; he grimaced.

"You can take the bedroom to the left; I'm going to take the one on the right." Bastien carried his luggage into his room, refusing to let anyone handle his suitcases as his weapons were secured in the hidden compartments.

"Hey, there's only one bed in that room. Where am I sleeping?" Orion asked as he marched into Bastien's room.

Bastien cocked an eyebrow. "With me."

"Funny." Orion looked around the elegantly decorated room. "There's only one bed in here, as well."

"What's the matter, wolf, don't you like to cuddle?" Bastien smirked as he started unpacking. "I heard all you furry types like sleeping in puppy piles. *Woof, woof!*"

"Blow me." Orion flipped him the bird.

"Love to." Bastien grinned.

Miranda laughed. "Now, boys, play nice. We're going to be working together for the next few days, and I don't intend to play referee. You can sleep with me, Orion. That bed is one of the most sprawling kings I've ever seen."

Putting his arm around Miranda, Orion smirked at Bastien.

"Not necessary," Bastien said. "We're taking split shifts, remember? Six hours on, six hours off, and since you slept on the plane—snoring very loudly I might add—I'm taking my rest, now. Miranda, if you need anything, all you have to do is call. I'm a light sleeper."

"To tell the truth, all I want right now is a hot bath and a nap myself. I still feel kind of jetlagged, and we're not scheduled to meet with Henri Duchamp until tomorrow."

"Sounds good. Do you want some company?" Orion asked as he rubbed up against her.

"I think I want some alone time, as well. After a nap, I'm going to go through all my notes and the information Valadon gave me one last time so I'm prepared for this meeting. Watch some TV in the sitting room. Did you see the size of the screen? There's a guide booklet that tells you what channels will tell you all about the city. Make a list of what you want to see, and I'll take you there. But, right now, I've got a date with the dream fairies."

After hanging his suits in the closet and tossing the rest of his clothes in the dresser, Bastien started undressing; when he was naked, he slipped under the sheets. He watched Orion enter the room. "Whatever you do, roomie, don't open the drapes or you'll give me a really bad sunburn. Okay?"

"Sure."

Bastien waited until Orion had unpacked and closed the door behind him to make his phone calls. Remare had given him explicit orders to call Francois Pascal once they landed and to make sure his men were in continual surveillance of Miranda and the painting.

Unfortunately, the problem wasn't with Miranda, but with Orion. The guy was decent enough, but the last thing Bastien needed was a watchdog—not with his true mission.

Smirking, he knew exactly who to call to keep the wolf busy while he completed his task in Paris.

After taking his own shower and making sure Miranda was safely napping, Orion rifled through the food baskets and snacked on some cheese and crackers. When he checked the other basket, he saw it contained *Crescent's Chocolates* with a note that simply said, *Taste Me!—V.* He shrugged. *Love to!* Then, he popped one of the chocolates in his mouth and stretched out on one of the sofas—careful that his weight didn't break the spindly legs.

It was during the video clips about Paris, the metro and other forms of transportation, he heard voices coming from Bastien's room.

Opening the door, he saw a sight he wasn't expecting. "I thought you wanted to get some sleep?"

"Got some." Bastien grinned at him. "Juliet, meet Orion. He's a singer and...a werewolf."

The stunning blond rolled off Bastien and didn't bother to cover her naked breasts. "Hello, I've heard your music. I liked your last song, 'Dream Within a Dream.'" She smiled seductively at him. "The lyrics are very cool."

"You've heard it? I didn't think my music made it to Europe, yet."

Juliet played with a strand of her long hair. "Oh, yes, it's very popular here."

Orion made a mental note to check with his manager when he got back to the States.

"So, wolf, you gonna stay there and drool...or join us?" Bastien asked as he got up and walked naked to get a bottle of water."

"I don't think your girlfriend would appreciate that." Orion had never been with a vampire before and didn't think they mixed too much with Weres. Humans, maybe, but he didn't know any Weres who dated vampires.

"Juliet's a friend I've known for years." Bastien sipped his drink. "We're not exclusive." He shrugged. "Join us."

"You can join us, Orion." Juliet rose and walked unabashedly toward him. "We don't bite." She smiled suggestively up at him, the scent of sex clinging to her. "Unless you want us to."

Orion grew hard as she slid her bare arms around his waist, but he wasn't ready to surrender to the seductive charms of the vampire just yet. "One of us has got to be on guard duty. I'm still on shift."

"Miranda's safe in her room. We're going to be busy the next few days so—" Bastien embraced Juliet from behind, fondled her breasts, all the while maintaining eye contact with Orion as if daring him to take part in their sexual escapades. The beast in Orion fully awoke. Juliet pulled him to the bed and began undressing him. But his eyes weren't on Juliet. It was Bastien he watched as the vampire grinned sexily.

Orion wondered what he was getting himself into and then realized he didn't care. When his clothes were finally off, he joined them on the bed.

Chapter Fourteen

Standing on her patio, Miranda enjoyed the cool night air as it skimmed against her freshly showered skin. As she looked out over the City of Light, somehow, Paris seemed colder—more remote than she had remembered. Cities like Paris, Rome, any of the European cities, had this old-world feel to it New York didn't—it was in the scent in the air and the sensations invading her body. Miranda placed her hands down on the cold balustrade, instantly warming the stone.

Centuries of history drifted over the Seine and caressed Miranda as if welcoming her home. Ancestral voices whispered to her of times long gone—it was almost haunting. When her phone rang in her robe pocket, Miranda woke from her reveries. Her toes curled when she saw the caller ID. "Hello."

"Bastien informed me you arrived safely and will meet with Duchamp tomorrow. How was your flight, Mir-randa?"

Still feeling heated from her hot shower, Miranda opened the sash to her robe as she contemplated the city and said whimsically, "Oh, you know those charter flights are so unpredictable. I swear the pilot must have been all of eighteen, and he hit every section of turbulence he could find." Miranda's voice emulated mock boredom. "Your doing, I suppose."

"Not at all." Remare laughed. "But I will have him fired if he caused you any such distress."

"No, don't do that. I was joking." Miranda smiled. "The flight was fine. And I'm glad we're not meeting with Duchamp until tomorrow. I'd forgotten how much jetlag affects me." Not wanting to discuss business with him, she changed the subject. "By the way, thank you for the nightgown."

"I thought you would like the bronze color. Cesare showed me the design before I approved it. Where are you, now?"

"Standing on the balcony, outside my bedroom, looking over the city."

"You're not cold?"

"No, I took a very long hot shower. Though I must say, as comfortable as this gown is, it's very gossamer and clingy." Miranda wanted Remare to imagine what she looked like wearing it. "No wonder Cesare had insisted I be naked when he took my measurements."

He chuckled, then became serious. "Bastien and Orion haven't seen you in it, have they?"

Miranda grinned at the worry in Remare's voice. "No, they're in the other room, setting up their schedules." A chilling breeze drifted over her heated flesh. "I have to tell you, this city, Paris, feels different from when I was here as a student."

"How so?"

"It's different. I don't know." Miranda rubbed her arms as if cold. "Something makes it feel colder—older." She could almost hear an echo in the distance. "I'm not sure what it is."

"Perhaps, it is not Paris that has changed, but you. You've been through much, Mir-randa. You're a few years older than when you were a student there."

Maybe, she thought, as another breeze made her skin tingle. But something was...off. "You're probably right." After a lengthy pause, she said, "I know you couldn't come with me, but it would have been nice if you could have come on this trip. I would have showed you my old stomping grounds. Where I hung out with the other art students. Out of the way places that aren't in any tourist book."

After a pause, he said, "I would have liked that."

Miranda knew Paris was six hours ahead of New York and wondered if Remare was at work. "Where are you, now? ValCorp?"

"Yes, I'm on the roof. I wanted privacy for this phone call."

Miranda wanted private time with Remare, as well. "Remember when you took me on your boat to get that bottle of wine for your friend?"

"Yes. It was a warm night—your first night back in the city after your trip to New Mexico."

Miranda remembered it well and had liked being alone with Remare. She knew being in a *romantic* relationship was out of the question. Valadon would never approve, and the vengeance he would elicit would be excruciating. But, if she couldn't be intimate with Remare, she at least wanted his friendship. "I've thought about that night. And you know what I wanted more than anything else? I wanted us to take a boat trip on the Hudson River up to The Cloisters—the museum at the northern edge of Manhattan. Have you ever been there?"

"Yes, but that was nearly a century ago. I haven't been there since."

"It's an awesome museum. One of my favorites in New York. I like the medieval artifacts and the tapestries. They're a wonder of this world."

"As are you, Mir-randa. If that is what you truly want, I will arrange to take you. But it must be kept between us. No one else."

"I would like that very much." Miranda felt the cold go through her and imagined what it would be like to have

Remare come up behind her and put his arms around her. She shivered at the thought.

"I have to go, Mir-randa. I will call you again, soon."

"All right. Tell Valadon I'll text him as soon as I start working on the Degas. It shouldn't take too long."

"I will. Be safe, Mir-randa."

"You, too." Miranda ended the call and felt a longing deep in her belly for something she could never have. But, if they couldn't be lovers—*damn Remare and his sense of loyalty*—she'd have his companionship. That she wanted very much. Valadon could dictate just so much of her life, but he couldn't control who she chose to befriend.

But it was Valadon's ballpark, and if she wanted to play, she would have to play by his rules.

For now.

***

Bastien checked over his motorcycle to make sure it was in fine running condition. He didn't like deceiving Orion, but the Were wasn't part of his mission. God, the wolf had as much stamina in bed as he had, and Bastien couldn't help but wonder, if the wolf lived as long as he did, if Orion wouldn't become an even better lover. Bastien admired the athleticism and muscle tone the Were had and tried to remember if he had ever been in bed with a werewolf before. Nothing registered in his memory.

At the moment, Juliet and Orion were taking a breather from their intense lovemaking session. But that wouldn't last long; Bastien needed a couple of hours away to meet with some of his contacts and had procured Juliet's services for the next few hours. That should give him enough time to meet with his informants and lay the groundwork for Valadon's plan.

***

Restless after her phone call with Remare, Miranda decided she needed some alone time without her bodyguards before she procured Valadon's painting. Dressed in jeans and a dark sweater, her hair in a ponytail, she reached for her sunglasses and backpack. When she glanced in the mirror, she almost resembled the grad student she'd once been. Leaving a note on her bed, she silently left the hotel and grabbed a cab a block away. Miranda wanted to visit her former mentor and friend, Monsieur Dourdain. But, first, she would stop at the open-air flea market.

Valadon had given her his card, and Miranda was almost tempted to use it, but the gifts she was intending to buy her friends she wanted to pay for with her own euros. When the cab dropped her off at the market, Miranda breathed in the Parisian air and felt like she was home, again. People watching was a thrill in itself. Here, in the noisy market, some of the best bargains in the world could be found. She made her way through the throng of people. She felt guilty for ditching her guards, but she could never get her shopping done with Orion or Bastien in tow.

"*Merci.*" Miranda paid the merchant for the gift she picked out especially for Lizandra. Stuffing her purchases in her backpack, she hailed another cab to go to Dourdain's apartment in the Latin Quarter. In exchange for hours of tedious modeling, he had shown her techniques for mixing paint you couldn't learn in a book.

Dourdain would be in his sixties, by now, Miranda mused as the cab pulled up in front of his place. Excited, Miranda climbed the stairs to Dourdain's third-floor apartment and knocked on his door. After waiting a while, she knocked again, and then, dread started in her stomach. She knew she should have called first, but she had wanted to surprise him. When she tried the knob, she found it locked. Checking the hallway to make sure no one was watching, Miranda used her *Elemental* gift of manipulating the cylinders inside the locking mechanism and sprung it free.

Quietly, she entered the apartment and called out, "Hello. *Monsieur* Dourdain, Jacques? Anyone home?" Disappointment made her heart ache.

As she scrutinized the apartment, cold penetrated her skin. Exhaling, she realized no one had been inside in some time. Any valuables in the apartment were long gone, and all that remained, besides the dust, were a few pieces of furniture. Miranda sighed. She'd only been gone a few years; she'd never imagined Dourdain would have moved. He loved the Latin Quarter, and so had she.

Miranda went to the window where the same blue curtains from when she had posed for him were still hanging. Looking out at the back alley, she saw the neighborhood boys playing soccer. Opening the window to let the scents of Mid-eastern cooking in, she breathed in deep. Her eyes drifted to where the couch had been. Dourdain had painted his last painting of her while she'd fallen asleep there.

"If you're looking for *Monsieur* Dourdain, he's not here."

Miranda turned to see the neighbor across the hall who had often baked her treats when she worked for Dourdain. "Claire, do you remember me? It's Miranda."

The woman's eyes studied her, then blazed in recognition. "Miranda! It is you!"

Miranda loved seeing Claire, again, and hugged her tightly, inhaling the scent of freshly baked baguettes. "I've missed you."

"It's been years." Claire stepped back and considered Miranda. "You've filled out; your face is fuller, better I think.

I hardly recognized you. You were so skinny when you modeled for Dourdain."

"Yes, I wanted to surprise him. Do you know where he moved to?"

"Oh, *ma chere*, *Monsieur* Dourdain passed away." Claire wrung her hands. "I'm so sorry to tell you this. You did not keep in touch?"

Miranda knew her face must have looked as crestfallen as she felt. "He can't be dead. He was only in his late fifties when I worked for him."

Claire brought her two fingers to her mouth in a gesture of smoking. "Too much with the cigarettes." She shrugged. "Come into my home. I'll make you that green tea you liked so much."

Miranda entered Claire's apartment, still in shock her friend was dead. The first year or two, they'd emailed each other every few months then once or twice a year. She wasn't sure who had written last and regretted she hadn't made more of an effort. "What happened to all of his stuff?"

"What always happens when a person dies?" As Claire put the tea kettle on and prepared two cups, she shrugged in a way that was unique only to the French. "Someone came and took most of it away. What is left is what nobody else wanted."

At the sound of the door opening, they both turned to see Evan, Claire's teenage son, enter with a soccer ball in his hands. "Miranda! You're back!"

She welcomed his embrace. "My God, you've gotten so big." Feeling his hand drifting down to her hip, she was surprised when he groped her. When she looked at him, Evan winked back.

"Evan, stop that and put your ball away. Where is your father?"

"He's downstairs talking to *Monsieur* Pauvelle." Evan snagged a slice of baguette as he ran into his room.

Claire turned to her. "Miranda, please stay for supper, Gustave will be so pleased to see you, again."

"I can't. I just stopped by—"

"Miranda." Gustave entered, grinning ear to ear. "So, you've finally returned. We expected you sooner. Why didn't you keep in touch?"

Miranda wasn't sure what to say. "I don't know. It's good to see you, Gustave—how's the flower shop doing?"

"Very well. Had I known you were visiting, I would have brought you some peonies."

"She came to see Dourdain." Claire spoke softly in French to her husband.

"Oh, the old fool. It was inhaling all those paint fumes." He sampled what his wife was cooking on the stove and added more spices.

Since she remembered Dourdain always keeping the windows open, she doubted his opinion.

"I was trying to get Miranda to stay for supper."

Gustave rubbed his belly. "Of course she's staying, aren't you, Miranda?"

Miranda looked at their two happy faces and didn't have the heart to disappoint them. "Yes, I'd love to."

***

Orion didn't think his hunger for sex could ever reach the peak it just did after having sex with Juliet; he'd lost count around the eleventh time. He'd been in threesomes before with different members of his band in different cities; he'd even remembered a fourth and possibly a fifth, but this had been way hotter. *Was it because they were vampires?* Juliet had been exciting, but knowing Bastien was watching him—daring him to keep pace—had turned Orion on even more. They'd fucked so many times, each had worked up an appetite that Bastien had volunteered to go out and get them some food.

After Orion felt his heart rate returning to normal and his head clearing, he turned to Juliet. "Where the hell did Bastien go?"

"I don't know." She shrugged nonchalantly. "There are several cafés in the area."

Glancing at his watch, he jumped out of the bed. "Holy shit, it's been hours." Knowing he'd just been had, he looked scrupulously at Juliet. "Bastien put you up to this, didn't he?"

Juliet smiled whimsically as she stretched. "He said he thought you could use some company."

"Oh, really!" Orion zipped his pants. "What else did he say?"

"Was it so bad?" Juliet pouted as she made mewing noises, then walked to him and stroked his chest. "I've never been with a werewolf before, but you were wonderful."

Orion could say the same about her. With humans, he had to be careful, but with vampires—as he'd just discovered—they could take vigorous amounts of sex play. "Juliet, do you know where Bastien went?"

"No, he didn't tell me," she whispered as she ran her tongue along the vein in his neck. "Forget Bastien; we still have time."

When Orion held her at arms' length and shook his head, Juliet said, "All right, just let me take a shower, then."

Orion sniffed his skin and smelled the scents of both vampires. He wasn't sure how Bastien's scent became embedded in his skin, but since they'd all been intertwined, he guessed it was possible. He needed a shower, too, but would wait until Juliet was finished or...maybe not. He looked at his rising cock and saw Juliet beyond the mist of steam in the shower. How he could even want sex after the marathon they'd just had amazed him. He figured one more round couldn't hurt.

Then, he would go in search of Bastien.

Chapter Fifteen

Bastien parked his motorcycle by the café where he'd agreed to meet with his contacts, Pascal and Touraine. This late, the neighborhood was nearly deserted, and Pascal had picked an outdoor table set apart from the others. Bastien checked the surrounding area, but didn't sense the presence of any other vampires. Valadon demanded answers, and Bastien's mission was to find the source of the rumors about the VHC contemplating ValCorp merging with some of the European conglomerates—something Bastien knew Valadon would *never* allow to happen.

"Sebastien de Rosemont. It is good to see you, again." Pascal and Touraine spoke French, then bowed in formal greeting.

"I gave up that title a long time ago. It's Bastien of House Valadon, now. Let's speak English." Bastien noted the gray hairs at Pascal's temple and the white whiskers of Touraine. Although an older vampire, Touraine still retained his vigor and good looks. And both were friends who Valadon trusted.

"Of course." Pascal nodded. "I just figured while you were in Paris, you might wish to resume your title."

Surveying the area, Bastien leaned in and whispered, "I don't have much time. Valadon is anxious for his report. What can you tell me about the High Council?"

"Regrettably, not as much as I had hoped to. The High Council members have become very secretive. They always were, but now, more than usual. Obtaining information on their activities has become difficult to monitor without risking being apprehended. Flaubert would have joined us tonight, but he feared his movements were being watched and thought it wiser to stay hidden."

"I can understand his reticence." Bastien knew Flaubert was a trusted ally Valadon spoke highly of. Although a younger member of the Council, his information had proven valuable many times in the past.

Touraine sipped his wine. "The economy here has everyone riled up. We had hoped to see improvement, but as yet, that has not happened."

"Yes. Valadon keeps a steady watch on the European Financial Commission. He is most disturbed by the trend. Even our Asian friends have shown concern."

Pascal agreed. "True, but not to the degree we've seen here."

"Tell me, *vieil ami*, just how bad have things deteriorated?"

Touraine leaned back in his chair. "Unfortunately, it is worse than what the news media has reported. Several banks have already gone under, and others are on the brink. Many fear that is not the worst of it."

Pascal growled as he nodded.

Bastien had read the financial reports, and although Valadon had assured him that trends like this weren't unusual, this particular downturn was becoming alarming. "Who on the High Council is most affected?"

"There are many, either directly or indirectly, who have much cause to be concerned. But, the ones who wear the deepest frowns are Calisar, Tobias and Merlinder." Pascal rubbed his chin. "Alone, they do not pose much of a threat, but together, *together*, they could cause Valadon much distress. They feel Valadon should be doing more to help."

Bastien held his temper in check. "Don't they realize how much he has to do in America? He's been instrumental in saving financial institutions not only in New York, but throughout the States and in Canada."

"The conservatives believe his duty to the VHC comes first." Pascal shrugged. "As many Council members have the majority of their fortunes tied up in financial institutions here, they are demanding action be taken by Valadon."

"How much more do they want him to do?" Bastien knew Valadon already tithed a significant amount to the VHC.

"You would have to get close to a Council member to obtain that information, *ami*." Touraine leaned forward. "I do know, however, that there have been secret meetings by those of the highest echelon. Magritte has even been in private consultations with the sages."

Bastien knew no matter how confidential some meetings were, with the proper inducement, information could be obtained. He looked at Valadon's two trusted allies. "Any clue of what's being discussed?"

Pascal shrugged, again. "They are resentful of Valadon's success. They have always been thus, and they will plot to arrange *something* they believe will work in their favor."

Greedy bastards, Bastien thought. "I need to find out more. Who else can I talk to?"

"I have watched the members carefully. There is one name who I think can be of benefit to you." Pascal eyed the street, then passed a slip of paper across the table. "But you must be vigilant."

Touraine's voice softened. "Your presence here has already been observed. They will be circumspect where you are concerned."

Bastien read the name Pascal had given him. "I'm only going to be in Paris for a few more days. Will Auriel meet with me?"

"Yes. But tread very carefully. Your actions will be monitored." Pascal exhaled then smiled. "Your father has not heard from you in some time. Perhaps, it is time for you to make amends."

Bastien knew, when he agreed to this assignment, he would have to meet with his parents; but he'd been hoping to avoid it. His father still had not completely forgiven him for leaving his court and becoming a member of Valadon's. He met Pascal's eyes. "Perhaps, it is."

"One other thing, Sebastien." Touraine sounded apprehensive. "Your sister, Isabelle, has been seen in the company of Caltrone. Her ambition to become Council is well known."

Bastien sighed. He knew his sister's associations were less than desirable, but Isabelle had always done as she pleased. No matter who was hurt in the process. "Thank you for meeting me, gentlemen. As always, Valadon appreciates your loyalty. His gratitude will be deposited in your Swiss accounts."

Pascal and Touraine nodded, then Pascal added, "Do send him our highest regards."

***

After leaving Dourdain's and still preoccupied with the news Claire and Gus had provided, Miranda wandered into an old section of Paris she was not familiar with and stopped—her senses in heightened cognizance. She peered upward. Something was rank in the Parisian air; the cloying, putrid scent of decay permeated the thick mist that was slowly drifting over the Seine and hovering over the city.

Her heart beating fiercely, Miranda tried to slow down her breathing as the muscles in her arms and legs tightened. She looked around the unfamiliar, deserted square with its many gargoyles standing sentry as if to ward off any transgressors. If she could just find the university, she could get her bearings straight.

Stupid! She was so stupid not to have left sooner. Miranda knew the buses and cabs didn't run this late at night in this old section of Paris. She should have left Claire and Gustave hours ago, but Dourdain had promised her the painting; by rights, it was hers. Thankfully, before she left, Gustave had remembered the old leather cylinder case Dourdain had instructed only go to Miranda. She would die before giving the painting up, and now, that was becoming a distinct possibility.

Miranda felt the hairs on her neck rising in awareness as several different pitches starting going off in her head in a cacophony of dread. The vampires were here, now, surrounding her from the far sides of the square, staying in the shadows, their whispers ricocheting off the buildings purposely designed to disorient her. Their vibrations grew louder in her head—echoing faster. She could block one voice, maybe two, but not all of them.

Run! Her instincts were screaming as the pitch of the vampires reached a crescendo that made her body tremble. If she ran, they would surely chase her. But, if she stood there any longer, it was certain they would capture her. Breathing hard, Miranda bolted to the far end of the square, her arms pumping, her feet pounding against the cobblestones. She then swung left down a side street, aware the vampires were tracking her. Until another scent—both familiar and formidable—appeared.

His shadow, dark and dangerous, elongated, and then, the howls of pain from the vampires echoed in the night and quickly vanished—taking the scent of decay with them.

Miranda recognized his muscular form, had seen him fight before. With the power of a Blueblood vampire rushing through his veins, he was at once handsome and terrifying.

He turned to face her. "A long way from New York, Professor."

Brushing the hair from her face, Miranda smiled in relief. "I could say the same about you, friend." She went into his arms, inhaling his comforting, masculine scent. "It's good to see you again, Gabriel."

Valadon's progeny had been her lover months ago, yet they had remained friends. Needing his embrace a moment longer, she peered up into his golden-brown eyes. "You're about the last person I expected to see. What are you doing in Paris?"

"Besides saving you from those goons, I'm attending a medical conference in Amsterdam. Some of the doctors wanted to come down to Paris for the weekend." Gabriel gave her one of his crooked smiles she found so endearing. "I joined them."

"I'm glad you did. Mind walking me to my hotel, Le Grand?" She hooked her arm in his.

"Sure." He caressed her hand. "But what are you doing in Paris?"

Miranda tapped the leather case. "Authentication." After only a few steps, she said, "You look great. How've you been?"

"Pretty good. The conference has been great." Excitement laced Gabriel's voice. "I've been meeting with geneticists from around the world. The research that has been going on is just incredible. There's a doctor from Finland who's been working on cellular deconstruction and making great strides at identifying different...and that's not what you wanted to hear."

"No, go on. It's all right." Miranda laughed, grateful to hear his soothing voice. "I know genetics has always been your interest."

"Yeah, but you also called it my little 'obsession'."

Miranda regretted saying that. Finding a way to turn himself back to human had been Gabriel's dream, and she'd had no right to criticize. Even though Valadon had told her there was no going back. "I think we were both just—"

"On different paths," Gabriel said as they walked along the low-lying bridge that would take her back to her hotel. "Have you been in contact with Valadon?"

"Who do you think I'm doing the authentication for?" Miranda glanced over the Seine as a fine mist coated the water, thinking Paris had the best views from their bridges. So many historical structures lined the shoreline; it was as if she could breathe in deep enough, she could inhale a piece of French history.

"Ah, I should have known." Dejection laced his voice. "I guess I figured it might have been one of the benefactors of the museum."

Miranda stopped by the lamppost on the bridge and watched as a late night boat filled with revelers passed them. "Orion's with me. So is Bastien. They're here to help me bring back a painting Valadon wanted.

"How's Orion doing?" Gabriel asked as he leaned against the bridge's railing and tenderly moved a strand of hair away from her face. In the lamplight, his light brown hair appeared blond.

Miranda wanted to cup his hand while it was still on her face, but he dropped it before she could. She looked out over the river and then down below. Beneath the misty water appeared a darker, more sinister mist with a terrifying specter. Gazing deeply, for a moment, she thought she saw a pair of eyes of darkest blue staring up at her, beckoning her. Her breath caught in her throat, and she had to fight to breathe. When she blinked, the momentary vision was gone.

"Earth to Miranda." He chuckled. "I see you still do your zone outs."

"I thought I saw something in the water." Miranda shook her head in an effort to clear the haunting image. "I'm sorry; what did you say?"

"I asked how Orion was doing."

"Good. He's probably worried sick about me, by now. I forgot my phone." Walking to her hotel, Miranda took one last look at the water and decided exhaustion must be pulling at her.

"Well, you're almost there, now. Tell him I said hello and that I like his new song."

"I will." When they reached the hotel, Miranda wasn't sure if she should invite him up, but then decided against it.

"You look good, Miranda." He smiled. "Are you happy?"

She looked into his golden-brown eyes that almost appeared green in the light and felt something melt deep inside her belly. "You know, I am."

"Then, I'm glad." He bent to kiss her temple. "Next time, don't go out alone so late at night."

"I won't." Miranda remembered Gabriel's black cat who used to snuggle between them. "Hey, don't forget to give Rexi some treats when you get back."

Surprise flickered in his eyes that she had remembered his cat. Gabriel grinned. "I'll tell her you were the one who reminded me."

Miranda watched him walk away and exhaled deeply. "There, for the love of God, goes a good man."

***

Guy de Montglat watched Miranda safely enter her hotel. He turned to go back to his apartment. The bodies of the vampires who had accosted her had already been dealt with by his associates. He had snapped the neck of the oldest one who barely had a second to register his presence before death's cold kiss brushed his lips. Guy had no fear of the others reporting his presence to their masters. He smirked. The only image they saw was the image he had wanted them to see.

The streets of the Latin Quarter were familiar to him; they would be, he'd lived here for nearly a century. When Montglat reached his building, he spread a mist so that his presence would go unnoticed. As far as the neighbors knew, Dourdain—just one of his many personas—was dead, and he wanted to keep it that way. If anyone recognized him, they would think they were seeing a ghost.

He silently climbed the stairs and unlocked the door to his former living quarters. Guy looked around the abandoned apartment, remembering every nuance, touching a shelf here, an object there. It had been some time since he had last visited the studio. Unlocking the window, he looked out over the city and inhaled its fragrance; Paris was a city of many fascinating scents, but the scent that intrigued him most...was Miranda's.

Montglat gazed down at the spot where his sofa had been. She had often napped there after hours of modeling for him. He smiled as a memory of Miranda posing for the painting he had titled *Lavender Dreams* surfaced. How he had adored painting her likeness. He remembered how she lay sleeping, and the need to touch her had been overwhelming.

His own blood had been calling to him. He'd known when he met Miranda, even though many generations separated them, she was his. No other vampire could detect her vampire blood because too much human blood had diluted it, but he, alone, could and did...recognize his kin.

Guy crossed his arms over his chest. Miranda didn't know it yet, but trouble was on the horizon. Old friends and old enemies continued to spin their wheels—each hoping to succeed where the other had failed. Montglat sighed. The machinations of the High Council never seemed to end. But there was one game in which he intended to play a major part.

And Miranda was his key to winning.

Chapter Sixteen

"These are the media reports you requested." Camille backed away after placing the articles on Vivienna's desk. "The digital ones have been sent to your e-mail account."

The Madame Lord of Paris barely glanced at her assistant. "Very well. And you are certain these are the most up-to-date images? There are no others I should be aware of?"

"*Oui*, Madame."

"Keep an eye out for anything else that should surface on Miranda Crescent. Especially if it pertains to High Lord Valadon. *Comprends?*"

"*Oui*, Madame, *je comprends*." Camille nodded as she left Vivienna's office.

Vivienna swiveled in her chair as she flexed her fingers. "So, Valadon is still involved with the human wench." Smirking, she perused the pictures. "Well, we'll just see about that." Caltrone thought the human an impediment to their plans and wanted her eliminated. Vivi saw her as a challenge, one that she fully intended to meet. Not that Miranda Crescent could ever challenge her. She had outmaneuvered far cleverer opponents, including the former Lord of Paris, Savinien—whose bones were currently resting on the floor of the Seine.

Vivi peered out her window up at the moon. What fun was a game if you had no one to play with? She was in the mood for some entertainment—then she would dispose of the wench.

***

When Miranda unlocked the door to her suite, she didn't expect to be greeted by the angry faces of Bastien and

Orion. Like sentinels, both stood with their arms crossed—mirror images of each other. If they weren't so serious, Miranda would have thought it comical, as if she were a teenager sneaking in after curfew.

"I wasn't gone *that* long." Actually, after glancing at the clock, she figured, yeah, she had been. "What's the big deal? We don't have the painting yet."

After clicking his phone off, Bastien politely asked, "Where were you?"

"I got restless, so I went shopping at the open-air flea market." Miranda shook her backpack for emphasis, then went to her room. "Why do you two look so concerned?"

"Because we didn't know where you were." Orion followed after her. "You left your phone on your nightstand. We had no way of reaching you."

"Yeah, sorry about that." Miranda dumped her backpack on the bed and put the leather cylinder in the closet. That was one painting she didn't want either of them to see. "It won't happen, again." When she came back to the living area, the two males just stared at her. "Fine." She exhaled. "I promise, okay?"

"I'm just glad you're all right." Orion hugged her. "But no more sneaking out."

"I didn't sneak out."

"Miranda, I'm glad you're safe, too. But I think you need to explain to Remare. He's quite irritated with me." Bastien frowned. "I'm not even sure he's told Valadon, yet. Here, use my phone. He said for you to call him immediately after you arrived. He was *very* upset."

"Seriously, people, I don't know what you're so upset about. I just went shopping." Miranda took Bastien's phone and went out on the balcony for privacy. After taking a deep breath, she called Remare.

"Mir-randa, how nice to hear from you." She could hear the snark in his voice. "Tell me, what part of 'you are not to go anywhere without one of your bodyguards' did you not understand, because I thought I was very clear on the subject."

"Remare, the painting is not in our possession, yet. I just went to the flea market to pick up a few things for my friends." A feeling of giddiness danced in her belly at hearing his voice.

"Doesn't your hotel have a gift shop?"

Miranda laughed at Remare's sarcastic tone. "Of course they do, but I like the flea markets; they're fun to browse. You find all kinds of unusual things there. Besides, if I brought them stuff back from the gift shop, they'd expect that every time I went away, and that's not happening."

"You didn't use Valadon's credit card?"

"I'm using that for expenses. The gifts I get my friends come from my wallet, not his. I appreciate your concern, but really, I'm fine." She rubbed one foot over the other. "Feet are a little sore, though, but other than that, I'm good."

"Promise me you won't go out again without taking either Bastien or Orion."

Miranda closed her eyes, relishing a breeze from the Seine blowing across her face. "Fine, fine, I promise I won't go out without Orion or Bastien."

"Good, because if you do, I will personally punish that lush round ass of yours."

"You and what army?" she murmured.

"I don't need an army, Mir-randa, and I'm quite serious. It's not just the painting I'm concerned about. Your life is...precious to me...and to everyone else here at ValCorp."

Touched by his words, she said, "So tell me, Remar-re, while you're punishing my 'lush round ass', am I naked at the time?" She laughed at the growl erupting from his voice.

"All right, all right! I've seen the error of my ways. I shall go nowhere without either Orion or Bastien under penalty of death. I swear on all that's holy and right. Happy, now?"

"I will be very unhappy if you should become injured in any way."

"Yeah, I don't think I'd be very happy either. Listen, I'm going to Château Venier tomorrow. There is no way I could become injured. Besides, who would want to hurt me? I'm just here to validate a painting. People don't go around hurting scholars; we're pretty much ignored by everyone."

"Is there a television in your suite?"

"Yes, Orion was watching it before."

"Could you please turn it on?"

"Why?" Miranda walked over to the television and flicked the remote.

"You don't watch much screen, do you?"

"Lizandra, the Weres and I watch old movies; that's about it. I don't have much time for media updates between the museum and NYU."

"Obviously. Turn to any news channel that has an entertainment segment."

Miranda flicked through the channels, not knowing what had gotten Remare's gander up. At least not until she saw her picture plastered across the screen leaving the restaurant with Valadon. "You've got to be kidding me. Fuck!"

"Precisely. So, you see there is reason for concern."

Miranda's heart sped up as she translated the broadcasters' words. "Not only do they have me in bed with Valadon, they've got me engaged to him!"

Orion stood beside her and watched the screen. "What is she saying?"

Bastien offered, "They're wondering if Valadon is set to marry her or if they're just fu—"

"Don't say it!" Miranda and Orion said simultaneously.

Miranda's mind started racing. She asked Remare, "There are people here who don't like him much, aren't there?" No wonder she'd been taunted earlier in the market and again in the square. Damn, now, she understood why Gabriel thought she was involved with Valadon. It was all making sense, now.

"Valadon has always had enemies, Miranda, as well you know," Remare said softly. "Many of them make Paris their home."

She barely registered Remare's voice as she sank into the couch. "I'll call you back another time."

"Be safe, Mir-randa. Bastien is there for a reason. Let him do his job. Please."

"Sure. Okay. I'll let you know how it goes tomorrow."

"Thank you. Now, please put Bastien on the phone."

Miranda handed the phone to Bastien and shut the television off. She heard a lot of capitulation on Bastien's part and then silence.

Orion rubbed her arm. "Want me to stay with you tonight?"

"Maybe later. Right now, I just want to be alone." Miranda went to her room and closed the door behind her, letting her head rest against the wood. She'd just become a target. And wasn't that just going to be fun? *Damn you, Valadon! That's why you insisted on dinner out! You knew the paparazzi would be waiting!*

Chapter Seventeen

After a long and thoroughly relaxing shower, Miranda sat back and combed her wet hair. The hot water helped clear her head of some of the stresses Valadon had heaped on her. She'd be leaving Paris in a few days, and if she kept to her schedule, she wouldn't be out in public much. Which went a long way in alleviating her fears.

Needing to see her painting again, Miranda retrieved the leather cylinder and unrolled the canvas. When Gustave had given it to her, she'd promptly taken it to Dourdain's apartment to study it. Disappointment still marred her face as she examined the subject—it wasn't the painting she'd hoped for. *Girl in Window* was an amazing work of Impressionism with its blue color variations and study in light, but it didn't compare with the enchanting figure highlighting *Lavender Dreams*.

Both were nudes, but unlike *Girl in Window*—which emphasized her profile—*Lavender Dreams* showcased Miranda's sensual appeal in full glory as she dreamily lay on a sofa surrounded by lavender swirls of color. He'd captured the whiskey color of her eyes perfectly with the subtle striations of red. "You promised me *Dreams*, Dourdain. You said you would never sell it." She shook her head in frustration. "What did you do with it?"

After rolling the canvas and securing it in the cylinder, Miranda felt exhaustion tugging at her and dropped into bed. Tomorrow, she'd focus on work and forget the drama plaguing her. Work had always been her way of coping with stress. After crawling under the sheets and pulling up the covers, she turned the lamp off and hoped tonight the nightmares wouldn't haunt her.

Hours later, still in a somnolent state, Miranda heard the lock turning and the door slowly opening. The scent of the forest drifted over her before she could make out his shape. Smiling, she turned toward the shadowy figure. "Remare."

"Mir-randa," he said as he closed the door behind him. "I can only stay for a short while."

Surprised, but grateful for his presence, she sat up quickly and rubbed the sleep from her eyes. "What are you doing in Paris?

"I had business in London, but I wanted to see you before flying home." Sitting on the edge of the bed, Remare pulled her close.

Welcoming his embrace, Miranda hugged him tightly and breathed in his masculine scent—something she'd always found comforting. "Does Valadon know you're here?"

"No. That's why I have to leave soon. He only knows I flew to London to speak with an informant."

Miranda rubbed his hand. "Did you see Bastien? He's in the other room."

"Yes." Remare kissed her knuckles. Chuckling, he rose to shed his jacket and tie. "It appears Bastien and his new bedmate don't get along. Orion is at one end and he, the other."

He toed off his shoes, undid the top two buttons of his shirt and then joined her on the bed. Having him beside her sent thrills throughout her body. "I'm glad you came." She wondered if she should tell him about the vampires in the Latin Quarter. "I ran into Gabriel. He called you, didn't he?"

"Gabriel?" Remare's brow furrowed at the mention of her former lover's name. "I wasn't aware he was here." He tilted his head. "What's Gabriel doing in Paris?"

"Medical convention." Miranda raised her hand and cupped his cheek. "How long can you stay?"

Remare's breaths deepened. Longing in his eyes, he kissed her palm and moved it over his heart. "A little while. Miranda, what I told you in New York still holds true. I can't defy Valadon. He loves you...dearly." Remare shook his head in futility. "He would not understand."

But Valadon wasn't here, now, and she'd be damned if the high lord dictated her love life any more than he already had. Miranda could feel Remare's beating heart under her palm. He'd come to Paris because he had wanted to see her, again. Being in the same room with the vampire made her feel alive, more sensuously aware. She took his hand and placed it over her heart. Whatever it was that bound them together intensified. She smiled. "Careful, Remare, I'll begin to think you care."

He smirked at her with devilry in his eyes. "As if you didn't know." He rolled on top of her. "I must not be doing a very good job, if you doubted it." He nipped her chin. "Let me see if I can convince you otherwise."

His arms embraced her as his lips captured hers in a heated kiss that had the butterflies in her stomach dancing. He tasted of wine as she passionately returned his kiss. It had been too long since the last time he'd kissed her. She thrust her fingers into his wavy hair, the thick strands caressing her fingers. Her heart pounded as she ran her hands up and down his back, loving the way his muscles flexed under her touch.

When they finally broke from the kiss, Miranda couldn't tell who was more out of breath. Remare's eyes darkened with passion—a hunger impossible to ignore.

"You are a sorceress, Mir-randa. I've often thought so. No other woman haunts my sleep and tempts me so." He buried his face in her neck and brushed his fangs over her pulsing flesh.

She laughed in pleasure. This was what she'd been missing. Remare and the terrifying, delicious connection they shared. He was hers—despite what Valadon might think or say. Remare belonged to her as much as she was a part of him. And there was nothing Valadon could do to change that.

When the heat in the room started surging with his taunting fangs over her jugular, she tried to shed her nightgown.

"Easy, Mir-randa. I like this nightgown. I told Cesare I wanted the finest silk for you."

She grinned. "I still can't believe you had me stand naked in front of him. But, now, I understand. It fits me like a second layer of skin." Eyes heavy, she looked at him with wicked intentions. "Help me take it off."

Remare's breaths came hard and fast as he thinned his lips. "He never finds out about this, Miranda." His fingers bit into her arms. "Not ever."

"He won't hear it from me."

He sat her up and gently peeled the nightgown away from her too-heated flesh. Staring at her naked body, he slowly unbuttoned his shirt and tossed it over a chair. For a moment, he hesitated, and Miranda was afraid he'd changed his mind.

But, then, his half smile emerged, the one that made her stomach flip flop. Next, he unhurriedly removed his belt, one loop at a time and tossed it away. His pants were next.

Miranda couldn't tell if he'd been wearing boxers or not, she was so transfixed by the beauty of his body. Remare, naked, aroused her more than any other man ever could. Her heart beating frantically, she peered up at his eyes. His red rims were glowing. He was pleased she hungered for his body. She lifted her arm toward him.

Caressing her hand, he trailed soft butterfly kisses up her arm and snaked one hand around her neck to bring her mouth to his. Warm sensations flowed through her.

Miranda was amazed at the rightness of her feelings for Remare. She knew it was dangerous—knew it was impossible—but in the darkest part of the night, when logic sleeps and instinct awakens, there's no denying the desire to be with the one your heart craves most. Miranda pulled his body over hers and reveled in the erotic nature of his skin rubbing against hers. Although his vampiric anatomy made his skin colder, she could feel the heat emanating from him and grew damp at his touch.

Trailing kisses down her neck and collarbone, Remare found her nipple and sucked it into his mouth. Miranda moaned loudly and arched off the mattress, forcing more of her breast into his mouth. She'd tried to forget him—forget his touch, the darkness of his eyes, the curve of his lips, and the way he made her feel when he smiled. But the denial had only made the desire stronger. She lifted her legs up and circled his waist baring her most intimate flesh.

Remare looked at her with heavy-lidded eyes, his fangs fully elongated. "I've waited too long for this, Mir-randa. For months, I've denied myself. I won't anymore." He lifted one leg up by her calf and kissed the inside of her thigh until his tongue found her core, then he kissed her there as passionately as he did her mouth.

Miranda's head spun in delirious rapture, her heart beating a frantic rhythm. No other male could ever make her feel this way—no other man ever would. When the heat became too much and she thought she would explode from the web of passion, Miranda slammed her nails into the sheets and screamed out his name.

Remare looked up at her with male satisfaction. Slowly, he lifted himself and positioned his cock at her core. "I will not rush this, Mir-randa. I've dreamt of this for far too long." He slowly entered her and then retreated. Watching her face, he entered her again, this time deeper, one tantalizing inch at a time—each thrust an agonizing testament to his patience.

Miranda tried to wiggle her hips to make him go faster, but he only slowed his thrusts. "Behave," he whispered, as stream after stream of pleasure flowed through her body. Like the waves over an ocean, the ebb and flow of their bodies beat out a rhythm that had ancestral voices singing secret arias to the moon.

Tears of passion swelled in her eyes. She knew the communion of souls they were experiencing was so rare, so fine—there was no escaping the raw truth of their union.

Minutes passed, maybe hours, there was no telling how long Remare tortured her with the rapture only he was capable of creating. Without warning, her head arched back, and another howl of passion broke from her throat, making her body tremble even more. A few strokes later, Remare tensed under her hands, and then, she felt the eroticism of his fangs piercing her neck. His vampire kiss reinforced the sensuality of their shared soulful coupling.

Moments later, Remare rolled to the side, and slowly, reality crept back into her brain. She glanced at his sweat-slicked skin and silently watched as his chest rose and fell in rhythm with his breathing. She raised her hand toward him, and he gently squeezed her fingers. Their bodies thoroughly spent, neither one said a word as they simply held hands in complete understanding.

When enough time had slipped by, Miranda turned toward him. "What did your informant in London tell you?"

With eyes dark as midnight, Remare reluctantly turned toward her. Miranda nearly gasped. She had never seen his eyes this black before. Gone was the man who had shown her such intimate tenderness and made her feel more alive than any other. In his place was the ruthless assassin, the monster who prowled the dark. His voice held the unforgiving, jagged edge of truth, a blade cutting her to the bone, as he uttered the phrase that made her shudder violently. "Brandon is in Paris."

Miranda screamed in horror as Remare's body dissolved into mist and floated away. At once, the dream dissipated, leaving her cold, shaking and alone. Anguish ripped through her that it had all been a dream, one where she had felt such intense yearning for Remare and had only imagined his desire for her.

But what had her heart thundering and the tears gathering in her eyes was the knowledge, the undisputable sense of knowing, that Brandon, Valadon's traitorous brother, who had once tortured her was, in fact, in Paris.

And Valadon had known it all along.

Chapter Eighteen

"What's wrong?! What's wrong?!" Bastien yelled, shaking Miranda by the shoulders.

"Brandon's in Paris." Miranda brushed Bastien's hands away. She was still in shock at the vividness of her dream and could still taste Remare's mouth on hers, feel his touch on her skin, feel him inside her body. Needing the fresh air to erase the memory of the dream, she slipped out of bed and walked to the balcony doors, thrust them open and relished the cool, crisp air on her flushed face.

Seeing and unseeing, her spirit drifted over the buildings, inhaling the scents of the city, allowing the reality of Paris to wake her. "That's what this was really all about. Your boss is using me to get to Brandon. It was never about *me* or the *damned* painting! It was all about finding Brandon. Wasn't it?"

"Miranda, I know nothing of Brandon being in Paris." Bastien's face twisted in confusion. "If Brandon were here in Paris, I would know it. Valadon would never keep that from me."

"He knows." Miranda knew in the deepest levels of her soul Valadon knew. He'd played her. *Bastard!* "He sent me here knowing the danger. He's using me as a lure."

"No, that's not true. You can't know that."

Miranda turned to Bastien. "I *know*." When she saw horror etched on his face, she knew her eyes had turned black. Orion had once told her after Dane's murder, her eyes looked like death, and when he had tried to talk to her, nobody was home. But she'd been home, at least the part she called the *Dark Angel*—where the psyche housed the darkest of our natures. Miranda knew, if she didn't contain her emotions, things were going to get bad fast. "Call him," she said. "Find out for yourself."

"Miranda, you had a bad dream. I know some dreams can *seem* real. God knows I've had a few of them, but Brandon is not in Paris. If he were, Valadon would be sending a whole battalion of vampires for him."

No, he wouldn't. He would save him for himself. Miranda said nothing as she looked over the city—the early morning breezes calming her. Her *Elemental* powers were always strongest at dawn. She was sure Brandon was somewhere in Paris. Remare's voice was echoing in her mind to that mental place where instinct and logic merged. *Truth,* the voice whispered. She'd had premonitions before, and they'd all come true, but that was not something she was going to discuss with Bastien. "Call Remare. He knows." Miranda placed her warm palms on the cold stone balcony.

"Remare wouldn't keep something like this—" When Bastien put his hand down on the balcony, he must have felt how heated the stone was and searched her dark eyes. She smiled boldly back at him. His shocked facial expression almost had her laughing.

"I'll get Orion."

After Bastien left, Miranda breathed in the cool breezes coming off the Seine. "Come to me. Come to me, now." She needed the calming coolness of the wind. It would be daylight soon. There would be no more sleep for her. Memories of how Brandon had taunted her in her cell surfaced. Bitter fragments better left forgotten floated in her vision; she quickly wiped them away as Orion surrounded her with his arms.

"I heard you had another nightmare, Mira. I'm so sorry." Orion turned her to face him. "Want to talk about it?"

Miranda hoped her eyes looked normal as she peered up at Orion. "No, not really. It wasn't like the others." Not wanting to be touched, she pulled away from him. "Brandon has the face of angel, you know. Oh so charming with his sexy smile. But he's a monster underneath."

Orion tilted his head. "Are you sure you didn't have some sort of flashback? Maybe to something that already happened?"

"I'm sure." Miranda briefly glanced at him. "It was no flashback."

Bastien joined them, his phone to his ear. "I called Remare. They have no intel whatsoever that Brandon is in Paris. He wants to speak to you."

When he tried to hand her his phone, Miranda turned away. "Ask him if he's lying."

Bastien and Orion looked at each other.

Orion asked, "Is there any way possible Brandon could be here and it hasn't reached ValCorp, yet?"

When she felt calm enough, she turned to Orion with her arms crossed over her chest. "I'm not wrong." Orion nodded at her with understanding. She knew he'd seen her when she appeared zoned out, drunk. She hadn't been. Orion was one of the few people who understood Miranda was a *sensitive*, his Cherokee grandmother told him stories of people who had gifts. He'd seen too much not to believe.

"Remare says it's highly unlikely Brandon is in Paris. Please talk to him." When Bastien tried to put his hand on Miranda's arm, Orion interceded and shook his head. "Miranda, we have a whole network of agents out there looking for him. We will find him."

"Or he'll find you first." Miranda took the offered phone. "Remare."

"Miranda. It's good to hear your voice, again. Now, would you mind telling me what makes you think Brandon is in Paris?"

"I know he is." Miranda wanted to run her claws across his face.

"Could you be more specific?"

Miranda thought about it for a moment. "Call it...instinct."

"I'm sure your instincts are very good, Miranda, but I need more than a woman's intuition to go by."

"Have you been in touch with Valadon, lately?"

"Yes, I have, and that is not something he would keep from me or any of his Torians. Did you happen to see Brandon when you were out sightseeing?"

Miranda wanted to brain him; she really did. "I know what you're getting at. Nothing I saw today triggered any memories." She hesitated then said, "Remare, I know Brandon is in Paris, and if this is yours and Valadon's idea of a sick game you're playing to lure Brandon out, I really don't appreciate being used as bait."

"Miranda! I would never use you in such a manner."

"Perhaps, but Valadon would, wouldn't he?" When she heard Remare's sharp intake of breath, she knew she was right. "*Au revoir,* Remare." Not wanting to talk to him or anyone else, Miranda handed the phone back to Bastien and went inside.

***

Remare tossed his phone on his desk and closed his eyes as he reclined in his leather chair. Miranda was a woman of intelligence, not one given to fanciful imaginations. If she believed Brandon was in Paris, he was convinced something must have set her off—something she saw or heard while she'd been out alone in the city. A feeling of disgust made his stomach turn that he barely heard the soft knocking on his door as Irina entered his rooms.

"I thought you might want some company tonight," she said in her Russian accent as she slinked closer to him.

Remare had once thought her one of the most beautiful women in the world. It had been some time since he'd given her much thought. "You did, did you?" He swiveled in his chair.

"It's been a while." She slipped into his lap.

When she bent to kiss him, Remare twisted her hair around his fist and pulled her head away. His lips were mere inches from hers. "How would you like to go on a mission? One that must be kept secret."

She stroked his face. "Do I get to kill anyone?"

"Perhaps." Remare smirked. Irina was one of the best assassins in the Torian Guards. Valadon had forbidden Remare from leaving New York, but he didn't say anything about sending one of his Torians to Europe. And, as leader of the Torians, it was up to Remare to make the call. "A situation has arisen, and I want you to fly to London to interrogate an informant."

"London? That's Herbert's territory. He's a friend of yours. Why don't you go?"

"Valadon needs me here. While in London, I will need you to visit one of the underground bloodclubs." Remare knew his agents in Europe and their habits. Few ever ventured to the more sordid, backward terrain of the bloodclubs the older vampires found fascinating. Humans sold themselves and their blood for the perceived passion only vampires could provide. Remare had lost interest in such clubs long ago. "After paying respect to Herbert, I want you to locate a vampire called Barusch. He has contacts in Paris. I want you to find out if anyone's seen Brandon."

"Have there been any reports or sightings?" Irina picked up a dagger Remare had on his desk and stood. The ivory hilt was beautifully carved and the blade dangerously sharp.

"Only one, but since the report is sketchy, at best, I want you to find out what you can then report to me." Remare stood and walked toward his door. "You leave immediately."

"And if I should find Brandon?"

"Do *not* try to apprehend him. You are to call me directly." He took the dagger from her. "Valadon does not want his brother killed. He will punish Brandon his own way. Do you understand?"

Irina leaned in and put her arms around Remare. "Absolutely."

"Complete your mission." Remare's mouth hovered inches from her face, as his arms locked hers behind her back. "And I'll give you a taste of what you've been craving." Remare kissed her temple, then released her. "Remember, no one is to know of this mission. No one."

"Understood." Irina turned and closed the door behind her.

If there was the slightest possibility Brandon was in Europe, Irina would procure that information. With her background, she could handle any of the criminals who hung out in the bloodclubs.

Tapping the blade against his thigh, Remare narrowed his eyes in contemplation. Irina would not welcome a partner on this mission. She would see it as an insult. But some of those clubs were dangerous—even for a Torian. His Grinch smile surfaced as he reached for his phone. There was one who would lay down his life to protect her.

"Gregori. I have an assignment for you."

Chapter Nineteen

The drive to Château Venier was splendid. In the serenity of the backroads, Miranda's mind quieted, and she relaxed. There was something magical about the old growth forests. A hidden mysticism called to her, beckoning her to discover its secrets. But what those secrets were, Miranda had no clue. She just knew the forest was a place of wonderment.

"Andre Brevet, the man handling the estate of Marta Venier, will meet with us and direct you to the painting." Henri Duchamp, Valadon's urbane solicitor sat next to her in the car. "Don't be too offended, if his attitude is prevalent."

"Attitude?" Miranda raised an eyebrow. She'd enjoyed chatting with Duchamp during the drive to the estate. Henri exuded confidence and old-world charm she sensed only in vampires of a certain age. With his graying hair and crystal clear blue eyes, he not only emanated social poise, but a degree of elegant sophistication Miranda wished more men possessed.

"Brevet had his own contacts from the Louvre examine the painting. He thinks Lord Valadon is being...overly fastidious."

"Perhaps, Valadon wanted the objective opinion of someone not so close to the family." Miranda knew there were certain older men who disliked younger scholars. The fact she was American and female probably factored in, as well.

"Dear girl, don't mention that to him. I worked hard enough to calm his indignation."

She smiled at Duchamp; he was one of those rare people she liked on first sight.

Duchamp peered out the window. "Ah, there's the house, now."

Miranda had Googled Château Venier as soon as she learned the location of the painting and had researched the surviving members of the family. Perusing the estate, she nearly whistled at one of the oldest buildings in France. At one time, the château must have been magnificent, but age and the elements had taken their toll. Although still beautiful, some of the façade of the building was in desperate need of repair.

The problem with estates this old was the upkeep cost a fortune. Probably why the family was selling off some of their works of art.

"Take my hand." Duchamp helped her out of the car and escorted her to the front door where he rang the bell.

Orion and Bastien, who had been keeping pace behind them, pulled up in Bastien's car. They quickly carried her equipment up the stairs. Despite their sometime posturing, she was glad the two seemed to be hitting it off.

"How long will it take you to complete the authentication?" Orion asked.

"I need to examine the frame, analyze the pattern of the brush strokes, the age of the wood stretchers, the amount of rust on the nails, the chemical composition of the paint." It was a painstaking process, and it took time, but Miranda was assiduously methodical. "A couple of hours." She exhaled. "Orion, I told you I don't need two bodyguards. I'm sure I'll be perfectly safe. So, if you want to go sightseeing—"

"After your little shopping spree, Valadon gave specific orders we're to keep an eye on you. One of us will be in close proximity to you...*at all times*." Bastien glanced at Orion.

Miranda wasn't sure what just passed between the vampire and the werewolf and shrugged. "Suit yourselves, but what I do could be pretty boring to an outsider." She smiled at Orion. "I hope you brought something good to read."

Duchamp spoke French to the servant who greeted and escorted them inside. There, they met Mirabelle Venier, the deceased's daughter, who smiled warmly and extended a handshake to each of them. Miranda got a good vibe from her.

However, she did *not* from her companion.

Andre Brevet scornfully looked at Miranda and spoke in French with Duchamp. She knew he probably spoke English as well as she did, but his attitude was rearing its ugly head. She watched the cruel nature of his lips and facial expressions. He'd assumed she didn't know French very well. After four years of French in secondary school and living three years in Paris, Miranda could understand him very well, even when he started using swear words. Her French friends at University had taught her those.

Brevet continued with his tirade until Miranda had had enough. Sounding bored, she turned and said in perfect French, "I may be short two courses of a PhD, but I excelled in the AGDP—Advanced Graduate Degree Program—under the tutelage of Professeur Auguste Treville. If you have any doubts about my abilities, you can contact him. I'm sure he could assuage your concerns." Miranda knew Treville was well-known throughout France as one of the world's leading authorities on forgeries. The American University had been lucky to obtain him.

She had surprised Brevet, who huffed, "He was unavailable." He turned on his heel. "Come along, *Professeur,* I will show you where the painting is."

Miranda wondered if she could use her *Elemental* powers to have one of the tall statues fall on his head. Probably not a good idea. Her Dark Angel whispered, *Oh, just do it!* The Light Angel was too busy laughing to offer a comment. When they reached the end of the hall, he pointed to the portrait of a noblewoman who sat sidesaddle on her horse—*Catrona.*

"Thank you, Monsieur Brevet, I'm sure Lord Valadon will be pleased to hear how polite and accommodating you were." Miranda enjoyed watching Brevet flinch as he turned and walked away. She thought, *ça soulage*—that was satisfying.

Henri Duchamp smiled. "I'll let you get to work, then." He reached inside his jacket. "Here is my card. Call me anytime." Then, he whispered, "Valadon has exceptional taste. I'm glad he hired you. *Au revoir.*"

"Please feel comfortable in my home," Mirabelle said. "My mother was good friends with Lord Valadon and spoke very highly of him. If you need any refreshments, Annette will bring you anything you want. *Au revoir,* for now." She left with Duchamp.

Both hands firmly planted on her hips, Miranda turned to face Orion and Bastien. "All right, what am I going to do with you two? I'm safely in the château; I'm going to be here for hours. I certainly don't need both of you ogling me while I work."

Bastien gave her the evil eye. "You promise you won't take off again on one of your strolls?"

"I'll be here for hours, I promise." Miranda unpacked her equipment.

"You okay to watch her, wolf? There are a few things I could be checking on." Bastien checked his watch. "I'll be back in a couple of hours, and then, you can take your break. Does that work for you?"

"Works for me." Orion took out his phone to check his messages. "My manager texted me. There's a club here in Paris that's invited me to play. I'd like to check it out. So, as long as you're on duty tonight, we're good."

Bastien nodded and then turned to leave.

"Do you trust him, Miranda?"

Miranda slanted Orion a look. "Not completely." She remembered how Bastien had once guarded her and had no reason to doubt him, but still...something didn't feel right. "After you're through with your engagement, I think it might be a good idea to keep an eye on Bastien." Miranda rubbed her arm. "You feel up to a little reconnaissance?"

"For you, always." Orion bumped shoulders with her. "I've done some surveillance work for Lizandra. I know how to stay hidden."

Miranda nodded then turned to the painting. "Now, Catrona, my beautiful horsewoman, let's see if Degas truly painted you." Degas had liked his ballerinas, but early in his career, he'd done portraits and had an affinity for racing horses. The pattern of brush strokes were seemingly of the proper angle, but Miranda would scrutinize the measurements for any variations. One of her talents at University her professors complimented her on was her ability to notice the minutest of details—especially when something was off.

Chapter Twenty

"It's good to see you again, Sebastien." Hugo smiled warmly. "We've all missed you. Your father is waiting for you in the library."

Bastien breathed deeply as he walked down the corridor. Seeing his father again after so many years made something knot in his stomach. Lord Rosemont never approved of his only son leaving to live and work in New York under Valadon. When Bastien reached the double oak doors, he wasn't sure if he should knock or not. He decided on a light tapping and then entered.

Lord Rosemont stood as Bastien approached. His father was still a handsome vampire with light brown hair, piercing brown eyes and an aristocratic nose. His angular features were clearly defined, and sculptors took pride in creating their likenesses of him. "Sebastien, why didn't you tell me you were planning on visiting us sooner? Your mother and I would have made preparations."

Bastien was relieved to see the warm look in his father's eyes and exhaled, unaware of the breath he'd been holding. "I'm here on business, Father. Valadon prefers anonymity in his business ventures." Bastien accepted his father's embrace and then watched him resume his seat behind his desk.

"How is High Lord Valadon?"

"Good." Bastien looked around the library he had often played in as a boy. "I've enjoyed working for him."

"I see." Rosemont darkened his computer screen. "And for how long will I enjoy the pleasure of my son's company?"

"Only for a few days. I'm scheduled to fly out the day after tomorrow."

Rosemont smiled slyly. "Then, you'll be joining us for dinner tonight."

Bastien knew his father wasn't making a request. There was work he needed to do, but the look in his father's eyes decided for him. "Of course. As long as I can bring a friend."

"Oh? Has my son finally found someone he deigns to bring home?"

"No. She's a friend. Only a friend." Bastien considered inviting Orion, but remembered the wolf said he wanted to check out a club. Perhaps, Orion could reschedule. "And I have a colleague I would like to join us, as well, if that's all right with you?"

"I'd be delighted to meet your friends. But, now, come with me into the gardens." Rosemont stood. "There's something I would like to show you."

Bastien was glad the sky was overcast. He could withstand the trellised gardens, but his father was sensitive to the sun's harmful rays. The Rosemont gardens were spectacular; his parents were especially fond of mazes and spared no expense in maintaining the beauty of their grounds. Walking with his father through the greenery brought back good childhood memories, and he wondered, just for a moment, if he could ever return on a more permanent basis.

He focused on the reason he was there. "Father, have you heard any disturbing news concerning Valadon?"

"There's always talk." Rosemont waved one elegant hand in the air. "Europe's economy is not as strong as it once was. That makes certain people nervous. And anxious people often act in a way that is less...desirable."

"And your accounts, Father?" Bastien's voice held concern. "Are you all right?"

Rosemont laughed. "Yes, my son, your fortune is well-protected. You need not worry."

"I didn't come here for that. You know the money has never mattered to me."

"Yes. Unfortunately, I do." Rosemont gestured to the wrought-iron table and chairs under a shaded trellis. "Let's sit." After a moment of shared silence, he asked, "Have you ever considered returning to Paris?"

Bastien knew all too well where this conversation was heading. His father had tried many times to encourage his return. "Other than for a visit, no. I'm quite content in New York. It's my home, now."

Rosemont exhaled. "All right, then." Resignation laced his words. "Ask the questions you wish to know concerning Valadon."

"We've heard disturbing gossip about the High Court desiring a merger between some European industries and ValCorp. Valadon was less than amused."

"I would imagine so." Rosemont breathed in deep as he viewed his gardens and then turned to his son. "Some on the High Court have grown very envious of Valadon's success. They covet what he has."

"They've always been jealous of him."

"Yes, but now the economy has reached such a low point, their envy has turned to hatred." Rosemont's countenance turned grave.

"Who, Father? Who's responsible for the adverse reports we've been receiving?"

Rosemont's eyes slowly turned toward the maze. "You play in dangerous waters."

"I'm a strong swimmer." Bastien grinned. "You taught me, remember?"

Rosemont nodded. "With most on the court, it is a matter of financial security, but there is one with whom it has always been personal. Merlinder."

Bastien sat back in his chair. Merlinder was one of the oldest vampires in the VHC—his resources wide and deep. But, more importantly, there were only a few on the Council who equaled his power. "We suspected him. Is there anything more you can tell me?"

"Yes. But it will keep until tonight. I want to enjoy my son's company." Rosemont smiled. "It is so rare that he shares himself with us. Tell me, have you heard from Josette?"

Bastien closed his eyes in memory of the one woman whom he'd almost stayed in Europe for. They'd grown up together, and no other woman had ever affected him the way Josette had. "No, Father, I haven't heard from her."

"Perhaps, you should contact her. I hear she does well working for Vivienna."

"Vivienna is one of the reasons my relationship with Josette didn't last." Bastien grimaced. "How is the Madame Lord?"

"You haven't kept up with society, I see. She is well. Her industry flourishes, as do most of the fashion houses in Paris." Rosemont smirked. "Shall I invite her to the dinner party?"

"God, no! She's a piranha." He rose. "I have to get going, Father. But I'm glad I came. I've missed you and Mother."

"And we've missed you. Your sister will be pleased to see you, again. Isabelle was quite excited to learn of your visit. And your mother will be overjoyed to see you, again."

"I've missed her, as well." It was Isabelle whom he didn't miss.

Not one bit.

***

Heads turned as Bastien walked down the hall to the design wing of Vivienna Industries. Living in New York, he wasn't used to the attention—few knew of his Blueblood ancestry—but in Paris, every vampire knew who the Rosemonts were. That had been another reason why he'd left.

When he spotted Josette engrossed in her designs, his heart sped up as his body tightened in awareness. She'd cut her hair short—her long platinum locks were gone and she sported a style barely more than a buzz cut. Her brows were still dark, he noticed. But her gray eyes were her most striking feature; when aroused, they turned a turbulent silvery-gray. She looked up at him as he approached her cubicle. He grinned. "Hello, Josette."

Her jaw lowered. "What are you doing in Paris?"

"I'm here visiting my parents." Bastien didn't like withholding truths from her, but fealty always came first. "It's been a while, and I thought I would see how they were doing." He smiled charmingly.

"I'm sure they're glad to see you. But what are you doing here at Fashions de Vivienna?"

"I can visit an old friend, can't I?"

"Does she know you're here?"

"If you mean Vivienna, I'm sure she's aware of my presence." He let Josette take his arm and lead him down a deserted corridor and watched as she bowed her head. Sensing her anxiety, Bastien asked, "Hey, what's wrong?"

Josette raised her chin. "A lot has changed since you left. Vivienna has always been difficult."

Bastien grunted. "You mean temperamental."

"Lately, more than usual." Her eyes held a wealth of emotion. "You probably shouldn't be here."

"Why, Josette? Are they treating you all right, here?"

"Yes, of course." She glanced down the hallway. "That's not it."

"I never understood why you wanted to work for Vivienna in the first place."

Josette raised her head. "You never did. Fashions de Vivienna is one of the best design houses in the world."

"So is Valadon Creations. New York is one of the world's best places for designs. You could work there. And be free of Vivienna."

"You assume I want to be free. Paris is my home, Bastien. Yours, too."

Bastien exhaled. They'd had this argument before. "Not anymore." He'd invited her to New York several times, and she'd refused, saying her loyalty was to Vivienna. "Haven't you ever been curious?"

"New York does have its appeal, but Paris is the world's capital of fashion. I have no reason to leave."

Bastien could think of several. "Won't you even consider coming for a visit?"

Josette shook her head. "We've been down this path." She raised her hand to move a hair off his forehead. "We always wind up in the same place."

Nowhere, Bastien thought. "My parents are having a dinner party tonight. Will you at least come to that?" Josette nodded. "They'll be happy to see you, again. I've gotta go." He lifted her chin to his. "It was good seeing you, again, Josette." He kissed her. "If you ever change your mind about New York, the invitation still stands." Though he knew in his gut, she would never take him up on it.

Chapter Twenty-One

Disguising her appearance as much as she could with the black wig and make-up, Irina stealthily stayed in the shadows and scanned the alley where Caress—London's notorious bloodclub—was located. She noted the few Bluebloods who frequented the club known mainly for its Rogue clientele. Irina thought the bloodclubs were crude— responsible for the bad rep vampires often received. On the rare occasions when the vampires of House Valadon tired of the bagged blood easily accessible at ValCorp's blood bank, they often satisfied their thirsts for human blood in modern vampire clubs like Nightshade.

Satisfied there was no imminent danger, Irina slinked inside the club and sighted Remare's informant sitting alone at a table near the back. His dark complexion seemed deeper because of the cigar smoke surrounding him. Dressed in a linen suit, he still wore the ruby earring she'd seen in his photos. From her research, Irina knew Barusch never went anywhere without his watchdogs; she easily spotted them at the nearby tables by the cut and style of their clothes. She made her way to him. "Barusch."

"Irina." He smiled, displaying tobacco-stained teeth. "Remare texted you would be contacting me." Barusch motioned for her to join him at his table. "My beauty, let me buy you a drink."

Irina raked her eyes over the club. "No, thanks, I didn't come here for a drink."

"Of course not." Barusch leaned forward. "Remare told me you were not one to socialize. What is it that you seek?"

Choosing a seat where she had a view of the exit and his associates, she said, "Information, but I'm sure you already knew that."

Barusch grinned. "Usually, Remare sends me a gift first."

Irina knew Barusch would try to illicit some sort of payment. "Remare has agreed to let you live. I think that a fair enough trade. Don't you?"

Barusch laughed. "He would, but then again, it would *not* get him the information he wanted."

In a swift movement, too fast for most of the vampires in the club to notice, Irina took the knife from her boot and pressed it against Barusch's throat. "It will get me the information *I* want or you'll be missing your head." Irina pushed the tip of the knife into his skin, letting a rivulet of blood drip down his neck. Her eyes on his men, she asked, "Do we have a deal?"

Barusch motioned for his men to remain seated then placed his hand over hers. "I see your point. Perhaps, a drink is in order?"

Irina lowered her knife and sat again. "I don't waste time on small talk."

"Like your boss," he muttered as he sipped his scotch. "Americans can be so impatient, though your accent says Russian."

"Russian or American. We save the bullshit for those whose time is not valuable."

"I see." He reached inside his jacket and took out an envelope. "The man you seek can be found at this address. I tried to bring him here, but he did not wish to be seen in public with either one of us. His liege would not approve."

Irina's voice iced over. "Who else knows I'm in London?"

"No one." Barusch downed his drink. "I swear it."

Irina kept her eyes on Barusch, then glanced at the contents of the envelope. "Is there anything else you're not telling me?"

Barusch seemed to consider her as he narrowed his eyes. "There's much turmoil in Europe since Valadon visited last. Tempers are much shorter, and the violence has been steadily escalating. Be careful where you tread, my beauty. Perhaps, you would consider one of my bodyguards?"

Irina scanned the crowd again for any watchers. "I work alone. If your men try to follow me, they will lose their lives. That is your only warning. *Das vi danya.*"

Out in the alley, Irina sensed the presence of other vampires. Her heart beat rapidly in covetous anticipation. Like vultures perched on their stands, they waited for her. Smirking, she let the knives in her wrist sheaths slide into her hands. She didn't get more than ten feet when Rogues jumped down in front of her. Her body was already primed for fighting, desperately needing to release her pent-up emotions.

In rapid succession, she broke the neck of one attacker then slit the throat of another as they lunged for her. The others rushed her, and their groans could be heard as they were hurled against the walls until one got lucky and slashed her across her side, the blood quickly dripping down her hip. Irina used her curved blade to slit his spinal cord and then was tackled from behind as a throwing star flew by where she had been merely a second ago.

The familiar weight of his body pressed her into the ground as he held her down. Irina breathed in his unmistakable scent. A scent she recognized from the many fights they had previously engaged in.

A deep masculine voice echoed in the shadows. "Good to see you, again, Irina. I've missed you." The bastard kissed her cheek.

***

"Your parents have a beautiful home." Miranda smiled at Bastien as the limo pulled into the circular driveway.

"I grew up here—centuries ago."

Curious, she asked, "Why'd you leave?"

Bastien seemed reflective. "I just wanted something different."

She raised a brow. "And did you get it?"

"Working for Valadon offered opportunities I could never get here."

She knew there were few Bluebloods left in the world, and Bastien probably left because, everywhere he went in Paris, people knew him as a Rosemont. "Autonomy."

Bastien nodded. "Valadon said you were intuitive. Growing up as a Blueblood sounds great, until you realize all the obligations that go along with it."

Miranda couldn't begin to imagine all the limits imposed with those obligations. "How do you like working for Valadon?"

"He's much better than working for Vivienna. I would have killed myself before submitting to her caprices."

Miranda had heard pretty much the same from Blu and Rosalyn. "Is she that bad?"

"Worse. We're here." He took her hand as they exited the limo. "I'm glad you chose the dark blue gown. It looks good on you."

"Thanks. You're looking quite handsome yourself. It's a shame Orion couldn't come, but he said he'd join us afterward. I hope your parents don't mind."

"No, they're expecting him." Bastien led her up the stairs to where an elegantly dressed couple waited. "Lord and Lady Rosemont—my parents. This is Miranda Crescent, my colleague and friend."

"*Enchantée.*" Miranda shook their hands. "It's a pleasure meeting Bastien's parents. Valadon spoke highly of you both and said to send you his warmest regards."

"*Merci.* It's a pleasure to meet you, as well. Welcome. Please make yourself at home." Smiling, Lord Rosemont gestured for her to enter the grand foyer as he spoke with his son.

Miranda made her way inside the impressive château and admired the many works of art the Rosemonts had acquired through the centuries. She spoke with several of the guests and watched as Bastien often glanced in her direction. Finally, as dinner was about to be served, Orion arrived in his tux, looking as handsome as she'd ever seen him. Even Bastien seemed impressed with his jaw slightly dropping and his eyes lighting up.

"I'm glad you made it." She kissed his cheek. "How was the club?"

"Great." Orion hugged her. "I had no idea my music was popular in Paris. They invited me to come back when I tour again."

Smiling, Bastien greeted Orion. "My parents would like to meet you."

"Of course." Orion took a few steps and then grinned back at Miranda with a look that said, *"Do you believe this place?"*

***

"Usually, by this time, you would have chosen someone to taste in one of the back rooms."

Remare nodded as Rosalyn stood beside him. From the second-floor balcony of Nightshade, they looked down at the partygoers who were dancing. "Perhaps, I haven't yet chosen who I wish to feast upon."

"You've chosen. She's the reason you no longer socialize with the patrons of my club." Rosalyn faced him. "And she's the reason you're standing here alone."

Remare exhaled. "That is a dangerous assumption you make, Rosalyn." If she could read him so easily, he wondered who else could.

"Not so dangerous. You know your confidences are safe with me, as are your other secrets, Lord Remare."

He knew Rosalyn was referring to his heritage. His father, a Blueblood, had been lord of the Roman territory, but his mother was born British and had been human before his father had turned her—a fact he had kept from many. "Do *not* refer to me by that title. I relinquished all claims when I joined Valadon's court."

Rosalyn nodded below to one of her security people. "As you wish. Besides, I'm quite fond of Miranda. I would never say or do anything to endanger her." Rosalyn smiled as a twinkle gleamed in her eyes. "She came to see me before she left for Paris."

Interested, Remare turned toward her. "Why did she do that?"

"Because, she wears the same face of longing you do." Rosalyn breathed out. "And she wanted to know about the European courts, especially Paris."

"What did you tell her?"

"Nothing she couldn't find out for herself. She believed Valadon was keeping her in the dark."

Remare kept his face schooled. "What did you tell her about the Parisian court?"

"I told her to be careful with Vivienna. Something Valadon should have warned her about."

Closing his eyes, he said, "Valadon has his reasons for doing what he must."

"Of that, I am certain, but I think she came to me for other reasons."

"Such as?"

Rosalyn's lips twitched in humor as she took his arm and led him to her office. "You."

After discussing their joint business ventures in Rosalyn's office and being reassured of her loyalty, Remare returned to the balcony and gazed down at the dancers. He wondered when he'd last socialized in public. With his ongoing hunt for Brandon, he'd given little thought to celebrations. But, perhaps, it was time he did.

Sauntering down the stairs, he was gracious as he smiled at the women who flirted with him and even danced a few steps with them. If the paparazzi took pictures of him laughing with the women, so much the better. After his conversation with Rosalyn, he would make certain no suspicion would fall on him or those he held dear.

***

After dinner, Miranda admired the way Orion easily conversed with the people around him, but the day's tension finally caught up with her, and she found herself yawning. Unlike most Americans, Europeans enjoyed late dinners. And with vampires, dinner didn't get served until almost midnight. "Orion, I'm getting tired. I don't want to disturb Bastien. He seems to be enjoying his family's company, but I want to go."

"That's cool." He nodded. "Let's just say our good nights."

Lord Rosemont smiled beneficently. "It was a pleasure meeting you *Mademoiselle* Crescent. If you should visit Paris, again, please feel free to call on us again. That goes for you, too, *Monsieur* Orion. Sebastien's friends are always welcome in our home."

"Merci." Miranda smiled graciously. "It was a pleasure meeting you both."

As they were nearing the entrance, the doors suddenly exploded open and the most vivacious, beautiful woman Miranda had ever seen entered. She was dressed in a sequined black gown cut low enough that it barely covered her breasts. Her body was slender, but curvy in all the right places. However, what was most captivating were the woman's lavender eyes that were focused on Miranda.

Vivienna, the Madame Lord of Paris, had arrived.

The breath in her throat constricting, Miranda backed up a step as a tendril of Vivienna's power reached out to stroke her.

Lord Rosemont greeted, "Vivienna. I didn't think you would make it tonight."

Miranda had heard much about the vampire, but nothing had prepared her for the powerful vampire's presence. The woman radiated a captivating charm, turning all the men's heads in the château in her direction. With her long wavy raven hair, fair complexion and features women would pay a ton of money to possess, the vampire was stunning.

Eyes still on Miranda, Vivienna smiled with a hint of cruelty. "Lord Rosemont, introduce me to your guest. I don't think I've had the pleasure."

"Vivienna, this is Miranda Crescent, an associate of my son's, and this is—"

Before Rosemont could finish introducing Orion, Vivienna said, "So, this is Valadon's human companion. I've been looking forward to chatting with you."

Miranda's headache became a splintering migraine because of the pitch of Vivienna's power. "I'm sorry. We were just leaving. Perhaps some other time." When dead silence followed, Miranda knew she had just committed a major vampire *faux pas*.

Vivienna's eyes blazed as she scrutinized her, and Miranda could swear the vampire knew she was causing her pain and reveled in the fact. "But you're here, now. Why not stay and socialize?"

Miranda didn't like feeling coerced. "Thank you, Madame Lord, but I've a terrible headache and was on my way out, so if you would excuse—"

Before Miranda could stop her, Vivienna clutched her arm, and the migraine shrieked through her head. Orion, sensing her pain, tried to pry away Vivienna's grip.

In a movement too swift to follow, Vivienna slashed Orion's throat, and the blood splattered in an arc across Miranda. When Orion went down, Miranda went with him, trying to stem the blood with her hand. She knew if he changed into his wolf form, he could heal the wound, but too much blood was gushing out too quickly. Locking eyes with the bitch queen of Paris, she frantically called out, "Bastien! Heal him!" Her eyes were on fire, her voice demanding. "This wasn't his fault. Heal him!"

Glancing quickly at his father, Bastien bent to lick Orion's throat—his saliva healing and then sealing the wound. Leaning close to Orion so the others wouldn't see, he slit his own wrist and let some of his blood drip into Orion's mouth.

When Miranda looked up at Vivienna, she was licking Orion's blood off her fingers. Hatred and anger iced Miranda's voice. "You nearly severed his vocal cords."

"Pity." Vivienna shrugged. "Perhaps, now, he will learn some manners."

Bastien helped lift Orion, his temper pitched, and his breaths were harsh. "You're in my house, now, Vivienna, and that was uncalled for or have you forgotten the rules of guesthood?"

Vivienna raked him with a scathing look. "The mongrel *dared* to touch me."

Bastien's eyes narrowed as his nostrils flared. "You didn't have to slit his throat."

"Have you forgotten whose territory you're in?" Vivienna casually strolled into the dining room without a single glance back. "You should know better."

"Take your friends home, quickly, Sebastien." Lord Rosemont helped his son with Orion. "I do apologize. I didn't believe Vivienna would come tonight, and I certainly didn't expect this."

Her eyes on Rosemont, then on Bastien, Miranda put her arm around Orion and helped him down the stairs.

Bastien nodded as he also helped support Orion's weight. "I'll be in touch, Father."

"As will I. Good night, my son."

Chapter Twenty-Two

Cesare accompanied Valadon as they walked down the hall to the high lord's spacious living room. "I've decided on our lead model for Valadon Creations. He's one of the most astoundingly handsome vampires and fits the image of sophistication."

"I'm sure if you like him," Valadon glanced at his chief designer, "he's impressive enough for my approval. I'll meet him some other time. Tonight, I have another in mind." Valadon smiled when he saw the blond songstress, Tiseira, by the piano. She was as beautiful as she was talented, and he loved hearing her sing. "Good evening, Tiseira." He kissed her cheek. "I'm glad you decided to accept my invitation."

"How could I refuse?" She laughed. "I believe the last time we spoke was in Paris nearly a century ago."

"Yes, I remember, but then, you sang opera."

"I still do, on occasion." She smiled graciously. "But my music is more mainstream, now."

"I believe our guest should have a glass of champagne." Remare joined them. "Some of our Torians will be sorely upset when they find out you've paid us a visit and they weren't here to hear you sing."

"Thank you, but water is fine. I don't drink liquor when I'm singing."

"Of course." Remare nodded to Escher, who quickly went to retrieve a glass of Pellegrino.

Valadon nodded at Remare. "Too bad Bastien is in Paris on business." He turned toward Tiseira. "He enjoys your music immensely."

"Then, I shall have to return again when he is here." Tiseira tilted her head. "Is there a favorite song you would like me to sing?"

"I have several favorites, but tonight, I think I will let you choose. However, there is one more guest we are waiting on." When Valadon turned to face the elevator, he was expecting to see his strongest ally, Queen Lizandra, and her entourage.

What he was not expecting to see was how intensely her eyes blazed as she strode toward him. Her Weres were equally rigid in their approach. Valadon's voice was severe. "What's happened?"

Lizandra nodded. "I think we need to talk."

Valadon gestured to the couches.

When Lizandra was seated with the rest of her Weres by her side, she said, "One of my Weres was viciously assaulted by a vampire."

"Who?" Remare asked.

"Orion. In Paris." Glaring, Lizandra extended her sharpened nails and began tapping them on the arm of the couch. "Does the name Vivienna sound familiar?"

Knowing Orion was acting as Miranda's bodyguard, Valadon worried for their safety. "How badly injured is he?"

"It appears...Vivienna has slashed his throat."

Tiseira gasped. "Oh, no! Not Orion. I've heard him play. He has a fantastic voice."

"As do you." Lizandra seemed mildly mollified by Tiseira's presence.

Valadon wondered why he had not been informed earlier of this incident. "Was he taken to the hospital?"

"No. Evidently, one of your Torians was nearby and helped him."

Remare's voice held barely restrained anger. "Was anyone else hurt?"

"No. Miranda called me after Orion was injured. She and Bastien made sure he was safely transported to the hotel." Lizandra rose, clearly agitated. "This attack was totally unprovoked. I have half a mind to get on a plane and seek out Vivienna and show her how Weres deal with unwarranted insults."

"That would be unwise." Valadon knew, if Lizandra unleashed her fury on Vivienna, the ramifications would be destructive—each would fight to the death. "I will deal with Vivienna."

"I thought you might." Lizandra continued pacing until she reached the piano. "What I would like to know now is what type of restitution I can expect for the injury done to one of my Weres?"

"We need to be made aware of the circumstances. Will you wait until my people have reported in?" When Lizandra nodded, Valadon turned toward Remare. "Contact Bastien, find out *exactly* what transpired."

Remare nodded, then took out his phone.

***

"Well, you don't need any stitches. There's some swelling, but with rest and plenty of liquids, it should go down." Gabriel shut the pen light after examining Orion's throat and looked up at Miranda. "I'm not that familiar with Were anatomy, but I've been told Weres heal almost as quickly as vampires."

"They do." Miranda rubbed Orion's hand as he sat up in bed.

When Orion tried to speak, Gabriel raised his hand. "Whoa. Try to rest your voice as much as possible. I can put a dressing on your neck, but the wound has already closed. By tomorrow, you should be fine. Try to get down as much liquids as you can."

"We were more concerned with the inside of his throat." Miranda glanced up at Gabriel.

"I didn't see any damage, other than the swelling." Gabriel nodded at Bastien. "It was good that you were able to heal him, otherwise the injury might have been more severe." He glanced back when he heard Orion growling. "I'm glad your vocals cords are fine. But I meant what I said. Rest your voice."

When Orion nodded and turned on his side, Miranda dimmed the light and ushered them out so he could rest in peace. She walked Gabriel to the door of the suite. "I can't thank you enough for coming. We were really concerned." Miranda rubbed her arms. "Bastien closed the wound fast, but we had no idea what damage was done internally."

"Weres are tough. I know that much." Gabriel gently caressed Miranda's shoulder. "But there shouldn't be any residual effects. He'll be fine."

"I'm glad you were still in Paris and able to come."

"Me, too." Gabriel rubbed his brow. "I'm leaving in the morning to go back to Amsterdam. Think you can stay out of trouble until you get back to New York?"

Miranda hugged him. "I think I can manage that."

"Try hard." Gabriel kissed her cheek and then closed the door after him.

Miranda then turned and met Bastien's eyes. Any warmth she had felt quickly turned to ice. Hatred laced her voice. "Did you call Valadon?"

"Yes." Bastien ran a hand through his hair. "He's been informed, and he is not happy. There isn't much Valadon can do about Vivienna as we are in her territory. But he said he was already taking steps to prevent another incident like this from happening, again."

"Such as?" Miranda's brow lifted as she crossed her arms over her chest.

"He didn't specify, but he did say he would consult with our solicitors. The Were Queen is already seeking restitution."

Miranda nodded. "I thought she might be."

Grabbing a bottle of water, Bastien followed her back into the bedroom and watched as she cuddled against Orion. He put the bottle down on Orion's bedside table.

"Weres like to be held." Miranda knew Bastien was eying her as she tenderly stroked Orion's arm. "Could you get me a warm wet cloth from the bathroom? I'll sponge bathe him."

When Bastien came back from the bathroom, he handed her the cloth, and she gently wiped at the splotches of blood that still stained Orion's chest. "I'm going to take a shower. Can you watch over him until I get back?"

"Sure." Bastien scrutinized the way she hugged Orion. "Are you two—?"

"Nah, we're just friends." Orion snuggled closer with his head between her breasts. When she lay sideways, her dress revealed a bit more cleavage than if she'd been standing. But, the pain meds Gabriel had given Orion seemed to have taken effect. When Orion's lips moved closer to her areola and his tongue licked out, Miranda chuckled in surprise. "Okay, definitely not what I expected."

Bastien's phone rang again, he read the text. "It's Remare. He wants to talk to you."

"Tell him I'm busy." Miranda was in no mood to deal with Remare or anyone else and went to bathe.

In the shower, she remembered how heated everyone had been during the drive back to the hotel. Orion had adamantly refused to go to a hospital, citing in hoarse whispers, "Bad publicity." When she'd told him Gabriel was in Paris, he had calmed and agreed to be seen by him. She knew Bastien had texted Valadon just as she had texted

Lizandra. She hoped the Were Queen was giving Valadon
hell.

After her shower, Miranda put on a sleeveless tee and a
pair of shorts, then went to join Orion in bed. "Thanks for
watching him. You can sleep in my room if you want. I'll
stay with him." At his suspicious look, Miranda sighed. "It's
no big deal. Weres sometimes sleep in puppy piles when
someone gets sick or injured. It doesn't imply sex, just
comfort."

Bastien nodded. "I'll take my shower, now." He grabbed
a pair of dark pajamas from the dresser then closed the
bathroom door behind him.

When he finished his shower, Miranda was surprised
Bastien sat in one of the chairs. Valadon must have ordered
him to watch over them. "You can join us on the bed.
Nothing is going to happen," she said groggily. "We're just
sleeping."

Bastien phone rang, again. "It's Remare, again."

"Tell him I'm sleeping, and I'll talk to him tomorrow."
Miranda heard him finish texting and toss his phone on the
end table. "Stop lurking and get some sleep." When she felt
the mattress dip down, she grinned. "Welcome to the puppy
pile."

Bastien muttered, "Puppy pile, my ass. At least this way
I can keep an eye on the both of you."

The last thing Miranda heard before falling asleep was
Orion's sigh of contentment.

***

Remare read the text. "They are both turned in for the
evening, and Bastien is keeping guard."

"I never imagined Vivienna would attack Orion."
Valadon stopped pacing as he gazed at the mood screen. He
had wanted his bedroom to have the illusion of windows.
Right now, the image was of the stars and moon.

Miranda's evening was over. His was just beginning.

"Vivienna has always done as she pleased with no regard for others." Remare leaned against one of the bed posts. "As you and I well know."

"Orion is Miranda's friend and under my protection." Valadon looked at his second. "This should not have happened."

"Perhaps not," Remare shrugged, "but Orion is a Were and unfamiliar with vampire protocol. He didn't know not to touch a vampire queen."

"Even so, Vivienna will never touch him, again." Valadon's eyes hardened. "I'll see to it."

A corner of Remare's mouth lifted. "Perhaps, we should send Lizandra to Paris to deal with Vivienna."

Valadon's brow arched. "Now that would be something worth seeing."

"My money would be on the Were Queen."

***

"Hold still. I'm almost finished. Bastard must have used a serrated edge." Gregori finished stitching the injury. Irina had lowered her slacks enough for him to clean and treat the wound, and he was working damned hard not to let her feminine scent distract him. They had sparred before, but he couldn't remember when he'd last been this close to Irina's body. "The skin's a little ragged here, but it should heal up nicely."

"We don't have time to waste." Irina hummed with impatience. "The sun will be up in a few hours. I want to meet with Barusch's contact before that."

Gregori liked how Irina's Russian accent became more pronounced when she was roused; her dulcet tones reminded him of home. Long ago, he had shed his own Russian accent. "We will. But you won't do anyone any good if you go smelling of blood." Gregori had Irina's scent memorized as well as her taste. He had licked the cut clean, but the wound had been deep, and he hadn't wanted to take any chances of her losing any more blood.

"Why did Remare send you? Does he doubt my skills?"

Gregori paused to look up at her; he understood her resentment. He'd feel the same if he thought Remare had any doubts about his abilities to complete a mission. "It's still your operation. I'm just your shadow here. You know well enough Remare has always believed in *all* of us." Gregori put both hands on her waist and grimaced. "Hold still. If you would stop jostling, I could finish faster."

Irina took a calming breath and then another. "I don't know why you wanted to come back to your hotel room. We could have done this in the car."

Gregori admired her resolve. "Yes, but without the antiseptic, your scent would carry for miles." He tied off the thread and then put a bandage over the wound. "We'll meet the contact before dawn."

"No, I want to go, now." Irina wobbled as she took a step toward the door.

"He'll wait for us." Gregori reached out to hold her in his arms. "We're paying him enough."

"I want to get there early and scout out the area."

"No need. I have our people already in place. We'll leave in a couple of hours. You need to get some rest."

Irina bristled at him. "I said I wanted—"

Gregori swooped her up in his arms and placed her gently on the bed. "I know what you want." He looked into those icy blue eyes of hers and felt himself hardening. "But I say we wait, and as the senior Torian here—"

"It's my mission." Irina gritted her teeth. "You're my shadow, remember?"

"Hmm, but when the mission commander is injured, the next senior Torian is in charge, and since you're injured, that's me." Gregori liked arguing with her and pressed his body closer to hers. "Now, lie still or I'll just have to hold you down if you don't behave."

Rage filled Irina's eyes at the thought of being held down, and Gregori realized his mistake. Irina had been held captive in Ivan's camp for too long before he and Remare had rescued her. He knew she had been treated badly by the members of Ivan's coven and detested being held down. Gregori lightened his hold. "Take it easy, Irina," he said comfortingly. "We're on the same side."

"Remare would kill you."

Gregori doubted that. He'd watched Remare over the past few months, and his leader seemed to have only one objective, finding Brandon. Even though Irina had been given him the eye, Remare barely seemed to notice, or care.

"Do you really think I would force myself on you?" Gregori studied her eyes for an answer. When there was none, he asked, "What's between you two?"

"Why do you ask?" She peered up at him. "You've never cared before."

Gregori had cared a great deal since he'd help get her out of Russia, but he didn't think she would welcome such news. "I just don't understand why a woman as beautiful as you longs for someone she can't have." Gregori rolled to his side and ran a hand over his jaw. He knew his looks didn't compare with some of the Torians. He didn't have the Hollywood charm of Bastien or the seductive appeal of Valadon or Remare, but he knew he was considered attractive, and that was enough.

Irina huffed. "Shows how much you know. Remare and I have been lovers for decades."

Gregori wasn't impressed. "Past tense, Irina. When was the last time you were with him?" When he saw the perplexed look of hurt on her face, he lay down and put the back of his hand over his eyes. "You have options, Irina. Maybe you should consider them." He shrugged. "That's all I'm saying."

Chapter Twenty-Three

Miranda woke as the sun was rising on the horizon. Turning to look at Orion, she was surprised to see Bastien had wrapped his body around Orion. *Protective, much?* Weres were often affectionate with each other, their gender not mattering. Touching was a way of life to them. She had thought vampires more remote. But, as she studied their sleeping forms, she admitted they looked good together, like two young brothers sleeping in the same bed. Bastien, the older sibling, protecting his injured younger brother.

Once in her bedroom, she quickly dressed. There was something she needed to do this morning, and it didn't include the somnolent twins in the other room. After leaving a note, Miranda made sure she had the keys to their car. Once on the road, she headed due south.

There were hardly any cars out, except for a few trucks and early morning risers. She lowered the window, letting the crisp, cool air in and breathed deeply.

It had been years since she was on this highway, but she knew the way by heart.

***

When Orion woke, he felt thirsty and guzzled the bottled water on the bedside table. Realizing Miranda wasn't there, he figured at some point in the night she'd gone back to her own bedroom. Turning on his side, however, he saw Bastien had also slept with him. God, what was in the injection Gabriel had given him last night? It had him out cold for hours. As Gabriel had assured him, the soreness in his throat seemed to have vanished, and he felt better than he had in a long time.

Laying on his back, he stretched and moaned in satisfaction.

"Stop hogging all the blankets, wolf," Bastien said in a groggy voice. "I had to keep pulling them back on my side."

Orion smirked. "I was wondering whose knee kept poking me in the night."

"You snore, wolf."

"Name's Orion, vampire."

"You know, you're the first person I know to be named after a constellation." Bastien's voice was muffled by the pillows. "Who the hell names their kid, Orion?"

"Hey, my grandmother was Cherokee, and she liked the name." Orion was mildly insulted. "She said she saw the stars shining brightly the night I was born. It kind of stuck. My mom liked it." Orion turned toward Bastien. "What the hell kind of name is Bastien? It sounds like a fort or something." When he saw Bastien using his hand under the blankets to pretend his cock was rising, he snorted. "Oh, yeah, like I'd be interested."

Bastien laughed. "It's Sebastien, but most call me Bastien or just Bas. I always thought it reminded me of soldiers." Using his elbow to support his head, he turned toward Orion. "And that's something I always wanted to be."

"You got your wish."

"Yeah, I did. But it caused a lot of heartache. My father didn't want me to leave France, neither did my mother. I don't think either one of them ever completely forgave me."

Orion cocked his head. "Do they want you to stay in Paris?"

"No, that's impossible, anyway. My fealty is to Valadon." Bastien faced Orion. "How about you; did you always want to be a musician?"

"Yeah. As far back as I could remember. Music was big in my house. My mom played piano, and my dad was the orchestra teacher in high school. It just came natural to me."

"Your voice sounds good. I mean not just your singing. You're not gravelly like last night." His eyes held genuine concern. "How do you feel?"

Orion thought for a moment. "Better. Whatever Gabriel gave me last night worked." He gave a half smile to Bastien. "So did your blood." He knew vampires didn't share blood easily with others.

"Yeah, well, you needed it." Bastien looked down. "I'm sorry about Vivienna. Most vampires aren't arrogant like she is."

"Something of a bitch, wouldn't you say? I could have taken a bite out of her ass for what she did."

"You'll do nothing of the kind," Bastien warned. "She's Madame Lord of Paris and a very, very powerful vampire. You don't want to mess with her."

"I don't?"

"No, you don't. And it was partially my fault. I should have warned you no one is allowed to touch a Madame Lord without permission. There's a lot of vampire protocols I should have warned you about—especially when it comes to vampire royalty."

Orion grinned. "Like waking up in bed next to one."

"That's *not* what I'm talking about!"

"Forget it." Orion threw the covers off. "I'm taking a shower."

Once inside the shower, the soap and warm water felt comforting as it slid down his body, and Orion relaxed as the water pelted his body. He breathed the steam deep into his throat and felt it soothing his voice. Letting his head drop back, Orion reveled in the way the heat of the water penetrated his muscles. He wasn't sure why, but he felt a sense of contentment he hadn't felt in a long time.

"Orion! Finish up!" Bastien rushed in. "We gotta get going. Miranda's gone!"

"What do you mean, gone? She's in her room sleeping."

"No, she's not. She left a note. She's gone to put flowers down at her parents' gravesite. Do you know where that is?"

Orion shut the water off and grabbed a towel. "Let me think. I know she told me her parents died when she was little. Yes! She told me they owned a small cottage an hour south of Paris. Damn it! I can't remember the name of the town."

"I'll figure it out." Bastien took out his phone. "Get dressed."

***

Miranda admired the view from the observation station on top of the hill. The countryside in central France was beautiful with its old growth forests, and Miranda remembered when she was a child how she loved the sun shining down on her and danced in circles trying to capture the sun's rays. Her family had enjoyed vacations here. There'd been much laughter as they played outdoor games. Her mother used to take her sister, Cassie, and her to the market in the neighboring town. Her father had liked playing bocce with the men in the village.

Lost in her reveries, she barely heard the car coming to a halt behind her.

"What the hell, Miranda?" Orion slammed the car door then put his hands on his hips. "I thought we had a deal and then you just leave without saying anything?"

Miranda sighed. The guilt had been haunting her. She'd been responsible for one Were's death and now the injury of another. "I'm the reason you got hurt, Orion. If you hadn't tried to protect me, Vivienna wouldn't have slashed you." She glanced at Bastien on his phone. "I needed some time alone. Can you understand that?"

Orion pulled her into a tight hug. "Of course I do, but you should have taken at least one of us. Especially after last night." He caressed her shoulder. "And it wasn't your fault. Bastien explained vampire protocols to me this morning."

"I hate seeing my friends hurt," she said into his chest. "Your voice sounds much better than it did last night. How are you feeling?"

"Better. But what are you doing out here in the middle of nowhere?"

Miranda sighed, then turned and pointed. "Do you see down there in the ravine? That's where my parents died. Over there," she gestured, "that's the tree I wound up in when I got thrown from the car."

Orion nodded to Bastien as he joined them. "They never found your sister's body, did they?"

"Nope, that was the worst part of it." Miranda studied the way the trees swayed with the breezes. "The local police couldn't find her. My Aunt Meg hired private investigators, but Cassie vanished without a trace. All they could tell us was that she was probably carried off by wild animals."

"There was no way to track them?" Bastien asked. "Even now with the new technology?"

"No." Orion shook his head. "Even Weres can't track after a hard rain. The scent is long gone. It's been what, twenty years?"

"Eighteen. I was eleven at the time." Solemnly, Miranda turned from them. "I want to put down flowers at my parents' graves. It's not far from here." She started her car as Orion slid in next to her. Bastien followed in his car.

When they reached the cottage, Miranda said, "I haven't been here in years—since I was a grad student." She walked around the cottage, inspecting all the locked windows and doors. "We used to come here during the summers. My mom loved it here. She said it was good to get away from New York for a while." She pointed to the backyard. "That shed in the back is where my mom kept her gardening supplies. She was an herbalist and grew all her plants over there." Miranda nodded to a patch of ground that had once been a garden. She gazed up at Orion. "Could you get me the flowers I left on the back seat?"

"Sure."

Turning to Bastien, she said, "He sounds good. The hoarseness is gone from his voice."

Bastien stepped closer. "Yeah, he woke up in good spirits—said his throat felt good."

"Thank you for what you did." Miranda met his eyes. "I know vampires aren't supposed to share blood with others, but he needed it."

"I was glad to do it." Bastien glanced back at Orion. "He's a good man." Then, he looked at her. "You scared the hell out of us. We were worried about you."

Miranda smiled. "I did leave a note."

His hand on his hip, Bastien narrowed his eyes. "If you think that's going to placate Remare, you can forget it. He was pissed you wouldn't speak to him last night, and after I told him you went missing—again—he nearly blew a gasket."

Miranda turned and smiled. "Good."

After placing the flowers down on her parents' graves, Miranda looked one last time at the cottage. She felt as if she was saying goodbye to a part of her childhood. "I'm probably going to sell this place." She thought about all the bills her brownstone incurred. "I don't come here much anymore. I should have sold it sooner, but I just couldn't bring myself to let it go."

Bastien tilted his head and appeared sympathetic. "If you do decide to sell it," he looked around the place, "let me know, I'll have friends of my family handle it for you."

Miranda reached up and kissed his cheek. "Thank you. That might make it easier. Okay. I'm ready to go back."

After stopping for a late lunch on the way, they drove in companionable silence. Miranda was tired of Paris and looking forward to being back in New York. The plane had been prepped, and they were supposed to leave that night.

When Miranda unlocked the door to their hotel suite, she was not prepared for the person waiting for her.

And, from the look on Remare's face, he was not happy.

Chapter Twenty-Four

Miranda stared at Remare, inwardly quivering, and knew she would always react that way to him. No other could make her heart hammer against her ribs the way he did. She was still angry with him for sending her to Paris without warning her of the danger. Her body might betray her, but her mind was resolute. *Courage!* After taking two deep calming breaths, she gestured to his sword cane. "How'd you get that past customs?"

Remare's eyes couldn't hold any more ice as she walked farther into the suite. "I didn't come through customs. I had business to attend to in London that had to be cut short." Noticing the envelope in his hand, Miranda heard the restrained rage in his voice and knew he was at his most dangerous.

"Bastien, would you and Orion wait for me in the bar downstairs? I would like to speak with Professor Crescent for a few minutes. Alone."

Miranda had nearly forgotten Orion and Bastien were still there.

"All right." Bastien reached for Orion's arm.

"Miranda?" Orion tilted his head, waiting for her assurance, and when she nodded, he joined Bastien and closed the door behind him.

So, Remare was pissed off. Well, all right, so was she. She opened wide the double doors on the balcony, and the setting sun's rays blazed into the suite. She breathed in the fresh air as Remare backed into the shadows. She knew she was being juvenile, but it was the only defense she had against the powerful vampire.

"Shut the doors, Miranda, and come inside." His voice was cold as steel and just as sharp. "If you force my hand, it will not be pleasant...for either one of us."

Miranda knew she was on dangerous ground, but since she'd already made her point by ignoring his phone calls, she took one last deep breath and went inside, closing the doors behind her.

While Remare silently studied her, she admired his custom made blue suit that clung well to his sculpted body and wished he would say something. After centuries of practice, vampires were too damned good when it came to the silent treatment. When he continued staring at her, she said, "I just wanted some time to myself." She rubbed the back of her neck with both hands and exhaled. "No one followed me, and I was perfectly safe."

"Perfectly safe, Mir-randa!? You were out of reach for hours. Valadon and I were worried about you." Tossing the envelope on the table, he began slowly circling her, reminding her of one of the large jungle cats about to pounce on its prey. "I do not appreciate the fact that you ignored my phone calls."

Sighing, Miranda wasn't sure how to answer him. "Vivienna slashed Orion's throat." She looked at Remare's penetrating eyes and swore she saw flames. "Friend of yours?" Miranda crossed both arms over her chest. "I guess you forgot to mention her to me. Thanks a lot, Remare."

In a movement too quick for her to follow, Remare grabbed her shoulders and held her tightly against the wall. He was so close she could inhale his sylvan scent.

"That's why I assigned Bastien to you." Remare's nostrils flared as he dropped his hands to her waist, his fingers biting into her flesh. "He was supposed to keep an eye on you, and from what I understand, he had been doing just that until you decided to ignore my requests." Eyes closing, his head drifted back, Remare breathed in deep and then lessened his hold on her. "There was no way to know Vivienna would visit the Rosemont home."

Miranda bowed her head, then peered up at him. There was no dealing with Remare when he was this angry. She hated seeing his anger burning so hot the red rims around his irises glowed. Resolved, Miranda steeled herself against his wrath. "Vivienna nearly severed his vocal chords, Remare." Knowing her voice sounded hostile, she gentled her tones. "Orion makes his living by singing. She could have ruined him."

"But she didn't. Bastien texted me he's healed without any scars." Remare backed away from her. "If Vivienna wanted to destroy him, she would have." He handed her the envelope.

Miranda examined the monogram on the dark velvet envelope. "What is this?"

"It's an invitation from Vivienna. It appears you and Bastien will be attending a dinner party of hers tonight."

"The hell we will!" Miranda threw the invitation on the table. "Our plane leaves tonight. I'm not going anywhere near her."

Remare closed his eyes and exhaled. "You have no choice, and neither does Bastien. Vivienna is the ruling vampire of Paris. You cannot refuse her invitation."

"Oh, yes, I can. I'm not a vampire, remember?" Miranda's temper surged. "I don't have to play by the ridiculous rules you guys set up."

"You're working for Valadon. He's your employer, so by extension, you fall under our rules, Miranda. Should you choose not to answer her request for your presence, she could make life difficult for you."

"Difficult, how?"

When Remare shook his head, she knew Vivienna would go to any extent to get what she wanted. "Why didn't you warn me about her?" Miranda wasn't about to inform Remare she already knew about Vivienna after reading the letters Blu had given her.

"You were never supposed to meet her. You were just supposed to validate the painting and procure it for Valadon. That is all."

"That's all?" Miranda's brow lifted. "Really? Ah, but Valadon wanted more, didn't he? That's why he arranged for the paparazzi to take our picture after our dinner in New York. He wanted his enemies to see it, so while I was in Paris, they would come after me." Her eyes narrowed. "I was supposed to weed them out, wasn't I? I'm his lure." Miranda took a few steps away from Remare. "He used me." She took a deep breath and faced him. "So did you."

"I told him I thought you should be told the truth. He thought it was best if you didn't know, so if you were ever questioned—"

Her heart sinking, Miranda refused to shed any tears at her profound disappointment in Remare, even though she could feel them building. Remare and Valadon were two of a kind; they deserved each other. She nearly asked him to leave, but remembered the invitation. "So, what am I supposed to do about the invitation?"

"Attend. There will be several in attendance. Vivienna has always enjoyed an audience. Bastien won't be the only guard there. I've already instructed my contacts here to keep an eye on you, as they have from the moment your plane touched down on French soil." He smirked. "They've labeled you as 'unpredictable'." He diverted his eyes. "Your protection has always been paramount to us both."

Miranda knew there was much he wasn't telling her, and she hated him for not being completely honest with her.

"And exactly what is it that you want me to procure for you? Eavesdrop on some of your adversaries? Find out who's conspiring against ValCorp?"

At his surprised look, she added, "I watch the news, Remare. I know Europe was affected worse than the States when it came to the financial crisis. When Valadon gave me the tour of the archives, he told me he used to be Minister of Finance for several of the European courts. He made them rich, didn't he? But, now, those fortunes are either lost or dwindling. But ValCorp is financially solvent." Miranda started pacing. "They want a piece of him, don't they?" She stared at Remare. "So, what is it he wants from me? Who does he want me to charm the pants off?"

Remare's eyes blazed and his nostrils flared as he shoved her back against the wall. "Be careful, Miranda. Vampires are known to be very territorial. Valadon would never suggest such an idea." He rubbed his body suggestively against hers. "And neither would I."

Miranda's heart thundered as Remare's breath caressed her face. She hated it when he became antagonistic with her. "So, what does he want?"

"Attend the party. That is all. Our spies will ascertain who pays you careful attention." Remare released her and stepped away. "Information has already come our way suggesting certain individuals we already had suspicions about."

"And Vivienna?"

"She will try to find out as much about Valadon and ValCorp as possible from you. Give her no details. Be wary, Miranda. Vivienna excels at dissembling her true motivations. She is good at deciphering information even when you think you are being prudent."

"Firsthand knowledge?" Miranda saw something flicker in his eyes. "You were once involved with her, weren't you? And so was Valadon."

"*Touché*, Miranda." He smiled appreciatively. "That was centuries ago. None of us are who we were back then." Remare reached for his cane. "I must go. I am illegally in her territory, and my presence here in Paris must not become known." When he reached the door, he turned to her. "Do not disclose our meeting to anyone." Grimacing, he met her eyes. "Even Valadon doesn't know I'm here. I would like to keep it that way."

Miranda was momentarily stunned, but nodded. As angry as she'd been, she hated seeing him go. So, when Remare opened the door, she waved her hand and used her power to close it. She smiled as he turned to face her. It was rare she was able to startle him, and she enjoyed seeing his look of surprise.

The corner of his mouth lifted seductively. "Was there something else you wanted of me?"

Miranda's heart skipped a beat. The vampire was infuriating. "I need you to do something for me." She reached for the leather cylinder and slid her hand smoothly over the tip. "This is a painting my former mentor did for me. He passed away and left it for me, but I have no paperwork for it. I don't want to have trouble at customs. Can you take it back to ValCorp with you? I'll collect it when I'm there next."

Nodding, Remare took the cylinder from her, one finger gently brushing over hers. "One other thing. I know Orion is close to you, but do *not* let him attend the party. Vivienna has never developed a fondness for Weres. It would be best if he avoided her altogether."

"I'll tell him." Miranda nodded, then held his eyes, reluctant to see him go.

Remare caressed her shoulder with his thumb. "I'll see you in New York, Mir-randa."

Miranda felt the butterflies in her stomach every time he rolled his *r's* when he said her name. She watched as he slowly closed the door behind him and a corner of her mouth slowly lifted. "Yes, you will."

And, then, she wondered at all the things he hadn't said.

Outside on the balcony, she breathed in the scents of the city. Paris, she thought, shaking her head, was one of the most romantic cities in the world, and instead of flowers, candlelight dinners, cruises on the Seine, the freakin' Eiffel Tower...she got violence, bloodshed and recriminations.

Damn it all to hell, she decided. It was Orion's first time in Paris, and she would show him the sights. He'd get a kick out of Notre Dame, the Louvre, the Eiffel Tower and, her personal favorite, the boat cruises on the Seine—the best way to see the most stunning sights of the city.

They both deserved some good memories of Paris, and she'd be damned if she couldn't give it to him.

Chapter Twenty-Five

Walking along the quays on the Left Bank of the Seine, Miranda and Orion watched the sun setting. After playing tourist at the Eiffel Tower and the Louvre, Orion said he needed some fresh air, so they enjoyed the architectural wonders of Paris from the boat ride on the Seine. Miranda knew, from his sullen face, he'd had his fill of art appreciation and had wanted to show him the bridge with the locks—where she had locked away secrets of her own by tossing the key into the Seine, but all the locks had been removed. She wondered if all the keys were still on the bottom of the river.

Bastien had tried to pretend he wasn't bored, but his interest had picked up considerably when they had toured the Catacombs. Miranda thought the caves morbid with its ossuary of bones and dank, musty smell, but since it was something Orion really wanted to see, she went along with them. The tour guide explained the tunnels went on for miles under the city. Why they had placed all the skulls, femurs and other assorted bones in separate sections was beyond her. Despite the creepy factor, several of her art student friends had liked to party there. Until a friend of theirs, Marie, had gone missing. It had taken hours to find her.

When it started getting dark, Bastien suggested returning to the hotel and getting some rest before Vivienna's party.

"I'm still not sure about you going." Orion watched Miranda getting ready. "I mean, without me."

Bastien adjusted his diamond cufflinks. "Hey, if you ever visit Paris with your band, I promise to give you the full tour. There's still a lot you haven't seen."

Miranda admired Bastien in his tux, but felt bad Orion was feeling left out. "I'm not planning on staying long. If *Madame Lord Vixen* insists on us making an appearance, we'll go." Miranda tossed her lipstick in her purse. "We'll just make it short."

"I hope you're right." Bastien grimaced. "Just don't call her that to her face."

Miranda hugged Orion. "And I'll be a lot more relieved knowing you're safe here in the hotel. I don't want you anywhere near MLV." Miranda slanted Bastien a look then peered up at Orion. "I still can't believe you wanted to come after what she did to you."

Casually leaning against the doorframe of the bathroom, Orion crossed his arms. "I just don't like the idea of being cooped up here while you two are out."

"Remember what Remare told us," Bastien added. "You're not to go anywhere near her château." He glanced at Orion. "And, if you do venture out, make sure you carry your phone with you at all times, and that it's charged."

Miranda double checked her purse for her own phone, then faced Orion. "Please don't go out. I know you can handle yourself, but we're leaving tomorrow, and I don't want anything to happen to you. And Vivienna is the Madame Lord. There's no telling how vindictive she could be."

They turned when they heard Bastien mutter, "God's truth."

"Okay, I'm ready." Feeling confident in her appearance, Miranda swirled the dark bronze dress with the tight bodice and flared skirt. She wished Remare was there to see her.

"Hot mama." Embracing her, Orion kissed her temple. "You be safe. And remember, if you need help, call."

At the door, Miranda turned and blew him a kiss. "Will do."

Smirking, Bastien also blew him a kiss.

Orion grabbed it in his hand and slapped it against his ass.

Miranda rolled her eyes. "Now, boys!"

***

In the limo, Bastien was unusually quiet during the ride to Vivienna's chateau. When Miranda noticed his fingers tapping out a tune, she realized the vampire was never still for long. He'd been the same way when she'd first met him in her home with Gregori when they were sent to guard her. "What's got you so concerned?"

"Nothing. We're leaving tomorrow." He glanced out the window. "Part of me is glad, and part of me—"

Miranda felt sympathetic. "You didn't have much time to socialize with your friends."

Briefly closing his eyes, he exhaled. "It wasn't that kind of trip. Besides, it will be good to be back in New York."

"I hope Remare wasn't too tough on you." She frowned. "He wasn't pleased I took off this morning."

"Remare is a good boss." Bastien shrugged. "So is Valadon."

Miranda sensed he was preoccupied with something, but didn't want to pry. When they arrived at Vivienna's château, he escorted her up the stairs to the double doors.

"Whoa! She's not exactly hurting for bucks, is she?" Miranda appreciated the finely designed gardens with the gazebo toward the side of the mansion and the magnificent fountain in front lit with multiple colors. At its centerpiece was the goddess of the hunt, Diana, pointing her arrow. Miranda wondered if it was meant for her.

Vivienna didn't spare any expense in decorating her home. Where the Rosemont home was tastefully understated, her château had ostentatious displays of artistic décor with rose veined marble dominating the floor and statues lining the walls. Miranda remembered something her father once said. *Some people like to make a splash, others—a tidal wave.* If that was true, they were definitely in the deep end of the ocean.

During dinner, most of the guests spoke French rapidly with mixed dialects difficult to follow, so she tuned them out. When Miranda became bored, she started perusing the portraits on the walls. She knew Vivienna was watching her and avoided eye contact. When she tried to read the Vixen Queen, she couldn't get a bead on her emotions. *Shields of granite. Whatever are you hiding?*

Vivienna's lavender eyes sparkled with a pleasure Miranda was sure was as cold as it was calculated. She made a mental note of who the VQ spoke to most.

After dinner, Bastien introduced her to a vampire who made Miranda's sensitivity to a vampire's pitch intensify to the point of pain. He appeared to be in his late thirties or early forties, was elegantly dressed in his dark suit and spoke eloquently, but Miranda felt like fire ants were crawling up her arms. Only very old and powerful vampires affected her this way.

"A member of our ruling council, Caltrone."

Caltrone looked at her with eyes dark as midnight as if he wanted to dissect her mind, and if she was damaged in the process, all the better. "*Enchanté.* I see Valadon has good taste in his associates."

Miranda didn't like his choice of words. "It's a pleasure to meet you." When he went to kiss her hand, she instinctively pulled away. "You knew High Lord Valadon when he lived in Europe?"

At first, Caltrone seemed disconcerted, then smiled. "Of course. Anyone connected with the courts would be familiar with Valadon." Mild irritation laced his voice. "We had hoped he would join our summits here in Europe."

Bastien explained, "Valadon was Minister of Finance, Miranda. Many here had dealings with him before he moved to New York."

"Some would say *abandoned*," Caltrone made eye-contact with Miranda, "for his new."

Miranda wasn't put off by his remark. "What else would they say, I wonder."

"Charming." Caltrone's tone all but said otherwise. Dismissively, he moved away to speak with another vampire. From his reserved frown, she didn't think his conversation was anything pleasant.

Bastien stiffened as a beautiful dark-haired vampire approached them. Instinctively, Miranda knew she was a Blueblood.

"Bastien, just don't stand there; introduce me to your companion."

"Miranda, this is Isabelle, my sister."

Noticing the way Bastien gritted his teeth, Miranda said, "It's a pleasure meeting you."

Isabelle laughed. "It could be. What brings you to Paris, Miranda?"

Before she could answer, Bastien said, "She's here on business."

Without warning, Vivienna appeared, her violet eyes sparkling.

Miranda couldn't remember ever meeting a vampire with such translucent skin. "Your home is beautiful, Madame Lord."

Vivienna glanced at Bastien. "I see you've taught her vampire etiquette."

"Thank you for inviting us." *As if we had any choice!*

"How is the handsome young Were doing? I do so regret his accident, but I am unaccustomed to being touched by those who have not received an invitation to do so."

Accident? Miranda wouldn't have called slashing someone's throat an accident.

Bastien answered, "He's healed and is resting."

"Good. I observed you admiring my collection of paintings. Perhaps, you would like a tour of my home?"

"Oh, I think your guests would miss you too much." Miranda gestured to the elegantly dressed people conversing around them. "There are many here who seem to want your attention."

"They can do without, and I would like the opportunity to get to know you. Bastien why don't you socialize with your sister, Isabelle? She's flown from Nice to see you."

Bastien's eyes narrowed as he looked at Isabelle. "It would be a cold day in hell before my sister would fly anywhere to see me."

Isabelle pouted. "Oh, brother dear, you wound me."

Miranda doubted that very much. The look on Bastien's face suggested he would like nothing better than for his sister to disappear. Preferably off a cliff.

His spine erect, Bastien said, "Given the unexpectedness of the last time we met, I think it prudent to accompany Miranda as she is new to our world."

Something Bastien said seemed to amuse Vivienna, and she laughed heartily. "Be that as it may, I'm only going to show Miranda my collection. I guarantee she will be perfectly safe with me."

Nonplussed, Bastien said, "Of that, I'm certain. But I do have my orders."

Vivienna's eyes glittered. "Valadon must think very highly of Miranda if he assigns one of his elite Torians to accompany her...or does he share?"

"I came to Paris to visit with my parents. Miranda accompanied me on my trip. She is my friend." He put his arm around Miranda. "And my traveling companion."

Miranda was quickly picking up on vampire politics. Bastien was being prudent—neither confirming nor denying Vivienna's implied questions. Remare nor Valadon could enter her territory without permission, but Bastien could as he had relatives in the area.

"And, tonight, she is my guest." Vivienna took Miranda's arm. "And under my protection."

Miranda remembered the rules of guesthood. If she was truly a welcomed guest, the host had the responsibility—no, the obligation—for seeing to her welfare. She wondered how much of a traditionalist Vivienna was. "Bastien, socialize with your family. I'm all right viewing Vivienna's collection." Remembering vampire decorum, she asked, "May I call you Vivienna?"

The Madame Lord smiled. "Of course, everyone here does."

Miranda glanced back at Bastien and Isabelle, who watched her with fevered eyes as she ascended the stairs. Strolling down the corridors, Vivienna was charming as she pointed out one portrait after another, introducing her acquaintances from centuries past. Miranda recognized most of the artists, but there were a few she wasn't familiar with.

At her curious look, Vivienna explained, "These are vampire artists who had kept low profiles. Asanti was one of the best. How did you meet Valadon?"

Miranda had been waiting for her to bring up Valadon, but was still surprised at her quick change of topic. Keeping her answers neutral as possible, she said, "I met him when I was authenticating his Matisse for the insurance company. He has a very varied collection."

"I'm sure he does."

Vivienna explained the histories of the paintings. In truth, it was a fascinating collection, and Miranda was intrigued by the artists she knew so little about and planned to do some research on them. Occasionally, glancing down the balcony, she noted the eye contact between Isabelle and Caltrone.

Bastien, casually standing near a statue, saluted her. When they had climbed the stairs to the third level, one of Vivienna's assistants approached.

"Vivi, there's a phone call for you in the study."

Vivi?

"Can't you see I'm entertaining a guest, Camille? I'm sure you can handle it; tell whoever it is I am indisposed."

"I did, but it's *Monsieur* Goering. He says it is very important."

Vivienna exhaled. "Very well. Do you think you can finish the tour yourself, Miranda? There's a painting in the room at the end of the hall I think you will find most...intriguing."

"Of course." So far, the bitch queen Blu and Bastien had warned her about wasn't as formidable as Miranda had expected. Yes, Vivienna was temperamental—vicious, when she didn't get what she wanted—but tonight, she seemed to be on her best behavior.

Miranda wondered when the curtain would drop.

Traversing the corridor, she studied the works of art in awe of the wealth of history the paintings afforded. When she came across a painting of courtiers enjoying a party, she leaned in for a closer look, and spotted Blu in the background, then gasped. Beside him was the likeness of

Dr. Walcott. Once before, Miranda had seen her mentor's image in an old painting, but now, she was certain the other woman had lived centuries ago. And the only way that was possible was if Felicity was a vampire. *Why didn't you tell me?*

Not wanting to solicit undue observation, Miranda continued perusing the other paintings.

The closer she got to Vivienna's room, the subjects in the paintings became more graphic in their naked sensuality. Humans couldn't possibly bend in the varied positions the figures were in. Their repertoire of hedonistic delights knew no bounds; their intense sexual satisfaction was clearly etched in their visages. But there was one picture of a nude, redheaded man tied to a post with such a profound expression of humiliation as another man took him from behind Miranda found haunting. Barely glancing at the other erotic paintings, she opened the door to the room Vivienna had wanted her to see.

Then, the Vixen Queen's true persona emerged.

Chapter Twenty-Six

"It's nearly dawn; Trubark should be here," Irina whispered.

Gregori nodded as he scrutinized the street and rooftops. He'd already had his people strategically placed for this meet and greet and wasn't taking any chances it was some sort of trap. Instinct said they were safe, but just in case instinct decided to take a nap, Gregori was being extra careful. Rarely did his gut steer him wrong, but with Irina by his side, he wasn't taking any chances. "There he is, now."

Trubark entered the early morning bakery and paid for his purchases. Once outside, he sucked in a sharp breath. Gregori grinned. He often had that effect on people meeting him for the first time. "Trubark? You agreed to meet with us."

"Yes, yes. But not here." He nervously scanned the dark street. "Come with me. I'll bring you somewhere safe."

"Not so fast. You said you had information you were willing to share. This area is secure. Spill it."

"The information you seek would be better presented indoors. Come with me. I mean you no harm."

Irina studied Trubark's features. "He's telling the truth. Let's follow him."

Gregori knew he was riding shotgun on this mission, but he also knew Irina was impatient to retrieve the data Remare had requested. "That may not be the best option."

"It's not far." Trubark motioned down the street. "It's just around the corner."

They moved cautiously down the street until Trubark unlocked a basement apartment and they went inside. A young girl on the verge of womanhood was resting on the couch with a blanket casually draped over her thin form. She gently smiled up at them. "Father, you brought them."

"This is my daughter, Cara. She will tell you what you want to know."

While Trubark went into the kitchen and started preparing breakfast, Gregori sat on one of the chairs and faced Cara. "You don't have to be afraid; we are only seeking the whereabouts of a certain vampire. No danger will come upon you or your father."

"I'm almost completely healed. The vampire took far more blood than I thought he would. Father told me not to go, but so many from school were going to the club, I didn't think it would be so bad."

"The students from the university like to travel in groups." Trubark set down a plate filled with pastries. "Eat. You need to raise your sugar level. I warned her about the clubs, but she insisted on going, even when I forbid it."

"My father worries too much." Cara took a bite of the cherry tart and sat up straighter. "Gilly and Sam go all the time, and nothing like this ever happened."

"What happened?" Irina chose a seat where she could keep one eye on the girl and the other on the door.

Seeing Cara's worried look, Gregori told Trubark, "Please wait in the other room." Then, he turned to the girl. "You can tell us."

"I've already let a vampire feed on me, so I didn't think anything of it." Cara shrugged. "Most of the time, it's all very controlled and efficient. But Gilly says she gets a high better than anything she's ever tried before."

"Did you know the name of the vampire who fed off of you?"

"No, I didn't ask." Cara sighed. "But he was one of the handsomest vampires in the club, so I felt charmed when he asked to buy me a drink. Everything was pretty normal until his friends showed up, and together, they— I'd rather my father didn't know."

Gregori knew the girl was sexually active, and her father probably knew, as well. "Go on."

"We stayed in one of the back rooms for a while. Then, I started getting dizzy. I think I passed out for a while, but I heard the men talking. They started discussing business. I didn't pay much attention, but then, I heard them speaking of the High Council and how they finally found a way to snare him and all they had to do was wait to spring the trap. Once they had him, they would be able to transfer some of his profits to their own accounts. One was furious, the hatred evident in his voice. The other spoke in civil terms, but he's the one who drank the deepest."

"Do you remember his name?" Irina inquired.

"I c-can't remember." Cara squinted and held her head in pain.

Irina and Gregori exchanged a look. Vampires sometimes veiled the memories of humans when they didn't want them to remember something. It was outlawed in America, but this was London. Gregori stared into Cara's eyes and, blocking her pain, willed her to remember.

"I heard him call the older man Cal. He was very angry. I didn't like him much. He said once Vivi got hold of him, she would never let him go."

When Gregori searched her mind, he saw a clear picture of Caltrone, but the other was too heavily veiled for him to lift. Someone had made sure to leave no tracks. "Cara, who were they talking about? Who's the mark they were after?"

Trubark re-entered the room. "Tell him, Cara."

Cara sat up straighter. "They said the High Council had wanted him for some time, and now, they had him."

When the headache returned, making tears form in her eyes, Gregori put his hand to her forehead, alleviating the pain. She whispered, "Valadon, the American Lord."

"How?" Irina stood and demanded.

"I don't know. But it had something to do with finances, and yes, I remember. They said something about old traditions, old customs. That it was as good as the written word." Cara looked down at her twisted fingers. "They didn't say which word."

Gregori softened his tones, knowing a vampire's voice could be persuasive. He didn't want to force her any further, knowing he could break her mind. "Can you remember anything else?"

"Not really." Cara twisted the edge of the blanket. "I'd already had a lot to drink, and by the time, they started drinking my blood—"

"Stay out of the bloodclubs. They're no place for kids like you." Gregori hated the clubs where vampires preyed on the weak. Cara was lucky to be alive. He'd seen far too many deaths resulting from careless Rogues who didn't value human life. Though the vampires Cara was talking about were anything but Rogues; they were members of the uppermost echelon of vampires, the High Council. Christ, they'd been jealous of Valadon's success for centuries, and now, they were conspiring against him.

"All right, I'll leave you my card. If you remember anything else, you call me. Anytime, day or night. Do you understand?"

When Cara nodded, Gregori rose to leave. "We're done here. Let's go."

Trubark shook his head. "I told her to stay out of those clubs, but she didn't listen."

Irina took out an envelope and handed it to Trubark. When they were out on the street, Irina said, "The High Coucil never accepted Valadon's leaving."

"I know," Gregori whispered. "Not here. Let's get back to the hotel and notify—" Gregori never finished his sentence. His senses on full alert, he inhaled the scent of fresh blood. When they turned the corner, several bodies lay dead in the street. Some were his own men.

A lone dark figure in a black leather coat was standing in the shadows at the far end of the street. Gregori barely heard Irina's voice telling him to wait. Growling, he charged the figure.

***

Growing restless, Bastien was about to climb the stairs and go in search of Miranda when a woman in a verdant dress approached him. She was stunning with her long blond hair, but her eyes, the color of her dress, held intelligence and gripped him. "Sebastien de Rosemont." She smiled benevolently. "I believe we have some mutual friends."

Impatience laced Bastien's voice. "And who would that be?"

She came closer and whispered softly in his ear, "Pascal."

That immediately got Bastien's attention. "What do you know of Pascal?"

She laughed as she extended her hand. "I suppose I should introduce myself. Auriel."

Bastien's eyes widened, but he kept his voice low. "Pascal told me you might talk to me about some other friends."

Taking hold of his arm, she led him into the shadows, away from any onlookers. "Come by the window. If it wasn't raining outside, I would suggest a walk in the gardens."

"Your accent's English."

"Yes, my mother is French, but my father's English. I grew up here in Paris, but my family moved to London when I was still fairly young."

Bastien had researched as much as he could about his potential ally. Her pictures didn't do her justice. "Your father's on the banking commission."

"Yes, but he doesn't always approve of those he is forced to work with." Auriel turned to face him. "And neither do I."

Bastien stealthily eyed his surroundings to make sure there were no listeners. "Will you help me?"

"If I can." She smiled warmly. "Ask your questions."

"What have you heard?"

Auriel turned to watch the rain pattering against the window. "As you know the economy in Europe is not as strong as it has been. Everything is cyclical, but there are those on the Commission who are panicking. Many have suffered severe losses. But there are only a few who have been meeting in secret." She laughed. "They are arrogant not to believe someone is always watching."

"Can you tell me who?"

"Yes, but first, I need your assurance neither my father's name nor my own will be mentioned in this regard."

Bastien raised a brow. "Valadon will want to know who his friends are."

"I believe he does already." Auriel's eyes twinkled. "Granted, my father has always spoken highly of him and his second."

"Remare."

"Yes, he came to our home once when I was between semesters at Oxford. My father and he seemed to get along quite well." A gust of wind blew against the window. "The ones you seek meet once a month beneath the Catacombs. Tobias, Merlinder and Lysette.

"Lysette?"

"She's invested heavily in transportation, specifically, Italian cruise ships. Her losses have been very substantial, though she denies it publicly. There is one other you should be wary of." Auriel pulled him farther into the shadows. "He's here tonight."

"Caltrone."

Now, it was Auriel who raised an eyebrow. "You know him."

"It's amazing how many times his name has come up."

"Be careful of him, Bastien. He's on the Council of Elders, as well as our High Court, and is very well connected."

Bastien sighed. "I know."

"I must leave, now. I dare not be seen with you too long. I return to London tonight."

"Thank you for your help." Bastien kissed her knuckles. "It was a pleasure meeting you, Auriel."

"Likewise. Tell Valadon, our family sends him our warmest regards." She turned and walked toward the front door.

Bastien blew out a breath. "Now, she's one woman Valadon should meet."

***

Remare knew, in another's lord's territory, he couldn't draw first blood so he carefully watched as his opponent circled him.

"You should not have come back to London, Remare. My lord wants a meet with you."

Remare had other plans. "That's where you're wrong, Gideon. Herbert has already given permissions."

Gideon smiled deviously as if he was one of the fallen. "You know who I'm referring to."

Unfortunately, Remare did know, and Lord Acton was the last vampire he intended to see. Herbert was Lord of England, but Lord Acton was the most powerful vampire in the North.

"You'll have to tell your master, I've made other plans, and if he wants to see me, he can petition High Lord Valadon for an audience." He returned Gideon's sardonic smile. "Though I doubt it will be forthcoming."

"Still hiding behind Valadon's power. How degrading, even for you."

"I don't hide, Gideon, unlike your master who sends a cur to do his dirty work."

"My master has plans for you." Without warning, Gideon lunged at Remare.

Remare thought, finally, an opponent worth fighting. Gideon was older, but less powerful, even with his master's blood running through his veins. Something that had once enraged Lord Acton's executioner. Centuries ago, Gideon and Remare had had their altercations, and Remare always won their battles.

Except for the one time when Gideon had cheated and caught him in a snare. But since then, Remare had trained in many places in the world and in the East under the most severe conditions. There were few who could test his resolve.

Gideon was one of them.

***

Inside Vivienna's boudoir, Miranda considered her erotic and visually stimulating art. Each painting was more sensuous than the previous one. But one work caught her eye, and she examined the full-length trip-tychs—the three panels Vivienna had depicting her sexual relationship with Valadon and Remare in bed. Each nude figure had taken turns in the middle—the position of honor—though Miranda couldn't imagine Valadon or Remare posing for the paintings.

So, the rumors concerning Valadon and Remare were true, Miranda mused, transfixed by the eroticism of the images. From the craquelure on the panels and the style of the clothes hanging off the chairs in the background, their relationship existed centuries ago; they had been quite a threesome.

"I see you found Valadon." Vivienna's singsong voice carried into her boudoir. "Of all my lovers, they were my favorites."

Placid, Miranda asked, "And between the two?"

"That would depend on the time and place." Vivienna ran her fingers down the image of Valadon's back. She turned toward Miranda with a wicked smile. "Are you not surprised?"

Miranda calmly exhaled. No way was she going to let the Vixen Queen get to her. "I did a paper on erotic art while I was a grad student here. I studied at the Musee de l'Erotisme. So, there's little in the way of eroticism that surprises me." *But the bestial nature of the painting in the corner comes pretty damned close!*

"I thought as an American, your Puritanical ancestry would have you astonished." Vivienna's eyes nearly glowed. "I'm glad to see that is not the case."

Miranda scrutinized Valadon's and Remare's facial expressions in the paintings. Of the two, it seemed Remare had had genuine feelings for Vivienna in the way he looked at her. Valadon appeared more detached. Miranda remembered reading how Vivenna had betrayed them by informing the Vampire High Court of Valadon's desire to leave Europe for America. "What happened?" she muttered half-aloud.

"In time, no matter how skilled a lover is, one feels the need to find new territories to explore."

I bet! Miranda arched a brow. "They loved you."

"As I loved them."

Then, why did you betray them? Miranda bravely faced Vivienna. "Why did you want me to see these paintings?"

"You're involved with Valadon. I thought you should know what *eclectic* tastes he has."

Oh, if she only knew! "You don't think he's changed since you were involved with him?"

"Perhaps." Vivienna smiled like the snake Miranda knew her to be as she casually meandered around her bedroom, inspecting one object d'art after another. Her movements were measured, each step carefully orchestrated as if part of some choreographed play she was silently directing. "Perhaps not."

Miranda was impressed with the elegant confidence Vivienna exuded. Lizandra also moved with the grace and self-assurance born of a lifetime of hard work, experience and a general consideration for others. Miranda had great respect for such women whose success was based on determination, ingenuity and intelligence. However, Vivienna moved with the cunning and icy calculation only one who had spent centuries manipulating others for her own interests possessed. Miranda sensed the viper was circling her prey, contemplating her next move. She just couldn't figure out what it was, so she kept her back to the wall and the door in view.

"Over time, tastes change, but not essential nature." While she stood silently near the window, Vivienna's fangs lengthened as her eyes darkened to deepest purple. Mischief danced with amusement in those violet orbs. There was one painting that had yet to be revealed. She slowly pulled a drape from what Miranda knew she'd been patiently waiting to reveal. "Don't you agree?"

A sharp gasp escaped Miranda's throat as echoes of laughter reverberated throughout the room.

Chapter Twenty-Seven

Remare wiped the blood from his brow. Gideon had been quick. Quicker than he had remembered. But he still was not as fast as Remare. "Tell your master I'm sorry to have missed him this trip, but perhaps, we'll meet again some other time."

Leaning against the building for support, Gideon gritted his teeth and held his hand over the deep wound Remare had inflicted. He nodded behind Remare. "I see you have your shadows following you. Don't feel too safe in London, Remare. Lord Acton's arm is longer than you remember."

Limping, Gideon turned and left. Remare knew well the length of Acton's arm and didn't doubt the day would come when he would have to face his former nemesis. "A pleasure to see you, too, Gregori."

"Jesus Christ, Remare, I nearly attacked you." Gregori huffed out of breath as Remare cleaned off his sword and then inserted it in his cane.

"A pleasure anytime." Irina slung her arm around Remare and traced the back of one fingernail down his face.

Remare covered her hand with his and slowly removed it. "I'm glad to see you're wearing your disguises. The beard looks good on you, Gregori." Remare smirked. "Let's return to your hotel room, before more Rogues show up. My time here is limited. You can tell me then what you've discovered. Our people have been notified and will clean up this mess."

At the hotel, Gregori removed his fake beard as Irina tossed her black wig on the sofa.

Remare listened intently to their report. "Stay in London a little longer. Interview the girl's friends. See if you can find out any more information." Remare leaned back in his chair. "I wonder if Herbert knows about the bloodclubs."

"He does," Irina offered. "But, like the ones in New York, every time he closes one down, another surfaces."

Remare exhaled. "And so it goes." He stood. "Now, I have a meeting I must attend." He regarded them both. "Under no circumstances is my presence to be reported to anyone. Understood?"

"Understood." Gregori and Irina watched as Remare departed.

Locking the door, Gregori said, "Let me take a look at your wound."

Irina avoided his eyes. "It's already healed."

"I know, but I want to take a look at it, anyway."

"Are you thinking the wound is what alerted the Rogues to our presence?"

"That's not what I said."

"But it's what you were thinking?" Irina asked as she lifted her shirt.

Gregori grabbed a chair and sat before her. Her skin was pale under her shirt. He slowly peeled the bandage away. Only a tiny drop of her blood had been on the bandage. But it was enough for a Rogue to have smelled it. "You heal up nicely." His fingers gently traced her skin. "By tomorrow, the scar will be gone."

"We should contact the girl's friends and set up meetings."

"I'll do that. For now, you should get some rest."

Irina felt the exhaustion of the rising sun pulling on her. "Make the calls. I want to interview them before dusk."

"We will." After making the contacts and arranging for meetings, Gregori made sure the thick drapes didn't let in any sun as they slept. He lay back on his bed and considered the fitful sounds Irina had made as she slept. He thought back to when they had raided Ivan's camp in northern Russia and freed her. She had been abused by his men, and Ivan had left his mark upon her lower back. She'd been branded like an animal. Gregori hated Ivan for that alone and was glad his coven had been destroyed.

"He sang to me," Irina whispered in the darkness.

Gregori turned to her. "What?"

"You asked why I've stayed with Remare for so long. The night you raided the camp. He held me in the back of the truck and sang to me as he kept me warm. Ivan didn't think the women in camp needed much clothes, so he barely kept us clothed. Remare covered me with blankets and held me. He sang an old Russian ballad to me."

Gregori rose up on one elbow and stared at her. He had driven the truck to the compound. But Remare had driven them back. "Remare didn't sing to you, Irina. The song you heard was an old Russian children's song my mother sang to me. I was the one singing in the truck. Remare was the one driving."

Irina looked at him in confusion. "You?"

***

Miranda stared at the portrait Jacques Dourdain had named *Lavender Dreams*. "Monsieur Dourdain told me he wanted me to have the painting. I was in my early twenties when he painted it." Miranda noted how much thinner she'd been and how Dourdain had been intrigued with her combination of innocence and sensuality. He certainly had captured her alluring demeanor in his sensuous nude painting. A painting he'd sworn he would never sell.

"A very evocative pose." Vivienna chuckled as she clasped her fingers and brought them to her lips. "I can see why Valadon finds you so fascinating."

Miranda strode to Vivienna and stood shoulder to shoulder with her. Her cloying flowery scent was nearly overwhelming. Miranda knew she was in murky waters and had to tread carefully. "How did you know about this painting?"

"When I saw your picture with Valadon—twice now—of course I was curious. You went to the American University here for nearly three years. How is it we never met?"

"Grad students are very focused on their work. I spent most of my time in libraries and museums doing research." Miranda glanced at the painting. "Though, at times, I did some modeling to help pay for expenses." She narrowed her eyes at Vivienna as she crossed her arms over her chest. "How did you know about Dourdain and the portrait?"

"One of your former classmates told me." Vivienna sauntered to her bed. "Calisto works for me, now."

Miranda exhaled. Dourdain had several models. Calisto must have seen the painting in his studio. Miranda knew she didn't have the funds to pay for the portrait, but she did have Valadon's necklace that was worth a small fortune. She considered a trade. "How much do you want for it?"

Reclining on her luxurious bed, Vivienna smiled slyly as she eyed Miranda. "It's not for sale, but it can be obtained." She leaned backward on the pillows, her breasts all but protruding from the top of her dress—a deliberate pose.

"What do you want for it, Vivienna? You didn't bring me up here to admire your art collection. You wanted me to see it. So, what do you want?"

Vivienna pursed her rosy lips. "Information only. On Valadon."

Miranda gestured toward the panels. "Obviously, you know more about him than I do."

"But it's been so long." A nipple peeked out of her dress. "I'm sure you know much you can share with me."

Miranda knew she was being played and needed finesse in dealing with the vampire vixen. Rosalyn and Blu had warned her Vivienna enjoyed playing mind games. "I'm not sure how much more I can tell you. So much has been written about him in the magazines, the news stories. Anything you want to know you can find on social media."

"Not *anything*." Vivienna's violet eyes glowed as she smoothed the duvet. "Why don't you join me and we can discuss what you know about Valadon?"

Miranda started stroking the amber necklace Blu had given her and hoped the ancient was awake to hear her silent call.

"*Miranda, I've told you repeatedly not to stroke the amber. It's disconcerting. And most distracting at the most inopportune times.*" Blu's voice echoed in her mind. "*I'm in the park, and one of the children just threw a Frisbee at me. I would hate to think his mother thought my hard-on was for the child.*"

Surprised, Miranda asked, "*Stroking the amber is like stroking... Oops! Sorry! Blu, I might be in need of assistance. I think Vivienna is trying to seduce me.*"

"*There is no thinking, Miranda. She either is or is not. Which is it?*"

"*Oh, I'd say she definitely is...and not too subtly either.*"

"I'm not sure what you hope to find out about Valadon, Vivienna. I only validate his art." Miranda shook her head. "Nothing else."

Vivienna smirked. "Nothing else?"

"*Miranda, you walk a fine edge. If you deny working for Valadon, you will* not *be under his protection in her eyes, and Vivienna will toy with you as a cat plays with a mouse. However, if you say you are a "Friend of the Court," she will try to pry you for information. Please be careful. OH! NO!*"

"*What's wrong?*"

"I may have thrown the Frisbee a little too hard. I nearly decapitated the child!"

Shaking the image out of her mind and choosing her words carefully, Miranda asked, "What do you want to know?" When she felt Vivienna's cool touch invading her mind, she slammed the door on her. Hard. From the startled look on her face, Miranda knew she had surprised the Madame Lord.

The amusement was back in the vixen's voice. "A challenge, then?"

***

In an exclusive area of London, not far from the financial area, Remare knocked on the door of one of the toniest homes in the affluent neighborhood, hoping Bastien's information was solid and Valadon had acquired a new ally. When Auriel answered, Remare was taken back at how the young woman he'd once met briefly had blossomed into a ravishing adult. He smiled graciously. "Auriel."

"Remare, why don't you come in?" Tightening the sash to her robe, Auriel returned his smile and led him farther into her home. "I'm not surprised to see you, but I didn't expect to see you quite this fast." She went to the bar and poured him a glass of blood wine. "I take it Bastien contacted you?"

"Yes, he did." Remare casually inhaled her scent and noted the stock indexes on the television and the financial newspapers on her coffee table. "He told me you were able to gather certain information on Valadon's adversaries. I was hoping you could share more with me."

Auriel used the remote to shut the television and poured herself a drink as well. Handing Remare his drink, she gestured to her sofa. "As Valadon's second, I'm sure you made sure no one followed you or saw you in this neighborhood?"

Remare nodded. "Of course. You need not fear." He could tell by her scent she was aroused, but if it was due to his presence or the prospect of entering into a potentially dangerous situation, he could not tell.

"Then, this conversation never took place." Auriel glanced up at him.

He knew she was intelligent, but could detect no subterfuge in her scent or her behavior. "Agreed, for both our sakes." In another time or place, he would have been attracted to the blond-haired beauty, but his interests lay elsewhere.

"What do you wish to know?"

Remare smiled. Like a cat. "Everything."

***

"Tell me about Valadon's Torians." Vivienna played with a curl of her hair as it covered her naked breast. "Does he have any favorites?"

Miranda saw Vivienna's nipple was pierced and wondered where the Madame Lord was going with this line of questions. "I wouldn't know. I never asked him."

Her voice was deceptively casual. "Surely, he has his favorites."

"I suppose we all do, but he's never confided in me."

Vivienna pouted as she sprawled on her canopied bed. "Never?" One of her perfectly arched brows rose.

Miranda shook her head. "I've met a few Torians at ValCorp. They all seem very efficient."

"So careful, Miranda. I'm just curious about Valadon. I haven't seen him in years." Vivienna's eyes were gleaming. "You need not be afraid of me."

Miranda wasn't so sure. "You slashed my friend's throat."

Vivienna made mewing noises. "He was only a Were. I'm sure he's healed perfectly fine by now."

No thanks to you! "Tell me what Valadon was like back then." Miranda motioned to one of the paintings.

A sensuous groan escaped Vivienna's mouth. "He was delightful, as was Remare. Together, they could pleasure a woman for hours and hours and sometimes even days."

TMI! If she didn't already have erotic images burning in her brain, she certainly did, now. "You do realize I dated ValCorp's doctor for a while." Miranda knew that information was easily accessible, but she wasn't sure how much Vivienna knew about Gabriel.

"Yes, Valadon's progeny, Dr. Gabriel. Very studious, but handsome. Is he as good as Valadon?"

Miranda was getting tired of being toyed with and figured two could play her game. "Valadon is successful as a financier." Miranda crossed her arms over her chest. "Are there people in Europe who are jealous of him?"

Vivienna watched her like a cat lounging on its favorite piece of furniture. "Of course."

"Anyone who would like to take a shot at him?"

"We like him very much alive." Vivienna shrilly laughed. "What good would he do us if he was dead?"

"I suppose not much." Miranda gazed at the panels and remembered Vivienna reported to the Vampire High Council. She had once betrayed Valadon and Remare by disclosing their plans to leave the High Court and wondered if Vivienna was set to repeat herself. "What about Remare? He's in as many paintings as Valadon."

"Our Minister of Defense. We were so sorry to see him go. But wherever Valadon went, he followed. He was our third, even though he believed he was the first." At Miranda's confused look, she added, "In a *ménage a trois*, one is usually the leader and the other the follower. Remare was our third." Vivienna seemed reflective. "He loved me. More than Valadon ever did, but I loved Valadon more."

Miranda didn't believe Vivienna ever loved either one of them or that she was even capable of loving someone. "Does Valadon have enemies here, Vivienna?" Miranda ground her molars. "Would you help him if he did?"

Vivienna's eyes were filled with silent laughter. "Would *you* help him, if he did?"

Miranda didn't hesitate. "Yes."

"Did he send you to Paris to search out his enemies?"

So, this was why Remare said Valadon thought she was better off not knowing. Vampires could smell a lie as quickly as Weres could. "He sent me here to procure a painting. That is *all* he requested of me." Miranda came closer to the foot of her bed. "You're Madame Lord of Paris and must have connections to the Vampire High Court." Miranda knew there was power in voice and lowered her tone. "Are there people here conspiring against Valadon?"

"I'm sure there are." Vivienna's scent became intoxicating. "Would you like to know who?" She ran her hands up and down her protruding naked breasts. "How far would you go to obtain what you seek most?"

Oh, bloody hell! The spider had just invited the fly to play.

Chapter Twenty-Eight

Bastien grew impatient and jogged up the stairs to the third floor. How long did it take to look at paintings anyway, he wondered as he texted Miranda. When he glanced up, he was shocked to see the person standing before him. "Josette."

"I wasn't sure I wanted to come tonight." She smiled seductively. "But, in the end, I decided I'd rather be a masochist than not see you, again."

Josette's revealing pink dress barely covered her slender body. His heart thudding in his chest, Bastien pulled her tightly to him. With all that had been happening, his emotions were on a hair trigger. Kissing her relieved some of the ache, but his body demanded more. Breaking the kiss, he opened the door nearest to him and pulled her in, locking the door behind him. When he read Miranda's text that she was fine, he shut the phone. Their clothes were off in a flash, and it took him barely a second to have Josette naked, under him on the bed.

She laughed at his speed. "Slow down, we have all night. Make it last, Bastien. Give me good memories."

"I'll give you more than that." Long ago images surfaced of him watching her picking flowers. She had turned and smiled up at him, looking so beautiful his heart had ached. More intimate images of when they'd been teenagers flashed in his mind—Josette running through his father's maze, her long blond hair flowing as he chased and then caught her. Darker images surfaced, as well. His father lecturing him in the study that, as a Blueblood, Bastien could only mate another purebred vampire.

"But why, Father, why?" he had demanded.

"Tradition! Your lineage and your future!" His father's words still echoed in his mind.

Not his future! He'd given up his title to join Valadon's service and had never once regretted it.

Bastien's fangs shot out as he kissed her neck. He rubbed them sensually over her neck and began his downward exploration of her body. His hand cupped her breast. Her rosy nipples were hard, and he bent his head to taste them. When she gasped, he smiled up at her as he moved his lips and tongue to her other breast. She tasted as sweet as he remembered. Trailing soft kisses over her sternum and ribs, he laved her navel as he spread her thighs wide with his knee. Hooking her foot over his shoulder, he kissed her slender ankle then plunged his head between her thighs.

Josette moaned when he penetrated her with his tongue, but when he used his fangs to rub against her most sensitive flesh, she arched off the mattress. He hadn't forgotten how she liked to be pleasured, and he gave her all that he had to give, sparing her nothing until her body twisted in ecstasy.

Unable to deny himself any longer, Bastien positioned his cock at her core and slid in one slow inch at a time. He loved watching her face as her warm, wet body welcomed him. Pleasure etched her mouth as she fought not to scream. He then twisted his hips and slammed home. Seeing the passion in her eyes, he pulled out slowly and found a slow, sensuous rhythm that would have him howling before long.

Bastien could feel his shoulders bunching as he kept himself erect over her. Her body was too thin, and he didn't want to crush her with his muscular frame. He felt the tension burning in his back and buttocks as the pleasure built higher and higher until he thought his jaw would crack from the intensity. Three deep strokes later, he heard her cry out in bliss as his body emptied itself into her, his release jetting into her, wave after wave, as he howled in rapture.

Exhausted, he rolled them over and brushed her bangs from her brow. He gently cupped her face with his hand. He could hear her heart beating against his own. He looked into her passion-filled eyes. "Come back with me, Josette. Come to New York."

Tears welled up in her eyes. "You know I can't." She breathed deep. "Not now. But you know I want to. You know that, Bastien, don't you?"

Bastien rolled to his side and listened to the wind and rain beating against the window. He knew she would never leave Vivienna. Paris was her home, where her work and friends were. In his absence, she'd made a life for herself. He exhaled. Anguish threatening to tear him apart.

***

"This is the dossier on Merlinder. You already have the others. I compiled notes on when and where they've met in the last month. I followed them to the Catacombs once. They don't seem to trust technology and keep their meetings far below the surface so as not to be detected."

"You're very brave, Auriel. I hope you made sure no one saw you." Remare looked at his newest ally and inhaled her alluring scent. "You could have put your life in great danger if anyone had seen you." The fact that she had subtly moved closer to him and had *accidentally* rubbed her leg against his wasn't lost on Remare.

"I was careful. As much as I respect Valadon, I did not take any unnecessary risks." She pointed to one of the photographs at a wall inside the Catacombs. "Under the fourth lamp, there is a loose brick; push it inward, and the wall will open. There's a staircase that will take you deep beneath. It's rumored that, in the Middle Ages, the kings stored some of their treasures there, so when invading forces attacked, their wealth would be preserved."

"Most monarchs had similar bolt holes they used to escape their enemies." Remare knew not only monarchs had used these passageways; members of the court and their spies had also used these escape routes. He had once fought one of his king's betrayers in those Catacombs. "I've heard how Henry IV used these passageways to visit his mistresses."

Auriel smiled, then took their empty wine glasses and brought them to her kitchen. "He had several and did not want the added attention of his political allies."

"I thank you again for your assistance, Auriel." Remare rose. "Valadon has been known to be generous with those he considers his friends."

She walked seductively toward him. "When do you leave to go back?"

"Immediately. I have a plane waiting for me."

Auriel stepped back and let her robe fall to the floor, displaying her feminine curves. "You could take a later flight."

Remare sucked back a hiss. Her body was as exquisite as her face. His jaw twitched once, then he met her hunger-filled eyes as he reached for her cheek and stroked it with his thumb. He slowly exhaled. "If I wasn't already spoken for, I would consider your generous offer." He bent down and handed Auriel her robe.

Auriel looked up at him and smiled as she tied the sash to her robe. "You must care deeply for her. Your lover is a lucky woman."

Remare nodded. He was not used to discussing his feelings with anyone and would not do so with someone he was just barely beginning to know. "At times."

Though there were moments when he wanted to strangle her.

***

"The weather is terribly frightful outside; you should consider sleeping here tonight. The country roads become impenetrable when it rains this hard."

Miranda considered Vivienna's offer as they walked down the hall toward the stairs. After giving up a slice of her integrity, Miranda rubbed at the pain still emanating from her chest where she'd been pierced. She never should have revealed her childhood fear of needles. The game of *Truth or Dare* had taken on new dimensions. But how else was she to have gotten the information Valadon needed?

Vivienna had been so cunning in what little she offered, but Miranda remembered her professors from University instructing the students to focus on not just the subjects in a painting, but to study the negative space. In this case, what Vivienna wasn't saying and what she was conveying through body language. When she thought Miranda wasn't looking, there had been one painting that made Vivienna shudder when she glanced briefly at it—*Magritte*. It had been subtle, but unwittingly, the madame lord had revealed a fear. Miranda would make it a point to learn what she could about the stunning vampire.

Glancing at the open stained-glass window, she saw the rain falling harder than it had been earlier. "Thank you, but I'm eager to get back. Let me find Bastien, and we'll be on our way."

Vivienna's nostrils flared as she sniffed the air and smirked. "I don't think you will have to search far."

Miranda watched as Vivienna pulled a painting that swung open from the wall to reveal a glass window. Apparently, there was another painting on the other side of the wall with gossamer canvas, and Miranda could see well into the dimly lit room. And Vivienna was right. She didn't have to search far for Bastien. His naked body was intertwined with a woman on a canopied bed.

"Shall I call forth your traveling companion?" One corner of Vivienna's mouth lifted. "Though I would hate to interrupt him, especially when he seems so close to com—"

Miranda closed the painting as Vivienna pouted. "He doesn't need an audience." She wondered how many other secret panels the vampire had in her home that she used to spy on her guests. "All right, then, you can give me a room where I can rest for a couple of hours. But, at first light, we're out of here."

"But, of course." The vampire led her down another wing of her château and opened the door to a capacious bedroom. Apparently, all the bedrooms were luxurious. But, instead of Vivienna's purple boudoir, this one was a combination of browns and tans. "I believe you will be most comfortable here."

"I won't sleep. I just want to rest until the rain stops."

"As you wish, *ma chère*. The closet is filled with clothes. Help yourself to any nightwear you wish. *Bonsoir*, Miranda." Vivienna stared slyly at her chest then met her eyes. "It was a pleasure meeting you."

"*Au revoir*, Vivienna." *Pleasure, my ass!* If it hadn't been pouring like a monsoon, Miranda would have left as quickly as possible. Opening the stained-glass window, she realized they must be a favorite of vampires for its diffusion of light and saw that the rain hadn't let up. When she spotted the closet, curiosity got the better of her. Inside, she found outfits for every occasion, but after seeing the spyware Vivienna had just revealed, she nixed the idea of changing.

After using the bathroom, she entered the bedroom ready to shut her eyes for a while and discovered the gift

Vivienna had sent her. A handsome, naked, redheaded man lying on her bed.

She could tell from his pitch he was a vampire. Exasperated, Miranda clenched her fists. "Who the hell are you?"

"My name's Eric." He seemed to grit his teeth as he jutted his chin toward her. "I'm your entertainment for the night."

"The *hell* you are!" Miranda marched over to the door and turned the knob, but found it had been locked. "What the hell is this?"

"Vivienna ordered me to pleasure you tonight," Eric said sarcastically, as if he was less enthused at the prospect than she was. "That door won't open until sunrise. It's on a time-controlled mechanism."

"We'll see about that." Miranda turned and pulled the knob, yanking and twisting to no avail. Then, she banged on the door and yelled for help. Her pleas went unanswered. Imagining Vivienna's sly smile and her grating laughter, she turned on her new roommate. "Mind going into the bathroom and using a towel to cover up."

"Why? Is my body not to your liking?" Eric stood, spread his arms and turned his muscular physique in a circle.

Shaking her head, she put her fists on her hips. "I don't do strangers." She glanced down at his semi-erect cock. "No matter how impressive. And I certainly didn't ask for an *'entertainment'.*" Narrowing her eyes, she pointed to the bathroom. "Get. A. Towel. Now!"

Eric eyed her as if waiting to see if she was actually serious, then went to the bathroom and came back with a towel around his hips. His expression held a hint of hurt and curiosity.

Now that Eric was covered up and she wasn't distracted by his male parts, she studied his face, focusing on his finely chiseled face and those startling hazel eyes. "I know you. I've seen you before."

"I'm sure you have," he said in his clear masculine voice. "Vivienna enjoys showing my portraits to her guests."

Miranda thought back to the erotic paintings lining the hallway and Vivienna's rooms. But, in the paintings, Eric hadn't been enjoying the sex. However subtle, his defiance had been etched in his eyes. "Who are you?"

"I'm no one." Eric huffed with indignation. "A whore. A toy the aristocrats play with."

Curious, she asked, "How did you wind up here? Your accent's not French."

"No, I'm Finnish by birth, but I've lived in England," he shrugged, "and other places, before here."

She had met another Finnish vampire with the same startling red hair, Rosalyn, Nightshade's proprietress. "Do you have any relatives in America?"

Eric raised an eyebrow. "Not that I know of. Why do you ask?"

Miranda shook her head. "No reason. Why'd you come here? Better yet, why don't you just leave?"

Eric snorted as he sat on a chair by the fireplace. "You don't know much about vampire royalty, do you?"

"I'm American." A painting above the fireplace caught her attention. "I try not to get caught up in vampire affairs."

"Smart girl." He looked up at her as he rubbed a hand through his hair. "You're from New York, Valadon's territory?"

Miranda narrowed her eyes. "Yes. I've met the high lord. I've actually validated some of his paintings." She gestured to the painting above the fireplace of a young boy, who couldn't be more than eight or nine dressed in the fashions of the seventeenth century. He had long dark blond hair and emerald green eyes—Valadon's eyes. "Who's the child in the painting?"

"Beats me." Eric shrugged. "I haven't seen any kids around here, and I've been here for decades."

Miranda tried to get a read on Eric, but there were too many emotions fighting for prominence. She didn't know what to make of him. But she could sense his restrained anger, and that was without hearing the tones in his voice or seeing the tension in his body. She sat on the bed and faced Eric. "How'd you wind up here?"

"It's a long story," he said as he exhaled. "Nothing I feel like recounting." Eric rubbed his hands together as if cold. "Could you tell me about Valadon?" He lifted an eyebrow. "Is he as calculating and capricious as the vampires here?"

Miranda didn't know who Eric was and suspected he was a plant Vivienna was using to obtain more information. She kept her answers simple. "No. The vampires at ValCorp seem to hold him in high-esteem. I've never heard anyone complain about him."

Eric leaned forward. "What's his court like?"

Miranda smirked, remembering Remare's words. "In America, they call them houses, not courts."

Eric smiled boyishly. "I knew that."

A yawn escaped before Miranda could stifle it. She glanced at her purse on the table and lamented not remembering to bring her migraine medicine. Whenever a storm was in progress, her head felt like it was being cut in half. She looked at the bed and then Eric. "I'm going to lie down for a while." She rubbed her forehead. "I've had one helluva day. You are *not* to touch me. Okay?"

Eric looked offended. "I don't force myself on others."

"If you're cold, you can have one of the blankets." She pulled off the duvet and handed it to him. "I don't need them all."

Eric looked at her as if a simple act of kindness was foreign to him. "Thanks."

"As soon as the sun comes up, I'm out of here."

"Take me with you," Eric whispered as he stretched out and covered himself on the settee. "I have a few years left in my service to Vivienna, and then, I'm leaving."

"Where will you go?" Miranda fluffed the pillows and lay down on the bed.

"I'm not sure." Eric's voice was barely audible "Far away from here, though."

She studied his form and thought back to the paintings she saw of him being enjoyed by others. In some, he seemed acquiescing; in others, a look of despair cloaked his features. "Why did you leave Finland?"

"I was no longer wanted there." Sinking lower into the cushions, he exhaled. "My parents politely asked me to leave."

Miranda didn't want to imagine what he must have done to be booted out by his own parents. "Will you go back to them?"

"That is one door which is permanently closed." He turned on his side. "No, I will not return there." After a while, he turned and looked at her. "Does Valadon welcome new people to his co—house?"

"I have no idea." Miranda wasn't sure she was being played. "What have you heard?"

"Bits and pieces from the guests who frequent Vivienna. Some seem respectful of him, others envious."

"Well, he is very wealthy."

"No. That's not it." Eric closed his eyes and seemed thoughtful. "Something else. I think they're jealous he got away and they didn't."

"Got away from where?"

"Here." As Eric turned over, the duvet slipped, and Miranda saw the scars crisscrossing his back.

She swallowed her gasp. "Did Vivienna do that to you?"

"Some, mostly her lovers." Eric rubbed his forehead. "One, in particular, gets off on inflicting pain. He says it arouses him."

"With all the erotica around here," Miranda huffed, "I shouldn't think anyone would have a problem."

"Brydon likes using a whip. I think he thinks of it as an extension of his cock."

Miranda quickly sat up from the bed. "What did you say?"

Eric shrugged. "Some men like to use whips. It helps them maintain an erection."

"Not that. Whose name did you say?"

"Brydon. He's been Vivienna's lover, off and on, for years."

Miranda's heart rate slowly returned to normal, and she laid her head on the pillow. Images of Brandon visiting her in her cell flooded her mind. She quickly locked the door on those memories. Nightmares were not welcome in her consciousness. It was only on the bitterest of evenings that they haunted her. She tried focusing on the paintings in the room, but the darkness was too deep, and sleep kept tugging at her. Slowing her breathing, she closed her eyes for a few minutes.

Miranda woke when she heard the barest of sounds. Her instincts on alert, her eyes opened to see a figure looming over her. Quickly thrusting her power out, she held the figure against one of the posters of the bed, realizing too late, she had just allowed Eric to see her power. Enraged, she quickly grabbed his throat with her hand and squeezed. "I thought I told you, I didn't want to be touched."

Gasping for air, he tried to peel her fingers from his throat. "I wasn't touching you." He coughed repeatedly as she relaxed her fingers. "I was just...watching you. That's all."

Miranda rubbed her hand across her thigh to lessen the burning sensation pulsing in her fingers. "Why were you watching me?!"

"I don't know." He rubbed his throat. "You looked so peaceful. Most women don't turn down my offers of sex. You did. I was just curious."

"Curious, huh?" Miranda huffed and walked away from him. "Remember what it did for the cat."

He looked perplexed. "What cat?"

Miranda shook her head. *Vampires!* "Go. Get some sleep." She gestured to the chaise lounge. "And no more sleep walking." Miranda slipped into bed and pulled the covers over her. She hoped Eric didn't realize what she had just done, but from his surprised expression, he might have. The last thing she needed was for Vivienna to realize she was an *Elemental*.

Chapter Twenty-Nine

Miranda was just drifting off when a cool breeze brushed against her skin. Slowly sitting up, she looked at the window; it was still locked. Wondering where the cold air was coming from, she rose and followed the coolness to a bookcase. The breeze was coming from *behind* the book shelves. After examining the wood frame, she pressed on the side, and the bookcase opened. The musky scent attacking her nostrils was cloying. *Oh, this is just* too *much!* A dark passageway lay beyond. *Could this get any more Gothic?* She peered down, but the darkness was too thick. When Miranda leaned in closer, she heard the whispering of voices.

She considered seeing where the passage went but figured, if it was secret, there must be a damned good reason why. Sitting on the bed, her fingers tapping on her arms, she considered her options. One, she could forget it and go back to sleep. That thought had great appeal. Two, she could follow the passageway a little and see where it went. If any danger presented itself, she could hightail it out of there. She looked at Option Three. Eric was sound asleep on the chaise. She could wake him, but did she trust him? *No, not really!*

But exploring in the dark was dangerous; she turned and looked at the candelabra. If she took it with her, someone would surely see her approaching. Miranda decided to use her powers to light one of the candles and hold the flame in her hand—a trick only *Elementals* could do. This way her path would be illuminated enough so she wouldn't trip and fall, but not enough to signal anyone of her arrival.

Opening the bookcase wider, she kept one hand against the brick wall, her bare feet silent on the cold stone steps. When the voices became louder and the sound of music echoed off the walls, she smothered the flame and quietly continued down the stairs. Immediately, the combined scents of incense and sex hit her.

Blu and Cyra had warned her that some vampires had a dark nature. She'd heard whispers of bloodclubs where vampires gave in to their more basic desires; she'd even been to an underground Rogue club.

But nothing prepared her for the Bacchanalian sight she was now seeing. Fascinated, Miranda crouched into a sitting position and smirked. Valadon had his underground conclave, his living area and archives elegantly modern and refined for civilized behavior.

Vivienna's was something entirely different.

The marble walls had variations of lapis lazuli, as did the floors and columns supporting the underground cave resembling the interior of an ancient Greek temple. *Vivienna must consider herself some sort of goddess.* There were several life-size statues throughout the temple. Along the side walls there were sections separated from each other by sheer lavender drapes where couples were enjoying the pleasure of each other's bodies. Miranda could hear their sounds of laughter and sexual gratification.

Nearly a year ago, Miranda had been at an estate where sex was public, but the Americans had treated sex as if it was a spectator sport or something Machiavellian and had worn masks to hide their identities. Here, the vampires enjoyed each other as it was their nature—without any fear of censure. They were simply being who they were. Miranda's eyes traveled to the far corner of the temple where musicians were playing their instruments.

Directly across the vast floor, high on their dais, Vivienna and Caltrone sat, nearly naked, and watched their people below. A woman with long dark hair had her head between Caltrone's thighs, and Vivienna had a handsome young man, wearing only a loincloth, massaging her shoulders. Behind them, etched in the wall, was the likeness of Bacchus, the god of wine. When the dark-haired woman rose from Caltrone's crotch, Miranda's eyes widened. *Isabelle,* Bastien's sister.

So, this was Vivienna's court. In the central area, girls danced in gossamer gowns barely covering their crotches. They hardly looked legal, but from the fashion magazines, Miranda recognized them as Vivienna's top models. They moved in intricate circles to the music, each holding a candle in their hands. The vampires who weren't naked wore short tunics resembling togas and were no less transparent than what the females wore.

Sitting on one of the marble tiers facing the center court was one of the most handsome vampires Miranda ever saw. Unlike the others, he appeared solitary and was reading poetry. The young girls danced around him as if he was the god, Apollo, and they his Muses.

When she studied the statues behind him, Miranda swore she saw them moving and rubbed her eyes to look, again. Her eyes weren't playing tricks. The statues weren't statues, at all, but live beings who were slowly, seductively becoming amorous with one another. Their dance carefully choreographed to evoke the most primal of sexual urges. Rodin's statue, *The Kiss,* was tame compared to the uninhibited eroticism of their touches. Her heart pounding, she looked up and saw Vivienna smiling as she whispered in her mind, *"Welcome, Miranda. Join us."*

Miranda's Dark Angel chose that moment to rise, her mouth, drooling at the prospect of the fun to be had, whispered, "*Yes, please. Go for it! You know you want to!*"

Putting her hand on her hip, The Angel of Light snorted, "*You wish!*"

Miranda huffed, "Not in this lifetime or any other."

Suddenly, Vivienna's command started vibrating inside her head, and Miranda knew the madame lord was trying to glamour her by bending her will—something Valadon had outlawed in his territory. But this wasn't New York; this was Paris—Vivienna's territory. And the Vixen Queen had her own rules. Miranda fought the compulsion by biting down hard on her tongue. When she tried to stand, a heavy weight forced her to her knees.

Vivienna was far stronger than she'd imagined. Miranda knew she would soon have a nose bleed if she kept fighting the compulsion, but she refused to let Vivienna overpower her. Feeling the seductiveness of cool hands caressing her body, she tried to crawl up the stairs. But each step was a lesson in futility. Turning, Miranda glared at Vivienna and heard her shrill laughter.

She would have crumbled on the stairs if a hand hadn't suddenly grasped her arm and pulled her upward. Eric had come to her rescue and dragged her up the stairs. Once inside their bedroom, they shoved the bookcase closed and stood panting.

"What the hell were you thinking?" Eric had his hands on his hips. "Do you know what they could have done to you, had they seen you?"

"No one saw me." *Except Vivienna.* Miranda rubbed her arms—not because she was chilled, but because she still felt Vivienna's cold power crawling over her skin. She went to the bathroom to check if her nose or eyes were bleeding.

"That was pretty stupid of you." Eric followed her. "If you were so curious, why didn't you wake me? I would have told you not to go."

"There was no need. You were sleeping, and I was curious." She looked up and saw Eric smirking, as if he was thinking, *"Really?"* "Are they always like that?"

"What?" he asked in exasperation. "They don't have parties like that in New York?"

Miranda shook her head. "Not that I know of." She glanced up at the clock. "We still have an hour before sunrise. Help me move the dresser in front of the bookcase." When the dresser was firmly in place, she said, "Let's get some sleep."

When Eric looked hopeful that she was inviting him to bed, she pointed to his lounge and nearly smiled when she saw his look of resigned rejection. He looked like a puppy that had just been relegated to the doggy bed.

Feeling secure they would not have any uninvited guests and confident she was a light sleeper, Miranda dozed off. When she woke, flecks of light were streaming through the stained-glass window. Eric was still asleep on the chaise lounge. She wasn't sure if she should wake him. When she saw the scars on his back peeking out of the duvet, she wondered what kind of monster got off on the pain of others.

Trying the door knob, Miranda found it unlocked. She quickly grabbed her purse, and with one last lingering look at the boy in the painting, she slowly closed the door behind her. She was halfway to the stairs when Bastien appeared out of his room. He looked spent, even for a vampire, but his eyes held hurt.

"I say we get the hell out of here."

Bastien rubbed his neck and seemed to come awake. "I couldn't agree more."

Once outside, Miranda hurried to their car, but movement to the side of the château caught her eye. Peering closer, she saw a form dressed in black sitting in the shadows of the gazebo. When she moved nearer, the vampire looked at her.

Miranda recognized him from the night before, even though he was wearing sunglasses.

"*Bonjour*," he said as she approached.

"Good morning." She looked around the area. "Shouldn't you be inside?"

"I like to watch the sunrise. It inspires my poetry."

"I'll bet. Not many poets around these days."

He laughed. "No, not many. My mother sent me to the University of Wittenberg to learn economics, but I preferred poetry." He smiled up at her. "I'm afraid I disappointed her gravely."

Miranda remembered how Valadon had tried to inspire Nick to take an interest in finance. "I know another young man in New York who seems to prefer the fine arts instead of economics, as well." She studied his face and wished he would take off the shades. "Shakespeare did say, '*To thine ownself, be true.*' People need to do what inspires them most."

"That's what I keep telling her." He smiled. "You're American."

"*Oui, monsieur.*"

He laughed. "I'm sorry. We haven't been properly introduced. I'm Vincent." He extended his hand toward her.

"Miranda." She shook his hand, a slight buzz creeping up her arm. When she looked up, Bastien started signaling to her.

"I'm sorry, I have to leave now. Got a plane to catch, and my friends are waiting on me."

Vincent bowed his head. "It was a pleasure meeting you, Miranda."

"*Merci.* I'm sure your poetry is inspirational, but if the sunrise truly inspires you, you should face west. I've always thought sunsets far more dramatic and visually stunning." Miranda signaled Bastien she was coming when a whim occurred to her. "Someday, you should write a poem about the boy in the painting."

"Which boy?"

"There's a painting on the third floor in a room decorated in browns and tans. The painting is above the fireplace. The boy is dressed in clothing of the seventeenth century. He has long dark blond hair."

"Miranda, we have to leave. Now!" Bastien's voice echoed in the morning light.

"*Au revoir,* Vincent. I hope we meet, again, someday."

"Perhaps, we will." He smiled. "Have a good flight home."

***

Vincent watched Miranda leave. He didn't have to check out the painting Miranda had described. He knew whose room was decorated in earth tones and who the boy was in the painting. He backed farther into the shadows of the gazebo and took off his sunglasses. His eyes were light sensitive, especially after several centuries of studying and then teaching classical literature in Europe's finest universities. Bluebloods, in particular, were known for their sensitivity to sunlight. Closing his eyes, he breathed in deep of the morning's invigorating air. When he looked over the expanse of lawn, his eyes shone emerald green.

***

"You failed to seduce her. I'm disappointed." Vivienna leaned toward the window.

"She was adamant about not having sex." Eric shrugged. "Did you want me to rape her?"

"With your body," Vivienna slid her hands down his abdomen, "I should think persuasion would have been enough. I would have had a nice gift to present to Valadon when I see him next."

"You were watching?"

"Of course." She peered out the window. "You did plant the bug as I instructed?"

"Yes. It's in her purse. You should be able to hear her conversations, now."

"As you should with Sebastien's."

Vivienna turned at the lithe figure entering the room. "Ah, Josette, join us."

"Excellent." A male entered from the door to her sitting room. Eric watched as the Blueblood circled his hands around his mistress's waist. The two of them looked equally devious as they stared at him. Over the years, Eric had learned to detest the games Vivienna played. What a fool he'd been to believe she'd ever loved him. He had given up his home, his family and his very name, to be with her; he had learned too late her promises were as hollow as her heart.

But, when they visited America, he would be a part of her entourage. Then, they would see who was good at deception. "I'll leave you two, then."

"Oh, don't go, yet. The day is just beginning. Join us," Vivienna purred.

Eric hid his look of defiance. "Of course. Who should I do first, you...or Brandon?"

"Why not both?" Brandon, Valadon's traitorous brother, smirked in lustful anticipation. "You almost gave me away. I'll have to punish you for that."

"Enough with your indulgent games!" Magritte entered, and Eric bowed to the vampire elder. "I see you let the human go."

Vivienna waved a hand in the air. "She was of no further use to me."

"Then, why did you waste valuable time on her?"

Vivienna waved her hand in the air. "An amusement."

Magritte threw the morning paper on Vivienna's desk. "Perhaps, you should spend more time on social media."

Eric glanced at the pictures of Miranda in the arms of a dark-haired man, but remained silent. He knew better than to interrupt the Bluebloods.

"Perhaps, it was Valadon who engaged in an amusement." Magritte waited patiently as Vivienna scanned the paper. "You may still be able to redeem your error in judgment."

"How?"

As Magritte walked closer to Vivienna, the temperature in the room dropped considerably enough Eric had to rub his arms. "Take away that which is dear to him."

Vivienna hesitantly glanced out the window, then said, "Very well."

Chapter Thirty

"Look, there's Chagall's! That's the shop Katya wanted me to stop in. Pull over; it will only take me a minute."

Bastien sighed. "Katya and her glass collection." But since he appeared too tired to complain, he did as she asked. "Just don't take too long. We have a plane to catch."

Miranda entered the store, not expecting any customers this early. Only one blond woman was perusing something in the showcase. After looking over the superb assortment of glass miniatures, Miranda went up to the proprietor, a middle-aged man who seemed to have a friendly demeanor. "Your collection is beautiful. My name is Miranda Crescent; I'm a friend of Katya's, from New York. She said you might have something for her."

He immediately broke into a grin. "*Oui, madame, oui.* Katya is a longtime customer and an old acquaintance. One moment, please." While he went to the back room, Miranda gazed around the shop and the many pieces of glass ornaments. When a set of intricately designed twin daggers caught her eye, Miranda giggled then muttered, "Well, you did say you wanted something shiny, Lizandra." When she peered closer, at the price, she whistled lowly. *Definitely out of my range.*

"I see you were admiring the daggers. They're quite beautiful." Effortlessly, the blond woman reached up and brought the box down to the counter. These are fashioned from the Age of Elegance, the time of Louis XIV."

"Yes, they are. The scroll work is finely detailed, but a little too expensive for me."

Chagall returned, carrying a box. "Here it is. It is a design I made especially for Katya."

When Miranda tried handing him some euros, he said, "No need; it is already paid for."

"Are you certain?" When he nodded, Miranda said, "Thank you. I will make sure Katya receives this."

"Let her have the daggers, as well. Put them on my account."

Miranda immediately shook her head at the blonde. "No. I can't accept them."

"Nonsense. If you are from New York, you must be familiar with Lord Valadon, an old acquaintance of mine. The blades are a gift for giving the high lord my fond greetings."

Suspiciously, Miranda eyed the woman. She was not in the habit of accepting gifts from strangers, but she really wanted the blades. "And who would I say was so generous with me?"

"Lysette." Smiling, she turned to leave the shop. "He'll know who I am."

Chagall packaged the daggers. "Please take them. Lysette is one of my best customers, and I would not want to disappoint her."

Miranda hesitated, but not seeing any danger, she took them along with Katya's glass figurine.

Opening the doors to their suite, Miranda told Bastien, "My suitcase is already packed. I just want to take a quick shower before we leave. I'm ready to go as soon as you get the okay from the pilot." After throwing her purse on the bathroom vanity, she slung off her gown and threw it in the wastebasket. The beautiful blue gown had been ruined with Orion's blood, and last night, the bronze gown, to a much lesser degree, had suffered a similar fate.

In the shower, Miranda let the steaming water soothe her. The tiny wounds Vivienna had inflicted had all but healed over. After a few moments of feeling clean again, she quickly dressed in a simple black dress and the sleek black suede boots Valadon had once given her.

"Is Orion all ready to go?" Miranda stopped dead in her tracks when she saw her Were roommate, who, from the satisfied smile on his face, obviously had "entertainment" of his own last night. Her hands went to her hips. She knew her expression screamed, *"Oh, Really!"*

"What?" Orion's face was a combination of indignation and innocence. "You two left me alone last night, what did you expect me to do?" Putting his bags down, he closed the zipper to his guitar case. "I went down to the bar. They told me their pianist cancelled at the last minute, I volunteered to play a few songs." He shrugged. "A fan volunteered to keep me company." Cocking his hip, he said sarcastically, "By the way, thanks for the phone call."

Miranda closed her eyes and thinned her lips. "I'm sorry. It rained hard last night, and Vivienna suggested we wait until dawn to leave." Miranda hugged Orion. "I lost track of the time. I'm sorry."

"It's okay. I would have tried to track you, but the rain..." Raising a brow, Orion looked at Bastien's spent appearance. "Rough night?"

Ignoring him, Bastien said, "I texted you last night, you didn't reply. Busy much?" A look passed between them. "I also heard from the pilot. The plane's fueled and ready to go."

Halfway to the door, Miranda remembered she left the little bronze purse on the vanity in the bathroom. No matter. She'd learned long ago to keep her essentials inside her boot. Her passport and the legal papers for Valadon's painting were in her carry-on. She looked at both men. "Let's go home."

***

During the limo ride, Miranda leaned her head on Orion's shoulder as they drove to the private airfield where Valadon's jet was waiting. It felt good to be leaving Paris, a city she had once called home. "It will be good to get home and sleep in my own bed with my own pillows."

"Same here." Orion hugged her shoulder and kissed her forehead.

Bastien said, "I texted the pilot. The skies are a little windy from the storm last night, but other than that—"

Seeing Bastien's concerned face, Miranda quickly sat up. When she looked out the rear window, two cars were speeding up. "Who the hell are they?"

"Vivienna's men. Apparently, she has no respect for vampire détente." Bastien retrieved his guns from his carry-on and handed one to Orion. "You know how to use it?"

He grinned as he handled the gun. "Shoot them with the pointy end?"

"Right. Bullets won't kill a vampire, but it will slow them down."

"Why are they after us?" Miranda's heart started beating frantically when one of the cars sped past them, effectively boxing them in. "Vivienna didn't threaten me last night; why would she be doing this?"

"News must have reached her that I hurt some of her men." Bastien loaded a clip and handed one to Orion. "My name alone should have been enough to keep her people away. Vivienna doesn't always play by the rules—she prefers to make up her own."

"This makes no sense. We were in her château last night." Miranda shook her head in confusion. "If she wanted to hurt us, she could have easily done it then."

"No." Bastien shook his head. "It wouldn't have been *gracious* of her according to the rules of guesthood. Knowing

Vivienna, she probably came up with some new protocol we don't know about."

Bastien and Orion checked their weapons as their driver, Paul, lowered the glass. "We're two miles from the airport. I don't think I can make it there before—" He didn't have time to finish his sentence as the car in front hit the brakes. They swerved to avoid crashing into them.

Miranda thought of Valadon's painting and remembered the look of disgust Brevet had given her before she examined the painting. "Damn it! They're art thieves! Brevet set us up. Who else knew we had the painting?!" Her mind was racing with the reports of stolen art work. Gangs of art robbers were notorious for hitting their marks in transit. "They're after the painting! Not us!"

"I don't care who they are," Bastien said harshly, his body tensed for action. "Stay in the car, Miranda." Meeting her eyes, he warned her. "Do *not* get out! Do you understand?"

"Yes, of course." Miranda accepted the gun Bastien handed her and placed it on the seat beside her. The men from the first car started walking toward them, then the guys from the other car started surrounding them. Bastien exited the limo with Orion beside him. She knew Bastien was a high-ranking Torian, and Orion was not only strong, but one of the fastest Weres she'd ever met. But they were only two men against nearly a dozen.

Bastien tried talking to the men. It didn't take long for the fighting to break out. Miranda ducked as bullets started flying. Paul opened his car door and started firing shots off. Most of the men were on Bastien, who was fighting fast and hard. When Orion took a shot to the arm, she grabbed her gun. Not waiting any longer, she opened her car door. If the badass vampires never met an *Elemental* before, they were about to, now.

Heart pounding, Miranda eyed the sharp pieces of metal posts on the ground near the wire fencing by the side of the road. Using her powers, she summoned the shards. Crouching low, she slung the spikes at the vampires who were fighting Orion, then at those who were trying to take down Bastien. Next, she summoned a longer section of the broken metal post and speared it at the vampire who was trying to tear out Orion's throat.

As one of the vampires rushed her; she flung out her hand and slashed his jugular with a swipe of her claws. The shocked expression on the vampire's face matched her own look of baffled amazement. Her bloodied hand resembled an eagle's talon. Trying to stem the blood spurting from his throat, the vampire fell to the ground.

When she saw Orion go down, she rushed toward him, but at the same time, the vampires were forcing Bastien into their car. She tried to throw more shards their way, but they quickly swept them aside. They got off a few warning shots as they hauled Bastien into their car and then rapidly drove off.

"You're hurt." Miranda inspected Orion's arm.

"It'll heal." Orion growled. "They got Bastien!"

"I know. *Fuck!* They weren't after me. They were after Bastien all along!" Miranda examined the nearly deserted stretch of highway—her eyesight far better than it had ever been. "Can you track him? Do you know his scent well enough?"

"Yeah, I know it very well." The last he said to himself. "When I shift, the scratch will heal. They won't know they've got a tail. I'll track him."

"Do it. I'll call Pascal; he's their contact here."

Orion slipped out of his T-shirt and jeans. Standing nude, he handed Miranda his phone. "Tie this around my neck when I change. I'll contact you when I know where they've got him."

Miranda ripped off her scarf. "Don't take any chances, Orion."

"I don't know about vampires," Orion hissed, "but Weres don't leave people behind."

"Great." Orion morphed into his wolf form, and Miranda had one moment to admire his rich black fur. She quickly secured the phone around his neck, and he was off bounding and leaping in the car's direction. She knew whoever the men were, they would take Bastien to someplace in Paris. She walked quietly back to Paul. "You're one of Pascal's men, aren't you?"

"*Oui, mademoiselle.* I've already alerted him. He says to see you safely on the plane."

Miranda raised an eyebrow. "And you will. Just not yet. Take me back to Paris."

"Pascal said to—"

"Take. Me. Back. To Paris!" If she'd been a vampire, she knew her red rims would be blazing. "Now!"

Paul stood staring at her for a moment. "*Oui, mademoiselle.*"

***

From a distance, Blu watched the limo leave, then drove his car to where Miranda had been. Wearing his Fedora and sunglasses, he exited his car and inspected the road. Lifting one of the metal shards, he felt its heat—her energy signature easily readable to him. Reaching in his pocket, he retrieved a smooth black stone with an eagle carving an Indian shaman had given him long ago. "Your powers are increasing, Miranda." Good! He smiled. They would have to become even stronger...if he was ever going to free a friend from a watery grave.

Then, those who had long opposed him would learn the true meaning of vampire justice.

***

Bastien woke in his cell with the mother of all migraines. He could smell the dank, musty air and knew he was deep underground near the river. Whatever they hit him with felt like they had fractured his skull. When he tried to rub his sore head, he discovered his arms chained to the wall. He could heal very quickly, but even Bluebloods felt pain when the affliction was severe enough. When his captor entered his cell, he snorted, "Well, Caltrone, I should have known only you would stoop so low. Have you forgotten all the rules of guest protocol?"

"Ah, but my dear Sebastien de Rosemont, you have forgotten that," Caltrone sneered as he walked farther into the cell, "you have forsaken your titles and privileges when you became a member of Valadon's court."

Bastien gritted his teeth. "The same rules apply!"

"The rules, perhaps, but not the privileges. In either case, I would not worry much. Negotiations are underway for your release. I should not think it will be much longer. Enjoy your stay...while you are still able." Caltrone gazed back at the door and extended his arm. "I've brought you a visitor to keep you entertained in the interim."

The door opened, and a woman of intense beauty walked in, carrying a metal rod. Isabelle smirked up at him. Her dark hair and eyes were similar to his; her complexion just as fair, but the icy calculation in her eyes was what had always separated them.

"Isabelle."

"Hello, brother." Smiling, she thrust the hot poker deep into his stomach.

***

After briefly transforming into his human form to read the text that Miranda had sent concerning Pascal, Orion had stayed in his wolf form until he found a secluded area where he could change without freaking out any tourists. As liberal as Paris was, he didn't think the Parisians would appreciate a naked man running around in a heavily populated area. *Yeah, that would do wonders for my career!* He grimaced. Following the car had been tough once they'd reached the city, and twice, he had nearly lost them, but with his wolf speed and sight, he'd been able to track them to the Catacombs. "How many men do you have?" he asked Pascal.

"We have a dozen, with another dozen standing by should there be need," Pascal said. "Your friend was quite stubborn about joining us."

"Miranda's like that." Orion snorted. "When do we go in?"

"Not yet. Our scouts have not yet reported in."

"When can we expect them to report?" Miranda asked as she joined them.

"Soon. The Catacombs are not to be traversed lightly. The section opened for tourists is nothing compared to the underground maze lying beneath."

Miranda snorted. "I may be able to help you there. I knew some art students who liked to party hearty in the Catacombs."

***

Bastien ground his molars in pain. "So, you've thrown in with Caltrone. Why am I *not* surprised?" He felt a combination of resignation and regret at his sister's choices. Even when they'd been younger, Isabelle had always made decisions that hurt the family and those closest to her. And for what? To further her own selfish pursuits.

"If you had had sense centuries ago, little brother, you would have done the same." Isabelle brought the hot poker close to Bastien's face. The stench of his burnt flesh still rent the air. "Flaubert said the same thing you did." Isabelle's eyes danced with delight. "Right before I gouged out his eyes." She seemed to reflect. "But I think he screamed louder than you...until the end; then, he didn't scream at all."

Bastien's nostrils flared. Flaubert had been one of Valadon's most trusted informants. He knew Isabelle had enjoyed torturing Flaubert before she eventually killed him, a fetish he was certain she had learned from Caltrone. "You're walking a very dark path, Isabelle. One that will only lead to misery. Can't you see that? Or has Vivienna blinded you to what you are becoming?" He had tried to reason with her, but to no avail. "Can't you see what Caltrone is?"

Isabelle ran her fingers along the stem of the poker. "I can see quite clearly. It's you, little brother, who has had his vision clouded." Isabelle's eyes glistened with confidence. "The Council here has the real power—not Valadon."

"You're a Blueblood—the same as me. Why would you sully yourself with the likes of Caltrone?"

Bastien breathed a sigh of relief when Isabelle put down the poker. However, the reprieve didn't last long when she slashed his face with her nails. "You were the one who deserted the family, Sebastien. Don't you dare question my motives when you, yourself, have shown little regard for our blood."

Never taking his eyes off Isabelle's darkened stare, Bastien braced himself when he saw her reaching for the poker. He knew there was no arguing with Isabelle. As always, she was going to do what she wanted, and no one was going to stop her.

He just hoped the damage wasn't too severe when the mists of deception cleared.

***

Following the trail of the wolf, Pascal moved steadily down into the Catacombs. Orion stopped to sniff the air and then continued downward. Pascal could hear voices below. When he recognized one, his smile widened. Caltrone. The Council member had long been suspected of several cases of duplicity, but had never been caught. That was about to change.

When his men were in position, Pascal gave the signal. His men quickly stormed the room. The fighting immediately erupted between his men and Caltrone's. But, when he searched for Caltrone, the vampire was nowhere to be found. The lion had escaped the hunter, yet again. Later, when the vampires were questioned, he knew they would deny any knowledge of Caltrone's involvement in Sebastien de Rosemont's abduction.

Pascal would stay on Caltrone's trail for as long as it took to get the justice his people sorely deserved.

***

Following Orion's trail, Miranda found where they were keeping Bastien. The scent of burning flesh rent the air. When they rushed into his cell, a woman flung out a fist in her direction. Miranda, her senses already heightened, quickly ducked. The wolf jumped high to clench the vampire's wrist in his jaws. He bit down hard as her scream reverberated around the room.

Using her powers, Miranda flicked her wrist, mentally releasing Bastien's chains, as Orion was brutally flung across the room, the impact shaking the walls. From the corner of her eye, she saw the injured Bastien, holding his side, crawling to Orion.

Fangs elongated, Isabelle lunged. Miranda created a fireball that quickly spread to her other hand, the flames growing with each of her breaths. She had never held fire with both hands and found the power seductive and exhilarating. Sensing her eyes turning black, she stared at Isabelle, daring the vampire to attack. *"Come and taste my darkness. I will show you a world you never dreamed of. A world from which you will never escape!"*

Eyes wide with terror, Isabelle hissed, then quickly turned and fled.

Miranda didn't know whose voice had just emanated from her mouth, but knew it wasn't hers. She had a moment to realize when you play with the darkness, sometimes, the darkness plays with you.

As the wolf lay on the ground panting in pain, Bastien knelt by him and soothed his fur, whispering words of encouragement. The look of sorrow in Bastien's eyes was heart-rending. Miranda gently ran her hands over Orion's back. Her body humming from her power, she used the heat from her hands to alleviate his pain and helped him heal.

Miranda exhaled. "I don't know about you guys, but I'm ready to go home."

Chapter Thirty-One

Safely inside Valadon's plane, Bastien discovered and cut out the implant in his hip. Grimacing, he quickly flushed the device down the jet's toilet. Shaking his head in bitterness, he knew only Josette could have inserted it. Shirtless, he checked his scars in the mirror and was glad his skin was quickly repairing itself. He wanted no reminder of Josette's duplicity or his sister's. Exhaling, he bowed his head in resigned disgust. He had suspected Josette's allegiance to Vivienna, but never imagined the depth of her treachery.

Bastien wondered if his parents were aware of his sister's alliances with certain Council members and their malevolent activities. He opened the satchel containing letters his father had Hugo deliver to the pilot. Some were for him, but one had been marked *Valadon* and sealed with wax containing his father's crest. Later, he'd read his letters. But, for now, he'd rejoin his friends.

Taking a seat facing the cot in the back of the plane, Bastien watched as Orion snuggled beside Miranda. "Just friends, huh?" The bed was designed for one person, but somehow, they managed to fit.

"Yeah, sometimes, she has real bad nightmares." Orion murmured, "We both do. It's no big; we just keep each other company." He rose up on one elbow as one arm draped protectively over Miranda's sleeping form.

Bastien leaned forward and whispered, "What does she have nightmares about?"

"Different things." Orion kept his voice low. "She hated being kidnapped and trapped in a cell by Brandon." He exhaled. "But the worst...the worst was the gift the HOL sent her—the head of her former lover." Orion stroked Miranda's hair. "Sometimes, she wakes up screaming."

When Bastien looked confused, Orion added, "Dane. He was my best friend. She told me the worst of the nightmares weren't about his death, but when he spoke to her in the dream... It felt so real to her, she thought he was still alive. Then, when she wakes and realizes it was only a dream—"

"Yeah, I can understand." Sighing, Bastien looked out the window. Flaubert had often visited him and his family while he'd been growing up. He could still hear his jovial voice and see the twinkling of Flaubert's eyes. "If you hadn't shown up when you did, I'm pretty sure *I'd* be having some pretty horrendous nightmares." He nodded to Orion. "Thanks, again."

"I'm sorry that happened to you." Orion tilted his head. "But having a relative do it, that's worse."

"Yeah." Not wanting to discuss his sister's cruelty, he said, "Try to get some sleep, wolf. We'll be in New York in a few hours.

"You, too, vamp. You look like you've been through hell."

"I'm a soldier. I'm trained to deal with pain." Bastien laid his head back against his seat and tried not to think of Josette, but images of their lovemaking flooded his mind and clawed his soul. "Did you ever have feelings for someone so much it almost hurts to think about them?"

"Yeah, of course. How do you think I write the songs I do? The rock songs are my biggest sellers, but my ballads get more hits than anything else."

Bastien had heard Orion sing and thought his voice soothing. "What do you think of Tiseira? I like her the best of all the female singers."

"She's hot, but c'mon, Weres have it over vamps when it comes to singing." Orion grinned. "No one howls like us."

"I beg your pardon," Bastien huffed. "Vampires can hit notes you can only dream of."

"We say the same thing about you."

Bastien tilted his head. "You know, you should play sometime at ValCorp. Valadon has parties and entertains many people from various businesses. I think he would like your music."

"I might. To tell the truth," he exhaled, "I'm getting tired of touring, even though that's where I make most of my money. I want to spend more time in New York." Orion carefully climbed over Miranda and went to the restroom. "Excuse me."

Bastien studied Miranda's face. She almost looked like she was having another nightmare—her brow began twitching, and her fingernails were digging into the cushion.

***

"The weather's getting a little fierce out there; please make sure you're strapped in." The pilot's voice buzzed in the cabin.

Remare barely glanced outside the window of his private plane at the pelting rain and lightning. He'd flown through bad weather before. But the storm hadn't passed as quickly as they had thought it would and seemed to be following them across the Atlantic. No worries; he had faith in his pilot. He continued reading through the data his informant had given him, memorizing names and places he would file away for future reference.

However, the turbulence was intensifying as they tried to outrace the storm. He had to hold his wineglass steady before it slipped off the table. When lightning struck too close for comfort, the plane dropped about twenty feet. The jet felt as if it was being ripped from the sky. Remare became concerned, his heart beating rapidly. His first reaction was to call Miranda, but what could he tell her? He quickly texted her, but didn't get past her name, when the plane shook violently from the force of the lightning.

"That last strike took out our right engine. Reykjavik Airport isn't far—" The pilot didn't get a chance to finish his statement when the lights went out, plunging the cabin in total darkness. Remare quickly switched his phone to camera mode and speedily photographed the data. If he didn't make it, at least Valadon would have the information he needed to deal with his enemies.

Another hit! Remare braced himself as the plane began plunging downward. The sounds of the alarms were deafening as the pilot tried desperately to control the plane.

***

Miranda tried to hold back the tears, but one slipped from her eye. She knew it was only a dream, but still her heart throbbed inside her chest. Remare would never fly out in such terrible weather like they had last night. He was too logical—too intelligent. When she opened her eyes, she saw Bastien watching her with sympathetic eyes. He leaned over and brushed away one of her tears with his finger.

"It was a bad dream." Rubbing her eyes, she sat up. "That's all. I'm fine."

"Orion told me you get them." Bastien looked concerned. "Are you sure you're okay? You look a little rattled."

"I'm fine. How much longer until we get to New York?"

Bastien glanced at his watch. "A couple more hours."

"I wanted to thank you again for helping Orion." At Bastien's confused look, she said, "When Vivienna slashed his throat. It scared the hell out of me. I didn't mean to raise my voice at you the way I did. You healed him." She exhaled. "Thank you."

Bastien shrugged the same way Orion did. "I was glad to do it. My father's the traditional one in the family. He had his concerns. Not many others know about the healing properties in a vampire's blood. We try to keep it secret. How'd you know?"

Miranda rubbed her cheek. "Mulciber slashed my face when I was in the archives. The first one down there was Remare. He used his saliva to close the wound. Later, when I was with Gabriel, he explained it to me."

One of the pilots opened the door and walked toward them. "I'm sorry, I have some bad news. Remare's plane went down over the Atlantic. The storm last night knocked out power, and we just now got word that—"

Miranda's world spun, and her heart beat frantically. "*No!* You're wrong! He can't be gone."

The pilot looked at her sympathetically. "I'm very sorry, but—"

Tears threatened to break free, and Miranda's lower lip trembled as she grasped her stomach. She hated, absolutely hated, her premonitions—they always came true. And, now, Remare was gone. "Oh, God! No!" Her voice sounded ragged even to her own ears.

"I'm sorry," the pilot repeated, "but you didn't let me finish my sentence. You misunderstood. Remare's pilot was able to land the plane at Reykjavik airport. He's fine. I heard Remare put up quite an argument when they told him the part they needed for the plane would take two days to arrive. When they told him the next flight was completely booked in first class, he refused to be seated in coach and chartered a flight out. He's already in New York. I'm sorry I alarmed you. I apologize."

Breathing deeply, Miranda waved off the pilot, who whispered something to Bastien then left. When she glanced up at Bastien, he was slanting her a look.

Orion exited the bathroom. "Why all the grim faces? Miranda, are you okay?"

Still grasping her stomach, she said, "Peachy," and gave him the thumbs up.

Bastien leaned forward toward Miranda. "Pilot says the weather is good flying into New York. With the wind currents, we shall be there in two point four hours."

"Great. I'm starving." Orion walked to the kitchenette. "Is there anything to eat in here?"

"Yes, there should be some sandwiches in the mini-fridge." Bastien continued studying Miranda. "You sure you're okay. I didn't expect you would...react so strongly."

She tried to brush it off. "I just don't want Valadon mad at me because I made his second come all the way to Paris."

Bastien smiled. "I'm sure he won't be. Besides, Remare had business in London. He didn't come just for you."

Closing her eyes, Miranda exhaled.

"There's ham and Swiss, turkey with lettuce and tomato, and roast beef with Russian dressing."

"No, thanks. I'm not hungry." Still shaken from her nightmare, she didn't think she could keep anything down. "You go ahead. I'll get something when we touch down in New York."

"Are you sure?" Orion took a bite of the roast beef. "I'm starving."

"Yeah, I'm sure. Go ahead." When Bastien offered her a glass of wine, she gladly accepted it.

Chapter Thirty-Two

Smiling, Miranda walked down the hall to the high lord's office. His scent of cool night breezes lingered in the air, making her skin tingle. There wasn't a vampire on the planet who was as alluring as Valadon. With his dark hair, penetrating green eyes and sculpted cheekbones, he could spellbound anyone. She wondered if there would ever come a time when he didn't affect her the way he did. Although her body reacted in ways that unsettled her, Valadon didn't own her heart. That she kept for another. "We need to talk."

"Miranda, it's good to see you, again." Even his melodic voice was mesmerizing. "I'm glad you made it home safely."

"So am I." She accepted his embrace. "Though Orion almost lost a chunk of his vocal cords." Miranda held his outstretched hand as he led her to the sofa in his sitting area. She liked his subterranean office better than his penthouse office. The lack of windows was comforting. She glanced at the mood screen. "Something new?"

"Yes. I find it relaxing. You can see the stars at night without being outdoors." Valadon went to the bar. "Would you like a drink?"

"Just water." Having drunk nearly half a bottle of wine on the plane, her throat was dry.

"As we speak, the Degas is being unpacked and hung in my upstairs office." Handing her a glass of water, Valadon sat beside her. "You will have to come see it when they are finished."

"I will." Relaxing, Miranda studied his eyes. Small talk was never her thing. She decided to cut to the chase. "It wasn't just the painting you wanted, was it?"

"No. But I think you know that by now." Valadon quietly exhaled. "Remare advised telling you the risks involved before you left. I thought it more prudent if you didn't know."

Miranda narrowed her eyes. "You should have told me."

"No." Valadon shook his head. "It was safer if you didn't know. Some of the old-world vampires excel at entering the minds of humans." Valadon pushed a strand of hair from her face. "You wouldn't have even known they were there."

Miranda wasn't so sure, but she wasn't about to tell Valadon that. She looked away. "I met your old girlfriend, Vivienna. Interesting woman."

"That she is." Valadon waved a hand in the air. "And very powerful and influential with our High Court. I heard you attended a party in her home."

"Yes, and I met a man named Caltrone who didn't seem to take a shine to me. He was very curious about you, though." Miranda's voice turned accusatory. "The night I left for Paris, you had photographers waiting for us when we left Le Cirque. The people in Paris knew me before I even arrived." She paused then met his eyes. "That was your plan all along."

Valadon nodded once, and Miranda was half-tempted to slap him. "As well as procuring a painting for me, I wanted to know who would seek you out. You were never in any danger, Miranda. My people kept constant surveillance on you. Except, of course, when you decided to elude my men for some personal time."

"My time *is* personal, Valadon. No one likes being used."

As Valadon stared at her, she had difficulty reading him. His emotions were far more complex and multifarious than anyone else she had ever met.

"Would an apology soothe your wounded heart?"

"An apology and *the truth* would go a long way in bridging our differences."

Valadon rose and stepped away. "The truth is not always pleasant, Miranda," he paused to exhale, "and it is often quite more complex and undesired than expected."

"Try me." Miranda glared at him. "I think I've earned it."

Valadon leaned against his desk and seemed to study her. After a while, he spoke. "While you were on your sojourn in New Mexico, rumors started surfacing of dissention directed at me by the Euro Council." The high lord crossed his arms. "Their economy has suffered greatly in the last few years and whispers pointed at a potential merger between ValCorp and the European industries." His brow furrowed, he looked directly at her. "That is something I will *never* allow to happen. ValCorp is my lifeline. I've worked for centuries to build her, and my people depend on me to keep her vital and autonomous."

"Why involve me?" Miranda angled her head. "My knowledge of economics is close to nil."

Valadon smiled. "That is precisely the reason I chose you. Many on the European Council know my people and evaded their attempts at discovering who is at the head of those rumors. And my people are *very* good at infiltration." He tilted his head. "You, however, are an unknown—an enigma—and the Europeans love a good puzzle."

"What exactly were you hoping I'd find out?"

"I needed to know who has been conspiring against me so I could prevent what they want to happen. I expected people to approach you with questions...and they did. The fact that you didn't have the answers they wanted is what kept you safe."

"I was angry when I realized you were using me as a lure." Miranda rose and walked to him. "But I was just a distraction, wasn't I? With everyone focused on me, Bastien could meet secretly with your people. And, with Orion doing guard duty, Bastien was free to meet with your contacts. That's why you agreed to have Orion on this mission."

Valadon smirked. "Lizandra threatened to use her piano tuner on me in a very uncomfortable place if I didn't agree to have Orion accompany you. She originally insisted on three of her people. We agreed one would be sufficient."

"Orion's popularity is growing. They knew who he was in Paris."

"Yes, and that worked in your favor. With you cavorting with him in the most public of places, you had the Europeans wondering who you were truly involved with."

Miranda rubbed her bottom lip with her thumb. "You play dangerous games, Valadon."

"I have to." Valadon nodded. "It's how I, and my people, stay alive."

She considered his words. "So, did you find out everything you wanted to know?"

"Not everything, but the investigation is ongoing. At least, now, my people have directions to go in."

"I met a few unsavory types, but the one who concerned me most was Caltrone. What does he want with you?"

"Caltrone is one of the ruling members of our High Court. He will do whatever is necessary to safeguard the interests of the Council, as well as his own. He covets ValCorp. He thinks if I allocate funds into his industries, it will help save their economy." Valadon shook his head. "It will not be enough, I'm afraid. I warned them years ago they were on the wrong path, but their greed dictated their actions."

"But don't you already tithe to them a vast amount of money?" Miranda remembered Valadon discussing his role as Minister of Finance when he gave her the tour of his archives.

"Yes, but it's only a fraction of what they need."

"Can't you serve as advisor of some sort?"

"I have advised several members. Some of the vampires have planned long term, like Lord Rosemont," Valadon smiled. "But some were more interested in short-term goals and invested unwisely. There is nothing I can do now to save them. Fortunes have already been lost."

Miranda wasn't going to pretend to understand all the nuances of the economic world. "I'll leave the finances to you. What about Vivienna? She was very much interested in you and asked several questions about you, ValCorp and your Torians." Miranda glanced downward. "She was relentless with her questions."

Valadon's eyes narrowed. "What did she want to know?"

"Everything." Miranda scoffed. "I told her to check social media. She wanted more. As I only know the basics about ValCorp, she was very disappointed in me. She thinks we're lovers."

"Yes." Valadon smiled. "A great many people believe that."

Miranda stared up at him and sensed he wasn't being completely honest with her. "Are there any other games you're playing I should know about?"

Valadon laughed. "Suspicious, now, are you?"

He didn't answer her question. She'd let that go, for now. "How could you have been involved with Vivienna? She's such a viper."

"I was much younger, then. And...she caught me at a vulnerable point in my life." Valadon's eyes drifted away from her. "It was before I called America home. This territory was remote, but even then, I saw the potential."

"Valadon. Let me ask you a personal question." Miranda wasn't going to tell him about the erotic paintings of him, Vivienna and Remare. Like Remare said, it was the past, and they weren't who they had once been. But there was one painting that had piqued her curiosity.

"Of course." Valadon gestured with his hand. "You can ask me anything."

Miranda wondered if that meant he would answer truthfully. "By any chance...do you have any children?"

"Do you mean made vampires?"

"Like Gabriel?"

"Yes, a few here in New York and some throughout the world. But I don't consider them children. They were turned a long time ago. Gabriel was the only one I ever considered a son."

Miranda was surprised. Valadon had never mentioned that to her when she worked at ValCorp. She wasn't sure how Gabriel thought of Valadon. At times, Gabriel appeared detached, other times—conflicted. She peered up at Valadon. "I meant have you ever had any naturally born children?"

"No. I never had any children." Valadon seemed remorseful. "Conception between vampires is a complicated matter. Many female vampires can't hold a child to term. And most vampires lose the ability to procreate after the first few centuries. Otherwise, the world would be populated with vampires. Only male Bluebloods retain the ability to have children for longer periods of time."

"You were with Vivienna a long time; isn't she a Blueblood?"

"Miranda, where are you going with these questions?"

She rose and began pacing. "While I was in her home, I saw a portrait of a child who couldn't be more than eight or nine. He was dressed in the fashions of the early seventeenth century." She looked back at him. "He had your features. Your bone structure, the curve of your lips and your emerald eyes. I thought he was your son."

Valadon threw his head back and laughed. "You thought Vivienna and I conceived a child together? I assure you that is not possible." Valadon shook his head. "She was too old by the time I met her and well past the age of conception. And, if by some miracle she had conceived, she would *not* have waited four hundred years to inform me. Vivienna would have used the child mercilessly to get what she wanted."

Not if she really loved the boy. Miranda shrugged. She believed Valadon and considered Vivienna had wanted her to see the painting and that she'd been set up. She rose.

"By the way, I ran into a blond woman in a shop who said to give you her regards." At his inquisitive look, she said, "Lisa, no, Lysette. Friend of yours?"

One corner of his mouth lifted. "Perhaps."

When no further explanation appeared forthcoming, she said, "All right, I'm tired, jet lagged, and I want to go home. Let me grab Orion, and we'll be on our way."

"There's a car waiting for you in the garage." He walked her to his door. "I've already taken steps to make restitution to Orion."

"Oh, I don't think—"

"I don't like people getting hurt on my behalf. I'll let him tell you when he sees you."

"Fine, where is he?"

"The last I saw, he was shooting pool with Bastien and the others." Valadon played with a strand of her hair. "What did you think of the photographs of us together?" He smirked. "Handsome couple, don't you think?"

Miranda rolled her eyes. "Yes, we were once a happy couple. Never again. Good night, Valadon."

She heard his seductive, melodious voice laughing in her mind. *"Never say never."*

Chapter Thirty-Three

"Oh, Katya, I got what you asked me for." Halfway down the hall to Remare's apartment, Miranda ran into Katya coming out of her room.

"Great! Come inside." Katya closed the door after them.

Miranda searched her bag, then handed Katya her package and stood staring at her collection of tiny glass bottles. The vampire had been collecting for centuries. "I met *Monsieur* Chagall; he said he made this one specifically for you."

"Thank you. Chagall rarely posts his best pieces online." Katya sighed with delight when she unwrapped the shiny black bottle with the intricate silver meshing and held it up to the light.

"It's a work of art and looks almost like a Faberge egg." Miranda smiled. "I thought so when he showed it to me in his shop."

"Yes, it does. It's exquisite. Thank you, again. This means a lot to me. I know you must have been very busy in Paris, but I'm glad you made time to do this for me."

Miranda shrugged. "I always bring back a few things for my friends. I'm glad you like it."

Smiling, Katya tilted her head. "Perhaps, someday, I can repay your thoughtfulness."

"It's not necessary." Miranda shook her head. "I love shopping in the out-of-the-way places. It was fun discovering Chagall's shop."

After leaving Katya, Miranda walked down to Remare's rooms and breathed deeply. The closer she got, the more her spine tingled in anticipation. She wondered if her body would always respond in such a way. When she reached his door, she hesitated in knocking. Grinning, she remembered another time when she walked in on another vampire pulling up his pants. She knocked, and when she heard Remare's voice say enter, she opened the door and walked in.

Immediately, she was not in a happy place.

"Ah, Miranda, it's good to see you," Remare said, dressed only in a black silk robe and trousers. He was closing the clasp on a diamond necklace with a ruby in the center around Irina's throat.

She looked at him and then Irina, who slyly smiled as she fingered the ruby. "If you're busy, I can come back another time." Her blood turned cold at the sinful symbolism of the ruby.

"Nonsense." Remare rubbed his hands together. "Irina was just leaving, and I am eager to hear about your trip."

Miranda kept her breathing even as Irina walked by and closed the door behind her. Her Dark Angel was seething in rage. *"Run after the bitch and yank the diamond necklace for yourself."* The Light Angel reminded her, *"Valadon once gave you a necklace of priceless black diamonds."* No contest, the Dark Angel had this one.

"Nice gift." Miranda crossed her arms and leaned her shoulder against the wall. "I'm sure she earned it." Hearing the snark in her voice, she could have kicked herself.

Remare poured himself a drink. "Do not begrudge Irina a trinket of my esteem. She just completed a difficult mission." He gestured with the carafe in his hand.

Miranda shook her head. She'd had enough wine on the plane and was still feeling the effects. She glanced back at the door.

"If you had come a moment sooner, you would have heard what I said before I gave her the necklace." At her raised eyebrows, he continued, "I told her it was not possible for me to give her my heart, but she had...one small piece." Nonchalantly, he waved his hand in the air. "That is the symbolism of the ruby, Miranda—nothing else." Remare smiled wickedly at her. "So, you don't have to run after her and try to snatch the necklace from her throat."

Damn! Miranda glanced downward. She had forgotten how easily he could read her mind.

Remare walked toward her and stroked her arm. "You have far more than she ever will. And, one day, I will give you a gift of far more value." The combination of his sexy voice and tender touch sent a ripple of pleasure through her.

Miranda shook off the sensation. She was still smarting from Irina's cold smile. "Remare, I have a good life. I have a job I love, friends I adore. If you want to give your girlfriend a diamond necklace, that's your business."

His face darkened. "Irina is not my girlfriend. We have not been involved in quite some time."

"Really?!" Miranda walked away from him. "I can remember a few days ago in the shower room when she was on her knees in front of you."

"Nothing happened then, and nothing's happened for a good long while." He smiled with male smugness. "You're jealous."

She opened her mouth to tell him he was way off, but that would have been futile. Vampires could sense human emotions as well as Weres.

"I like that you're jealous, even though you need not be." Remare's voice deepened. "I have no plans to be with another woman, Mir-randa. No other woman interests me...the way you do."

She didn't know what to make of his comments. Instead, she focused on the reason she was there. "Do you have a very sharp knife, one that's razor sharp?

"I have several knives, but why would you need one?" Remare went to one of his dressers and retrieved a black lacquered box with Asian characters carved on the top. Facing her, he opened a drawer containing several knives with jade handles.

She chose a blade thin as a scalpel. *Perfect.* "I need you to do something for me."

Remare placed the box down. "If you are planning on using that on me, I assure you—"

His words cut off as Miranda handed him the knife, then slowly pulled the zipper down on her dress and lowered the front to reveal her breasts. Remare stood speechless, then met her eyes. "They are exquisite—with or without the adornments." Humor made his eyes glint. "I didn't think you went in for piercings."

"A gift from your *other* girlfriend, Vivienna." Miranda's fists tightened on her hips. "She doesn't give information away for free. This was her price for what I was able to learn. I tried to take them out myself, but she has little— and I can't believe I'm saying this—*booby traps*, in them." Miranda covered herself with her hands and turned away from him. "She would have exacted far more...had I let her."

Remare tried to hold back his laugh. "Vivienna would have played with you. She would never have revealed anything she did not wish to divulge." He took her hand and led her to his sofa. "Come sit."

Miranda wasn't so sure. Vivienna had enjoyed playing cat and mouse with her too much. "You're probably right, but Valadon did send me there for information, and I wanted to know more." She looked down at her nipple rings. "Can you cut them out? Use your saliva to close the wounds?" Miranda exhaled deeply. "I considered going to a hospital, but I didn't want stitches, and then, I thought of

Lizandra, but she probably would have laughed her ass off and left them in as a reminder of my stupidity."

"Why didn't you ask Valadon to take them out?"

"Because that was exactly Vivienna's point. She wanted him to see the mark she left. I think I embarrassed myself enough." She looked at him. "Will you take them out? Please?"

Remare scrutinized the rings and went to touch the ball on the side.

"No! Don't!" Miranda grabbed his wrist. "If you turn the ball, tiny blades shoot out of the shaft." Miranda exhaled. "I know; I tried."

"Vivienna always did enjoy her amusements." Remare examined her nipple rings. "I can make a tiny incision on top. You will not need stitches."

"Great." Miranda breathed deeply. "Do it. I want these out as fast as possible."

Remare eyed her. "If I do this, I'll want answers, Miranda. Agreed?"

"Agreed. Just get them out."

When Remare shifted the knife toward her, she gasped and grabbed his arm. "Stop. Sorry, I just needed a moment." He repeated his motion, and again, Miranda flinched and grasped his wrist. After the third time of halting him, Remare exhaled. "If you keep jerking your body, I will not be able to take them out. You have to remain still."

"If someone was coming at you with a knife and aiming for your penis, wouldn't you react?"

Remare smirked. "I would not allow someone that close to my cock with a weapon of any kind."

Trying to calm down, Miranda steadied her breaths. As he moved closer, she grabbed his wrist. "This isn't working." She looked around his room and up at his bed. She remembered his headboard had slats. "You're going to have to restrain me."

He followed her up the two steps to his bedroom.

"Do you have any ties or scarves you can use to restrain my hands?"

Smirking, he retrieved two navy ties. "Sorry, all out of gray."

Miranda glared at him. "Har, har!" She removed her boots and was relieved when she realized his bed was neatly made without any wrinkles or mixed scents.

When she leaned against the headboard, Remare lightly tied one wrist and fastened it to his headboard. "Of all possible scenarios of having you in my bed, this is not one of them." He then tied her other wrist.

"I never thought to be here." Her heart fluttered at the heat in his eyes.

"Are you ready?'

"Yes. Just be careful."

"Do not doubt my abilities. I've done surgery on countless soldiers in battle and removed shrapnel much larger than this. I think I can remove something this miniscule."

The fact she was in bed with Remare wasn't lost on Miranda. Her heart racing, she inhaled his magnificent woodland scent and felt soothed. Staring at his eyes, she tried not to focus on the knife in his hand. When he glanced down, she twisted her head to the side and tightened the muscles in her arms and fists. Gritting her teeth, she tried to restrain her gasp.

"Try to relax. Breathe."

His hypnotic voice had a calming effect. Miranda closed her eyes and tried to slow her heartrate. There was a slight sting, then she felt his mouth on her breast and the touch of his tongue as he closed the wound. Instantly, her back arched. When she looked down he held the ring in his palm, then he placed it on the bedside table.

He met her eyes. "Did I hurt you?"

"No." She shook her head. "I barely felt the knife cutting me."

Remare smiled. His voice was sultry. "Then, try to relax. One more."

Miranda tried to remain quiet as he cut her. When Remare dipped his head to her breast, she used her *Elemental* powers to slowly undo her binding. Her hand drifted to the back of his head. She liked massaging his neck and ran her fingers through his hair. He looked up at her with hungry eyes and then turned his attention back to her nipple. But, this time, his tongue lingered longer.

His lips brushed the top of her breast. He glanced at her and gently kissed her palm. Untying the other hand, he said, "Interesting abilities you have."

"I know." Miranda's heart beat rapidly, and she knew she shouldn't let her feelings for Remare surface. He'd told her he couldn't have her—he wouldn't go against Valadon—but in this private moment, she wanted him.

By the way he was looking at her, she knew he wanted her, as well. And that's why she moved her legs to the opposite side of the bed. "Thanks." She put her boots back on, and when she tried to stand, she wobbled. Remare caught her before she fell.

"Whoa. Woozy there." She grasped his arms to steady herself. "I didn't eat much on the plane, and I think I'm jetlagged."

Remare kept his arms around her and then gently lowered her to the bed. "Stay for a while."

When she looked at him apologetically, he said, "I have rounds to make and you'll be perfectly safe here. No one will bother you."

After tossing off his robe, he grabbed a black shirt from the closet. His body was beautiful. All lean muscle. Some men bulked up to proportions that looked too superficial, but Remare's physique was naturally toned. His muscles moved fluidly, and she enjoyed watching him as he dressed. "I'll only close my eyes for a few minutes."

"Take as much time as you need." Remare caressed her hand and sat beside her. "When I come back, I'll take you home." He moved a strand of her hair away from her face and kissed her forehead. "I'm glad you came to me tonight."

"Me, too."

After he left, she turned her head into his pillow and inhaled his scent. She smiled in sensual bliss as a gentle veil of darkness blanketed her, whispering she was safe.

***

Remare joined the others in the living area and nodded his approval as he observed the Torians. Orion was playing pool with Bastien against Tristan and Katya. The Were seemed comfortable in his new surroundings, and Remare wondered if Orion had accepted Valadon's offer. He stroked his chin with his thumb and thought Bastien could use a new partner because he planned on sending Gregori out on more missions with Irina.

As he passed the kitchen, he considered bringing Miranda some food, but knew she needed her sleep. When he entered the communications room, he found Aiden. "Have we had any more transmissions from Europe?"

"No. Everything's been quiet."

Too quiet! Remare checked his phone, again. There was one message from his friend, Pascal, in Paris. He pressed the button to retrieve the message.

"Remare, Flaubert was found dead tonight. Earlier, he was searching the Catacombs as instructed. His body had been tortured and his spinal cord severed. Flaubert was a

good man, careful in his movements. Before he died, he was able to turn his cell phone on, and one of my men was able to track it. I think you should hear the transmission."

Remare heard Pascal turn on the device. *"He's one of Valadon's. Well, we can't have him reporting our private sanctuary, can we?" Another voice said, "I'll take care of it. Sweet dreams! Say hello to Savinien at the bottom of the Seine."*

There was a pause, and Remare could hear something falling to the ground. *"Really, Brandon, your sense of humor leaves much to be desired."* Remare's blood turned to ice. *"Savinien could use the company. He's been at the bottom of the Seine for centuries. I'm sure his bones would welcome a new visitor. You need to enjoy life more, Caltrone. Shall we visit that café you like so much?"*

Pascal's report continued. *"Flaubert's body was found floating in the Seine. Whoever dumped his body didn't properly weigh it down, as if they were in a hurry or afraid of being discovered. I think we should wait before sending any others to investigate. Let us stake out the area, and I will report to you who's been seen entering and leaving."*

Remare texted him back to proceed with all caution. He sighed deeply. Flaubert had been a good friend for centuries; he should not have died so callously. Remare would track Brandon down if it was the last thing he did. "Do all of our subsidiaries have the latest technology?"

Aiden looked up from the monitor. "As far as I know. What's up?"

"Find out for certain, then make sure our contacts in Paris have the best surveillance equipment available." Near the door, he turned toward Aiden. "A friend of mine was killed tonight. I don't want another dying, as well." Remare left to inform Valadon they finally knew of Brandon's whereabouts.

Miranda had been right, after all, he grimaced. Her instincts were unusually perceptive for a human, and he wondered what had set her off. He would discuss this with her. But, first, he would meet with Valadon.

When he heard Valadon's voice, he entered his rooms. "I've had a transmission from Paris I think you should hear. Miranda was correct, and Brandon is in Paris...or he was at the time of the transmission."

When Valadon looked up at him, his eyes were blazing. "I've had a transmission, as well, you might find interesting." When Remare took a seat facing his desk, Valadon pressed a button on his phone.

"Don't bother with trying to trace this call. I won't be on long enough. It's been so long I hope you haven't forgotten me. Flaubert was such a good friend of yours. Now, he sleeps in a silent grave. Pity. I always liked him. I bet you're wondering who's next. Keep your Torians close, Valadon. I plan to make a trip to New York very soon. Au revoir.*"

"There's only a few select people who have my private number." Valadon swiveled in his chair. "Any bets whose voice that was?"

Remare shook his head. "We can run it through the voice identification equipment and see who comes up a match." Remare didn't like seeing Valadon's solemn look, but he had information the high lord needed to hear. "I've had a transmission where Brandon was meeting with Caltrone. Brandon killed Flaubert."

Valadon sighed. "That wasn't Brandon's voice."

"I know. I've been trying to place it. I will run it through our equipment." Remare played him Pascal's transmission.

Valadon didn't say anything as he listened intently with his fingertips tapping together. Then, he looked up and said, "Find out whose voice that is. Then, report directly to me."

"I'll have Aiden personally work on it. Should we send more of our people to Paris?"

"Not yet. Let's see what we find out first. If Brandon was there, there's a good chance he's already gone."

Maybe, Remare thought as he bowed and left.

In the communications room, Aiden said, "We'll run it through, but it could take hours before we have a match. I'll let you know as soon as we have results."

"Make it a priority." After relaying the information to Valadon, Remare returned to his room.

Chapter Thirty-Four

Miranda woke moments before hearing Remare quietly enter and move around in his apartment. Feeling the mattress dip, she cracked an eyelid as he loosened his shirt at his neck and lie back against the headboard. Miranda could hear her heart beating heavily and feel her stomach flip-flopping as it usually did when he was near. Remare was one of the handsomest vampires she'd ever met, and ValCorp had its plethora of gorgeous men. But he was also a dangerous assassin, one of the reasons she had stayed away from him.

Even though his bedroom was dimly lit, she could see him clearly. When his hand casually drifted to rest on her backside, she smiled. Hardly a grope, it was more the familiar touch of a man comfortable being with his partner. For too long, Miranda felt like she'd been drifting in a freezing snowstorm and somehow had wandered into his cave seeking shelter. Remare was like a sleeping bear, but instead of slashing her with his powerful claws for her transgression, he offered her safety and the soothing warmth of his body.

She'd been in other people's caves who welcomed her with friendship, but none of them ever gave her what she felt with Remare.

"I'm awake." Her voice sounded throaty. "I just wanted to rest for a few minutes longer before heading out."

Remare quickly removed his hand. Immediately, she felt the cold absence of his touch. "Take your time. Orion is enjoying himself playing pool with the others, and Valadon is in his office."

Gazing up at him, Miranda bunched the pillow under her. "You know what I was dreaming about? I keep picturing how great it would be if we could take your boat and go north to The Cloisters." She exhaled. "I've seen a lot of your world, the violence and the bloodshed. I'd like to show you something of my world. Something a little less dangerous. The history and the art there are beautiful."

Relaxing into the pillows, Remare studied her then spoke softly. "If that is what you want, then that is what we will do."

"Let's wait for an overcast day." She smiled. "The summer is too hot with the blazing sun and too crowded with tourists. I like the fall better when the leaves are changing colors and the air is cooler."

"I can tolerate some sunlight, but autumn is better." Remare turned and looked tenderly at her. "My world isn't always so dangerous, Mir-randa." Sorrow etched his face as he exhaled. "It is unfortunate you've seen the worst of it." He moved a strand of hair from her face. "We are a strong house full of loyalty and laughter. When Bianca, Nick's mother, was alive, the mood of this place was far more jovial. You haven't seen that part."

Miranda was often transfixed at the life-sized portrait of Bianca in the archives and wondered what she'd been like. There were times when it felt like she was whispering to her, but Miranda could never make out the words. "I've seen beauty here. The love Morel and Cyra shared, I see it with Aiden and Bree. I've seen it in the way Valadon looks at his people. I know love exists here."

"You've also seen the darker parts." He stroked her cheek. "You never should have been allowed so close that it touched you so."

Miranda covered his hand with hers. "It was my choice. I chose to work for Valadon." She smiled. "I loved working with Nick in the archives."

Remare chuckled. "He misses you. I've heard him groaning a thousand times the work would have gone much faster had you been there with him."

"I've missed him, too." Turning on her side, she flexed her feet. "With all that's been happening with the Paris trip, I haven't had time to have a real conversation with him."

Remare turned his body toward hers. "We should talk about Paris. I know you're an independent woman, Mirranda, but it was dangerous of you to go off by yourself."

She shrugged. "Nothing happened. I was perfectly safe."

"You should have waited for your bodyguards. That's why we hired them. For your protection."

"Is that why you came to Paris?" She stroked his hand. "For my protection?"

Lips thinning, Remare slowly exhaled. "You said you sensed Brandon. You half-convinced me he was there."

Miranda felt guilty for having believed Brandon was in Paris and making Remare travel across the Atlantic. "I was *so* sure he was there." Still holding his hand, she massaged his knuckles with her thumb. "I'm sorry you made the journey for nothing."

"I'm not, Miranda. I was able to complete some necessary work and see for myself you were unharmed. But what was it that had you so certain Brandon was in Paris?"

Letting go of his hand, she turned on her back. She didn't want to tell him about her dreams and how they were like premonitions. Her gifts of being an *Elemental* were scary enough, but he deserved the truth. "I dreamed of you in Paris."

One corner of his mouth slowly lifted. "I hope it was a thoroughly erotic dream where I made passionate love to you," he teased.

His seductive voice made her toes curl. Oh, if he only knew! "It was. Remare, have you ever had a dream, that when you're dreaming, it feels *so* real you believe you're awake? You see things so clearly, hear voices so distinct you believe the dream is real?" She faced him. "But, just before I woke, you turned to me and told me Brandon was in Paris. It seemed so real, I can still hear your words echoing in my ears. It scared the hell out of me."

Remare hesitated, then said, "You were right, Miranda. Brandon *was* in Paris while you were there."

She quickly sat up. "Where? Was he the one following me?"

"You sensed Brandon following you?!"

"I sensed a shadow. I couldn't make out who it was. I just had this feeling someone was following me."

"And you didn't tell me or Bastien this?"

Miranda snorted. "I didn't want you to think I was certifiable. You didn't seem to believe me when I told you I thought Brandon was there. Where is he, now?"

"We don't know. We have our people scouring the city for him." Remare sat up and faced her. "We *will* find him, Miranda." He clasped her hand. "There are just so many places he can hide."

Nodding, she slowly averted her eyes. When Remare lifted her chin, she saw a side to him he rarely showed anyone. She knew how he was feeling because she was feeling it, too. She exhaled slowly. Over the past few months, she had thought about him. Even when she had been with Gabriel, memories of being with Remare had surfaced. She'd convinced herself he was too dark, too dangerous—even though she had sensed something very human about him.

Valadon had scared her, overwhelmed her with his hunger, his inherent power. She'd never once felt overwhelmed with Remare. His body hummed in cadence with hers, arousing feelings long buried. Deep within her soul, an ache awakened that Miranda had been determined to keep protected. Remare could reach that ache, soothe her where no one else ever could. And that's what made him dangerous. If she was being honest with herself, she knew it had never been about him being an assassin. He did what was necessary to protect his people.

She had convinced herself Remare could only desire another vampire; a human woman wouldn't hold his interest. She had wanted to believe he had scorching sex with Irina, but knew now that wasn't the case. Her fears had dictated her decisions. Remare had terrified her by making her feel vulnerable; she'd convinced herself there was no way they could ever be together.

Lizandra had once told her she purposely chose men who were safe. Men who couldn't or wouldn't commit when, in fact, Miranda was the one who couldn't commit because she didn't want to feel that dizzying, devastating feeling of vulnerability.

Gazing into Remare's hunger-filled eyes, she realized he'd had the same fears. Only he hid it behind his loyalty to Valadon. Pressing a hand to his chest, she pushed him to the bed. "Brandon isn't the only one who's been hiding." She bent down and brushed a tender kiss to his lips, the barest of touches, and felt him stiffen at her gentle touch.

"Miranda, don't." She watched his eyes darken as he shook his head. "This can't be."

She took his hand in hers. "Valadon rules ValCorp and his house. But he has no dominion here." She waved a hand around his apartment. "These are your rooms, your bed, and what's between you and me he cannot touch."

Remare's voice was a raspy whisper. "You have no idea what he's capable of."

Miranda remembered how Valadon had once had her flat on her back in his penthouse office. "I don't fear him. I know he cares about me, and I care about him, but it doesn't touch what I'm feeling, now."

"You should fear him." Remare's voice was heavy with emotion as his thumb brushed her cheek. "He still desires you. I had hoped in these passing months, his feelings for you would have abated. They have not."

She knew Remare's loyalty to Valadon was born of centuries of friendship and fealty. Regrettably, she would not cross him. Smiling, she rubbed her cheek against his hand and noticed his sapphire and gold ring. "A sword and star."

He glanced at his ring. "Yes, my family's sigil. I have worn it for centuries."

Miranda met his eyes, resolve laced her voice. "If we can't be intimate, Remare, I still want your friendship. Whatever it is between us," the attraction too intense between them, "it's too real to deny."

"Friendship I can give you." He kissed her hand. "I want you in my life, Miranda. I want to work with you, again." His eyes glinted. "It gives me pleasure to have you by my side."

Impulsively, Miranda kissed him hard and fast, then swung her legs over the bed and zipped her boots. She felt Remare lift the zipper of her dress. "Don't zip it all the way. Let my skin breathe a little. The nipsters are still a little sensitive." She nearly laughed when she heard his growl.

Miranda glanced at the leather cylinder in the corner. "You remembered my painting. Thank you for bringing it here. Did they give you a hard time at customs?"

Remare gave her an insulted look. "Miranda, please. Customs wouldn't dare question my authority."

"Did you look at it?" She pulled the canvas from the leather carrier and unrolled it.

"Yes, curiosity got the better of me, and I opened it. The girl in the painting is you, isn't it? Even though you're in profile, I recognized it as you by the colors of your hair. It's a beautiful painting."

"My mentor, Monsieur Dourdain, painted it for me."

"He was quite fond of you. You can tell by the way he painted he was quite taken with you. He left you a letter." At her curious look, Remare pointed to the cylinder. "It's at the bottom. And before you ask—no, I did not read it."

Miranda opened the bottom and took out the envelope.

My dear Miranda. If you are reading this letter, you know I've passed on. Try not to be too disappointed with me. I know I promised you Lavender Dreams, *but months ago, a woman came to me and asked to see my work. When her eyes lighted on* Dreams, *she offered me a ridiculous amount of money for it. When I still declined her offer, she doubled the amount. I tried to dissuade her and showed her other works, but she would have no other.*

I had hoped to make a copy of the painting, but my time here is coming to an end. I've always wanted to live near the sea, and now, I have the means. Be happy with your painting, Miranda. I adored painting it. But, if you feel the need to see Lavender Dreams *once again, the name of the woman who purchased it is Vivienna.*

I'm told she is quite easy to find. The sea is beautiful; I wish you could see it through my eyes. I often think of you running along the shore with the wind in your hair. I can never tell if you are running to or from something.

I hope you have found what you were searching for and hope that you think fondly of me from time to time.

Yours always,

Jacques Dourdain

Miranda knew she would always remember Dourdain. As disappointed as she was he didn't leave her *Lavender Dreams,* she was happy with *Girl in Window.* Vivienna had visited him *months* before Miranda had arrived in Paris. The Vixen Queen must have seen the original pictures of her and Valadon when they'd had dinner out months ago. Vivienna had known about her long before Miranda had even known there was a Madame Lord of Paris.

Remare asked, "Is everything all right?"

"Yes. Dourdain passed away months ago." She rolled the canvas and inserted it back into the cylinder. "I miss him." Miranda grabbed her bag and slowly made for the door. Once there, she rested her palm against the door and exhaled. She didn't want to leave. What she had with Remare was too precious. "You know, Remare, you're not someone—"

He walked toward her with a sarcastic smile. "What, Miranda? I'm not someone you thought you could trust— not someone you imagined you would ever become attracted to?"

"No." She met his eyes. "What I was going to say was that...you're not someone I would want...*to have* to say goodbye to."

Remare's eyes darkened, and his red rims started glowing. Something she said had set him off. In that moment, she saw the depth of emotion he'd always kept hidden. It was dark, deep, unfathomable. His breaths intensified as his nostrils flared. The air around them became electric; whatever was between them magnified.

Her heart was hammering when he rushed her. She threw her arms around him as he kissed her fiercely, almost brutally—passion too long denied. One hand fisted her hair, and his other arm tightened around her back. Reveling in his desire, she wrapped her legs around his hips, her ankles locking him to her. She could feel his heart beating against hers in ecstatic harmony. Their tongues caressed, fought for dominance, dancing in sensual delight with the sensations feeding their hunger. She loved the way he tasted of fine wine.

When Remare broke from the kiss to lick his way to her throat, Miranda felt him shoving her dress up, his hands caressing her thighs and hips. She knew the minute he realized she wasn't wearing any underwear.

His eyes on fire, he asked, "Where is your thong?"

Her breath still heaving, she said, "I'm not wearing one."

Remare's heated voice was a harsh whisper against her skin. "You spent hours on a plane with two virile men, one a Blueblooded vampire and the other a very healthy Were," he cupped her between her thighs, "with no covering here?!"

Miranda groaned at his touch and nearly melted. Her legs slowly drifted down. "No. I was wearing pantyhose before. They became uncomfortable when I was lying down." She panted. "I took them off while you were away. They're in my bag."

As Remare stared at her with eyes of darkest passion, his breathing became arduous. Then, he kissed her, again, and she wanted to laugh at the sheer joy of finally being in his arms. His powerful arms slid down to her waist. He slowly went to his knees before her and, spreading her legs, kissed the inside of her thighs. His eyes never leaving her, he nipped and then licked her, sending erotic sensations throughout her body that funneled into her core. When his tongue licked her swollen flesh, Miranda could no longer hold back her moans. Her head knocked back against the door, and she grasped his hand in ecstasy.

Clawing her nails in the wood with her other hand, she tried desperately not to scream in delight at the sensations Remare had her body vibrating with. When he sucked hard and gently bit down on her clit, she saw stars and howled her pleasure.

Giving her a final lick, he rose. Impatiently, he tore off his shirt and unzipped his pants. Miranda pulled her own zipper down and flung off her dress. Except for her boots, she was naked before him. Remare caressed her swollen flesh, bringing the evidence of her arousal to her lips.

Grasping her hand tighter, he entered her, and Miranda's knees quivered. Only Remare could elicit the intense vibrations streaming through her body, sensitizing her to his touch. His eyes on fire, he moved slowly, one glorious inch at a time, savoring the pleasure. He seemed to take delight in teasing and tormenting her. Inching in and slowly, oh so slowly, he would pull out. Miranda's eyes started glistening at the punishing denial of his cock.

When Remare saw her tears, he whispered, "Now you know the hell you have been putting me through."

Then, he lunged in all the way. The orgasm rocked her body and had her crying out in passionate ecstasy as she shivered in his embrace. Unsatisfied with only one orgasm, he continued thrusting until he heard her scream again, and only then, he emptied himself inside her, his head nuzzling her neck.

Miranda would have fallen limply to the floor if Remare hadn't been holding her up. Her breaths ragged, her heart hammering, she thought she would pass out from the intensity of their lovemaking.

Still trembling, she felt him inside her as he walked backward to his leather recliner. Once settled, he gently rocked her hips. Miranda moved at a slow cadence, reveling in the hungry look in Remare's eyes. She wanted him to know how much she felt for him and that she wasn't afraid, anymore. This soldier, who slew his enemies and defended his own, had his own warrior riding him, protecting him from any harm, giving and returning the passion he so freely gave to her. When their bodies erupted again, her head drifted to his shoulder.

After a while, when the mists of magic retreated and logic prevailed, she asked, "We're in trouble now, aren't we?"

"Yes, but only if we're not very careful." Remare kissed her brow, then letting his forehead meet hers, he sighed deeply. "You need to go, Miranda."

She knew he was right, but the thought of leaving him still stung. Nodding, she slowly disengaged their bodies and looked around for her dress. When she saw it lying on the floor, she bent to retrieve it. Remare was on her before she could straighten. She smirked at the sight she must have presented, with her ass in the air, wearing only her boots. His hand glided up her sweat-slicked spine, keeping her head down while her body was bent over. When he penetrated her again, her body quivered. He slid in deeper than before. Miranda loved the way he stretched her, demanding she take every inch of his glorious, thick cock.

When she twisted around and looked up at him, she saw a trickle of sweat glistening at his temple and his fierce features as he continued pounding into her. His fingers were biting into her flesh. Miranda knew she'd be bruised, but didn't care. It gave her a heady feeling, knowing she could drive Remare near to insanity with pleasure.

Three deep thrusts later, she screamed again as her hand slammed into the carpet, her nails digging deep into the fibers. She heard his growl, then felt painful delight as his fangs pierced the flesh of her shoulder. The action wasn't lost on her. It was the way Weres marked their mates. Remare shuddered as his cock trembled inside her.

She collapsed onto the floor, his body pressed tightly to hers as he licked her wounds closed.

When his breathing evened, Remare stood, then lifting her in his arms, he walked to his bed and gently laid her down. Then, he went to the bathroom and she could hear the water running. He brought back a warm, damp washcloth and cleaned her inner thighs and core. When he tried to unzip her boots, she twisted away. "My scars."

At her dejected look, Remare said softly, "I know you have scars, Miranda. I saw them when you were in the infirmary."

She didn't remember him visiting her in the infirmary after she'd been nearly burned at the stake by Mulciber's daughter. At her confused look, he said, "I visited you nightly when you were still in a coma. I had to wait until your friends left. Lizandra and Orion came often. And, when Gabriel wasn't with you, Valadon was. I waited until they all left."

Miranda was surprised and touched at Remare's revelation. Somehow, she found the courage to let him see her scars. "I never healed completely. The scars are only on the backs of my legs, just beneath the calves to the ankles." Exhaling, she lay on her stomach. "I suppose, if I had to have scars, they're in a good place."

After Remare removed her boots, his hand smoothed over her scarred flesh. "It's not so bad, Miranda. I've seen far worse."

She frowned. "I've seen the women you socialize with. They're drop dead gorgeous. I didn't want you to think I was less than."

"I should spank you for such imbecile thinking. Do you think me so superficial that I would think less of you because you have a few minor imperfections?"

Imperfect! Yes, she was that and more. When he slapped her ass, she quickly looked up and saw him smirking. "All right, you're not shallow."

Remare tenderly kissed her scars on one calf and then the other. He then joined her under the blankets.

Holding her in his arms, he said, "I was rough before. I'm sorry. Did I hurt you?"

Miranda snuggled closer. "I'm a little swollen, but in a good way." Her voice was throaty. "You didn't hurt me, Remare."

"You screamed loudly." He caressed her cheek. "I wasn't sure. When I saw the eagle on your shoulder, I hated the thought of another man marking you."

"That man is seventy-seven years old and a grandfather." She wasn't completely certain, but she thought it was Chief Angel Fire who had tattooed her. "I don't think you have anything to worry about, Remare." Miranda enjoyed looking at him and reached up and stroked his handsome face. When he smiled at her, she felt a deep sense of connection. In the afterglow of their lovemaking, she imagined their auras connecting and creating something wondrous. Their undefinable essence flowed freely around them, enchanting her with a newfound sense of happiness.

She saw it in Remare's face, too. His eyes held more than he had ever shown her before—a well of emotion so deep, so profound in its intensity. When she placed her hand over his beating heart, he lifted it to kiss her palm, then returned her hand to his heart, his hand covering hers. Each of them was smiling at their shared intimacy. Feeling safer and more secure than ever, Miranda absorbed Remare's warmth. Burrowing deeper into his chest, the lulling of their heart beats music to her ears, Miranda surrendered to sleep's sweet serenity.

***

Irina stood curiously outside Remare's rooms, unsure of the sounds she heard emanating from behind the door.

Gregori came up behind her. "It's good to have a Were in our midst, don't you think?"

Turning, Irina knew her eyes were frosted over. "If it's what Valadon wants."

"It is." He spotted her necklace then met her eyes. "And what is it that you want?"

Ever since they returned from London, she'd been noticing how he watched over her and wasn't sure how she felt about it. He'd surprised her when he told her he'd been the one who sang to her when she escaped from Ivan's camp. How could she have not known it was him? He'd seen her vulnerable, nearly fragile, something she wasn't sure she could ever forgive him for. "A drink. I could use one, right now."

Chapter Thirty-Five

In the main living area, the Torians were gathered to play pool, and Valadon silently watched them.

"Yes!" Orion sank a bank shot and pumped his fist, the others cheering him on.

Valadon was pleased, he had plans for the handsome Were. He wanted to join them, but first, he needed to speak with his second about the results of the voice identification system.

Walking down the corridor toward Remare's room, he heard Aiden behind him.

"There you are. I checked your rooms first." Aiden exhaled excitedly. "I ran the VIS as you requested and none of our people are a match."

Valadon's shoulders sagged in relief. "Who's in the communications room tonight?"

"Morel's on tonight."

"Did you check for matches with our European affiliates?"

"Yes." Aiden nodded. "I ran the voice pattern with all our people in the European divisions and there still was no viable match. However, the more I listened to the recording, the more I thought I detected a slight accent. So, I ran it simultaneously through the linguistic program. The voice has traces of three different dialects, French, Scottish and Finnish."

Valadon crossed his arms. "Do any of our people have similar backgrounds?"

"I knew you would ask." Aiden smiled as he placed his hands on his hips. "No one here does, but I thought the

Finnish aspect sounded familiar and ran the system through known affiliates. One came up."

Valadon lifted one eyebrow. "Well, don't keep me in suspense. Who?"

"Rosalyn." Aiden exhaled. "She's the proprietor of Nightshade."

"I know who she is. Rosalyn has always been an ally. Call her in. Set up a meeting with her and me tomorrow. It's a long shot, but she might recognize the voice."

Aiden nodded, then turned and left.

Approaching Remare's door, Valadon was about to knock, then thought how diligently his second had been working in trying to track down Brandon. Remare's unfailing resolve and loyalty were commendable. Too often, he worked to the point of exhaustion, but Valadon decided this was news Remare should have. As he raised his hand to knock, Katya opened her door.

"Would you like to see the new ornament Miranda brought me back from Paris?"

He thought he'd smelled Miranda's scent in this wing. "Yes, I would."

Katya handed him the exquisitely crafted piece of glass shaped like a boot. But it was what was hidden in the compartment below that interested him more. "The flashdrive?"

"Chagall hid it in the heel of the boot." She handed it to him. "It amazes me how tiny they make these devices."

"Yes, but even more amazing is the information they contain. Tell me, have you been in contact with your mother recently?"

"No. She thought it more prudent not to have any transmissions between us."

"Lysette has always been cautious." Valadon examined Katya's face and easily recognized the family likeness. "I think you should take a trip to Geneva. Your mother likes to spend a holiday at the spa they have there this time of year. Take Tristan with you."

Katya grinned. "Will do."

Valadon crossed the hall to Remare's room and was about to knock when Escher approached him, "My lord, dinner is ready."

"Thank you." He nodded to his servant. "I'll be there momentarily."

"Very good, sir." Escher turned and walked away. Glancing again at Remare's door, he decided Aiden probably sent him a copy of the report and Remare was either working thoroughly through the data or resting. He knew his second had once been involved with Rosalyn and wondered if she was the reason he no longer seemed to be interested in Irina. Deciding to let Remare enjoy his rest, Valadon went to join the others.

Nearing the dining area, he motioned for Bastien to join him and spoke softly. "How's Orion fitting in with the others?"

"Fine, they were kidding him about a missed shot." Bastien shrugged. "But they seem to accept him."

"Good." Valadon considered Bastien and his burgeoning friendship with the young Were. He'd been watching them closely for a while and didn't think his next request would be too difficult. "I want you to seduce him."

Bastien's face flushed, then held concern and confusion. "Has Orion done something wrong?"

"Not at all. As a matter of fact..." Valadon smiled as they watched Orion raise his fist in victory at sinking one of the pool balls. "He's done something *very* right."

Valadon sensed Bastien's relief and heard his silent question. *"How?"*

There were many ways to seduce a person. Some desired riches, some pleasure, others coveted power and would go to any extent to possess that which they yearned for the most. And then, there were those who craved something entirely different. Valadon grasped Bastien's shoulder. "You'll figure it out." He then went to take his seat at the head of the table.

The Torians finished their game and joined Valadon in the dining room.

"I hope you made the steak with those Canadian spices I love?" Bastien inhaled the pungent aromas drifting in from the kitchen.

"In honor of your return from Paris, I have done exactly as you like." Escher served a platter heaped high with steaming carved meat. The table was already set with roasted potatoes and broccoli and carrots drenched in Hollandaise sauce.

Orion stood in the doorway. "Is there any place I should sit?"

"As you are our guest of honor, please sit at the end of the table." Valadon watched as Bastien sat beside him; Tristan and Katya took one side of the table and Gregori and Irina took the other side.

Bree walked in with her husband, Aiden, who nodded to him. "The meeting with Rosalyn is scheduled for early tomorrow. I've sent you and Remare an e-mail with the specifics"

Valadon nodded his approval as his Torians were seated. He whispered to Escher, "See that a plate is taken to Morel."

"I always do," Escher replied.

"Now that we're all assembled," Valadon directed his words to Orion, "I would like to offer my apologies for your unfortunate encounter with Madame Lord Vivienna."

Orion looked uneasy. "I think I should be the one apologizing. I didn't know there were rules about not touching, but when she grabbed Miranda's arm, I just reacted."

"If anyone's guilty of an impropriety, it's me," Bastien interjected. "It wasn't until afterward that I was able to explain proper vampire etiquette to Orion."

"There's no need to explain." Valadon waved his hand in dismissal. "If anyone's guilty of anything, it's Vivienna." He looked directly at Orion. "Had you been a member of my house, I would have waged a formal complaint against the madame lord. How is your voice?"

When all heads turned in his direction, Orion said, "It's fine. She came close to slashing my vocal cords," he nodded to his partner, "but Bastien closed the wound fast."

"Still, the fact you suffered needlessly when protecting Miranda has not gone unnoticed. This dinner is only one way of showing my gratitude. When news reached us of your injury, your queen was quite upset with me that I failed to provide adequate protection for the people under my care." All heads turned his way. "In fact, she met with me, and we agreed, in this instance, that restitution was appropriate, if not required."

Orion glanced at all the Torians seated and then at him. "There's no need for that." He shook his head. "My voice wasn't harmed. I'm okay, so there's no need for any restitution."

"Perhaps." Valadon took an envelope from the inside pocket of his jacket. "But I would like you to consider accepting a position with ValCorp." At Orion's incredulous look, he continued, "Before you say no, understand that Lizandra and I have discussed this matter at length. We agreed on all the particulars. And my offer would benefit not only the members of my house, but of Black Star Clan, as well."

Confused, Orion asked, "What position?"

"I have long considered naming a liaison to Lizandra and her clan. In light of events that happened several months ago, when Lizandra was able to send aid when I needed it most, I want to make certain communications stay open and work at optimum status." Valadon peered at Orion. "How would you like to be *Liaison to House Valadon*?"

"Whoa," Bastien said, as he started clapping, the others following his lead. "Something to consider, wolf; it's a prestigious status and one hell of a compliment in your abilities."

Orion appeared confused. "But I'm a Were; how would it be possible?"

"I wanted someone who would feel comfortable in my house, as well as in the clan. You would act as a sort of ambassador between the Were Queen and myself." Valadon slid the envelope down the table, and the others passed it along to Orion.

Orion held the envelope in his hands then met Valadon's eyes. "You must understand my first loyalty is to Lizandra and always will be."

"That's not a problem, and I would be sadly disappointed if you felt differently. As liaison, you would spend part of your time there and part of your time here. You would train with my Torians and work out with them, as well."

"You do realize I'm a musician, and I spend months on the road."

"Yes, I was aware of that; however, I was informed you no longer wished to travel as much." When Orion nodded, Valadon continued, "I'm also told you desire to tour Europe sometime in the future. If you accept my proposal, I will send one of my Torians," Valadon glanced at Bastien, "with you as your bodyguard. No lord would dare attack you, again."

Valadon gestured to the envelope. "Consider my offer. I don't expect an answer tonight. But, sometime soon, contact me with your decision." As he rose, he said, "Ladies, gentlemen, enjoy the rest of your evening. And Orion? I hope you accept my offer." He grinned. "This place could use some diversity."

***

When dinner was over and everyone had turned in, Bastien said, "Come to my rooms; we can hang out there for a while."

"Okay." Orion checked his messages as he walked alongside him down the hall.

Unlocking his door, he put his hand on Orion's shoulder. "Wolf, you have no idea of the honor Valadon just bestowed on you."

"I still can't believe the amount he's offering." Shaking his head, he followed Bastien inside. "I still think he added too many zeroes."

Flicking the lights on, Bastien sauntered to his fridge and took out two Sam Adamses. "Valadon has always been generous with those who work for him." He handed a beer to Orion. "Miranda must have told you as much when she worked for him in his archives."

"We never discussed the finances." Orion sat on the couch and ran his hand through his hair. "Holy shit! I can't believe this." He grinned. "I thought he was going to rip me a new one for touching Vivienna. I never imagined something like this." He shook his head, again. "I don't know what to think."

"What's to think about? Take the position." Bastien shrugged. "You're home half the time, anyway. This will give you something to do when you're not touring."

Orion rubbed his face. "I'll have to talk with Lizandra first. She has to okay it."

"So, talk with her." Bas swallowed his beer. "If she's okay with it, will you take it?"

Orion relaxed back into the couch and draped a hand over his eyes. "I don't know. Maybe."

"You guys really helped us out when Valadon fought Mulciber. I watched the way you fought with the Rogues." He gulped down his beer. "Wolf, you have moves."

Orion lifted a shoulder. "Nick was with us at the time. He told us Valadon was in trouble. We were itching for a fight, anyway." Orion smirked then quickly sobered. "A rival clan was encroaching on our borders." He pursed his lips. "If I do decide to tour Europe, would you really want to come? Be my bodyguard?"

"I'd be willing to try it." Bastien shrugged, then stood with both hands on his hips. "But we'd be partners. You understand? I wouldn't put up with any prima donna shit from you or anyone else."

Orion nodded. "It would be great to tour Europe. Just once. My grandfather was from Ireland." Orion let his head slip back. "I would love to see all the sights."

"Sleep on it." Bastien reached over on his bed and threw a pillow at Orion. "Valadon said take as much time as you need."

Orion exhaled a long breath and then looked up at Bastien. "How would the others handle having a Were in their ranks? I can't imagine they would all be pleased at having a *mongrel* in their presence."

"Don't say that. Not all vampires are like Vivienna." Bastien shook his head. "No one here looks down on Weres. You're our allies. You'd be like one of us."

"Would you introduce me to the other vampires? I'd like to find that out for myself."

"Sure." Bastien leaned against the doorframe to his bathroom. "If that's what you want." He seemed to be studying him. "What's holding you back? It's a great opportunity."

"What if a situation arose that compromised the Weres?" Orion leaned forward and rested his elbows on his knees. "Or something came up here that I couldn't tell Lizandra about? Don't you see the potential for a conflict of interests?"

"Maybe." Bastien tilted his head. "But Valadon knows you're a Were. He'd expect you to be loyal to Lizandra. He wouldn't put you in a compromising position."

"How do you know?"

"Because I know him." Bastien pulled his shirt over his head. "He doesn't work that way. He takes care of his people." He went to his bathroom. "Listen, I'm going to take a shower. Crash here tonight. That sofa opens up to a queen size bed." He gestured to a door. "Blankets are in the closet."

After making up his bed and turning down the lights, Orion pulled the blankets up to his bare waist and clasped both hands behind his head, feeling more comfortable than he should have been. He had much to think about and not the least was the vampire who was currently in the next room. When the bathroom door opened, Bastien was only wearing a towel around his hips. He put his watch and ring on his bedside table then turned toward Orion.

"You okay, wolf?" Bastien's voice was soft. He wasn't.

"Yeah, I'm fine."

Bastien turned toward him. As a Were, Orion could scent the vampire's emotions, and Bastien's were strong. When he walked slowly toward him, Orion smiled.

Meeting his eyes, Bastien's voice was seductive. "You're sure?"

Orion's heart was beating out a staccato. "Yeah. But I think there's something you should know." He met his eyes. "I've already decided to accept Valadon's offer." Grinning, Orion glanced at Bastien's crotch. "So, if that impressive salute is for me, you don't have to 'seduce' me."

Orion thought the look on Bastien's face was priceless.

"How?"

"Did you forget I'm a Were, vampire? My hearing's astute. Just like yours. Probably better. I heard what Valadon whispered to you."

Bastien's shoulders relaxed as he exhaled. "You fucking could have said something sooner!"

"I wanted to see how far you would go." Orion smirked as he glanced at Bastien's crotch, again. "Pretty far, huh?"

Bastien's eyes became heated and his breaths labored. "Fuck off." He turned and marched to his bed. Before reaching it, Bastien whipped off his towel and threw it against a chair, giving Orion a good look at his naked ass.

Orion laughed. "Oh, yeah. This is going to be fun."

Bastien punched his pillow. "Shut up."

That only made Orion laugh harder.

Chapter Thirty-Six

Waking, Miranda felt more relaxed than she'd felt in a long time and blissfully inhaled Remare's scent. It was even imbedded in her skin. She wasn't sure why he always smelled like the forest, but she liked his scent. Looking up at his furrowed brow, she saw the tension. "Please don't tell me that look on your face is remorse." She ran her fingers through his smattering of chest hairs, cherishing the way they felt. "Guilt doesn't belong here."

"It's not guilt, Miranda." Briefly closing his eyes, he turned to her. "It's concern."

"We'll be careful." Her voice softened. "Valadon won't find out."

"It's not just Valadon." Remare exhaled and spoke quietly. "I have as many enemies as him, maybe more."

"I can take care of myself." Miranda covered his hand with hers. "You don't have to take this all on yourself."

"My brave warrior." He stroked her arm. "You know not what you speak about."

"Oh, and Mulciber was nothing?"

He cupped the side of her face. "No. He was evil. But we have other enemies. You'd become a target, Miranda." Remare's body tightened. "There's no telling what they would do to you if you should fall into their hands. Or what I would do to preserve your life. They could force my hand to compromise ValCorp's security." He rubbed his brow. "The only way you would be safe is if you lived here in Valadon House." Remare sighed. "But I know your life is out there with your job and your friends." He met her eyes. "And I would not want you to be 'caged'."

Miranda remembered she had once told Valadon she wouldn't live in a cage. She knew Remare was making sense, but that wasn't their only option. "We could be careful. Meet in places where nobody would think to look."

"We would be found out. Long ago, another trusted me. It was in England." He closed his eyes and leaned back into the pillows. "I was in the service of a dark lord. Back then, we allied ourselves with human aristocrats for hunting grounds. He ordered me to seduce and defile a young girl no more than fourteen, who was to be the wife of one of his competitors. I refused the order, knowing I would be punished."

Miranda caressed his hand, knowing this story wouldn't end pretty.

"When I was led to the dungeons and bound with chains, I did not fight them. But I did not know the full extent of Lord Acton's cruelty. He had his men bring in the girl and had her bound to a table. Her clothes were ripped away, and his men took turns with her. She screamed for me to help her. I tried to break free of my bonds, but the chains were too heavy." Remare turned to her. "He knew I had grown fond of the girl. I'd been enchanted with her spirit. He did this to teach me a lesson."

Miranda knew there was much he wasn't telling her. "What happened after?"

"I hunted down the men and killed each one. When I was eventually caught, they tortured me. I escaped again and made it back to our main court. When Valadon saw the condition I was in, he bargained for my release with our ruling members." He met her eyes. "The cost of my freedom was exceedingly high." He stroked her cheek with his hand. "So you see, Miranda, I can't allow my enemies to ever learn how dear to me you have become."

She wouldn't ask how severe a cost it had been, but she knew it had to have been brutal. "I'm not a child, Remare. I do have some talents." She waved her hand in the air. "And, if you remember, Mulciber and Brandon already tortured me. I'm a survivor." She kissed his hand. "So are you."

Remare regarded her with heavy-lidded eyes as he brushed a strand of her hair away. "If there's a way, Mirranda, I will find it." Kissing her, he slowly moved the blankets away and covered her body with his.

Miranda gloried in the way Remare's body felt against hers and welcomed his weight. Usually cooler than hers, his body emanated heat. She wondered if part of his attraction to her was because she could give him warmth no female vampire ever could. Returning his kiss, she felt their bond growing deeper and stronger. As they tenderly made love, the air around them became enchanted.

Remare's eyes glowed as he moved slowly inside her. Intuitively, Miranda knew it would be a while before they were together, again. She would not think about that, now; there would come another time for thinking. Now was for enjoying what they shared together. How strange it was that, sometimes, in the daylight, people were so focused on facts and figures, they forgot their primitive desires. But the night—the beautiful, liberating night—presented a gateway to sensations only the darkness offered.

Together, she and Remare created something wonderful in the magical dark of night.

Miranda ran her nails down Remare's back, luxuriating in the smoothness of his skin as his muscles rippled, grateful for the passion he evoked in her. He was her magic man, weaving erotic spells of sensation as he rocked both their worlds, sharing a part of his soul with her. She stared into his dark brown eyes as he moved sensuously inside her. She saw his world, the good and the bad and accepted him anyway.

Thrusting inside her, Remare wove a world of impossibility into something that was not only possible, but precious as it transcended her darkest fears.

Miranda cried out as Remare's jaw locked and he came with her. Their combined scents enveloped them in a world of beauty. He collapsed on her in exhaustion. Breathing heavily, she held him as he lifted his head and stared down at her. The red rims of his irises pulsed with hunger.

"Go ahead," she answered his unspoken question. "We've shared everything else."

Remare nodded, bending his head to her neck and grazed her skin with his fangs. Then, shaking his head as if changing his mind, he met her eyes and ran his finger over her heart.

Miranda nodded in understanding and arched her back as his fangs pierced her breast. His bite gave her a sense of completeness, making her feel whole.

When he'd taken enough blood, he gazed up at her. "I would give you the same, Miranda. I want nothing more...than for you to taste me."

"But I'm not a vampire, Remare." She shook her head, her voice barely a whisper. "Humans can't tolerate vampire blood."

Remare smiled at her. "Some cannot. But you, Miranda, can."

"How do you know?" Everything she read about vampires suggested their blood was anathema to humans.

"I know." His eyes sparkled with mischief. "Trust me, Miranda. I would not willingly endanger your life. See for yourself." Using his thumbnail, he cut a slight incision over his heart and blood glided down his pec.

She saw the truth in his eyes and slowly licked the rivulet. "It tastes like copper, not all that different from human blood."

Remare seemed pleased. "There are some other elements, Miranda, but nothing harmful I swear to you." He pulled her closer to his blood. "Finish it. Use your tongue to seal the wound."

Miranda sensed he wanted more; he wanted her to drink from him, to share his life's essence. But she wasn't that daring. She gently sucked at his wound, swallowed a little of his blood and then sealed the small cut, but not before biting down to leave her own mark.

"Thank you, Miranda. Thank you." Remare rolled to his back, blissfully spent.

As was the night. She enjoyed watching his chest rise and fall with his breaths as he rested, but she could sense dawn was on the horizon.

She reached under the sheet and cupped him. "I can't stand the thought of another touching you here."

"No one else will." He slid his hand between her thighs and caressed her. "No one else, Miranda."

"No one else, Remare," she promised. She bent and kissed his lips. It was time for her to go. "I'll miss you."

Miranda quickly found her clothes and dressed. She hoped she didn't run into any vampires out in the hall. She knew most would be sleeping. Remare rose, and after fastening his pants, he looked around for his shirt. She found it, but on a wicked impulse, she shoved it into her bag instead. Loving his scent, she planned to sleep in that shirt.

"I'll walk you to the elevator. We have drivers waiting in the garage." Exhaustion made his voice sound gravelly. "One of them will take you home."

"Go back to sleep, Remare." She grinned. "You didn't get much last night."

"Oh, I think I got some." He smiled wickedly as he kissed her knuckles. "Everyone should be asleep in their rooms. Let me at least look out in the hall." He did. "No one is there. I'm not quite sure what I would say if anyone saw us together."

Miranda smiled. "I'll be fine." She embraced him one last time, inhaling his masculine scent, taking it deep into her lungs, and smiled in satisfaction. She studied his face. "You know, I kinda miss the goatee. As handsome as you are without it, I think I got used to you with it."

He rubbed his jaw. "I usually grow it back when the weather gets cooler."

"Get some sleep." She tenderly patted his ass.

"I will." Remare held her tightly, then let her go. "Get home safe. I will call you later."

Remare was right—no one was in the hallway. Miranda rode the elevator to the garage. But she was surprised at the person waiting for her once the doors opened. Her spine straightened. Belatedly, she realized Orion had driven his car to ValCorp and was currently leaning against it, jangling his keys.

He looked up at her and smiled in warm welcome as the elevator doors closed behind her. From the condition of his hair, Miranda knew he'd been with someone. As she walked closer, she gasped at the bite marks on his neck peeking out of his shirt.

When she stood before him, Orion bent his head to kiss her cheek and then inhaled. "Jesus, Miranda, I thought I was the one who got royally screwed." He laughed. "But I think you got me beat." He threw his arms around her and hugged her tightly.

She breathed in the cologne that clung to his body and grimaced. She'd inhaled that scent often enough to know who it belonged to. "I don't think either one of us should talk of this night, Orion."

"Yeah. I agree. But there's something you should know." He let his hands drift to her shoulders. "I accepted Valadon's offer of *Liaison to House Valadon*. I'm going to be an envoy between the Weres and the vampires. Lizandra's already approved the deal."

Miranda shook her head and didn't try to hide her concern. "Be careful with the vampires, Orion. They're not always forthcoming."

"I know." He smiled. "I'll be careful. Look, the sun's coming up."

She kept her arm around him as she felt the sun's rays on her face and her body awakening. It was a new dawn, not only for her, but for Orion as well, and hope pervaded the mist swirling in her mind. "Let's go home. I'm exhausted."

"Yeah, me, too." Orion opened her door and then got behind the wheel and headed out and away from ValCorp. "I know you're concerned. But, I'm not afraid."

Miranda glanced at him and then out the window. "You will be."

Chapter Thirty-Seven

Remare quickly walked down the hall to Valadon's office. He'd slept later than usual and was partly annoyed with himself that he was already late to the meeting. The other part of him—the lower half—was still glowing. He smiled when he realized there was a newfound jaunt to his steps. It had been incredibly foolish of him to have had Miranda stay so late with him. Ordinarily, he didn't take chances like that, but Miranda was no ordinary woman. No other woman affected him so deeply, could touch his heart the way she did. *Damned Sorceress!*

Once inside Valadon's office, his smile quickly vanished. Rosalyn was seated in front of the high lord, and Aiden stood nearby with his arms crossed over his chest. Rosalyn was the only other person who knew of his attraction to Miranda. Surely, she wouldn't have betrayed him. He glanced at Valadon, who was eying him. No, not willingly, but if Valadon threatened to unveil her memories, she would have no choice. His heart rate quickened. *Had someone seen Miranda leaving his rooms?* He could not decipher Valadon's expression. Surely, he would be dead by now if Valadon knew.

"Have a seat, Remare." Valadon gestured to the empty chair in front of his desk. "I came by your rooms last night." He hesitated for a moment, as if examining Remare's face, then glanced up at Aiden. "But I decided to let you rest."

Remare sent Rosalyn a silent question. He could hear the rapid beating of her heart and sense her confusion. She had no clue why she had been summoned to the high lord's chambers. Remare kept his voice even. "Was there something I missed?"

Valadon gestured for Aiden to speak. "I replayed the transmission Valadon received last night and was able to distinguish three different dialects. One of them is Finnish."

Silently, Remare breathed in relief and nodded for Aiden to continue.

"When I checked our databanks we saw that you're originally from Finland, Rosalyn, and we're hoping you could identify the voice on the recording...or give us some clue as to who it might belong to." Aiden turned on the recorder and played the transmission.

Rosalyn listened intently to the voice. "Can you replay it?" She closed her eyes as if searching for any distinguishing nuances. "I can hear the way he pronounces certain vowels the way the people do in the North Country near the Finnish/Russian border. The man was either born in Finland, or lived there for a long period of time. His dialect is not easily copied, and most students of the language don't have the ability to accurately pronounce certain words the way natives do."

Valadon leaned forward. "Can you identify the speaker?"

Rosalyn kept her eyes closed in deep memory, as if replaying the recording in her mind. "I've been trying to put a face to the voice." She shook her head. "I'm sorry, but I cannot place it." She looked up apologetically. "I don't know whose voice it is."

"It was a long shot." Valadon exhaled. "We knew that when we called you in, but hoped we might get lucky." He nodded to Aiden, who quickly took the recorder and left, closing the door behind him.

Remare rose and went to Valadon's bar and poured a glass of blood wine. "Can I get you anything to drink, Rosalyn, Valadon?"

Valadon shook his head as did Rosalyn.

"I tried as hard as I could." Rosalyn shook her head in frustration. "But I have no memory of whose voice that was. When I lived in Finland, I traveled a great deal to the other courts. I may have heard it there, but I can't distinguish him from so many others."

"We knew the chances were slim, but we didn't want to overlook any possibility. However, now that we're alone, there is one more thing I would like to discuss with you before you leave." Valadon looked at Remare and then at Rosalyn. He paused for a moment. "I would like to book your club for one night in the next week or so. I have an affair I would like to have catered there."

"Of course." Rosalyn's spine straightened. "Just tell me when, and I'll make certain the club stays closed for anyone not on your list."

"Thank you. My assistant, Lee, will be in touch with all the specifics." Valadon rose and took Rosalyn's hand as he led her to the door. After she left, Valadon went to his desk, but didn't sit down. He studied his second, as if searching for something. "Is Rosalyn the reason why you no longer have relations with Irina?"

Of all the questions Remare expected of Valadon, that was not one of them. "What makes you ask that?"

"You have not been with Irina for some time now. You haven't been with *anyone* that I can ascertain." Valadon sat and faced Remare. "And that's not like you." He gestured for him to sit. "You haven't been seeing Rosalyn clandestinely, have you?"

"I did not think my love life would merit such attention, but no, I have not been romantically involved with Rosalyn for several decades, now."

"Good." Valadon seemed pleased. "You do realize she is involved with Jason Morgan, the son of Wilson Morgan, two of our strongest allies. I would not want Jason put off because my second had become entangled with his paramour."

Valadon thought he was sleeping with Rosalyn? "I know the Morgans are our friends, and I would do *nothing* to jeopardize our relationship with them. I'm fond of Jason." Remare raised his glass as if in salute. "He's proven his loyalty to us several times over, as has his father."

"Excellent." Valadon rose. "Then, I don't have to worry about you and Rosalyn."

"My relationship with Rosalyn is professional only. I have used her club in the past to meet with informants who would rather not come to ValCorp." Remare knew Valadon was already aware of this. There was very little he didn't share with his lord, until recently. "She has been accommodating to our needs. Our *business* needs," he emphasized the last. "We are lucky to have her."

"Yes, we are." Valadon's eyes darkened. "So, there will be nothing to endanger that relationship."

"Nothing at all." Remare knew he had just dodged a bullet and exhaled deeply. The message he just received from Valadon was crystal clear. If he had become involved with Rosalyn, Valadon would have ordered him to break it off and had him censured in some *uncomfortable* way. With Valadon's keen eyes watching him, there was no way he would be able to meet with Miranda. Remare sighed. He had promised to contact her.

And, now, he would have to break that promise.

***

"I'm sorry, Miranda. I had no idea he was planning this. I am *so* sorry."

"Calm down, Orion, what exactly are you sorry for?" She put down the crackers and cheese on the table in anticipation of the movie they were going to watch. He had picked some classic war movie that wasn't a favorite of hers, but since it was his turn to choose, she was okay with it.

Orion pushed his hand through his hair as he paced in front of her. "I had no idea he would run with it. We talked about it, but that's all we did was talk, I swear to you, Miranda. I didn't think he was serious."

Not having a clue what was bothering him, she looked at him in confusion. "What are you talking about?"

He took a deep breath and another, then sat beside her. "Remember when I told you about those college students who gave me a ruffie and then started taking pictures?"

"Yes, you said that you were able to shake it off and took the camera away from them." Miranda narrowed her eyes. "Was there more to the story than what you told me?"

Orion wrung his hands and looked pained. "Yeah, there was." He rubbed the palms of his hands together. His face held guilt. "One of them was a male."

Oh, shit! Depending on the severity of the pictures, Orion's career could crash and burn. "Please tell me you got all the camera phones away."

"I was too distracted trying to shake off the drug and didn't realize he took pictures. I thought only the girl did. In one of the pictures, it *appears* I'm giving him a blow job. I didn't! I tripped, trying to sweat the drug out, but the angle of the shot makes it look like I'm going down on him. He contacted my manager and demanded money."

"Jesus! What did he do?"

Orion looked at her with his silver blue eyes and shook his head. "You're not going to like it much."

She took his hands in hers. "I don't like it already, but you're my friend, and friends are there for you when you need them the most."

"I just got off the phone with Frank. I think he meant well and thought I had discussed it with you."

"Discussed what?"

"He let it leak to the media that...we're engaged. You know all those touristy places we visited in Paris? The Eiffel Tower when I kissed you for bringing me there? Someone posted them on social media, and it looks...like we're lovers on vacation."

Miranda just stared at him—not blinking, not sure if she was hearing him correctly. "What did you say?"

Orion slowly shook his head. "You heard right." He threw his arms in the air. "The world thinks we're engaged. Turn on the TV—any of the media channels, they're running it now."

She flicked on the TV and punched in the number for a popular music station.

"*And, in a major revelation, Orion, the hot, young musician whose hit song, "A Dream Within a Dream," has been steadily climbing the charts, has recently became engaged to Miranda Crescent, who was rumored to be dating New York's premier vampire, Lord Valadon. Pictures surfaced of them in Paris where insiders hint of a pre-honeymoon. The couple has been living together for...*"

Pictures of them at the Eiffel Tower, the Louvre and other places where they were seen hugging and holding hands quickly flashed across the screen. They'd been happy and excited, and it showed in the images. Miranda's heart began hammering. From anyone else's viewpoint, it did, indeed, look like they were lovers. "Holy shit! You've got to call them and get this straightened out."

"Yeah." Orion exhaled and winced. "I can't."

"What do you mean, you can't?"

Orion looked miserable. "If I recant the article, there's a good chance pictures may surface of me with that guy." He looked up at her with despair. "Ninety percent of my fans are female. Those pictures could kill my career."

Miranda put her hand over her eyes and leaned back against the couch. Lizandra was going to go nuts. The people in her office were going to go crazy. "What are we going to do?"

"I know it's asking a lot, but could we let the story fly, at least for a little while? If the public thinks we're engaged, it's damage control." Orion stroked her neck. "Please?"

Miranda held her chin in her hand and tried to process all the implications. Her life was going to get complicated real fast if she agreed. People would start harassing her with questions and congratulations. She'd be followed, and the media would try to pry her with questions. She liked her privacy and hated the limelight. But, if she said no, his career—his life as he knew it—would be over. There'd been another famous rock star whose gender preferences were made public, and his career had nosedived. She didn't want the same for Orion. "How long?"

"How long what?"

"How long would we have to act like a couple?"

He shrugged. "I don't know—a month, maybe two."

Miranda exhaled. For two months, she could put up with the media circus. If she didn't, she'd be letting down one of her best friends so badly, it would be career suicide. Two months. Orion was worth a helluva lot more. "You know I value my privacy."

He looked deflated. "Yes."

"You'll owe me." She narrowed her eyes. "I mean, big time, you *will* owe me."

Orion's eyebrows nearly hit the ceiling. "What are you saying? You just said—"

Miranda exhaled. "If it's only for a month or two, I think I can manage it. You're my friend. There's very little I wouldn't do for you." She grinned. "Hell, you're the only one who remembers the baklava."

Orion grabbed her in a bear hug. "I love you, Miranda. I love you." He kissed her temple. "I didn't think you would agree. I thought you'd kill me."

"I just might if you ever invite strangers to your dressing room, again." Miranda lifted her index finger at him. "And there's going to be certain rules in effect if we get engaged. And you're going to follow them. To the letter. Understand?"

Orion's face beamed. "I really do love you." He bent and kissed her. This time square on her lips.

She knew he was being affectionate and grateful, his arms tight around her back massaging her muscles, but when she felt the tip of his tongue against hers, she pushed him away and rubbed her lips. "That is *definitely* against the rules."

"Sorry. I got carried away." Smirking, he stroked her arms with his thumbs. "Thank you, Miranda. Thank you." He hugged her, again, but this time, it was less arduous.

Inhaling his scent, she felt his relief. She had absolutely no clue how she was going to handle all the craziness of the next few months, but like anything else, she guessed she would deal with it one day at a time. "You better call Valadon and let him know."

"Yeah, I'm going to have to call a few people—"

It didn't take long for both their phones to start ringing. "Sheesh, is this what it's going to be like now?"

Orion chuckled. "Yeah, pretty much."

***

Sitting in his penthouse suite, Valadon smiled at the latest media reports. After his spies in Europe had informed him of his adversaries' interest in Miranda, he'd found a way to alleviate their potential threat. He'd made sure the tourist photos were delivered to the media. Now that the world believed Miranda was engaged to Orion, his enemies would have no reason to pursue her; her safety was, once again, assured.

Remare frowned at the screen. "Do you really think this is necessary?"

"For now—yes. It will shift the focus from my involvement to Orion. You disagree?"

Remare waved a dismissive hand in the air. "I'm told you bought Orion's contract from his current label and signed him to your new subsidiary. I wasn't aware ValCorp *had* an entertainment division."

"It does now. I recently acquired a fledgling music company with a great deal of potential. Especially since I was able to persuade a very popular female singer, who was not happy with her current organization, to sign with ValCorp Entertainment."

Remare's brow knit. "Who?"

Valadon's smile widened. "Who's one of the world's hottest singers with a voice that sounds like heaven itself?"

Remare's eyes narrowed for a brief second then his brows lifted. "You did not! How? Tiseira is one of the best singers in the world."

Valadon swiveled in his chair. "Yes, she is. Some would say *the* best singer. I offered her a contract very amenable to her desires."

"I am certain you did. But all this to lure Orion to ValCorp?"

"Not all." Valadon swiveled in his chair. "I've been thinking of investing in the entertainment business for some time. Now, I've found the perfect vehicle."

"I also heard you've hired contractors to build a music studio here at ValCorp, complete with engineering and recording capabilities."

"Yes. It will be a pleasure to have my people close and watch them evolve."

"And who will be heading this new division of yours?"
Valadon smiled. "You'll see."

Chapter Thirty-Eight

Two weeks later

The party for Orion signing with ValCorp Entertainment was in full swing at Nightshade. Valadon's PR department head, Katya, had organized the photo shoot of Valadon with Orion and various business associates. As Orion's fiancée, Miranda had to submit to the hype and glamour of the occasion. Orion stood with her, and Remare was alongside Valadon, as they posed for the cameras. She peered up at Valadon. "I have to give you credit. I didn't see this coming."

Standing together on the raised platform with ValCorp's emblem blazing behind them, Valadon glanced her way. "Didn't see what coming?"

In his black tuxedo, Valadon was stunning, and always, his emerald eyes held her spellbound. "Signing Orion. Since when did you become interested in the music world?"

Valadon smiled for the cameras. "Let's say, it's been an interest of mine for some time, now."

"I'll bet." Miranda thought her face would crack from all her smiling. "It was you who had those pictures of Orion and I released to the media, wasn't it?"

His smile widened. "Miranda, do you always have such a suspicious mind?"

"Where you're concerned, yes."

His hand drifted across her back as he spoke silently in the way of vampires. *"My adversaries no longer see you as a vulnerability of mine. It makes good business sense. Don't you agree?"*

"This arrangement is temporary. I did it for Orion."

"I know. And I'm grateful you did."

A reporter asked Orion, "How does it feel to be engaged?"

Grinning wide, Orion answered, "Like heaven."

Before she knew it, Orion grabbed her in a bear hug and passionately kissed her for the cameras. Miranda's breath felt sucked away. When the photographers abated and finally drifted away, she glanced at Remare, who hadn't said a word to her since the night she left ValCorp. She had received one text from him stating the timing was wrong and he would contact her when he could.

A commotion sounded near the entrance, and several females in the crowd rushed toward the door. Cesare and Valadon Creation's newest model, Jeremy, had entered. She'd seen his drop dead gorgeous face on the cover of several bath items in the hotel in Paris. With his golden hair and eyes and sculpted features, the vampire was as close to male perfection as anyone could get.

Cesare introduced him. "Lord Valadon, our leading model, Jeremy. I'm promoting him to our runway for the spring collection."

Jeremy shook hands with Valadon. "It's a pleasure meeting you, sir. Everyone at Valadon Creations speaks very highly of you."

"As does Cesare of you." Valadon took a step back and seemed to scrutinize the model. "I must say the photos Cesare showed me don't do you justice. Your likeness does our products proud."

"Thank you. I'm honored."

Miranda tuned out the rest of the conversation and made her way toward the stairs. As Orion conferred with Bastien, his new best friend and manager, she drifted to the second floor. She preferred the shadows, away from the bright lights, and watched the people dancing below.

"You should be down there celebrating with your people." Rosalyn stood alongside her.

Miranda perused the crowd below. "I'm not sure they're all my people. I don't know half of them."

Rosalyn gently laid a hand on her shoulder. "He has to put up a good front. That's why he keeps his distance."

Miranda knew Rosalyn was aware she was gazing in Remare's direction. "I know." But that didn't mean it didn't sting any less. "His first loyalty is to Valadon. Always."

Rosalyn glanced at her and then below. "Be patient, Miranda. He does what he must."

Just then, Jason Morgan hugged Rosalyn from behind, and Miranda felt a twinge of jealousy at their shared happiness. "Congratulations, Miranda, on your engagement. With Valadon backing Orion, his career is sure to skyrocket."

She wasn't sure that was such a great prospect. Fame and fortune changed people and not always for the better. "I'm sure it will. How are you doing, Jason?"

"Great. We just got back from Scotland." He sipped his drink. "Dad had me close a business deal with some of our associates there. But I think he had ulterior motives. While I was conducting business, Dad was off playing golf. The golfing in Scotland is some of the best in the world."

Miranda smiled at the image of the octogenarian on the greens. "How's Wilson doing?"

"Fantastic. Great. Semi-retirement agrees with him wholeheartedly. I think, if he ever decided to retire full time, he'd go mad."

Rosalyn's face was glowing as she whispered fond words to Jason. After they said their goodbyes, Miranda looked down as Valadon and Remare prepared to leave. Apparently, business called, and they were leaving the party. Near the door, Valadon looked up at her and blew her a kiss. Miranda gasped when she felt it as it brushed her lips. Smirking, he then departed. She hoped Remare would glance up at her, but he left without turning to look at her.

She sighed in silent resignation.

"You look beautiful tonight, Miranda."

She didn't have to turn around to recognize the voice. She'd know it anywhere. "Hello, Gabriel."

Turning, she saw Gabriel was dressed in a dark gray suit. His golden brown eyes glimmered in the shadows; the red rims around his irises barely noticeable.

"Hello, yourself." He grinned. "I hear congratulations are in order."

"Yeah, about that—"

Gabriel's brows lifted. "Yes?"

If not for his grin, Miranda would have almost felt guilty. "I guess Valadon told you it was all hype, to further Orion's career."

Gabriel nodded as he gestured to the crowd below. "When he invited me to the festivities, he mentioned something about it being a PR ploy. I would hate to think that, when we were dating, you and he were—"

"I would never!" Miranda was shocked Gabriel would ever consider such a thought. "Orion and I have only ever been friends. We were never involved. Especially not when you and I were dating."

Gabriel's lips twitched into his usual crooked smile. "Glad to hear it." He looked over at the bar. "Can I buy you a drink?"

"Sure. But, I'm only drinking cranberry juice. The last thing I need is a hangover. Orion's the one who likes to party hearty." Miranda gestured to Orion and Bastien as they drank and laughed.

When Gabriel extended his hand to lead her to the bar, she accepted it. "It's good to see you, again." He looked handsome when he was relaxed and not immersed in his work. She remembered all too well how worn and aggrieved he became when he overworked himself. But, then again, having Valadon as his sire ensured he was physically attractive.

"It's good to see you, too." Gabriel seemed to study her as they sat by the bar. "I'm glad you're not being chased by Rogues in the middle of the night, again."

Miranda didn't want to tell him she was pretty sure they weren't Rogues, but Vivienna's agents. "Yes. Me, too."

"I have to admit, when I first saw the photos of you and Orion on social media, it stung a little." Hurt was evident in his eyes.

"Yeah, I should have called to warn you, but everything happened so fast. Even Orion didn't know his manager was going to make the press release."

"And, now, he's got a new manager."

"Yes, but Bastien is only his manager at ValCorp. Frank will still be his manager when he tours or when Bastien's on assignment." Miranda felt a tinge of regret while talking with Gabriel. Sentimental thoughts hovered over her. If things had been different, if they could have made it work... Gabriel was one of the best men she had ever met, and she was grateful for his friendship. After his goodbyes, he left to socialize with some of the Torians. She hoped one day he would return to ValCorp and to Valadon.

Sipping her drink, Miranda felt the familiar vibration only an ancient possessed.

When she turned to greet Blu and Felicity, she gasped. "Felicity, is that you?" Her former mentor appeared younger than the last time Miranda had seen her. Now, Felicity seemed to resemble the same college age as Blu.

"Yes, Miranda. It's me. I feel like a new woman." Felicity laughed. "Stop looking so shocked. What did you expect?"

Miranda's words stumbled. "I-I'm not sure."

"I suppose I should have told you sooner."

Miranda guessed Felicity's secret from the old paintings she had seen of her former mentor's likeness. "You've been a vampire for centuries, haven't you?"

"I told you she would figure it out," Montglat said as he took the glasses the bartender handed him.

Remorsefully, Felicity looked at Miranda. "My family are conservatives who didn't believe in *coming out* the way Valadon asserted. They still keep their identities secret...as I am hoping you will with mine."

Miranda remembered how Felicity looked dressed in the fashions of the eighteenth century. "Of course I will. Felicity, you have nothing to worry about. Your secret is safe with me."

"Then, a toast is in order. To your engagement," Blu said as he lifted his glass.

"Really, Miranda," Felicity said, "you should have told us sooner, so we could help with the arrangements."

"What arrangements?"

"The wedding, of course. It's so rare, especially in our world."

Miranda's eyebrows shot up. "Oh, I don't think you have to worry about that. I'm sure it won't be for a very *long* time." She dared not tell her the truth, at least not yet.

After they left, Miranda stifled a yawn when her bestie, Lizandra, appeared and sat beside her. "We need to talk."

"Okay." Miranda raised a brow. "Am I correct in thinking you put Valadon up to hiring Orion?"

"Of course. Did you think I would accept that bitch queen hurting one of my Weres without restitution?" Lizandra looked around the club. "Anyway, this place is far too public for what I need to discuss. Can we go to your place?"

"Sure. Let me just text Orion."

"Good. Gavin is bringing the car around front."

***

Even with the warning Lizandra had given her in the drive to her place, Miranda wasn't ready for the person who had flown in to see her. He was waiting on her steps with Lawe, one of Lizandra's enforcers. Still in a state of detached awe, she barely heard Lizandra making the introductions. Her heart in her throat, her body on autopilot, she climbed the few stairs. Lizandra stood by her side.

"Miranda, this is Drake, Dane's older brother. He flew in from California on business and wanted to meet with you."

She didn't hear whatever else Lizandra was saying as the Were Queen unlocked her door and led them inside. Miranda's eyes were glued on Drake, who was the spitting image of her former lover, Dane—only older. Both had the blond hair and gleaming tan so many Californians sported, but Drake was taller and more ruggedly built.

"Miranda."

She tried, but couldn't get any words to leave her mouth. Finally, she said, "I'm glad to meet you."

"Gavin and I will wait in the kitchen." Lizandra kissed her cheek and hugged her. "Courage, now. He means you no harm."

Courage?! Maybe after her knees stopped knocking. When she entered her living room, Drake was standing by the fireplace examining her photographs. She found her voice. "Dane talked often of you and the rest of his family." Drained, Miranda grabbed on to the couch.

Drake went to her and held her arm as she collapsed into the cushions. "I'm sorry. I see my presence has upset you." He grinned. "People always said how much Dane and I resembled each other."

"I'm all right." Miranda tried to control her breathing; her blood was pounding in her ears. "I'm fine. It's just that... I wasn't expecting... God, you look just like him, even your voice sounds like his."

"I know." He exhaled as he rubbed her arm—a soothing gesture. "I didn't come here to upset you. Dane had written many good things about you. I just wanted to meet you. If you prefer I leave, I will."

Miranda steadied herself. She owed it to Dane to stay strong, and Drake deserved whatever answers he needed. "No. Stay. Let me get you a drink. I know I could use one."

***

Remare had wanted to talk with Miranda at the party, but didn't think it wise with Valadon watching her. He knew her engagement to Orion was just PR hype, but when he saw the way Orion kissed her, the beast within him wanted to do damage to the young wolf. He'd seen her glancing in his direction, but dared not return her look.

He checked his watch. It was late, but she might still be up, and he could talk with her without a crowd or watchful eyes on them.

Driving up Seventh Avenue, he saw a late-night deli was still open. On impulse, he decided to buy some flowers. Roses would be too simple and unimaginative. Miranda was unique and deserved something worthy of her.

He chose lilies with a beautiful orchid in the middle.

***

Miranda told Drake as much as she could about Dane. With Lizandra's okay, she told him about Dane's death and the reason he was killed. When she peered into his soft brown eyes, she lost it.

"I'm so sorry." The sobs came uncontrollably. "It was all my fault. If I hadn't asked him to do some research..." The harder Miranda tried to fight against the tears, the more they poured out of her as if someone had turned on the flood gates and she couldn't stop the torrent. "I'm the reason he's dead."

Drake gathered her into his arms. "It wasn't your fault." He rubbed her back and held her close to him. "Shhh, it wasn't your fault." In silent communion, he seemed to be offering her the forgiveness she had so long denied herself.

Miranda looked up at him with tear drenched eyes. "How can you forgive me?"

"I never blamed you. No one in our family ever did. But I'm glad you killed those responsible."

Miranda cast her eyes downward. She couldn't tell him she and Lizandra weren't completely sure they had gotten everyone, but they did get most.

Drake slowly lifted her chin and kissed her gently on the lips. "You need to forgive yourself. It's what Dane would want you to do."

***

Remare was lucky to find a parking spot one block away and smiled when he looked at the orchid. The grocer had tried to jack up the price when he saw his Mercedes and the clothes he was wearing. But Remare didn't care, he had tipped the guy handsomely, regardless. Exiting his car with the flowers in hand, he walked to Miranda's door.

From the street, he could see into her living room. He was relieved when he saw the lights were still on. When he glimpsed inside, his heart sank as if someone had sucker punched him. Miranda was in the arms of a handsome blond-haired man. Remare sniffed the air; only the scents of Weres were prevalent. Who the hell was she kissing? He had told her he would get in touch when he could. She couldn't wait for him?!

Incensed, a growl tore from his throat as he turned and flung the flowers in the nearest garbage can and stormed off. If he confronted her and her lover, there was no telling the damage he could do.

Chapter Thirty-Nine

Miranda sat alone in the dark at her kitchen table, staring at the bottle of vodka. After Lizandra and Gavin had taken Drake back to Werehaven, she pretended to get some sleep. But tonight, Morpheus, the god of sleep, would not visit her. And Miranda was grateful because she knew the nightmares would be brutal.

Sighing, she studied the pictures in the paper one last time of Remare partying his ass off with some hot blond at Nightshade. *No wonder the bastard hadn't returned her calls.* Shaking her head in bitter disappointment, she refused to torture herself over it. Exhaling, she stared at the bottle and imagined it staring back at her. The abyss was patiently waiting for her decision.

Miranda glanced at the clock. Dawn was on the horizon, so she would have to make a decision soon. Get drunk and finally, *finally,* get some godforsaken sleep or soldier on and keep on keeping on.

The ticking of the clock never sounded so loud. Even the angels who stood on her shoulders were silent. She'd have no one to blame for her decision. This was on her all the way. "Fuck it!" She grabbed the bottle and dumped the contents down the sink. "I've gone without sleep before."

"You know, if you hadn't poured the booze down the drain, I was going to break your fingers."

Smirking, Miranda tossed the empty bottle in the recyclables. "Who let you in?"

"You did." Lizandra dangled the key she had once given her and held two boxes in her other hand.

Miranda could smell chocolate a mile away. "What's in the box?"

"I thought you might be needing a little something—fucking insomniac that you are—so I stopped at the bakery."

She took out two plates. "I would've thought you and Gavin would be doing the horizontal mambo by now."

"We did. It roused other hungers." Liz grinned. "Put on a pot of hot water."

Smiling, Miranda did as she was told. "Yes, ma'am."

"Good answer." Liz's brows rose. "You get to choose first from the assortment."

When Miranda peeked into the box, her stomach picked that moment to heave. She quickly turned and vomited into the sink. Memories of opening another box with far more graphic images of death flooded her mind.

"Let it out." Lizandra held her hair as she vomitted "Let it all out."

Miranda continued retching until the dry heaves set in then rinsed her mouth out with water. "I think I'm done." After wiping her mouth on a towel, she embraced her friend. "Thank you for coming back."

"Just what I wanted to do after a night of great fucking—watch my best friend puke out her guts. Have a seat. I'll make you that green tea you like so much. I suggest the plain muffin. Leave the chocolate chip one for me."

"Yes, ma'am."

Opening the bag of loose tea, Lizandra stopped and turned. "By the way, if I find another bottle of vodka hidden in this house, I'll break more than your fingers."

Miranda smiled and shook her head. "You won't."

Lizandra stared her down. "I won't because there won't be any bottles or you'll just get better at hiding them?"

Miranda narrowed her eyes as she leaned in closer. "That's the bitch of it, isn't it?" Then, she leaned back and exhaled. "It's over. Drake was right. I never really forgave myself for Dane's death. You, Gavin, everyone else told me it wasn't my fault. I never believed it until tonight." Miranda looked up at her friend. "I believe it, now."

"Good to hear." Lizandra stared at her. "Now, eat."

Miranda took a bite of the muffin and sipped the tea Lizandra had made for her. She shivered at the morning cold. She'd been numb for so long she hardly registered the cold. "Thank you."

"You're welcome." Lizandra flipped the newspaper open to the pictures of Remare dancing with a blond and met Miranda's eyes. "Is this what's got you all upset?"

Miranda shrugged. "He's free to dance with whoever he wants."

Knowingly, Lizandra eyed her. "I wouldn't put much stock in those photos. I can't picture Remare crawling on his stomach for any of those bitches."

Miranda quirked her head in confusion. "What do you mean?"

"When you were nearly burned at the stake at ValCorp...Gavin told me he saw Remare crawl on his belly with his back all bloodied and bruised to get to you when you were unconscious."

Miranda ran her fingers slowly over his picture. She remembered Mulciber flinging Remare against the cave wall. The pain must have been excruciating. "He did that, huh?"

"Yeah, so stop with the dreary."

Miranda remembered Remare telling her he'd visited her in the infirmary every night after everyone had left. Smiling, she tossed the newspaper in the recyclables. "What's the folded paper?"

"It was in the bag of tea leaves." Liz opened it and read it. *"Miranda, I noticed you were almost out of the Moroccan Mint tea I've grown accustomed to so I bought you a pound.*

For some reason, I can't seem to drink tea without thinking of you and the time you made it for me. Enjoy—R."

"Well, it must be love if he buys you tea."

Miranda snorted. "It's not love until someone buys you chocolate."

"Truth!" They knuckle tapped.

"So, what's in the other box?"

"I don't know." Liz pushed the small box to Miranda. "It was in your mailbox."

When Miranda opened the box, she found a shiny dark stone.

Liz leaned forward. "What is it?"

"It's a totem. The Native Americans spoke of old magic embedded in the rocks." When Miranda turned the stone over, she found the carving of an eagle. "This is the stone they pressed into my forehead." She looked up at Liz. "That dream I told you about flying. It was no dream."

Liz huffed as she examined the box. "There's no address, no card." Her eyes widened when she saw Miranda's hand. "Look at your fingers, Miranda."

When Miranda glanced at her nails, they were shaped like an eagle's talons. She quickly dropped the stone back into the box and pushed it to Liz. "Here, you take it."

"I don't want it. It's your stone." She pushed the box back to Miranda. "Look, your fingernails are normal, now."

When Miranda looked at her nails, she exhaled in relief. She quickly took the box and put it in one of the drawers. "Do you believe me, now?"

Liz opened her mouth, then shut it. "I say, let's eat and forget that *ever* happened."

"Oh, yes."

She grinned when Liz started humming the tune to the old *Twilight Zone* theme then laughed as Lizandra made orgasmic sounds when eating the chocolate pastry.

Friends, Miranda thought, were priceless. Men came and went; some made promises and actually kept them. Some didn't. But, if you were lucky enough in this world to have friends who checked up on you, brought you chocolate when you needed it, and held your hair while you puked up your guts, you were blessed.

And, if you had a man who opened his cave to you, gave you shelter when you needed it, and remembered to buy you tea because he knew it was one of your favorites, you were doubly blessed.

When Miranda's phone started vibrating on the table, Liz checked the caller ID. "ValCorp2."

"That's Remare's number."

Liz's sensuous smile nearly melted the chocolate. "Are you going to answer it?"

Miranda was feeling very blessed. "Maybe."

Epilogue

Vivienna sat back and reviewed the video disks in her bedroom. Eric stood naked before Miranda's sleeping form on the bed. He was a carved masterpiece of masculine perfection. Vivienna had enjoyed his body every way possible and often shared him with other lovers. Miranda should have at least enjoyed his embrace. Then, Vivienna would have had something to entertain Valadon with when she went to New York, and she was very much looking forward to that trip.

She watched, in a flash of movement, as Miranda's arm sprang up and held Eric by the throat. Only her hand wasn't making contact with Eric. An invisible force was. Vivienna's eyes narrowed as she replayed the disk to make sure of what she'd just seen. She laughed in devious delight. "Now, that is interesting. So, Miranda, you have more in common with us than you think."

Vivienna ejected the disk and sealed it in the drawer of her desk as Vincent knocked, then entered her room. "*Mon coeur*, are you all packed for your trip?"

"Yes, Mother. I'm eager to start my position at McGill University in Montreal."

Vivienna sighed. Her son was eager to explore new territories, but she would miss him terribly. "Remember to extend my regards to Dione." The Madame Lord of Montreal hadn't been one of her friends, but neither had she been an enemy. However, she had agreed to Vivienna's request to make certain her son was protected. "Be well, my darling." She embraced her only son in farewell.

"I will, Mother." Vincent kissed her cheek and turned to leave.

After he was gone, Vivienna made her way down the hall to Vincent's room. Opening the door, she moved closer to his painting and smiled. "Your mother would have been very proud of you, Vincent." Vivienna clasped her hands together in front of her lips. "Had she lived."

She walked with confidence to her bedroom until she opened her door. She stood in shock and then screamed loud enough to have all the servants come running.

***

Exhaling, Jeremy took off his jacket and casually tossed it on the chair. Their apartment was small, not at all like Mulciber's luxurious townhouse, but that would soon change. Kaylee was still up and staring at the night sky. He bent down to brush a lock of hair from her face. "I met our father's murderer tonight. I've been working for him for months now and finally got to meet him."

Kaylee remained unresponsive as was her usual. Mulciber had succeeded in turning Jeremy before he died, but he hadn't had the time to complete Kaylee's transformation. Her mind had fractured, and she would forever stay in that twilight world of being neither human nor fully vampire.

Jeremy stared up at the night sky. "Soon, we'll be able to afford a better place where you'll be more comfortable." He had gathered what valuables he could from Mulciber's place before Brandon had arrived to empty the safe. Not long after that, Valadon's men had entered the townhouse and cleared out all of Mulciber's electronic equipment. But they hadn't known of the ancient's safe room where Jeremy had watched them.

He glanced at his reflection in the mirror. With the blood of an ancient flowing in his veins, his night vision was superb as were some of his other talents. He examined his face. His transformation had refined his already handsome features, and for the past few months, he had used his looks to earn a reasonable income. But his goals were set much higher.

He looked back at his sister and thought of his other sister, Persephone, locked away in Valadon's dungeons. At night, through their blood bond, he could hear her cries for help.

In a few short months, he would graduate with his MBA from NYU, and then, he would use his talents to worm his way into Valadon's good graces. Mulciber had a mole in the organization they still hadn't discovered, and Jeremy had his cooperation. The vampires who had reported to his father would report to him, and Valadon would never know it until it was too late. It would take time, but he would take back all that Valadon had taken from him.

And, then, he would destroy the high lord.

***

Feeling content, Guy de Montglat gazed outside the window of his private jet. His trip to Paris had been most beneficial. His meetings with his contacts had gone according to plan, as did his other enterprises. Sipping champagne, he admired his painting, *Lavender Dreams,* that he'd had mounted on the interior wall of his jet. His model had been as captivating as she had been courageous. He lifted his glass and saluted Miranda.

Reaching inside his pocket, he retrieved the listening device he had removed from the back of the painting and smiled. The newer devices Glatt Industries produced were far more sophisticated and impossible to detect. And, now, they were currently on the backs of paintings in the homes of various vampire lords who required monitoring.

Guy reached in his other pocket and held the miniature lizard with the golden eyes he had bought at the open-air flea market when he'd been shadowing Miranda. He entertained the idea of making the reptile his company's logo. Perhaps in time he would.

They didn't know it yet, but *Le Cameleon* was back. With a warm sense of contentment, he smiled.

His only regret was that he was not there to see the surprised look on Vivienna's face when she realized her *Dreams* had disappeared.

"*Au revoir*, Madame Lord." Blu's laughter echoed throughout the plane.

Available Soon

Veil of Darkness, Seven Deadly Veils, Book Three

When Nickolas Valadon, nephew of the High Lord Vampire of New York goes missing, the mission of finding Nick goes to Remare, a ruthless, but intensely sexy investigator. To assist him in the hunt, he contacts Miranda Crescent, an *Elemental*, and a former lover he has never forgotten. Valadon has made his intentions known regarding Miranda: She is not to be touched by any member of his house. But as Remare and Miranda work together to find Nick, Remare's desire increases to the point where he will defy the devil himself to pursue her, despite the punishment that will be meted out: Death.

Miranda Crescent was authenticating one of Valadon's rare paintings when she met the High Lord and discovered the dark world of the vampire. When Remare shows up requesting her assistance, she balks at the idea. Having been forsaken for Valadon, she refuses to trust the dashing vampire she once fell for and decides to search for Nick on her own, because if Valadon or Remare ever found out Nick had become involved with the niece of the local werewolf king, blood would be spilled.

And Miranda does not want it to be hers.

Diana Marik is the author of the Seven Deadly Veils Vampire Series. She grew up in New York City and has her MA in English Literature from Hofstra University. Before becoming an author, Diana worked as an educator, mental health therapist, yoga instructor and camp counselor.

Among Diana's passions, traveling is her favorite. One of her favorite places to visit is the American Southwest and her home away from home, New Orleans. When not writing, Diana loves discovering museums. In her leisure time, she enjoys going to the movies and hanging out with her friends.

Diana is currently at work on her latest novel in the Veilverse and would love to hear from her fans. She can be contacted at www.dianamark.com

Printed in Great Britain
by Amazon